Children of Destiny

ALSO BY JAMES K. MCVEY

Children of Ennaris
The Children Return
The Blood Rises
Ennarisi Unite
Children of Destiny

Children of Destiny

Children of Ennaris IV

James K. McVey

ISBNs:

EPUB: 978-1-923211-07-0
Paperback: 978-1-923211-03-2
Kindle: 978-1-923211-11-7

First Printing 2024

Book Cover Design by M. Yankevich, Novelized, at https://www.novelizedbookcovers.com/

CONTENTS

For Stephanie, whose support and encouragement made this and many other things possible.

Prologue

The pieces were coming together, the elements lining up as the Prophesy had predicted. Odruf, who had been spending a lot of time considering recent events and potential outcomes, remained nervous for the resolution. Yes, the Prophesy had been written by him but it was written without his volition. That had been put into his head and hands by The One, the entity that had created this universe, and Odruf had no sense of certainty about what would happen. No matter what the outcome was, he and the Guardians were limited in what they could do, unless the existence of Ennaris or the Ennarisi as a whole were endangered.

The Children walked Ennaris and they had such enormous potential that almost anything was possible. In Drewflin and Marjory Ennaris had the most powerful Mages of its long history, although they were assisted by very few others. Goroth had been released from his stasis prison and had returned to his single-minded drive to wrest away control of Ennaris and, ultimately, the galaxy. He was supported by the last two of his lieutenants from the rebellion, both of whom were powerful in their own right. However, as was his wont, Odruf was optimistic about the outcome.

In the northlands, Goroth was in a very different mood. He had started working with Grensor's set of gifted northers, with mixed results. If there was a need for overwhelming force, then Goroth was prepared to expend those gifted northers completely. While there were none of true power, what he did have were sufficient to defeat the powers that Drewflin would have available, especially so when joined with Likud and himself. Grensor had repeatedly assured Goroth that he had been removing the gifted children from the population as they were located, either by using teams of norther and local agents to deal with them or, in more recent times, sending ghazrak cells to eliminate them. Killing those children did not sit well with Goroth but he had been responsible for many deaths during the rebellion and it was necessary to ensure that there was no real opposition, so he quashed those few qualms in the name of the greater good.

His forces were weak, at least as he saw them. He realised that the current population of Ennaris did not allow for large armies, but the paltry numbers available to him were a concern. The northers were vicious, undisciplined and unruly, often drunk and always prepared to fight and brawl. Of the available population of the twin kingdoms, there were around thirty thousand of them available to fight, women and men both, although getting a good count was difficult given how widely dispersed they were at any point in time.

The regular army of the Twin Kingdoms was much better and its leadership was confident in its abilities, but they had never been tested against a disciplined opposition. There were relatively few full-time soldiers, however, so Goroth would have to use them carefully. Between them, however, the army and norther rabble should be enough to overwhelm Drewflin's force that, it seemed, would comprise representatives from the various peoples across Ennaris. Such was Grensor's reading of the Prophesy, at least, and it made sense tactically. However, it seemed unlikely that he would be able to build a coalition in the same way, as he had in the past.

Grensor's ghazrak were fewer in number than he wanted, although there were more then he had during the rebellion. Goroth kept the pressure on Grensor to deliver more, of course, but he recognised the extreme difficulty that the old Mage had worked under for the thousands of cycles since the Rebellion. That he had developed a cadre of norther gifted who could create electrical power as their gifts was a stroke of genius that Goroth would not have thought of. And the range of ghazrak that he had created was impressive. There were not enough of them for Goroth to feel comfortable, although when added to the northers they provided a formidable edge.

However, Grensor had allowed himself to deteriorate, which was unforgivable to Goroth. He had never been as resilient as others, of course, and had relied on Goroth as the last of a line of Mages who provided motivation and support. With no-one to do so during the relatively short period since the Rebellion's end, at least as a Mage viewed time, he had lost heart and failed to maintain *himself*, which did take some small effort. Rather, Grensor had given up, had surrendered to despair. Goroth was unsure as to what the future held for Grensor once this business was done. He needed to consider that some more.

He also knew that he would have a problem with Likud, and that was a further topic for deliberation, too. Not for the first time, Goroth found himself questioning his lieutenant's grip on sanity. Likud was inherently vicious, with a depth that proved to be frightening during the rebellion. Although Goroth was blamed for the action, it had been Likud who ordered the great battleship *Scaliba* to enter the atmosphere and turn its massive weapons on the group of opposition Mages, completely ignoring the potentially catastrophic effects to Ennaris itself. Even when confronted with those effects on his return recently, Likud had been fascinated rather than aghast, as Goroth had been. His policies with the Andorethi appeared to have reduced that race to no more than subservient lackeys, which Likud enjoyed but that left Goroth cold. While he would use the Andorethi as a tool for now, he would try to reverse that damage when he could. Likud expressed confident that his fleet would account for the opposition fleet. Goroth was unsure, given Likud's track record to date, but he had no better option.

In the Citadel of the Faero, the young Faero, Corm Ramesa, looked out a small window that overlooked the Citadel's main square, and gave himself over to his own doubts. He was unsure that he was right for job, but he was what there was. He missed his father hugely, and a lump formed in his throat at the thought. He was not ready for any of the responsibilities that had been thrust onto him. He was being trained hard by Almin Bor, a highly respected former general of multiple armies at a young age, and by Blaine, one of the Children of Ennaris, and had progressed quickly. However, militarily he was untried apart from the foray when defending Escar. He had no experience with the other, administrative, side of being a civil leader. With a barely audible sigh, he forced himself to push past those doubts. He was far from alone and was supported by a truly awe-inspiring array of people, from the people of the Blood to the Mages and then, of course, the three Children, Varna, Blaine and Jalor. Their examples were inspirational. He hardened his thoughts. He would defend his people, all Ennarisi, with every fibre of his being.

Elsewhere in the Citadel, Flight-Colonel Vinca Jalor of the Union of Sentient Planets was pondering also. He and his team of the Union's elite Warriors of the Light had been on Ennaris for more than half a year, and the mission plan was little more than a memory. Dropped onto Ennaris by Grand Admiral Mavin Serra with very little preparation to determine the fate of the previous team and to disrupt the plans of the Empire, the three Warriors had found themselves battling terrifying manufactured creatures, legends of the past that were coming back to life and, in Varna's case, the planet itself. Varna had found that Clay Anders, Champion of the Light, had survived but that he was the sole survivor of the first team. Blaine and Varna had taken on identities of legend from Ennaris' deep past. The team had thrown its support behind the young and inexperienced Faero, Corm Ramesa, who appeared destined to be the leader of this planet if he survived, and were helping a small group of Mages who survived from Ennaris' days of glory. Furthermore, he had accepted the role as general of Corm's army and had been trying to drum up support for that army from the disparate elements of Ennaris' fractured civilisation. That needed unity remained incomplete. The Grand Admiral obviously knew more about the situation than she had divulged, which was not unusual in Warrior missions, but in this case the potential sub-plots were a danger.

Throw into the mix the small group of Mages who been been struggling to keep alive the memories of the past and the need for the people of Ennaris to join to battle against Goroth, a rebel Mage who had caused more destruction to a civilisation than Jalor had ever seen or heard about. Every indication was that the loyal Mages, as Jalor thought of them, would be out-gunned by Goroth, Likud and Grensor, and yet they fought on without flinching.

Then there were the Guardians, a group of extremely powerful super-beings who appeared to have guided Ennaris' development and, through the Ennarisi, the development of both Earth and its main enemy, the Likudian Empire, but who were bound not to provide material assistance except in dire circumstances. That rendered their great power nearly worthless, in Jalor's view.

All signs indicted that the battle with Goroth would be soon. The twin Mages, Raglin and Ragnor, had explained the Prophesy to Corm and the Warriors in as much detail as they could, and events appeared to be moving towards the battle against this ancient evil that was foretold. Corm's army had representatives from many parts of Ennaris, but that did not mean that all of Ennaris was united behind the Faero. The great Rocs had joined the fight, although Jalor suspected that they had never left it. The Clans of the enormous grasslands had been brought into the fold. Jalor had planned to go to the southern continent to recruit the desert people, but Balgor had informed him that the situation with that group was in hand, and then said no more.

Spies told of the norther forces building once again. Their attack on Escar had been a tactical mistake, as Jalor saw it, because it revealed in part what could be expected later. However, it probably also provided a lot of information for the enemy commanders and it did have the effect of reducing numbers in Corm's army and the experienced knights. The Rocs also told of some sort of eastern force being formed, but Jalor could not see how they would get across the precipitous mountain range that had divided the northern continent in two since the devastation caused by the rebellion five thousand cycles earlier. Still, Jalor had to be aware that it could mean that Corm's army would fight on two fronts.

The Union fleet was in orbit and in conflict with the Empire fleet. Jalor had managed spasmodic contacts with *Starfire*, the flagship of the Union fleet, but they seemed to have occurred during battles, and so he had little sense of whether the fleet was in good shape or not. He had only had one mysterious contact with the Grand Admiral, leaving him with more questions than answers. The planetary AI system that he had used to make contact with *Starfire* left him astounded when he thought about it. In a medieval-level world this massively advanced and powerful system remained from the civilisation that had been Ennaris to provide a jarring juxtaposition. That it survived at all after the devastation of the rebellion was astonishing in itself, but the latent power represented by the AI caused Jalor to wonder about the future, should they win through against Goroth. What role would Ennaris play on the galaxy's stage?

The situation was coming to a head. Jalor had no doubt in that regard. The misgivings he had about joining with the Mages and the Faero against Goroth had faded under the weight of events. As Warriors of the Light they fought against the Empire, which it seemed had been a proxy extension of Goroth's forces for millennia. There was an acceptance by the team now that they had been given a different set of roles, too, whether by fate or by chance or by someone's machinations. Those roles could be the most important ones to be undertaken by any Warriors.

In doing so they had the chance to decide the future of this galaxy, perhaps even to save that future, if the Prophecy could be trusted. Jalor no longer doubted that it was he and his team who were referenced by the Prophecy. They were among the best the Union had to offer and they seemed destined to lead the Ennarisi in this climactic conflict.

They were the Children of Ennaris!

1. The Easterners March

High Priest Hardog was angry and worried. His task was to forge an army from the peoples of the eastern seaboard so his master, the First Prophet of Groks, could fulfil his destiny and extend his power across all Ennaris. For so it was written in the Chronicles and so it would be.

The build of the army had started well. The small force of temple guards was instructed to prepare, and the order was issued for those designated to be volunteers to assemble in front of the Grand Temple of Yster. Any who did not appear on the day and at the time designated would be hunted down by the Temple Assistants and their families would be obliterated, starting with the youngest. Hardog was sure that would be an effective means of raising the army needed, for the people of Groks were accustomed to obeying the First Prophet. However, it proved not to be the case.

As the Temple guards moved around delivering the order many of them were set upon, quite a few were killed. There had also been a small number of riots which were put down only by stern measures and the hard use of the Temple Assistants. Whole families had been eradicated, as promised, and still the people did not respond as required. If anything, resistance had hardened.

Hardog was at a loss to understand why this should be the case. Dedication to Groks was absolute among the people, as the First Prophet had stated repeatedly. It was only a short time since the great Mage Grensor had appeared to inform the First Prophet that the time had come to take up arms and assist the even greater Mage Goroth to destroy those who had caused the destruction and anguish of the past.

How could the people not respond to such a great opportunity to fight and die for the First Prophet's enduring glory?

However, they had not responded as expected and so here he was, standing in front of the Great Temple with an army of fewer than five thousand, largely made up of the dregs of the northern Grokog, the northern part of the people of Groks, as the First Prophets of antiquity had named them. Oh, there were firm adherents to the Temple and the First Prophet, those who wanted to sacrifice for the greater good and out of devotion to the god Groks. But to make up numbers the many gaols had been emptied and those who had been incarcerated for crimes of violence, theft and, worst of all, refusing to believe that Groks was the one god, had been forced into somewhat ragtag uniforms and issued short spears. The Temple guards were better equipped with swords and short bows and arrows, and the Temple Assistants who would be accompanying the army to ensure the recruits fulfilled their obligations were even better armed and armoured.

Hardog was unsure if he had done enough. The space in front of the Great Temple was filled to the brim, but only because he had brought all of the wagons and carts into the space. He now waited nervously upon the entry of the First Prophet to survey the army. Assuming all went well, they would then form up and march to the Passage of Groks. This was the tunnel through the mountain chain that had confined the Grokog to their strip of land. It had been uncovered by the great Mage Grensor only a short time before, and access to the tunnel was zealously guarded by the Temple Assistants. The ancient map that the First Prophets guarded just as zealously showed that this land was but a small part of the huge expanse of land that was Ennaris. Images of great cities whetted the appetites of the Temple adherents, who all dreamed of the wealth and abundance offered to those who led the way. Hardog was determined to be one of the leaders of those who took the religion of Groks to the unbelievers of whom the great Mage Grensor had spoken.

Finally, a stir went through the Temple guards. A small procession of ten Temple Assistants moved from the First Prophet's door. Their fine robes swished as they walked, and their ancient chain mail could be seen where ceremonial robes ended just short of their feet and hands. The procession halted and the Temple Assistants moved aside to form an honour guard, through which the palanquin of the First Prophet was carried, his great girth testament to the favour in which he was held by the god Groks. The palanquin was gently placed on the huge stones that formed the entry portico and tilted to assist the First Prophet to alight from it and to stand, assisted by two of the Temple Assistants. A massive chair was brought out. Two slaves struggled to carry it without having it touch the floor until it was in place, whereupon the First Prophet was lowered into the chair. The ancient plush cushioning sagged alarmingly, and the chair creaked in objection to the weight deposited on it but, finally, all was in readiness.

Hardog made his way to the side of the First Prophet and stood perfectly still, hands folded in front of him. The First Prophet surveyed the gathering for a long time, squinting through rheumy eyes whose sight had diminished significantly in recent times. His huge fleshy jowls quivered as he tried to count the army and failed to do so, being unable to make out clear details of those standing in the Temple forecourt. Finally, he held out one sagging arm, into which a goblet of fine wine was placed by one of the slaves, which he shakily held to his mouth. He gulped the contents. Wine trickled from each corner of his mouth and dripped onto his robe unheeded. He dropped the goblet to the floor with a resounding clang. It had been used and so would not be needed again.

The First Prophet waved Hardog closer, and the latter moved in and bent so that he was within range of the former's fetid breath and distinct body aroma. Unconsciously, he held his breath while he waited for the First Prophet to speak.

"So, Hardog, you have brought me my army," the First Prophet wheezed, barely louder than a whisper. "What number do you have? The square of my Temple is filled with those who seek to bring glory to the First Prophet and Groks."

Hardog held back the sigh of relief he felt as he watched the First Prophet squint through his failing porcine eyes, obviously unable to see anything much at all.

"Indeed, First Prophet," Hardog whispered back, "the Grokog have risen in great numbers to fulfil the Temple's destiny. I am pleased to state that we have, um, twelve thousand soldiers from the northern Grokog. My messengers inform me that we have almost as many from the southern Grokog to join with us on the other side of the great mountains."

"I am pleased," the First Prophet managed to mutter. "You have my leave to commence the march. Go swiftly, Hardog, and carry my destiny with you."

Hardog bowed and stood, moving with alacrity out of range of the odour of rot, old sweat and various other bodily fluids that clung to the hugely obese First Prophet. He gestured and the Temple Assistants moved to assist the First Prophet from the chair and escort him back to the palanquin. As the chair was removed once again, Hardog gestured a second time and the Temple forecourt resounded with a roar, as the army members had been instructed to do on pain of punishment. The First Prophet briefly waved a fleshy arm as he was conveyed back into the Temple.

Much further to the south, the other Grokog army was of a very different character. In the warmer, more balmy climes the dour personality of the northern Grokog was not at all evident. In fact, the call to arms that went out received a splendid reaction, with many adherents to Groks and non-adherents alike flocking to the slightly smaller Temple forecourt in Yftrel. And, true to the nature of the southern Grokog, it became a party.

But not just a party. Wine and spirits flowed freely at the Temple, and the priests of Groks joined in the festivities fully. Men and women, scantily clothed in the heat and humidity at most times, took the opportunity presented by rich food and potent alcohol, both laced with a range of narcotic substances, to drop their few inhibitions, and then to remove most of those scanty clothes and have a memorable orgy.

Bernis, the southern Temple's High Priest, watched proceedings from his throne on the Temple portico, modelled on the same lines as the Great Temple of Yster, but slightly smaller. Bernis, however, was not corpulent like the First Prophet, nor was he oblivious to the true state of worship of Groks in the south. And, being of the south, he understood his people well. Most of those who turned out were there for the bacchanal, not because of any fervour for Groks. So be it! And yet, an army he would have.

For now, though, there was a party to enjoy, and Bernis and his fellow priests made the most of the opportunity. Picking his first partner for the night, Bernis pressed a sweet treat on the already inebriated young woman, toying idly with one pert breast as she nibbled at the cube of jellied sagu fruit. Bernis watched as the narcotic in the treat took effect and then led the woman into the Temple where piles of felt had been arrayed.

The priests of Groks of southern Grokog did enjoy their Temple festivities.

The northern army marched from the Temple forecourt looking more like a rabble than an army. This, Hardog thought, was because they truly *were* a rabble rather than an army. Temple guards and Temple Assistants kept them in some form of order and prodded them onto the road. Officers rode the few hrss that the Grokog had. Hrss did not breed well in the east for some reason, and not at all in the hot and humid south, so there were relatively few, and they were all claimed by men of influence.

In slow stages the mass of men - no women, as the religion of Groks in the north did not acknowledge women as being capable of more than waiting on the needs of their menfolk and breeding - moved along the road towards the mountains. A few men sought to resign their services without notice and slink away and, as a salutary lesson for all, were caught, brought to a point in front of the route of march, and beheaded in the centre of the road. Their heads were carefully placed alongside their shortened torsos such that they appeared to be looking at the column of men as it approached the place of execution.

The column split to go around the bodies and heads. A grim mood settled on the men as they gazed on the deceased former army members. Life in Grokog was difficult. Men and women served mostly at the whim and wish of the priestly class, of whom there were many. Life was cheap to the priests, especially if those lives were those of the common people. Terror was a key tool used to maintain public order so there was little surprise at the executions. Still, the men all understood that, for most if not all of them, a return to Grokog was unlikely. For some, that would be a welcome outcome; for others, those who left family behind as hostages, a grim day became one of even deeper despair.

A brief break for a meal stopped the column after only two hurs. A tasteless flatbread was supplemented with a nondescript paste made from local tubers and other starchy vegetables that were staples of the Grokog diet. The food was handed out from carts and was eaten while sitting on the road. After the meal the march continued. The day wore on and the march slowed slightly as the men's resilience began to flag.

Finally, the head of the column reached the mouth of the tunnel. It had been opened up further than had been the case when the great Mage Grensor and his small force had pushed through it to visit with the First Prophet. Now, the tunnel mouth was wide and high. The huge mounds of debris and vegetation that had blocked it and hidden it from view had been moved painstakingly to the side and now towered over the reluctant army. The advance force stood still and stared at the opening. The waning light of day cast a wan twilight for the first short distance inside, after which the tunnel was pitch black.

Hardog considered the forbidding tunnel. At the top, poking from the blackness, was the end of what looked like some sort of rail, for what purpose he could not fathom. The road was pitted and potholed where the mountainside had collapsed unknown ages in the past, and yet remained passable. It obviously was from the time *before*, and he had seen remnants of other roads in various places throughout Grokog. Usually, they were short stretches only and often ended with the roadway being sheared off and badly weathered and worn at the point of the break, the effects of the devastation from so long ago and the long times since. And yet the ancient road surfaces that existed often were otherwise intact and could not be destroyed by ordinary tools.

Hardog made his decision. He called his captains to him, Temple Assistants all, and ordered them to herd the men into the area in front of the tunnel and bed them down for the night. While he wanted to keep moving, he also wanted to make sure that the first part of the tunnel was scouted. He then moved away from the tunnel mouth, getting a fresh appreciation of its size. His gaze wandered from the top of the tunnel mouth and up the side of the mountain, into the gathering dusk. He was unable to see very far up the mountain. A flicker of movement caused him to peer into the darkening sky where he could have sworn he saw a bird gliding. He snorted and shook his head. Impossible! Given the evident height of whatever it was he saw the bird would have to have been huge, and such did not exist.

The next morning something had changed. Hardog exited his tent at the frantic urging of one of the captains, who pointed to the mouth of the tunnel. Hardog frowned at the man's excitement, which was tinged with something like fear. His own mouth dropped open as he saw the tunnel. Where it had been as dark as a Mage's morals - a common saying in the east - now the tunnel was brightly lighted as far as he could see. And he could see quite a long way, for it appeared to follow a straight path into the roots of the mountain before making a bend.

Hardog walked to the mouth of the tunnel, trying to display a level of confidence that he was far from feeling. Never had he seen anything like this, and he truly did not know what to make of it. Trembling slightly, he stepped into the tunnel. He was dwarfed by the dimensions of the opening. Gingerly, he made his way to a point around fifty paces inside. There he paused and looked around. The walls of the tunnel were smooth and seemed to gleam. It was smooth to the touch, almost but not quite cold, as though there was a gentle fire burning just behind it. Vaguely, Hardog could make out a light thrumming noise, but he was unable to locate the source.

He moved a little further into the tunnel. A huge picture was displayed on the wall of the passage. With a thrill, Hardog realised that it showed the same map that the First Prophet had locked away in the Temple storerooms, but much larger. This map, however, included the tunnel in which Hardog stood, and it showed where it exited the mountain. There were the great cities, marked in various colours and shapes as though the artist tried to give each a different character. Around all four sides of the map were small images of fanciful buildings, graceful spires and incredibly tall structures, squares and fountains. Lush settings reminded him of the unruly and impenetrable southern Grokog jungle but with signs of intense cultivation. Fields were laid out in regular patterns and various crops grew. And there were people in some of the images, tending crops or walking through the cityscapes. With a thrill, Hardog realised that he was looking at images of the ancients, those who were before the great terror, before the execrable Mages had tried to destroy the world.

For a long time, Hardog stared at the map and the images that surrounded it. He was thinking, considering. Finally, he brought himself back to the present and turned towards the tunnel mouth, where a group of Temple Assistants awaited him. He strode back to them with his shoulders squared and purpose re-established.

"Get the army fed and moving through the tunnel," he ordered Margred, the senior Temple Assistant and captain. "Groks has provided us with the means to move from Grokog to the west and has lighted the way. We must make use of it. That map and those pictures show the world that the Mages tried to destroy. We will win that world for the greater glory of the First Prophet and Groks."

And Hardog, he thought to himself as Margred started to give orders. That lush and rich land, and those soft-looking people, would be no match for the Grokog army, even though there were many forced conscripts.

Stepping out of the tunnel he looked around once again. In the morning light, the mountain looked more substantial. The line of mountains that had locked the Grokog into the narrow coast presented vertiginous cliffs that could not be surmounted. But he, Hardog, now had a way through those mountains. Grensor had told them that the Mages were few and were far from the western opening of the tunnel. Hardog had every intention of falling on that land and creating his own Temple.

His hard grin of anticipated triumph did not fade as he watched preparations get underway. He made his way to his tent where he would have his own simple morning meal.

Far above, the Roc that Hardog had dismissed the previous night as an impossibility soared, maintaining a watch on the Grokog as the guards and Temple Assistants pushed and prodded and whipped the First Prophet's army into line.

As the first elements made their tentative way into the tunnel Nogar, wing second of the Roc scout wing, left his patrol station and sped back to the eyrie.

In Yftrel, Bernis took note of the glassy eyes and lethargic motions of his army and nodded. The effects of the drugs administered to the revellers remained and, while they were not enthusiastic, Bernis was sure self-interest would come into play when they met the enemy. If not, then he had other drugs that would make berserkers of them. However, Bernis had also been assured that they would meet little opposition. Grensor, the great Mage of Groks, had told the First Prophet that the people they were likely to meet would be unable to stand against an army. Bernis felt that with a little more than three thousand men he had enough to get through the jungle and, he thought wryly, to fall upon the unbelievers like the First Prophet fell upon a feast.

First, of course, his army had to get through the jungle. Here, again, the great Mage Grensor had provided great assistance. Two troops of ghazrak, which were themselves modelled after the great god Groks, had been left by the great Mage Grensor to lead them through the jungle. The ghazrak were a difficult group and had caused significant trouble while the army was being formed, what with their tendency to erupt in violence and then eat their victims. As fighters, however, they looked to be invincible. The old Mage had boasted that he had many more of them forming the core of his army on the western side of the jungle. These ghazrak would be the ones to forge the path through the jungle, and Bernis and his army would follow.

Bernis waited until he was sure that all was ready and then gave the signal. With a flourish the band of pipes and drums started playing and the Temple Assistants formed alongside the troops, the better to ensure that the reluctant and unwilling were identified should they come out of their drug-induced state too early. Bernis was arrayed in what he thought was a fine set of crimson-dyed boiled leather chest and back armour, complete with shiny metal studs worn over a crisp white tunic and well-fitted black leggings. The whole outfit was tied together by sturdy leather boots in black and fine kid-leather gloves in crimson. He followed the pipe band from the Temple forecourt. He acknowledged the cheers of those southern Grokog who had bothered to come to the march, and while a little disappointed at the small number he also knew that southern Grokog were not early risers. Just after dawn was not going to see many of them awake.

The army of the southern Grokog made its slow way from Yftrel. It wended its way through the outskirts of the city away from the coast and towards the jungle that lurked but a day's journey to the west. In many ways the southern Grokog had been formed by the jungle. Those hardy enough to make their way part-way into the thick, steamy interior of this seemingly endless expanse of trees both great and small, of hanging vines, thick undergrowth and myriad insects intent on biting, sucking and chewing on unsuspecting travellers, told of huge creatures with massive teeth and enormous tails, strange predatory animals that crouched in wait to spring on the unwary, poisonous crawlers that hung between trees on webs too fine to see, small slithers that coiled in wait to spring on those coming too close to them or other huge slithers that would wrap around the unwary and strangle them. The one common thread told by all who knew the jungle was that every part of the jungle sought to kill, maim or use as foodstuff those unwise enough to seek a path through.

Many had tried. There were legends of Grokog from the time of the great destruction making their way to the west and back again. Whether that was true or not Bernis did not know, but no-one was thought to have done so successfully for many centuries. Of course, any who made it through the jungle probably would not have sought to return. Perhaps there were some who made it through and whose descendants were living and thriving on the western side. Bernis thought it unlikely.

There were stories of some of the great creatures of the jungle coming out to prey on those who made their homes too close to the jungle edge. Bernis had seen the great skin of one of them, all tough knobbly bulges and hard ridges. It was easily greater in length than a tall man's height, and he shuddered to think about encountering one of these brutal beasts. The one that he saw had been killed after devouring three scroffers and at least one cottager, and had been sleeping when the hunters slayed him, although three of them also lost their lives and one lost several fingers. After an unsurprisingly short time, no-one lived close to the jungle.

There were also rumours of people living in the depths of the jungle. These stories were taken by most to be fanciful at best and injurious of good civil order at worst. For nothing good could come of believing that people could live in what was the most unwelcoming environment imaginable. Those rumours were quashed wherever they could be found, but still they persisted. Everyone knew at least one of the rumours - the cannibals who roasted their captives, the white robed priests who cut the hearts out of women young and old, the small people who were able to melt away and yet reach out to kill via a range of poisons that were familiar to the Grokog and other concoctions that were as yet unfathomed by the priests of Groks, who prided themselves on their dark knowledge of such things.

The pipes had long stopped playing and the drums stopped beating when the leading edge of the snaking column reached the pathway into the jungle. This was shown on the ancient map as a major road. On that map it skirted the southern reaches of the great mountains that blocked the northern Grokog from the interior. Now, however, it was little more than a track, for unlike the road Hardog and the northern Grokog were taking as they entered the bowels of the mountain, this road had not survived the forces that had been unleashed by the execrable Mages and the subsequent heaving and twisting of the land. Very few sections of the old road existed and where they did exist the grasses, shrubs and trees had managed to push through cracks and breaks. Thus, Bernis found an overgrown track reaching into the twilit depths of the jungle.

The ghazrak had already started to clear the track, under the control of three of the dark-robed soulless ones. The edges of the path had been widened for quite a long way. The beast-men proved to have extreme stamina once started. Bernis had hit upon this tactic to remove them from the environs of the populace when their murderous nature was recognised. Now it would play into his favour. The army was halted, and the men fed their daily dose of initiative-robbing elixir, along with a basic meal, while Bernis conferred with his captains. Like Hardog he had made the Temple Assistants the army captains. They agreed that, as dark was falling, the army would encamp slightly further back from the edge of the jungle and enter as soon after first light as possible.

The night was an uneasy one for many, being so close to the forest edge. The general mood degenerated into outright fear that forced its way through the effects of the drugs when a blood-curdling scream rang out in the middle of the night. None were of a mind to investigate until morning. As a result, although no further incidents took place, there was little sleep taken that night. In the morning a short investigation revealed a patch of churned grass where one of the sentries had been stationed. Marks of a body being dragged pointed to the obvious conclusion that one of the giant creatures of the jungle swamps and waterways had emerged and taken the guard. When the guard's shattered spear was found alongside the drag marks there was general agreement that any further search was useless. The investigating party returned with some alacrity.

The morning meal was reinforced with extra elixir and the men were formed into their troops. The Temple Assistants selected three of their number to lead the column and the rest formed up behind them. Bernis was placed behind the first rank of the army. The first rank was largely composed of free-will volunteers and Temple guards. Additional Temple Assistants rode between him and the rest of the army. The baggage train followed the second rank, and several Temple Assistants followed the third and final rank, mostly to deal with deserters.

Slowly, and then with increasing confidence, the column moved into the jungle, following the path carved through the foliage and vegetation by the ghazrak. The last of them were well into the jungle when there was a huge *crack!* from behind them. A Temple Assistant raced back to ascertain the cause and returned to report that an enormous tree had crashed down across the trail, rendering return next to impossible.

Bernis turned to look back the way they had come, lips pursed. For a count of ten or more he stood like that and then turned to his captains.

"Well, we were not planning on returning until the job is done, anyway," Bernis said with as much insouciance as he could muster. "So, we should just be pleased that Groks, in his great wisdom, held that tree from collapse until we had passed through."

As Bernis moved back to his place in the column the captains shared an expressive look of doubt and made their respective ways to their own places. The march continued.

Behind them the group of Waslit scouts moved onto the trail. Their tree-felling tools were once again carried on their backs or by their sides. Carefully, they followed the Grokog at a distance.

2. Leader Of the Tued

Breathless, shaken, with tears running freely down her cheeks, Marjory remained on her knees before Morrig's pavilion. She did not notice the pavilion's walls rise to reveal the Guardian within, nor did she see the compassion on the face of the Guardian that blended oddly with the habitual fierceness.

Morrig was not one to hold back from doing what had to be done, even though the Guardians were not permitted to take part in this action. She had convinced Odruf that Marjory should be delivered to herself, and had decided to watch the Battle Mage for a time before revealing herself. She was glad that she had done so. Morrig had given of her power to the defence of Ennaris in the past, and had just done so again, responding to the Archmage's cry as had every one of the Guardians and the remaining Mages. Interestingly, so too had the woman who the Guardians thought was Dharmoney-to-come, Varna.

Morrig stepped from the pavilion and walked quietly to where Marjory knelt still with tears streaming down her face. She waited and watched as the Battle Mage gathered herself and stood, turning towards the Guardian without surprise and not at all ashamed of the emotion that had washed over her. Morrig remembered Marjory as one of power and she had watched with interest as the most extreme of the weapons used during the rebellion were shielded by the young Battle Mage, drawing on Drewflin and a host of lesser Mages to deflect the worst effects. Knowing that some of the third rank Mages were unlikely to survive the drain, still Marjory had drawn on whatever she could, protecting the lesser ones where she could with a skill that Morrig had not guessed at. Morrig was aware that Marjory had been assisting one of the client races to achieve its secure place in the galaxy, holding back the forces of Goroth from establishing an overwhelming presence. And it was Marjory's sacrifice in leaving Ennaris for that time that allowed the Children to exist at all, for Likud was unlikely to allow a competitor race to survive had he been able to remove it.

Marjory nodded briefly. "Morrig?" she asked.

Morrig nodded. "Yes, Battle Mage. I am Morrig."

Marjory went back to one knee, bowing her head slightly. Morrig and Ogun were two of the Guardians of battle, along with Menra. And while the school where Mages learned the arts of battle was named for Ogun, Marjory had been drawn to the legends of Morrig, changeable in mood as she was reputed to be. Of course, as with all of the Guardians, there had been few reputed meetings of Ennarisi with her once the Ennarisi had developed into what they thought was a sophisticated civilisation, and none had been proven.

"Stand, Battle Mage," Morrig said, glaring at the kneeling Mage. "You have been told that we're not gods. You're being watched by three of the desert people, and they need to see you as strong and proud, for only then will you be accepted to lead them to the final battle."

Marjory stood, finding herself to be slightly shorter than Morrig. "You wish me to lead the people of the desert?"

"In battle, yes. The Guardians have seen the depths of your strategic capability over the last five hundred or so cycles with the people of Ordoreth, and we know that you're a capable leader. Furthermore, we know that you have great power and the judgement to use it wisely, as well as the skill to protect and defend those with lesser powers. And I know that you have the passion still. But it is the people who must choose their leader." Morrig stared at Marjory, her sharp gaze pinning the Mage in place. "Will you take this charge?"

Marjory paused for a moment, considering. "You are aware that I must re-join Drewflin and fight alongside him? If I am not there Goroth will defeat him. Drewflin has great power, but the ability to defeat Goroth and Likud rests with me."

"I understand that," Morrig said quietly.

"And you also understand that once that battle is joined, we will be consumed by it. Your people will have to be part of what is likely to be a larger force, and work accordingly."

"I understand such also. The Faero has acquired a general who has great experience and expertise. He has much to learn about Ennaris but is doing so as we speak. It will be your task to get my people to agree to join with the Faero and to lead them in that task."

Marjory nodded slowly. "The Prophecy calls for the sand and the ice to join together in common cause. I expect your people are the sand. So be it. I agree to lead your people, Morrig, if they will have me."

Morrig just nodded, but the fierceness faded from her gaze. "Come, then, Battle Mage of Ennaris, and meet your charges. They can be a little child-like at times," she added with a fond smile, "but I must admit that I'm pleased with what they became in our long absence. They need your guidance, but they may surprise you also."

Morrig led Marjory over the sands by foot, travelling in as straight a line as could be managed. After a time, Marjory became aware of a soft murmur, a gentle sound coming from not far ahead. They crested a last dune. In front of them was a large flat area that was roughly circular in shape and clear of the blowing sand. Staked around the rims of the clearance were tents large and small of varying shape and configuration but all were of a uniform colour that was designed to blend into the sand dunes. The murmur Marjory could hear came from the centre of the clearance where there was a gathering of some nature under way. Morrig looked over at Marjory and smiled.

"I told them I would bring a great warrior to lead them against Goroth," she said. "They are unsure what that may mean, and so have been meeting about it for two days now."

"Two days?" Marjory glanced askance at Morrig.

"They do like to discuss things," Morrig said. "But once they decide to do something they do it, and there is little chance of stopping them."

Marjory merely nodded to say she understood. They started to move down the slope of the dune. There were no lookouts that Marjory could see, nor any guards ready to defend the small settlement.

"Is this the entire force?" Marjory asked of the Guardian.

"No, this is merely the leadership group. The desert people have developed a tribal system, as you know already, which makes it easier for them to deal with life here. The tribes are no more than about a hundred families each, so they have developed traditions that allow them to meet and work together. This is one of them."

"Like the northern steppes people," Marjory said. "They have regular conclaves. Is this also where shared problems are dealt with?"

"Yes, and there are social aspects also. The larger gathers allow the young people to mingle so tribes don't become too inbred. It seems to have worked for them so far. Oh, and you can expect to be challenged, although that will be a matter of form."

Finally, someone noticed the two women walking from the sand and through the tents. A cry went up as Morrig was recognised and, by the time that she and Marjory emerged from between the last row of tents, the gather was waiting. All were on their feet and shouted for Morrig, although not, as Marjory initially thought, in a form of adoration but in welcome. Faces beamed and hands clapped. This was a welcome that Marjory had never seen for any of the ones who claimed to be kings or queens. In fact, this was the first instance that she had seen of direct contact between Guardian and people, and she was unprepared for the joy that overflowed and the accompanying clamour. The noise was deafening as she walked beside Morrig through the crowd until they reached a point in the centre where there was a low speaking platform raised.

Without pause Morrig stepped up onto the platform and held her hands out to quieten the crowd, which subsided quickly, leaving no more than a few mutters. Almost all of the gathered people were now sitting cross-legged. Marjory was impressed at the immediacy of the reaction and awaited Morrig's words with interest. The latter paused as the crowd settled and then started to speak.

"You know that Goroth has emerged from his captivity. Elmani has carried my messages to your tribes. You have seen some of the handiwork of his people in the ghazrak that attacked one of your settlements. Those in the north of Ennaris have fared much worse than you have and have fought skirmishes and battles against the same evil creatures. I have told you how the Archmage has been working to create a defence against Goroth and his minions. And I have promised you a warrior to lead you." She paused while the crowd gave voice to their approbation, several looking around to find the great warrior who would lead them to glory, and then gestured Marjory forward. "This is that warrior."

Morrig allowed a space for puzzlement to find voice and then subside. This was no warrior but a soft woman from outside the desert, wearing clothing unsuited to the environment. She did not even carry a weapon. How could she be this great warrior? However, the desert dwellers had trusted Morrig during the long ages of her absence. Once again they gave her the benefit of the doubt. Morrig grinned to Marjory.

"Some of you doubt," she continued. "Some of you cannot understand why I would call this woman the greatest warrior of Ennaris. I call her the greatest warrior of Ennaris' history." More hubbub arose and subsided. "For this is Marjory, Battle Mage of Ennaris, she who held back the forces of ultimate destruction, she who fought the battle that resulted in Goroth being captured and imprisoned. This is who will lead you to the last battle where Goroth must be defeated."

Morrig waited. All eyes were turned to Marjory, who merely stood at the foot of the speaking platform and waited. She did not know what was about to happen, but she was prepared. Morrig had mentioned a challenge, but not the form of the challenge. Finally, at the rear of the crowd one stood.

"I do not doubt the word of Morrig," he announced to the crowd, "but I would know more of this Battle Mage. I would test her to see if she truly is the one to lead the Tued."

"And would you do this yourself, Topil?" Morrig asked with a tone of formality.

"I would, Morrig, by your leave," the man replied, moving forward and threading through the sitting crowd.

Marjory regarded him with interest. He was tall and lean, which she could see even with the voluminous robes of the desert people. He walked steadily, confident in his own body and sure that he could hold his own against his opponents. Even the fact that Morrig had introduced Marjory as the Battle Mage of legend did not seem to concern him at all. As he approached the platform those seated at the front moved back, opening a space for what was to come. Whatever that would be, Marjory thought. Her personal battle skills were not rusty, but she had rarely relied on them entirely for either attack or defence. And whatever she did she had to convince those watching that she was fit to lead. Morrig dismounted the platform and it, too, was whisked away.

Topil walked to where Marjory stood, slightly bemused, and bowed formally. Marjory returned the bow and then started as Topil quickly doffed his robes to reveal the tight-fitting outfit of a desert fighter, ostentatiously dropping his robes in a bundle. Marjory nodded to herself and smiled, very deliberately removing the cape that Odruf had included when he transformed her on the bridge of *Starfire*. She too dropped it in a bundle and stood ready, waiting. Topil reached to his back and extracted from its guard a short but wickedly curved knife, holding it expertly and measuring Marjory.

Okay, Marjory thought, this is a little more than I expected. Still, fight with what you have. She had learned much living on or near Earth, including several inventive forms of fighting to supplement those taught at Resgalar and elsewhere. And, of course, she had her gifts.

With a thought the silver stone centred on her forehead flared and settled into a muted silver glow. Topil paused, uncertain as to what that might mean. The description of Battle Mage took new significance in his mind. But he had made the challenge and challenge was what he had to do. Suddenly he leapt at Marjory, a whirling leap with his knife whipping around through the space that Marjory occupied - or rather, had occupied a moment before. With a fluid move that of which Ogun would approve, Marjory had stepped back so the strike missed and now stepped forward again, grasping the wrist of Topil's hand holding the knife and seemingly with little effort flipped him onto his back.

Topil sprang back to his feet, unsure of just what had happened but sure that she had used some strange sorcery on him, which was enough to make him angry. He turned and leapt again, only to find that she met him in mid leap, the two of them clashing and his knife sliding over her shoulder. With another strange move, this one using her legs as levers as she fell onto her own back, Topil was flipped again, landing hard. He struggled to his feet to find the stranger standing on the far side of the cleared space. This time, he acknowledged, there was no sorcery, just expertise in a strange form of fighting.

For a third time he charged and for a third time he landed on his back as his legs were whipped from under him. And now Topil found himself facing the Battle Mage. The silver glow flared, and the desert fighter found himself two spans in the air, held in a tight grip from which he could not break free. He was slowly spun around so all watching could see him suspended, and then was gently lowered to the ground. The strange bonds released him.

Facing him once again, Marjory stood relaxed. Topil smiled, a genuine smile of satisfaction, and then gestured to one who sat nearby. Seemingly from nowhere Topil was handed a desert scimitar. The large, wickedly curved blade was held firmly and confidently and whistled as Topil swung it back and forth vigorously. Topil's smile faltered as Marjory reached into the air and suddenly held a long, straight blade, created from pure energy that leaked from its edges such that when Marjory slashed the sword through the air it left a light path behind it.

Topil leapt once again, driving the scimitar through an intricate set of moves that usually left many opponents unsure, only to be rebuffed as Marjory's sword sliced through his blade as a knife through butter. Marjory's sword rested on Topil's breast, above his heart, which was suddenly beating much harder. Topil stood for a moment, feeling the heat flowing from the tip of the sword and then stepped back, throwing down the truncated sword and bowing once again. Marjory released her energy sword as the assembled crowd roared approval and rose to gather around the two combatants. Marjory looked around to see Morrig nod and smile approval, and then fade away.

The gather held a feast that night to welcome their new leader. This would be the only time the desert tribes had allowed an outsider to lead them. Plentiful food was consumed, and drink flowed freely. The desert dwellers lived their lives on the edge largely, and when they celebrated, they did so with gusto. Marjory found that she enjoyed herself. She started to understand what Morrig had meant about these people having something of a childlike approach. They saw their lives as a series of battles against nature but had no real conception of what true warfare would be like. She was saddened that it would be down to her to change that. She was saddened further that some, perhaps many, of these people and their fellow tribesmen may be lost.

The food had been cleared away, and music was being played from several instruments ranging from pipes to stringed instruments, drums and other odd things, when Marjory found herself facing Topil again. The latter gave her a broad smile and offered her a toast, which she accepted and reciprocated.

“I apologise for destroying your sword,” she said.

“It’s not a problem,” Topil replied gravely, with a twinkle in his eye. “It was an honour to be bested by the Battle Mage.” He bowed and started to turn away, then stopped. “Besides, it was not my sword.” And with a roar of laughter, he moved off to join a group sitting around a fire and singing.

Marjory stared for a moment and chuckled to herself, before moving to the tent that had been pointed out as being for her. This had been a long day and she needed rest. She looked up into Ennaris’ sky, wondering if anyone was looking back.

3. The Eastern Army

They were three days into the trek through the tunnel. Hardog was getting worried again. The army was travelling at an increasingly slow rate and the atmosphere inside the tunnel was oppressive. Fights among the army conscripts were becoming more common. The few regular guards were used to quell disturbances. The criminals among the conscripted army were pushing against Hardog's authority, looking to foment mutiny. Already the priest had ordered five to be executed and their bodies, complete with the obligatory severed heads, were arraigned on the path behind the column.

But Hardog was at a loss now. After three days the lead elements had reached a region of the tunnel where there was a large gap in the road. Standing at the edge of the gap Hardog stared down at the floor of a large square pit. The smooth sides appeared to be made of the same material as the road itself, and there seemed to be no way across and certainly there was no way around. What to do!

He stood and stared. After standing and staring he still had no idea what to do. Turning back, he saw one of the captains approaching with ten men. The captain directed four of the men to stand in specific locations and lock arms, and then four others clambered up to stand on shoulders and clamped arms. Hardog saw what was being attempted and looked up. The top of the tunnel was not within reach, but the rail running along the centre of the tunnel may be. The ninth man held hands in a cradle to boost the tenth up the structure. The tenth was lightly built and climbed adroitly, trying to put as little pressure as he could on individual members of the structure. Even so, the pressure on the lowest men took its toll and the last climber, obviously aware of that, reached the top and without pause half leapt and half reached for the railing. His two hands clasped the large rail from both sides. Hardog smiled as the men of the structure cheered.

The tenth climber blew apart. There was a great flash and a noise like a huge clap of thunder and the rail was clear again. However, parts of the climber were spread in a ring centred on the point where he had gripped the rail. Hardog stared anew and the cheering died away. He looked down to see that his robe, which he had kept pristine till now despite the travel, had turned an ugly shade of crimson-red in places, and globs of flesh clung to it. Others closer to the point of the explosion were covered in even more of the noisome mix of flesh and blood and were scrubbing at exposed faces and arms that had been peppered with shreds of body and clothing.

Disgusted, Hardog turned away and walked back to the gap in the road, his anger spilling over.

“Damn you,” he shouted at the road, “close this Groks-damned hole in the road.”

“Maintenance hatch closing,” a calm voice said, seeming to be so close to Hardog that he spun around to find the speaker.

There was no-one. However, with a loud grinding noise a section of roadway moved from each wall. After a short time, they met in the middle of the gap and the road was now unbroken.

“Wha... what... what was that?” Hardog stammered.

“Maintenance hatch thirteen has been closed,” the same calmly impersonal voice stated in a matter-of-fact tone. “Ground transport capability has been re-established in this sector.”

Bernis was livid. The captain of the march had explained to him that approximately two hundred of the army could not be accounted for.

“How can we lose two hundred men?” he demanded, glaring at the captain.

"They must have deserted, sir," the captain said carefully. "I can think of no other explanation."

"And the Temple Assistants at the tail of the column?" Bernis hissed.

"Also missing," the captain stated. "Perhaps the deserters killed them."

The latter was said in hope more than with conviction. The army had yet to be issued with their weapons, while the Temple Assistants had been fully armoured and well armed. The likelihood of that scenario unfolding was somewhere between unlikely and ridiculous.

"Or your precious Temple Assistants were the ones who deserted and took the two hundred with them," Bernis shouted.

This was yet another setback. The army had penetrated four days into the jungle and each day threw up additional challenges and problems. After the tree fall that blocked the return path had come the extreme humidity, which caused the men to suffer more as time went on. On the second day some sort of sickly-sweet vapour had issued from the surrounding trees along the trail. Soon after that a swarm of slithers had erupted from the undergrowth. Hardog lost over a hundred men from poisonous bites. The men died hard, screaming from the pain, their skin quickly blackening and rotting where they were bitten.

The next day, stinging insects descended on the march, and almost everyone now carried welts and stings. A range of assorted injuries had been incurred as the troops tried to avoid the insects. The drugs that had been fed to the men meant that they had less volition to avoid those injuries, and more than fifty of the men had severe stings and were incapacitated. Several had died. Bernis had been told that most of the other severe cases would do likewise. And now this on the fourth day. So far, almost five hundred men were either dead or had disappeared. Unbidden, Hardog recalled the tales of the supposed jungle dwellers, but he pushed that thought aside contemptuously. There were no jungle dwellers.

The ghazrak were suffering also. Their armoured body plates made them heavy and somewhat unwieldy. While their stamina remained almost as strong as when they started, each of them had sores that leaked a greenish-black fluid. The black-robed soulless appeared not to be affected, however. They continued to drive the ghazrak mercilessly, for the army had almost caught up to the ghazrak. Should that happen then they would have to slow down or stop and wait for the trail to be cleared further. Bernis liked neither option.

Day five dawned as had the others. A wan light filtered through the jungle canopy and made its uncertain way to the army. The rounds of the captains told the continuing tale of attrition. All of the serious bite cases had perished during the night. None of the myriad drugs brought with the priests had served to effect cures. In addition, it was this day that Bernis expected to reach the ghazrak as they continued to drive through the jungle. One sixth of his men were gone, and from the information they had received from the great Mage Grensor they had come only one-fourth of the way, if that.

Hardog calculated that they were half-way through the tunnel. Two more of the open pits had been encountered on the march, but each time Hardog had told the mantenhash to close, on the orders of the First Prophet of Groks. He had no idea whether invoking Groks had any effect, but it was always a good idea to make it seem like Groks had a hand in things, whether they be good or bad. As Hardog was Groks' representative, even if it was via the First Prophet, he expected to receive some of the benefit at least. Nor did he know what a mantenhash was, but it seemed to close when he told it to, so he decided that was good enough.

His confidence was rising as the column halted for the evening meal. His army was intact, mostly. The grumbling had stopped after a few more of the lead troublemakers had been identified and fresh examples made. The speed of march had improved. Now, after eight days in the passage between the east and the west, Hardog was looking forward to the end of the journey beneath the mountains and what was to come after that. He ordered the officers to start training the conscripts in the basics of being soldiers, for which purpose many non-lethal withies had been included in the wagons. No weapons were issued yet apart from the short spears, but they could learn how to wield them and a sword.

Trouble came upon the army as they prepared to start the march for the ninth day. The small guard that had been placed at the tunnel mouth into which the army had ventured were shocked into immobility by the sight of six huge birds swooping from the heights in the early morning twilight. Even more shocking was the sight of six riders harnessed to the back of the birds, riding easily. The final and last shock came as each of the riders selected a target and fired their short crossbows in unison. The members of the small guard died, and the six Rocs gained height after the attack. The scout wing circling above them watched closely for any potential attackers. None were found. It was decided that the attack on the guard was a success, and the second phase was initiated.

No-gar sent the agreed signal. From the heights of the mountain range Hel-nor and the four Roc battle wings of the Alnar-kun swept down. Forty-one Rocs, each with its designated rider, formed staggered arrow formations to make sure they did not touch walls or each other, and flew into the mouth of the tunnel, making slightly more noise than a whispered conversation. Within moments the tunnel mouth was quiet once more. The six dead guards lay where they had fallen. The scouts pushed higher above the pass and winged their way back to the eyrie. The guards would be discovered later in the morning with no clues as to how they had been killed apart from the crossbow quarrels embedded in each chest.

In the middle of the tunnel Hardog felt something from behind. It was a whisper of air at first, then it became a steady beat, like a drum being heard from far away. He stepped away from his tent with a quizzical glance around. He finally determined that the noise, which was more than a whisper now, was coming from behind the column. The air was moving as though being pushed forward, like the bow wave pushes ahead of a small boat. He walked towards the rear of the column. He was more curious than worried. However, curiosity became concern and rapidly gave way to fear as the shifting currents and soft beats took on a different character. Something was coming and Hardog could not imagine what it was.

He turned to shout a warning to those at the rear. His words died in his throat as he saw an impossibility. Appearing from around the slight curve of the tunnel and driving towards him were giant birds and on the backs of those birds were riders. As Hardog's words died, the lead Roc gave voice to the mighty war-cry. The tunnel reverberated as the shattering cry was taken up and repeated by every one of the forty-one Rocs winging their way through that tunnel. The Grokog army was thrown into utter confusion. And then, to make matters worse, the lead rider held up some sort of staff and a brilliant silver-green light shone forth. Legends of nightmare come true!

Into the terror engendered by the sound of the challenge and the rush of the Rocs through the tunnel came crossbow bolts. Each of the riders except the first triggered a bolt and reloaded quickly, smoothly, to fire again and then again. From the staff of the front rider, balls of silver fire were flung into the massed troops. The riders would only have time for three crossbow bolts, but most of them found a mark. None of the army tried to return fire. The Temple guards, easily identified by their bright garb and body armour, were especially targeted. Neither they nor the ordinary guards had been issued bows in any event, and of course the rest of the army was unarmed except for the short spears. Then, from the centre of the winged terror more fireballs rained down, targeting the supply carts. Hardog watched as most of his supply of extra spears, bows and arrows was decimated by fire.

With a final defiant cry, the Rocs of the Alnar-kun accelerated down the tunnel towards the western end. It had taken them almost four hurs to cover the distance from the eastern tunnel mouth to the mid-way point where they found the Grokog army. It took them slightly more than half that to reach the other side. With a breathtaking display of aerial skill, the flights accelerated smoothly and sped down the ancient passage. Finally, with cries of victory, the huge birds swept from the western end of the tunnel, swinging in prearranged patterns and seeking the heights. The four wings formed into their battle formations and, with a final defiant cry, arrowed for their eyrie.

In the tunnel, automated fans kicked in with a great whine, sucking the smoke from the fires into great vents so it could be expelled via exhausts, some of which remained partially intact. But, for the Grokog, the sounds and effects only added to the confusion and fear.

Bernis stared in horror. Through the camp rampaged enormous creatures. Their giant tusks ripped at the southern Grokog army. High-pitched, ear-splitting squeals created confusion and panic. The beasts were much larger than anything Bernis had ever seen in Grokog. They trampled the men, their tents and implements into the spongy surface of the trail. Further towards the back of the column Bernis could hear shouts and cries of pain. Something was happening there also.

He felt helpless. The rampage was over quickly but the damage it caused was huge. Men ran to assist those who were injured. Bernis grabbed one harried Temple Assistant and directed him to go to the other end of the army column to see what had happened. He tried to create some form of order, but it took a long time. Finally, after an age of shouting and threatening, he was able to achieve some semblance of order. The news from the other end of the column was no better than where he stood.

All up a further hundred and thirty men were killed but over four hundred suffered injuries from the two stampedes. Half of the injured would not be able to wield a weapon, which meant that he had lost almost one third of his army since the march began. At least the ghazrak had not been affected, and they continued to forge ahead mindlessly. Or not mindlessly perhaps. Bernis now was aware that the three soulless were, in fact, controlling the ghazrak somehow. At all times at least one of them was exercising that control.

After a long night while the damage was assessed, the dead were left at the back of the column on the line of travel. They had already -

only once - made the mistake of laying the dead out near the army only to find a truly terrifying array of predators become interested in them. Bernis decided to put distance between the site of the latest disaster and the bulk of the army. The injured were left behind to follow when they were able, and the army marched on.

Behind them the Waslit emerged from the jungle. None of the injured would ever join their erstwhile comrades.

The northern Grokog army was in complete disarray. Hardog had lost half of his Temple Assistants during the surprise attack and a large quantity of his weapons. Surprisingly, the army's losses numbered less than one hundred, which was a tiny percentage. However, there were many injured, some critical. More worrying, the effect on morale of seeing those giant birds and that silver-green light shining forth from the front of the pack, of hearing what could only be a challenge shrieked at the Grokog during the attack, was shattering. The sense that this force of previously unknown creatures was now waiting for them at the tunnel's end created a palpable feeling of terror. It was difficult to enforce the order to proceed, but Hardog and the remaining Temple Assistants and guards managed to do so.

On the eleventh night, once the army had been fed and was bedded down, and with too few guards available to maintain an adequate watch, over five hundred men deserted. The drugs had lost their impact, and too much had been given to maintain the docile state required by Hardog, so the cooks reduced the dose to make sure the supply lasted. This allowed some of the men to break free of the effects. It started with a small cadre of men from the same village. They, using the residual effects of the drugs to make others compliant to their orders, slipped away in small groups. They avoided the few guards or, in at least two instances, were accompanied by the guards. Others noticed what was happening and made their own moves, pulling friends with them or just exhibiting fellow feelings for other victims of the priests and their perfidy.

On the twelfth morning, Hardog was greeted with the news of the desertions. When Hardog demanded that the Temple Assistants go after them and execute them all, he was informed that there were insufficient Temple Assistants remaining to undertake such a duty.

Hardog was seething but was forced to recognise the truth of that statement. He ordered the march to be resumed. He also ordered the remaining Temple Assistants to place themselves ahead of and behind the army to ensure that others did not follow the example of the deserters, but the damage was done. As he sought to understand how the men could break away from the effects of the drugs, so efficacious in the past, he was made aware of the reduction in the quantity of the drug provided to each conscript. Of course, he ordered all the cooks to be executed, which was duly done. Now he had to find cooks.

Gritting his teeth at his bad luck, Hardog ordered the true volunteers, many of whom remained firm adherents to the tenets of Groks, to replace the cooks. He made sure that they were aware of the required quantities of the different powders needed. Because of the reduced numbers, there should be enough to get through this everlasting tunnel and maybe slightly further. At that point they should be taking plunder and he was confident that the men would stay with him then.

That, at least, was what he hoped. His store of confidence was dropping all the time, however.

The small river should have provided few obstacles. Bernis, however, was taking nothing for granted now. The reduced southern army had come upon the river - it was better described as a large stream - early on the thirteenth day of the march. Steep vertical sides looked like the banks could have been constructed and were being maintained, which Bernis now thought possible.

During the previous night, a further thirty-seven men had died, apparently in their sleep but, to a man as adept with drugs as Bernis was, it was clear that they had been poisoned. It was a very subtle poison, perhaps, but he could tell by several minute signs. Eyes were slightly rheumy where they should not have been, even in death. Several had tiny abrasions as if something had brushed against them and their skin had reacted. Pondering on the deaths took a very short time. The Grokog army was not alone in this damnable jungle. Once again, the stories of the jungle dwellers returned to the front of his mind. This time he did not dismiss them.

The stream offered several paths across, all of them via thick, sturdy looking logs that spanned the width of the waterway from raised bank to raised bank. The logs' ends rested on equally sturdy looking logs that extended along each bank so that they were level with the ground. The stream was quite a long way below the level of the banks and its surface was smooth and unbroken. A few ripples caused the surface to undulate from time to time. The upper surfaces of the crossing logs were worn smooth, as though they had supported many crossings of many people. The path widened so it was quite broad at the point where it encountered the stream. This obviously was so that more people could avail themselves of the multiple logs. On the far side, the clearing shrank again in size after a short distance until the exit was no wider than the path they had been following for more than a tenday now.

The carts with their remaining equipment would not make it across and there remained quite some distance to go. Resigned, Bernis ordered the weapons to be distributed to the men, and packs were stuffed full of provisions, medical supplies and water bags. Cooking utensils were attached to belts.

With a gesture Bernis sent the ghazrak across and watched as the not-men made their strange shambling way across the logs to the other side. They were closely followed by their not-men shadows in black robes. Bernis shuddered. When first he had seen the ghazrak, he had been astounded to see these creatures that were so nearly of the likeness of Groks. He had been surprised when the black-robed ones had been described as their superiors but accepted the fact. Now, he was beginning to reconsider his opinions. The ghazrak were nothing like what he expected Groks-like beings to be. They were almost elemental beings in their ferocity, from what he had seen. They had caused considerable mayhem before being dispatched to commence driving through the jungle, so this overly docile behaviour was somewhat bewildering. He was unable to rid himself of a feeling of impending doom.

However, the ghazrak were across the stream and the captains were awaiting orders. Bernis gestured curtly and the first group made their way across the stream, gingerly stepping along the length of the logs. One man in the middle of the first group made it half-way along his log when he turned to speak to the man behind. His foot slipped on a mossy section that he would have easily avoided had he watched where he was walking. With a sharp cry he slipped into the stream. Bernis' irritated frown turned to horror as the smooth surface of the water became a seething cauldron. A second sharp cry was cut off as a huge creature from nightmare erupted from the stream carrying the fallen man in its huge saw-toothed mouth, shaking the body of its victim as it fell back into the water. Water-crawler! As it hit the water, a second water-crawler latched onto the head and a third onto the lower legs and, as the horrified army watched, the unfortunate victim was torn into three sections. A few moments later all were gone. Only a red stain was left, moving slowly in the direction of the stream's travel, to provide evidence of the calamity.

The men who were still on the logs had frozen in place. The action had taken but moments. The sudden violence caused those who had not yet stepped onto the log to stop and regard them with terror. Those few on the far side watched the water surface and the tops of the stream banks on their own side with suspicion. Bernis could hardly blame them and found himself staring into the water. It was then that he realised that the water had sprouted many small bumps, bumps that had not been there when they started to cross the stream. They were the eyes of the water-crawlers. Staring into the shadowed depths, for the light remained dim even with the wider spaces on each side of the crossing, Bernis thought that he could see long serpentine shapes swimming slowly towards the crossing.

The men on the logs had seen the same, and several sought to turn back. With a curse Bernis walked to the bank of the stream.

"Move across, all of you," he shouted angrily, turning to the Temple Assistants. "Get them moving across."

When the men stood and stared uncertainly, Bernis snarled another curse and stepped up to the fourth of the seven logs, the one in the middle. He stepped onto the log and started to make his way across. He strove to appear confident when all he felt was rising fear. He did not look down at what he knew would be the watching monsters.

"Move," he snarled once again. "If I find any of you in my way, I'll feed you to those crawlers myself."

With a start, the men standing on his log started to move across once more, followed by those on the other logs. That started the movement once again and the men started to stream across. Once on the far side, Bernis stood and watched as his army moved into motion once again. As they reached the far side, the men were marched towards where the path started once again. The ghazrak had not stopped as the horror had unfolded and were moving doggedly forward once again.

Some of the first men across carried long ropes which they now tied off to trees growing along the bank near the edge of the clearing. The ropes were used to transfer additional packs of foodstuffs and other supplies, held in slings.

The movement had now reached the best cadence it would do, with around twelve or thirteen men on each huge log at a time. Most of the supplies had been transferred and were being re-divided among the men who were across. About two hundred men remained to cross and around a hundred were on the bridge when the Waslit dropped the logs. Watching for the opportune moment, teams of Waslit both upstream and downstream of the crossing gripped their sturdy spliced liana ropes. At a signal from a spotter perched high in one of the trees that offered a clear view, both teams heaved at the ropes - once, twice and then a third time.

The men on the logs had a momentary warning as the logs shuddered slightly at the first pull and then shook at the second, causing the men to grip the logs tightly. On the third tug the upright supports under the huge east-side cross-log that, in turn, supported the eastern end of the crossing logs, were pulled into the river. The cross-log fell a moment later, followed by all seven of the bridge logs. The hundred men on the logs were pitched into the water. A feeding frenzy ensued. While several were pulverised by the logs as they collapsed into and then spun in the water, most were victims of the water-crawlers, and their screams of pain could be heard for long distances. Bernis could do little but stop and stare, aghast at this latest outrage. He stayed on the far bank for a long time watching his men die.

The two hundred men left behind looked around themselves. The Temple Assistant who had been detailed to trail the column stared at Bernis. The despair etched on his face changed to nothing more than a blank look. As Bernis watched he pitched forward. One by one the men yet to cross followed suit, several clutching their necks as they did so, and Bernis understood. Blow darts! Almost three-quarters of the remainder started to run back down the path, away from the stream, away from the horror, away from the killing. Bernis watched them go, knowing that none of them would make it. Several fell as he watched.

Now he knew! Bernis' column was under persistent attack. Those stories were not tales made up to scare gullible listeners. They were true. Even as Bernis had that bitter thought, the tales became reality as from the jungle on the far side to Bernis stepped a short, nut-brown man, wearing little but a breechcloth and carrying a short bow. Oddly, in one hand he carried a standard, the bright red flag limp in the still, humid heat until he held it on the diagonal and Bernis saw the insignia. His heart sank as he recognised it from his studies far in the past.

The sigil of the Faero of Ennaris!

The small man thrust the standard pole into the ground and stepped back into the shadows of the forest.

4. Ennaris' Moon

The two shuttles had taken a very circuitous route but were almost in position. Having left *Starfire* some hours earlier, they had taken a path via the rear of the fleet and then made a wide swing around the planet until they intercepted the moon, following the instructions left for them by Odruf and the Grand Admiral. It was hoped that the Empire fleet would see the movement as nothing but repositioning of personnel or the transfer of equipment. Admiral Jord, who had been tasked to lead the mission, remained unsure of what he would find. No, change that, he thought, he just had no idea.

With him were a command crew, several engineers and two full wings of pilots whose stingers had been destroyed when their ships' hangers had been targeted successfully by one of the earlier enemy attacks. All wore close-fitting regulation zero atmosphere suits. At least he knew that this mission must have something to do with ships, hopefully some fighters. Serra's cryptic warning before she departed had been to tell the pilots that they may find themselves with something more potent than they were accustomed to. Jord found that hard to accept, given that *Starfire* was the most advanced ship since *Sunburst* and the fleet's fighters were the latest generation. But he also knew better than to guess against Mavin Serra - Marjory. He shook his head. He'd need a whole lot of time after all of this was done to process what happened.

The shuttle pilot watched her screen intently, before calling to Jord.

"Captain, er, Admiral, I mean - sorry, sir - coming up on the waypoint now."

Jord grinned. "No problem, Ensign. How far until you relinquish control?"

"Thirty seconds, sir." The pilot shook her head. "Is this a good idea to let an unknown facility take control, sir?"

"If it had been anyone except the Grand Admiral then I would say no, Ensign. But it *was* the Grand Admiral and there are things going on here that we just don't understand. So, let's flow with it."

"Aye, sir. Waypoint in four, three, two, one. Control has been passed over, Admiral. Both shuttles show change of control." She sat back, nervously rubbing the back of her neck.

Jord had to admit the he felt apprehensive, too, but he reminded himself once again that it was Serra's plan, and she pretty much never got it wrong. A few lights blinked on above the pilot's screen and a faint tone sounded. The screen blanked and restarted.

"Sir," the Ensign called, "we just had a new control program initiated. It doesn't match anything we've had previously. It looks like it has always been there but was partitioned away."

Jord nodded. Yep, this was Serra alright.

"Steady, Ensign. Has the second shuttle initiated the same control program?"

"Yes, sir. The shuttles are being challenged and the control program is responding." She paused. "This is amazing, sir!" she continued, awe in her voice. "According to this we're entering a facility designated Nova on a base called Escantil. The facility is online but was not picked up by our previous control system. Sir, Nova is huge! It occupies almost the entire centre of the moon and seems to have docking facilities on the permanent dark side."

Jord released his constraints and walked the two steps to the pilot's station, looking over the ensign's shoulder. The schematic on the screen did look impressive, although it was hard to make out details. But he could see what appeared to be hangers and launch tubes. His eyes opened wide - twelve hangers each with their own launch tubes? Around each were what seemed to be engineering facilities, repair bays.

"Sir?" The Ensign pilot called out urgently.

"I see 'em, ensign," Jord replied. "Stay calm."

Directly in front of the shuttles a section of the moon's surface appeared to disappear, almost to fade away. And pointing at them were cannons, enormous cannons, and the new control system said that they were powered and locked onto the approaching ships. Beneath the cannon emplacements a slit appeared, as though a huge door has slid up and the two shuttles altered course slightly to head directly toward the slit. As they approached it appeared to grow larger. It would easily have accommodated much larger ships than the two shuttles. Ensign and admiral were quiet as the shuttles approached the entrance, mesmerised at the sight of the huge muzzles of the cannons following them all the way. Finally, after what seemed to be a very long time but was only two minutes by the ship's clock, the shuttles passed through the huge hatch, and into darkness.

The shuttle's front lamp ignited, as did that of the second shuttle, now ranging alongside Jord's. A long shaft was revealed, clad in a translucent material that absorbed the light and seemed to glow in response. In the distance, a set of lights came on and, after a short time, the shuttles emerged from the tunnel into a large cavern, brightly lit. Around the walls were arrayed enormous empty brackets, various closed pods of some sort, multi-story bays and equipment that Jord knew his engineers would salivate over. The shuttles stopped, spun in place so they were facing the tunnel and set down gently.

"Sir, we have passed through some sort of force field. Atmosphere is being generated in the landing site. Atmosphere is ready. Near enough to ship normal, sir. Gravity is slightly less than ship normal but close enough."

"Very well, Ensign. Well done." Jord reached for the communication stud and stabbed it once. "All personnel, this is Admiral Jord. Disembark but do not disperse until we are better acquainted with this facility. Squadron Captains Horwen and Kurzil, please assemble your wings and await orders. Security, secure a perimeter."

He stood back and watched the screen that now showed the external view of the shuttles. The rear doors cracked open and were lowered, creating ramps for disembarkation. First out from each shuttle were security personnel, wearing full combat suits and with pulse rifles at the ready. They spread out in a cordon around the two shuttles, the squad leaders both examining wrist displays intently. Finally, they conferred with each other.

"Clear to disembark, Admiral," one of the squad leaders reported.

"Very well," Jord said. "All personnel disembark."

Jord was one of the last off, as he had been at the front of the shuttle, and he looked around with interest. He walked to the chief engineer who was standing with the two Squadron Captains. All three nodded without saying anything. The chief engineer contented himself with a gesture that expressed amazement.

"Chief, let's find out where we are. See if you can find out." He thought back to Serra's comments and smiled. "I have a feeling you will find much of this familiar. Horwen, Kurzil, get your wings ready to move as soon as we can orient."

The chief engineer nodded and pointed to what looked like a view panel, while the Squadron Captains moved to where the pilots were gathering. At the view panel the engineer examined it for a moment, shrugged, and reached out to touch the screen. It glowed to life immediately, displaying a row of icons down the left side while the main image showed live footage of the landing bay from above. Jord could see the organised chaos coalescing into defined groups. The image was wiped away as the engineer, after examining the icons for a moment, exclaimed in satisfaction and touched one.

"This should be the schematic. It's almost exactly like ours," he said to Jord. "How is that even possible?"

Jord smiled. Realisation was sinking in that, in Serra, the Union may have been handed one of the most important people in human history, and almost no-one would know.

"Serendipity, Chief," he replied, "just think of it as serendipity."

"Huh," the Chief Engineer responded, "no such thing. But look, this is where the pilots need to go. A couple of the fitters will go with them to help get things ready."

He pointed to a section of the screen where the twelve hangers were clearly outlined.

"Okay, assign each squadron to one of them, I think. Any idea how many craft there might be in each hanger? We have about fifty pilots per squadron to get fitted out."

"Should be able to get that," the chief engineer said, studying the screen again. "There are a few differences but, this ... oh!" He pressed another icon and stopped as he realised what he was seeing. "Admiral, this shows each hanger has three hundred craft. That's incredible!"

"Three hundred? Well, now, that makes a nice change." Jord thought swiftly. "Assign both squadrons to the same hanger and leave the others. See if you can make it one where the launch tubes come out on the dark side." He touched a stud on his communicator tab. "Squadron Captains, to me, please." Then to the Chief Engineer again, "Can you get visual of the hanger we will use?"

"Aye, sir, I think so."

He touched another icon, and the screen went dark, resulting in fresh muttering to himself as he examined the set of icons anew, then a soft curse as he realised what he had forgotten. As the two Squadron Captains arrived, he touched another stud. On the screen, the dark image was replaced by a progressive reveal of the hanger, with row after row of lights switching on. The hanger extended into the far distance. Revealed via the lights were the craft of the hanger, and the sight drove any thought of speech from any of those clustered around the screen. Large, bulky craft, obviously shuttles or transports, occupied the immediate front of the scene, with some form of land craft next in line. But it was what followed that caused the four officers to stare. Rank after rank of needle-nosed space craft, their rear quarters hidden by the mountings, extended down the length of the hanger on both sides and up five rows.

"Oh my!" breathed Squadron Captain Horwen as she saw the fighters revealed. "Oh my, oh my, oh my!"

"Admiral, if I'm not mistaken, they seem to be very similar to the new X5 fighters," Kurzil breathed.

"I think you may find that they are more advanced than ours, Kurzil," Jord said softly. "Warn your pilots. I think we may have found our edge."

"How can they be more advanced, Admiral? The X5 is the best we have and they're ahead of the Empire by a long way." Kurzil looked quizzically to Jord for an answer.

"Because we were not ready for these, Kurzil, so we were building up to them. Over this long time, we were being made ready." He stopped momentarily as the sheer scale of Serra's strategy and effort became clearer to him. He was stunned. This one woman had single-handedly turned what had been a shambolic military capability five hundred years ago into an effective and modern fighting force. He must remember to go back through the archives and find out how many names she had used across the centuries. Jord roused himself. "Nevertheless, there are your horses. Go get 'em."

"Aye, sir," the Squadron Captains replied simultaneously, and moved away.

"Right, now for the other side of things. We need to find the repair docks. Apparently, there is something there we need to locate also, a ship I imagine given we had to bring a command crew with us."

The Chief Engineer brought up the schematic again and with a flick of one thumb shifted the perspective. He located and expanded a plan of what seemed to be an industrial complex.

"Here, I think," he said. "And there are the transport tubes. I thought a place like this would have to have something like them." At one end of the landing bay a set of lights came on. "Over there, Admiral. We should have shuttles waiting for us."

In no time, the pilots, along with a few support personnel, were in shuttles hurtling through the core of the moon, while Jord and his command crew were in another shuttle moving in a different direction. Jord watched through the front window of the shuttle as lights came on progressively in the distance and the shuttle sped through the transport tube. Occasionally one side of the tube fell away to reveal some sort of facility, but it was travelling too fast for Jord to get any idea of what it might be. He caught glimpses of machines that he did not recognise, of buildings set back from the tube and once what he thought was a rank of armoured suits. He decided he would have to get clearance to come back and look around, even while he took note of that location.

The pilots arrived at their destination first and disembarked at a spacious, flat station. A large hatch stood in front of them, and the still lighted hanger could be seen through the hatch. The squadrons separated, one going to each side of the ranks of fighters. The pilots stared at the array of craft with astonishment. One of the support staff, an engineer, examined a panel like the one in the landing bay and started to press icons. The schematic for the hanger displayed, and each craft was indicated, most of them with green overlays, and a few with red. The shuttles and land vehicles all showed green.

"Okay," he called out. "Green light means operational, red means the opposite. I'm sending each of you assignments. This is enough like our own that you won't get lost, the Light knows how but that's the case."

The pilots one by one received assigned positions and moved to their designated vessels. Nervous uncertainty gave way to amazement and various utterances of surprise, satisfaction and even of exhilaration as they settled into their fighters, only to find that while these ships may look and feel like the Union equivalents, their performance potential was significantly greater. Whoops could be heard across the closed channels as pilots discovered that these needle-pointed warships were faster and carried a much greater punch. Their various control dials told the story, and that story excited these warriors. Veterans and fresh graduates alike mentally rubbed their hands together, even as they went through their pre-flight checks.

And then there was Flight-Major Grechsly. He was a veteran of several space battles, most of them fought against the Empire, although two were against smugglers and pirates. He was recognised as one of the best pilots of the fleet. Grechsly was amazed at what he found. He examined the dials and read-outs once he had powered on and saw the extent to which this ship expected to be pushed. He started to run through the checks and was stopped in his tracks as the ship spoke to him.

"Asditra Grechsly, nefterdis e mitrel andit," the ship said.

"Er, Control," Grechsly called into his closed channel, "this ship is speaking some strange language. But I swear it called me by name."

"What did it say?" Control asked.

"I said, it spoke a strange language," Grechsly responded, "so I have no idea what it said."

In the background, the ship AI recognised that its pilot did not comprehend what it had said and made a request to the hanger AI. In turn the hanger AI discussed the situation with the Escantil Base control system AI. That entity communicated with the planetary defence control system and received a reply. The Escantil Base control system sent a flash request to another system, which responded with a language file, which was uploaded to all the systems at the same time. That took just over one second.

"I apologise, Pilot Grechsly," the fighter's AI said. "I was not aware that you did not speak our language. I have rectified the problem. Preflight checks have been completed."

"Control," Grechsly said, "the ship's now conversing with me in Standard. It's completed the checks in automatic mode. Anyone else have this happen?"

"Negative, Grechs," Control replied. "Looks like you lucked out."

"Excellent," muttered Grechsly, then addressed the voice. "Uh, who are you and how do I address you?"

"I am this ship. In your language we are designated Andar-9. I have detected that you are capable of enhanced mode and will complete the interface shortly."

The ship's systems reconfirmed that Grechsly carried the correct DNA sequence and commenced reconfiguring itself. A moment later it activated the enhanced mode, the small unit behind the helmet rest coming alive. *Interface active*, Andar-9 said directly to Grechsly. *Ready for instruction.*

"Control, this ship is speaking directly to me now, like straight into my brain." He paused and wondered why he was not feeling anything like panic. The Union ships did not do things like this.

"Grechs, I have no idea," Control replied. "We're getting ready to punch out, so try to roll with it."

"Great," Grechsly muttered again. "Okay Andar-9, let's see what we can do here."

Certainly, Pilot. You may now converse with me via thought rather than speech. What do you wish to know?

"Uh, really? Thought? Let's see," and Grechsly considered. *Can you show me the planetary system and position of the fleets?*

Overlaid onto his vision was a three-dimensional map of the Ennaris system, with the moon and the position of the two fleets. Grechsly could see the ships starting to manoeuvre. The Empire ships were launching their fighters.

"Control, the Empire ships have launched fighters and are on the move," Grechsly said.

"How do you know that?" Control asked. "We only just received the word."

"It looks like I have a neural interface into this ship, and it's tapped into the defence grid," Grechsly replied. "I can see it happening real time. Control, this dance is starting."

"Roger, Grechs. All ships, we will launch in ten seconds. Take up position at the dark side of the moon. Your position is coming up. Form by squadrons and flights."

Grechsly noted the position. *Can you show me the dark side?* He asked his ship.

Yes, was the reply, followed by a clear image again overlaying his normal sight. It took Grechsly a moment to understand what he was seeing, and then his eyes opened wide in shock.

The Light preserve us, he thought, *maybe we have a chance after all.*

Affirmative, Andar-9 replied.

Jord, along with the command crew, watched the lights speed past the shuttle. The occasional station flashed past too fast to make out any detail, but it was enough to understand that whoever built this was so far in advance of the Earth-based force as to be farcical. *And this was Serra's home*, he thought wryly, struggling to take it all in.

Finally, the shuttle slowed and stopped alongside a platform. The doors opened and the small crew moved out onto the platform.

"Okay, Chief," Jord said, pointing to what was obviously a monitor on a wall, "do your stuff. Find out where we are and what's waiting for us."

With a nod the Chief Engineer strode to the monitor and confidently began to work the interface. Jord watched as schematics came and went, followed by a long moment when the Chief stood and examined the display.

"Admiral," the Chief Engineer said. "Apparently, we go that way. There's a docking station down there. This is some sort of repair and service facility." He pointed down a long dark corridor.

Jord nodded in return. "Okay, people. We still don't know what we'll find so stay together. Security, lead the way."

Two security personnel moved to the fore. Pulse rifles held at the ready, they walked into the corridor. As they did so the first section lit, and a moving walkway came to life. Jord smiled slightly, recalling Bard's stories from the distant past about how Serra used to complain to her young ensign about space stations that made you walk everywhere. The crew stood on the walkway as it took them along the corridor. Lights came on as they went. The corridor was featureless for most of its length, finally ending in a large control room. Jord looked around as the lights came on, noting the consoles and a hatch on the other side. Several large windows displaying nothing but darkness were part of the wall into which the hatch was set.

"Welcome, Admiral Jord," a voice said from somewhere, seemingly all around. "Please move to the exit hatch. Systems are being brought online and will be ready shortly. Repairs and upgrades are complete. All power banks have been regenerated and weapons systems have been recharged. Munitions have been replaced with Ennarisi specification for greater reliability."

"Thank you," Jord replied, having no idea what was being repaired and upgraded. "Please show the ship," he continued, moving to the windows, followed in a group by the command crew.

Rork, newly promoted to Major, moved to his side.

Outside, the darkness was banished progressively. The rigging of the yard was first illuminated. Then, in sections, a huge ship was revealed. The lights played off its flanks, then its enormous central fin. Jord gasped, knowing what would be revealed even before the ship was completely illuminated. Rork and several others glanced at him.

"Sir?" Rork asked.

"I'm okay," Jord replied brokenly, staring at what was being revealed.

The final lights came on.

"Admiral!" Ensign Endoris breathed into a silence so profound that the muttered sound was shattering.

Jord shook himself and just nodded, struck dumb as he looked at the ship's symbol, huge on the near side and with a score mark through its middle, as a new voice came through, the ship's voice.

"Register change of command," the voice boomed from the speakers in the control room. "Recognise Admiral Blair Jord, commander of *Sunburst*. Welcome aboard Admiral."

Seated in the command chair, Jord glanced around. *Sunburst!* The crew were arrayed around the bridge. Not all stations were occupied but Jord knew they could fly and fight this ship with the numbers they had. They were tense and on edge. Surprise had given way to fresh uncertainty.

"Admiral, communication from the defence grid. The enemy fleet is manoeuvring and have launched fighters," Rork reported.

Jord nodded. "Release all umbilicals, retract the boarding gangway."

"Aye, sir. Umbilicals released. Gangway retracted. The ship is ready for undocking."

"Move us away, helm," Jord said calmly.

"Aye, sir," Ensign Endoris replied, as the huge ship gently slid sideways though the mass of spars, enormous clamps and other structures of the repair dock.

"Steady as she goes, Ensign. If you scratch this ship I'll dock your pay for the next hundred years," Jord said with a smile.

"Aye sir," Endoris replied. "Don't scratch the ship."

A chuckle went around the bridge and the tension broke.

"Sir, Squadron Captain Kurzil reporting in." Rork turned to Jord. "Both squadrons have launched and will be with us in two minutes."

"Very well, Major," Jord replied. "Ensign, move us to a position five klicks out from the dockyard. Then hold station."

"Aye sir."

Just under two minutes later Squadron Captain Kurzil's voice came over the Union's ship to ship channel, his voice tinged with awe. "Admiral, Hammer and Shield squadrons are on approach. Admiral, is that *Sunburst*?"

"Yes, Squadron Captain, it is. Welcome to the party. How are your new toys?"

"Sir, if we have to give these back at the end of this, you're going to have a mutiny on your hands," was the dry reply. Then, "Squadrons in position, Admiral. Hammer is on point. Shield is on cover."

"Very well," Jord said, unconsciously settling himself in his seat, last sat in by Grand Admiral Serra over fifty years before. "Here we go. All ahead two-thirds, bring the weapons systems on-line, shields up. Major, sound battle stations!"

5. The Eastern Army

It was day sixteen of the march of the northern Grokog and still they were in the tunnel. Hardog had expected to be through it by this time. Rations were now running short. The make-shift cooks had over-fed the army for the first few days, and the always tricky balance of numbers and food stocks had been shifted too far to one side.

He had around three thousand men left. A minor riot had occurred the previous day, day fifteen, and had been stamped out by the remaining Temple Assistants and a few of the volunteers. The ring leaders were executed and so were a few more men who had been heard muttering blasphemies about the great god Groks. *Just over fifty more men down now, which at least made for fewer mouths to feed.* Hardog snorted at the thought. Over one-fourth of his army was gone, and they were yet to get to the other side of the mountains.

It was a good thing that the remaining weapons had not yet been distributed, although Hardog knew they soon would have to be. If nothing else, the surviving draft animals could then be eaten - the weapons scavenged from the destroyed carts were most of what they carried now, anyway.

Hardog's sour musings were interrupted by a Temple Assistant hurrying back to him from the advance guard. What now? The march had been far more difficult than anyone would have thought, certainly more so than the great Mage Grensor had guaranteed. He would have words with that old man when he made it to the field of battle, ancient Mage or not.

"My lord," the Temple Assistant said, breathing heavily. "We can see daylight ahead."

At last, Hardog thought. He pushed past the winded man and hurried forward. Sure enough, as he neared the front of the column he could make out, far in the distance, bright light. A few swift orders and the Temple Assistants rode forward, still being careful where their mounts stepped, although the tunnel lights continued to burn or glow or whatever these strange things did. Hardog knew that he was seeing something from the time *before*, but he really did not want to think about the types of people who could make something that continued to work so long after the shattering events that ended that time.

The front of the column reached the western mouth of the tunnel as first sun was starting to wane and second sun due to peak shortly after. Light was good as a result. Piles of debris stood to left and right of the exit, where the great Mages Grensor' people had moved it when they re-opened the tunnel. Hardog looked out but was unable to make out any features of the land. He had expected to see something like the land of the Grokog. That land was terraced and manicured to the point that the original contours of the land were long lost, even after the destruction. The relative scarceness of land, especially of land suitable for crops, had forced that result. For some reason, Hardog had thought that it would apply on the other side also. Apparently not.

As his eyes became accustomed to the scale of the land, he could make out more details. The first thing he saw was distance, real distance. As far as the eye could see there was land. In Grokog, from the point where the road had entered the tunnel, Hardog could have seen the Eastern Deeps had he been high enough. The small and relatively narrow stretch of land to which the Grokog had been confined since the land had been broken did not provide this sort of view. Hardog struggled to take it in. He found himself sweating, although the air temperature was not overly warm. Nor was the air as humid as it was east of the mountains. Here it felt dry, almost parched.

The distance was brown and grey, dusty almost. It was like there was a pillar of dust hanging in front of the tunnel, and it was growing slowly. Hardog watched the curious spectacle for a time, noting that the cloud was growing. Only belatedly did he realise that it was growing because it was moving towards him and doing so rapidly. As his eyes and senses became more accustomed to the scale and light, he saw that it was, in fact, a windstorm, spinning wildly, lifting items off the ground only to throw them outwards. And it was moving almost directly for the tunnel mouth.

Turning, Hardog gestured for the men in the tunnel mouth to get back, realising too late that the first troop of around one hundred men had already left the tunnel and was picking its way down the slope towards a potential camp site below. Hardog shouted as loudly as he could but to no avail. The wind noise was rising such that he could not be heard. Down the slope, the troop leader realised that the rising wind meant that there was some sort of problem and turned to look back. Hardog gestured wildly, trying to pull the men back to the tunnel. They turned and started to run and stumble back up the slope. Hardog ran back into the tunnel again.

"Back, everyone back, right back!" he shouted as he ran, waving his hand.

The men picked up on the urgency and began moving back along the tunnel. The wind hit the mouth of the tunnel like nothing Hardog had ever heard. More than that, it reached into the tunnel and picked up the stragglers, flinging them against the wall of the tunnel like rag dolls. Hardog was lifted and dropped by a last tentacle of wind. He turned to see broken bodies. Billowing dust and some of the debris drawn from the mounds left beside the tunnel mouth made its way up the tunnel. The men turned their backs on the dust and tried to wrap cloths over their mouths and noses to help them to breathe, hunching over to create spaces in front of them as they would do if caught in a spray storm on the coast.

The tunnel remained blocked by the windstorm for long enough that many of the men, Hardog included, slept. The noise of the wind, now that it was no longer attacking them in the tunnel, was almost soporific, a melodic rise and fall that played a strange tune. *This land*, Hardog thought as he drifted into a troubled sleep full of flying creatures that shot flaming bolts or tunnels that tried to eat men or wind that played with and then destroyed those same men, *this land is not what I was expecting*.

None of the men of the first troop were seen again.

Bernis lost half of his remaining men during the five days of the trek after the river crossing. Each day, more and more of the men fell from blown darts, stingers, slithers or, for those who lagged or moved for any reason off the trail, a range of knife wounds. Nothing he did had any effect. Guards saw nothing. No-one heard anything. There was no smell out of place, although nothing about the increasingly fetid atmosphere of the jungle smelt right to any of them. The men had their weapons but many others were lying along the path of travel where they were dropped when their carrier died, for there were no pack animals to carry them.

Almost four hundred men were lost on the first day, which was the fourteenth day of the trek. There were three hundred more killed the day after that and two hundred the day after that. Only fifty Grokog died on each of the following days, so maybe the attackers were running short of whatever poisons they used in their darts.

Bernis had no illusions. They were going to die, and none of them would have the chance to take the rich pickings that the great Mage Grensor had promised them. These people were not even supposed to exist! These creatures were from legend! The jungle at least had been understood correctly - it was truly deadly. Even the ghazrak were struggling now. Finally, the heat, humidity and clouds of biting and stinging insects had taken they toll. At least half of the ghazrak were limping along behind their fellows, trailing raggedly from side to side. Even the soulless ones were having trouble, although still they glided above the ground, and the insects appeared to have little effect on them. However, the humid air did.

Now, the nineteenth day saw the members of the much shortened column dragging themselves along an ever narrower path, as the ghazrak could no longer maintain both pace and breadth. It had been remarkable, Bernis thought, but it should be close to done. As he had that thought a giant something reached out of a huge tree ahead and wrapped itself around one of the ghazrak that had drifted out of formation. Effortlessly, the sinuous creature, as thick as a man was round, lifted the ghazrak into the tree. It coiled itself around the torso and squeezed. The ghazrak tried to fight and failed once, twice, a third time. Bernis clearly heard the *crack* as the ghazrak's inbuilt bony armour gave way. There was a further moment of struggle and the ghazrak hung limp.

Bernis stared. Those man-beasts appeared to be unbeatable and yet that huge, truly gargantuan slither has destroyed it easily. As he watched a second and a third ghazrak were harvested - there could be no other word - and the rest redoubled their efforts to cut through under the urging of the soulless ones. The remaining men held back until one of them was taken, effortlessly, soundlessly, followed by a second and a third. Then there was a general scramble to catch up to the ghazrak, who were wielding their giant misshapen machetes or swords or whatever they were like nothing Bernis had ever seen. The remaining seventeen drove forward, followed by the soulless ones, all three of which were now working together.

Then, suddenly, there were only two soulless. With a sigh, the rearmost of the soulless trio died. A throwing knife remained tangled in the collapsed folds of the black cloak and hood. A second followed, another throwing knife ending its life. The third soulless drew closer to the ghazrak, perhaps to hold control more closely, perhaps to take shelter amongst the massive creatures. However, it was unable to maintain control of all seventeen remaining ghazrak and with shakes of their massive heads five of them broke free of its control. Immediately their baser instincts re-asserted themselves and the five turned back. With inarticulate roars of rage, all five started back along the trail, brushing men aside or swiping them aside with their machete-swords. More men died as the ghazrak lumbered through the shorter column, passing the place of the giant serpents, which claimed two more. The other three ghazrak crashed off the path and through the underbrush to avoid the many strands hanging down from the trees, each of the strands being one of those slithers.

Bernis listened to be sure the three escaping ghazrak were not returning. He could hear them heading away still, although he was sure that they would not survive. Not that he cared! Because the first of the ghazrak at the head of the column had broken through the tree line and reached open ground. With a roar the remaining ghazrak ripped down the shallow screen of vegetation and rushed into the open, followed by the remnant of the small Grokog army.

At last! Bernis almost shouted it aloud, eyes closed in relief. *Thank you Groks for helping us to survive this journey. For now, we go to create glory in your name!*

Shouts of dismay worked through Bernis' moment with Groks. He opened his eyes to yet another disaster. All of the remaining ghazrak were mired in some sort of sinkhole and they were sinking fast. A few men tried to throw them ropes to haul them out but they proved to be either too clumsy to grasp the rope, or too heavy to pull out, or were too infuriated to even try for the rope and lashed out all around trying to fight the unwinnable fight. The final soulless floated nearby, seemingly unable to effect any change. Bernis could never be sure what they were doing, so maybe it was trying to save them or maybe not. However, it moved too close and a slashing, flaying sword from the nearest ghazrak shredded the black cloak. The same odd sigh issued forth and the cloak collapsed.

There was nothing to be done for them, so Bernis did nothing. Besides, they had made it through that damnable jungle. They were almost a thousand strong and ready to wreak havoc on the soft lands of the Faero, the enemy of Groks and thus all Grokog. Looking around, though, Bernis saw that the large clearing they were in was more like a funnel, with what seemed to be a natural path to the south-west. Bernis only had two Temple Assistants left, a small fraction of the number he started with. However, he still had the true volunteers and he put them to work getting the men into some sort of order. Finally, with the ghazrak all having been dragged below the surface of the sinkhole, they started across the waist-high grass for the far end of the funnel, where the trees almost came together. To Bernis' inexpert eyes, they seemed to leave a sufficiently large gap for them to pass through easily.

Bernis put scouts a short distance out in front of the column and urged the men to stay close together. Even so, they were strung out over too long a distance. They were half-way by Bernis' estimation to the gap when the drums started. A steady beat sounded, starting low, at an almost visceral level. It was felt as much as heard, slow and bleak, like a dirge to the fallen. The men were staring around all sides of the clearing, trying to identify the source, but there was no single source. It came from all around them, and it held to the same beat, the same tone, the same cadence. Bernis moved through the halting men, encouraging them to keep moving, driving them, threatening them, and found himself at the front where the men had come to a complete stop.

In front of the line of march was planted a standard. The red flag fluttered in the fluky breeze that had arisen on their exit of the jungle. The sigil of the Faero of Ennaris appeared and disappeared at each gust. Bernis felt little more than a sinking feeling as he walked towards the standard, ready to rip it from the ground.

The drums stopped.

Bernis stood quite still for five heartbeats. Five heartbeats at that time felt like a shorter time than five heartbeats may have at other times. He slowly turned. From the grass all around rose the Waslit, hundreds of them armed with blowguns, javelins or throwing knives, and as though on a signal they all released as one. It was over in moments. The darts and javelins were, of course, tipped with the most potent poisons known to the Waslit. The knives even carried some of the venom on the blades. None were spared, none survived, none died easily.

Except for Bernis. He stood alongside the Faero's standard. He stared witlessly as he looked on at the end of his army. His plans of glory were nought but ashes. Why he was alive he had no idea, but he was, and the small brown men - and women he saw, his enemy included women! - did not attack him but merely watched and waited.

"Who are you and why did you invade this land?" a voice came from behind him, and he turned once again.

A woman stood in front of him, not one of the forest dwellers, but taller, more evenly proportioned to his eyes. But still a woman. Bernis could not see the man in charge.

"I said, who are you to invade the land of the Waslit?" the woman repeated.

"Who are you to question me, woman?" Bernis rasped out.

"I am Credar, first acolyte of the Guardian Likki. I am she who will decide your fate," Credar said and waited.

"A woman does not decide the fate of the High Priest of Groks," Bernis sneered, drawing himself up to stand slightly taller than this upstart woman.

"Groks? I have never heard of this Groks, but you travelled with ghazrak and those others, as described by Likki herself, and that condemns you. What were your plans?"

"I was to join the forces of the great Mage Grensor to defeat the abomination that is the Council of Mages, they who created the destruction of this world so many cycles ago." Bernis held himself proud. "I was to have stood by the great Mages Grensor and Goroth and free this land."

"This land is free already," Credar said with disgust. "It does not need you."

She gestured once and nineteen darts pin-cushioned Bernis.

Credar turned to look around the circle of Waslit. Once fearful of these people, then uncertain of her role, now Credar was ready.

"If there are those who feel the need to return to your homes, go now and go with honour. Those who wish to follow me to battle the great evil in the name of Likki and the Faero, then follow. We go to join the armies of Ennaris."

Turning, without looking to see how many followed and how many departed, Credar strode forward, sweeping up the banner of the Faero as she passed it. Behind her the Waslit formed a tight column and followed. As one they broke into the short-stepped trot that the Waslit used when covering significant ground. Scouts moved out soundlessly to shadow the line of march. None had felt the need to return to their homes.

The day after the great wind storm Hardog moved the troops out of the tunnel, down the slope and into the western lands. He had done it! He had brought them through the tunnel of the ancients and out the other side, an almost impossible task. He had fewer than four thousand men, most of his Temple Assistants were dead and they were almost out of food. But they had made it through.

Now it was time to get the men into combat order.

For three days the men were drilled in the use of their weapons, given some basic training in tactics and how to respond to the shouted commands of their remaining officers. After the three days were up the last of the food was cooked, distributed and eaten and the army of the Grokog started out.

Almost four thousand men, Hardog thought, will be a good number to add to the army of the glorious Mages Grensor and Goroth, for the glory of Groks. And with the thousands of men from the south, the Grokog would make a handy contribution indeed and the First Prophet of Groks would take his rightful place among the rulers of this world. Represented by Hardog, of course.

Far above the line of march, higher than the untrained eye could see, a Roc patrol soared through the brassy sky with their wings held wide to catch the thermals that came off the mountains and rose from the rough, hot country through which the easterners now marched. They watched long enough to be sure of the direction being taken. Then the surveillance patrol of two Rocs turned and sped across the sky.

6. Waslit Reunion

The four tendays after meeting with the militia Commander fell into an odd pattern for Likki's acolytes in the twin cities. Emdur and Ester found themselves playing host to an increasing number of Waslit society members or sympathisers, initially only from Killfor. However, after the first tenday the visitors were more evenly spread between the two cities. To each group of visitors Emdur repeated Likki's request and Nersli told of the Guardian's appearance to ask for the society's help. It became a well practiced routine, so much so that Emdur became concerned that they were being used as entertainment rather than progressing their cause. When he mentioned that to Nersli he was told that those with whom he had been meeting were important members of the Waslit community of both cities and that the meetings were, in fact, instrumental in growing the support for the Faero's cause.

It helped that reports were received during that time of two leaders of the Faero's army uncovering norther spies and helping to slay some sort of monsters in cities along the northern shore of the inland sea. Those reports told that the spies had been working to undermine support for the Faero. A detailed drawing of one of the monsters was received and caused great consternation, especially when other travellers confirmed that the monsters were real. The image was copied and circulated widely in both cities. The news was also told that the two men were two of the Children of the Prophecy and that several Guardians were known to have returned. Speculation ran wild and the words of Emdur, Maxnil and Ester were recalled. The Assembly decision started to be questioned openly. Emdur and Ester received even more visitors.

It was, Emdur thought, only a matter of time before their location was reported to the Assembly.

Maxnil left the storytelling to the other two. He spent much of his time with the Waslit Society, rapidly becoming an integral member. He was taller than most in the Society and deceptively strong. He also was rapidly growing skilled in javelin throwing, and his javelin throws went further and carried greater power than the others. His blowgun work, however, frequently left his newfound comrades rolling in laughter, even more after he missed his target entirely during a demonstration and instead punctured the watching Commander Joplin's arm.

The routine was broken early one morning when Perslil hurried into the safe house and reported that the Assembly had ordered the arrest of Commander Joplin on the grounds of treason and sedition. Joplin was charged with conspiring with Killfor's enemies to leave the city defenceless and open to attack. No enemy was named, however, and there appeared to be little detail about the supposed plot. It came as no surprise that Klors was the Assembly member who accused Joplin.

"So, I was expecting something like this," Emdur said once Perslil had finished his report. "It was only a matter of time before the extra training being given to the militia was noticed. I'm surprised it took this long."

"Most of the militia are Waslit," Perslil said, "and they're pretty thoroughly vetted before being allowed to join. But one of them may have betrayed the Commander."

"Or Klors just made the right connections. It doesn't matter how it happened. What does matter is what Joplin plans to do. Do you know?"

"No," Perslil replied, "but Klors has ordered the Commander to surrender himself in two days' time."

"Very well," Emdur said thoughtfully. "And the Society?"

"We will stand with the Commander!" Perslil declared, to a nod from Maxnil.

"So, this may invoke some sort of civil war? That's probably just what Klors wants," Ester mused. "It may result in severe loss to the militia and quite a bit of mistrust."

"Then it may be time we re-appeared," Emdur said.

The mood in the city was uncertain. The mistrust of the Assembly that arose from the revelations of monsters being fought, Guardians being returned and the existence of the prophesied Children, deepened overnight. Anger was directed towards Klors and the Assembly by some, and towards Joplin by others. Old arguments arose once again, spurred on by the revival by unknown people of tales of Waslit atrocities towards any who entered or even came close to the jungle, including cannibalism. These were met by vociferous denials. Insults were hurled. Fights broke out. Injuries were taken on both sides, and Killfor started to descend into turmoil. The citizens were on edge.

The deadline for Joplin to surrender himself to the Assembly came and went. Klors took the opportunity to denounce Joplin and those who held to the old Waslit ways, declaring them to be enemies of Killfor. He called for citizens to take up arms to protect Killfor from those who would harm it. His call was answered by numbers of men, most of whom appeared to be newcomers to the city. They used the old temple of Gel as a base. This temple had changed character dramatically since the sham trial. The older temple priests had been driven out after Gel was declared a false god and a new cohort of priests took their place. All of the new priests were newcomers to Killfor, although they had lived nearby without showing any priestly leanings. Klors greeted them and made them welcome to the city, declaring that at last Killfor had a proper city god that could be called on for help and guidance. The temple rapidly became a place for a party, and many men and women of the city accepted the hospitality offered, often day after day. It appeared that the new priests had established a solid support base.

Finally, several days after the deadline had passed, news was passed to Klors that Joplin was approaching the city, alone. Klors wasted no time in assembling his supporters to await Joplin's arrival. Almost two hundred men were spread along the road leading to Assembly House, mingling with the crowd. Each wore a yellow armband, a sword and a knife, and carried a stave. Emdur thought that he recognised several from the trial, but he could not be sure. Nor could Ester. Maxnil probably would know, but Maxnil was not with them.

The mood in the city was tense. Several of Klors' men were jostled by angry townsmen as they awaited the Commander's entrance. Small parties of men and women stood in isolated groups looking mournful. Joplin was a popular figure in Killfor, as he was in Port Killnar, and few of the older city inhabitants wanted to see him arrested.

A rustle passed through the crowd as the Commander entered the city, walking down the centre of the wide road unhurriedly. He was in full ceremonial uniform. A dark green tabard had the emblem of the twin cities picked out in white, representing jungle and sea. This was worn over pale grey uniform blouse and trousers. A black leather belt held sword and knife while, somewhat disconcertingly to some, a blowgun was hung on a thong around his neck. A map case was slung from one shoulder. Shiny dark grey boots completed the ensemble. He was confidence personified. Klors' men gripped their staves and felt for swords and knives for reassurance. None of them believed that the Commander of the militia would just saunter up to Assembly House and hand himself in, which meant that his militia could be expected to support him. Word had come that the militia had halted just outside the city, however. Uncertainty prevailed.

The crowd closed in behind Joplin as he walked at the same steady pace. There were several curious glances as men with yellow armbands collapsed in the resultant crowd, only for their armbands to be transferred to another man's arm, who proceeded to follow the Commander. Several grabbed their necks before falling. Close observers may have noticed small darts protruding from their necks as they fell, but the darts were retrieved as the armbands were removed. The pattern repeated as Joplin progressed. By the time Joplin reached the steps of Assembly House he walked before almost two hundred men with yellow armbands and many other men and women without such an accessory. Still he appeared to be unworried. Klors, watching from atop the steps, was puzzled at Joplin's relaxed demeanour but took comfort in knowing what would soon befall this fool.

Joplin stood at the bottom of the steps and looked up at Klors.

"Klors, I was told that you wanted to see me," he said evenly. "And so here I am."

"You were to be here four days ago," Klors snarled.

"Yes, well I had business in Part Killnar and I felt that it was more important." Joplin smiled easily. "Still, I'm here now. What did you want?"

"I am placing you under arrest," Klors said with relish.

"Oh, why?"

"You are charged with treason and sedition," Klors replied with a scowl as a wave of muttered comments swept around the gathered crowd. "You are charged with dereliction of duty and plotting to hand Killfor over to the enemy."

"Which enemy?" Joplin asked.

"The enemy that would have invaded Killfor when you abandoned it," Klors shouted. "And for that you will be tried and hanged. Your new second in command will take charge in your absence and ensure the security of Killfor. You are removed from command of the militia. By order of the Assembly, Allfors has taken command of the militia."

Klors was joined on the top step by a stoop-shouldered thin man wearing a nondescript pale-coloured robe. His hands shook slightly and his pale blue, watery eyes were slightly unfocused. He looked over the gathered throng and was re-assured by the sea of yellow armbands, although he could make out no faces clearly. Around his neck he wore an amulet with an image matching the one that adorned the face of the temple opposite Assembly House.

"This man is an abomination in the eyes of the great god Groks," he proclaimed in a strong voice at odds with his appearance. "You loyal men of Groks, take this man and kill him."

Klors stared and the priest of Groks grew confused as the yellow armbands were ripped off and red headbands were donned by the men and women who surrounded Joplin. The Commander merely stood and looked up at Klors for a long moment before speaking.

"You mean these loyal men and women of the Waslit Society?" he said clearly. "It appears they are loyal to the people of Waslir, not those of the east."

Klors looked around, trying to find his own supporters when his face lit up. Along the main road leading to Assembly House came the militia, marching in two columns of two. They were in full battle gear, with oiled leather breastplates gleaming, spears held upright and shields that showed the symbol of the twin city militia polished to a fine shine.

"Ha, now you'll see," Klors shouted at Joplin. "You are declared outlaw and your own militia will arrest you."

Several in the watching crowd that now ringed the square looked at each other nervously. Joplin appeared to be unmoved. The militia swung into the square where they came to a halt. At a signal from their captains each column of two shunted aside, leaving a wide gap between them. Puzzled looks were exchanged in the crowd. Then, from behind the militia rose a new sound. The two columns of militia turned to face each other.

Through the gap between the militia columns came the remainder of the Waslit Society, nearly five hundred men and women. All wore the urban version of Waslit attire, plain dun-coloured sleeveless tunics and long trousers, soft boots with solid soles that hit the ground in perfect unison. Blowguns were slung around each neck, and small leather pouches were hung from belts, along with knives and the occasional sword. Each carried a buckler, a simple lightweight rounded shield. Many carried javelins. Long hair was tied back with simple thongs and red headbands were tied around each head.

The Waslit Society moved at a sharp trot in perfect unison, each foot fall sounding distinctly. They were tightly grouped in a column four abreast. At the head of the column trotted Maxnil, facing to the front, running easily with three javelins held in his right hand and his buckler held by the left. The column swept through the gap left by the militia. As the Waslit Society moved past them, the two columns of militia turned to the front again and the gap was closed.

Unnoticed as the spectacle of the militia and Waslit Society unfolded, the members who surrounded Joplin had separated and now formed two short columns of two of their own, with the head of each standing beside Joplin. Maxnil brought his larger column to a halt just behind Joplin. The sound of rapid, sharp footfalls stopped abruptly. An eerie quiet prevailed. The citizens of Killfor stared in awe and shock, some recognising neighbours and friends among the Waslit Society's numbers, others trying to fathom what they watched. Klors merely stood with mouth open, stunned to his core.

Joplin finally stirred. He glanced around, acknowledging the Waslit Society with a faint smile before locking glances with Captain Derslin, his militia second - not Allfors, who Klors believed had taken command. Joplin nodded once before turning to face forward again. At a gesture from Derslin ten militia ran from the column into the temple facing Assembly House. At the same time several of the Waslit Society dashed up the steps of Assembly House and formed around Klors and the priest.

A minor commotion ensued as the militia dragged several other men from the temple, followed by two statues of Groks. These statues, however, had horns atop the grotesque visage where the face that was affixed over the temple door had the horns removed. Both were placed near the foot of the steps leading to Assembly House, while the priests were held separately. A hubbub arose as the watchers saw the horned statue and recalled the images of ghazrak that had circulated a short time before. The noise slowly abated.

"Klors, your time in Killfor is over, along with your fellow easterners," Joplin said into the relative quiet. "As for whatever these are ..."

"They are statues of Groks," a voice said from one side, somehow amplified so all could hear.

Joplin turned to face the speaker. He saw a medium tall man with a friendly, open expression, dressed in travelling clothes over which was worn a brown cloak. The cloak was edged with a red material. The man carried a walking stick, Joplin thought, but then he looked again and his breath caught. This was no walking stick, for the stone embedded at the top of the staff - it could be nothing else - showed a very faint light buried deep within it. The man was accompanied by a young woman who seemed unsure of herself.

"And you know this how?" Joplin asked the stranger, watching the stone in the staff.

"Oh, I've had to deal with Groks and its friends before," the man replied easily.

"Groks is the greatest god ever to walk Ennaris!" the priest declaimed loudly. "I call on Groks to smite these enemies!"

"You can call on Groks all you want," the man replied, "but it won't hear you. Groks is dead! Groks was a demon, brought into our world by Goroth and Grensor during the rebellion. It was killed by Marjory, the greatest Battle Mage of Ennaris."

"No!" the priest shouted, spittle flying from his lips as he did so, as a loud murmur went around the watching crowd. "Groks is not dead! Groks demands this man be killed!"

"Again," Joplin said to the man, ignoring the priest. "You know all of this how?"

The young woman grabbed the man's arm and spoke urgently, pointing at the group of priests who had formed what seemed to be a circle where they were being held. The man nodded and strode over to the group, where he raised his staff and crashed it down on the head of a man in the middle of the circle. The struck man collapsed. The stone flashed a cerulean light, almost in complaint at being used in such a manner. It stayed lit, even as its wielder returned to stand before Joplin.

"Sorry," the man said to Joplin. "That fool was trying to raise a demon. I doubt he would have succeeded but you never know. I know because I was there. I am Trabor, Mage of the Council of Mages. I stood with Marjory when she defeated Groks and turned it into, um," he paused as the stone in his staff spat two globs of fire which quickly turned the two statues into puddles of metal, "well, into that. I've always wanted to do that."

"This Groks was a demon?" Joplin asked askance.

"It was," Trabor nodded. "But it also was the pattern for an abomination call ghazrak, monsters that were raised to fight for Goroth and that have started to be encountered again."

Another murmur rolled around the square.

"These?" Joplin asked, opening his map case and drawing forth a piece of parchment.

Trabor glanced at the parchment and nodded.

"Yes, that's a pretty good rendering of a ghazrak," he said. "If you come across them be very careful. They're extremely hard to kill."

"I thank you, Mage Trabor," Joplin said formally, bowing to the Mage. "And I am honoured to meet you. Please allow me to offer you our hospitality while we deal with these traitors."

"Thank you Commander," Trabor replied with a smile. "We are merely passing through. We came to seek support for the Faero and the Archmage as we take up the battle once again. We hope the people of old Waslir will do likewise. Goroth has returned, as the Prophecy said he would. For now, though, I think we will gladly accept your offer."

Emdur stayed at Killfor following the revelations while Ester and Maxnil went to Port Killnar three days later, much later than planned, to continue to spread the message. They were accompanied by a troop of militia for protection and a demonstration of support. In a complete anti-climax, they faced no opposition to their message, for the news had been passed back to that city by several well trusted people who had seen the events of Killfor.

Ten days after that the two acolytes returned to Killfor, with Maxnil leading the four hundred members of the Waslit Society from Port Killnar. Word had been received that the Waslit would move out from the jungles shortly and would join the Faero. The mood in the twin cities was uncertain, for the jungle Waslit were people from stories for many.

There came the morning, only a few days later, when Emdur and Ester were called from their lodging. They reached the main square to find Joplin standing alone facing the road that led to the jungle. The square was empty of people, but many stood around its boundaries. The sense of anticipation was palpable.

"Commander," Emdur acknowledged Joplin with a nod. "You are alone?"

"We felt that it would be less confronting to our jungle-dwelling relatives if they were not met by a large military force," Joplin replied. "So, I will meet them alone."

Emdur nodded, bemused. He doubted the militia would have caused much concern with the jungle Waslit, based on what he had seen of them.

"Oh, and I assumed you would be joining the march to the Faero's camp, so we procured hrss for the two of you."

Emdur nodded again. No mention of Maxnil, he thought.

"Ah, they come," Joplin said as a signal flag was raised and dropped in the distance.

From the direction of the jungle there now came a muted and continuous *shush* sound. Rounding a corner in the distance came a single person, a woman, running with the short trotting gait of the Waslit. Around her head was tied a red headband and she wore a red tabard over her clothes. Even at the distance Emdur and Ester recognised Credar. Ester was about to comment on the lone runner when his breath caught.

Around the same corner, trailing Credar by several spans, came the Waslit, running with that ground-eating trot. They wore their usual breechcloths and soft skin footwear rather than bare feet, along with red tabards with an emblem that Emdur now knew was the Faero's. Red headbands encircled their heads. Hundreds of Waslit pounded along the road. Credar reached the square and headed directly towards Joplin, Emdur and Ester. She stopped in front of the three, breathing easily.

"Commander, may I present Credar, first acolyte of Likki," Emdur said as the Waslit came to a stop a short distance behind Credar. "Credar, this is Commander Joplin of the militia. He will join us to confront the old evil."

"Commander," Credar replied. "Alone?"

"I'll have a few friends along too," Joplin said with a smile.

Credar nodded.

"And Maxnil?"

"He seems to have found those same friends," Emdur replied with a wry grin. "I expect you'll see him soon."

"Well, we won't tarry," Credar replied. "I had hoped to find the whole militia coming with us."

Joplin pursed his lips and gave a peculiar whistle, which Credar now recognised from her time with the Waslit. A grin split her lips.

"Your friends?"

"Indeed," Joplin replied with a grin. "Lead the way, First Acolyte. The Waslit will follow."

Credar turned to face the group of Waslit behind her when she heard the familiar short trot echoing around the square. From the jungle road came Maxnil leading the joined Waslit Society, while from the road that led from the square towards the south came the militia, all wearing the same red headband. Credar stared before she turned to the Commander and laughed in delight. She nodded once and raised her right arm.

"We go," Credar said and swung around to face the road out of Killfor towards Port Killnar. "Oh, and we will meet others outside the city. You may find it a little confronting."

Emdur and Ester hustled for their hrss as Credar broke into the short-stepped trot, followed by the jungle Waslit. Behind them came Maxnil and the Waslit Society. Joplin waited for them to pass and then took his place at the front of the militia, who followed at the same pace.

The Waslit were going to war.

7. The Hides

They approached the small community carefully, walking softly. None of the cottages showed any sign of life. No smoke issued from any chimney. There were none of the sounds that would be expected from what should have been a small farming community at the start of a working day.

Clay gestured to Varna and moved off the small road - more akin to a large trail - that they had been following. The trees had changed from the tall evergreens of the forest through which they had walked to smaller, almost scrubby trees, with odd wind-sculpted shapes. All appeared to lean towards the inland areas. Varna realised that this was because they approached the western shore. The steady breeze was blowing scents of the sea to them. She halted close to the edge of the village, stepping behind a bush to hide her to some extent. Her wider senses told her that this village had no-one at home. Still, she waited until Clay appeared - just appeared - in front of her.

"No-one here," he said shortly. "It looks like they left in a hurry, though, and some time ago."

"Ghazrak?" Varna asked, remembering Anhard Springs with a chill. Clay shrugged. She took a deep breath and opened her senses wide but could not pick up any traces of the sort of bloodshed that she had 'seen' at the other village. "No, I don't get anything like that here."

"Well, people were here last night, I think," Clay replied. "But not many and probably not for long. They may have been checking on the village rather than staying here. I think we need to trace them."

"I agree. I can feel something, but I'm not too sure what it is. Nothing dangerous, though."

Clay nodded thoughtfully. He turned to look at the village and took his time as his gaze roved from cottage to cottage and across the small openings between them. He could see nothing that gave a hint of where the occupants had gone. Slowly, carefully, they moved along the single road that ran between the two rows of cottages. All of them were neat and tidy, with small gardens and paths to front doors edged by whitewashed smooth stones.

"Picture postcard," Clay muttered. "This is too perfect. It's been lived in and some cottages are very old, but the village is too well maintained to match every other village I've seen here. Even the plants are better."

Varna nodded. It was almost an idealised version of a small village, designed for show or perhaps to distract. Varna had been on Ennaris long enough now to realise that even the better villages had some aspects that were not picture perfect. But why, and why here?

They came to the end of the village and paused. Clay ranged along the road a little further, and then moved into the scrubby bush and trees on one side and then the other. Finally, he returned to Varna.

"That way," he said, pointing towards the coast. "There's a small path, almost a game trail, about fifty metres to that side of the road" - pointing to their left - "and they went down there. It's well used. I would guess about forty people, although it's likely that any young children were carried. Last night there were only a few, though."

"Let's go, then," Varna said. "Maybe they don't like visitors, so we'll just have to be careful."

They moved away from the village, following the thin game trail. Varna could see where there were several faint scuff marks. She knew the few marks were readily apparent to someone like Clay. The scent of the sea became stronger and the trail wound behind a low barrier of scrub. Varna pushed through the thin screen and found herself standing atop a low cliff. In front of her, the ocean stretched to the far horizon. Closer to shore, it was broken by several large rocky protrusions arising from the water, one of which had jagged shards on its crown and towered at least fifty metres above the waves that crashed at its base. Three others were lower and, if anything, more jagged. A confusion of small rocky shapes protruded from the water around the larger ones.

Varna moved back to the trail and followed after Clay. He had continued alone and was now well in advance of her. Too late, Varna sensed several people converging on the location where Clay now waited for her. Trusting in Clay, Varna halted and moved into the brush on the side of the trail further from the cliff edge. Very carefully, she moved towards the place where she knew the group had intercepted Clay. She came up behind them, being very careful where she stepped, and stopped where she knew Clay would see her but where she was hidden from the small group. Four young men and an equally young woman stood in an arc in front of Clay with short spears held tightly in what, to Varna's eyes, seemed to be nervous hands. No experienced warriors, these.

"...cannot be here," Varna heard the woman say, addressing Clay.

"And yet, here I am," Clay said reasonably, standing relaxed.

"You must leave," the woman said. "There are dangers around here that you do not understand."

"All the more reason to stay, then," Clay replied. "I would not want to wander into something dangerous."

The woman was nonplussed.

"No," she said, becoming uncertain at Clay's lack of concern. "I'm unable to allow that."

"And you would force me to leave?" Clay asked, his voice remaining mild and his demeanour relaxed. Varna knew that he was on a knife edge of readiness, depending on what the group decided to do.

"We have the spears," the woman said unevenly, "and if you force us to use them we will."

"Ah," Clay said, nodding as though in understanding. "But then again, you probably can't do that."

"You think not?" one of the men said, stepping forward, his spear held ahead of him in what he probably thought was a stabbing position.

He was wrong. With a blur of movement Clay grasped the last speaker's spear. He pulled it towards him so that the man lost his balance and so released his hold on the spear rather than falling. Clay spun the spear in a whirl and stepped into the others before they had a chance to move. The spinning shaft clattering against each of the other spears and knocked them suddenly from inexpert hands. The woman gasped and grabbed her hand where Clay had struck her, looking up in shock to find Clay watching her, the confiscated spear now held in very expert hands. The four men stared. The suddenness of Clay's movements stunned them.

"Don't ever believe you have control," Clay said as though to raw recruits, "and never put yourself too close to your prisoner when you don't know anything about him. Or if he has a friend."

That was her cue, Varna knew, and she stepped from the shrubs before speaking.

"What Clay says is correct," Varna said, and paused while the five whirled at her voice. Chagrin coloured the woman's face. "And you're lucky it was us you encountered, for others would have killed you on the spot."

"Maybe we would not die easily," the woman said, although she looked at the four spears on the ground as she did so. "We do not rely on spears alone."

"Maygry, hush," one of the men said, not the one whose spear had been taken.

Varna glanced to Clay, to see an eyebrow raised. She turned back and looked at Maygry, the young woman, more closely. Her aura was strong, Varna thought, and shot through with blue shards indicating at least one gift. Turning her sight on the other four Varna saw they all had strong auras, and all had similar blue veins running through them.

"What gifts do you have?" Varna asked Maygry, quietly.

Maygry gasped. "I know not what you mean," she said quickly, but Varna sensed that she was building up some internal force, as were the others.

"You do know," Varna said, "and please don't try to use them on us. Clay, I think you can give that back."

Clay nodded. He reversed the spear with a flourish and held it out for the young man who had lost it to reclaim it. He did so uncertainly and then held it as though not sure what to do with it.

"My name is Varna, and this is Clay. We come from the Citadel of the Faero, following rumours of a village of people with the old gifts," Varna said, and smiled as she sensed a sixth person, older and more experienced, moving up the trail behind Clay.

Clay, always aware of his surroundings, moved aside to let the newcomer pass. The latter, an older but far from old woman, glanced at him as she passed and smiled wryly to acknowledge the warrior's skills. She looked at the spears still lying on the ground, assessing the tableau facing her.

"Once I could have made it up here and you would not have known," she said to Clay.

"But you would not have done so without Varna knowing," Clay replied.

"Indeed?" the woman replied, turning to Varna. "So, Varna from the Faero, you would wish to meet with gifted people?"

"I can see that Maygry and the four men here are all gifted and all seem to share the same gift. You, on the other hand, appear to have several gifts, with different strengths. Yes, I would like to meet the people of this village." Varna looked from villager to villager as she allowed the woman to process her statement. "We come from the Faero, who will be leading Ennaris in its fight against Goroth, and Corm needs all the help he can get."

The older woman nodded, regarding Varna as she thought. With a thrill of surprise, Varna realised that the woman was seeking out her aura, and gently she released the constraints that she had been taught by the Guardians. The woman gasped, eyes wide and suddenly trembling, as Varna's aura shone forth, all the colours of the rainbow shifting and whirling through the whiteness of her spirit.

"Lady," the woman said, going to one knee and bowing her head. "Are you a Guardian? I have heard that the Guardians have returned."

"Please," Varna said, suddenly embarrassed, "don't kneel to me. No, I'm not a Guardian, but yes, they have returned to aid the Ennarisi in their battle. Tell me your name, please."

The woman raised her head but remained on one knee.

"I am Jorphy Bart, Lady," she said.

Varna moved forward, through the five who were now completely unsure of what was happening, and reached down to take Jorphy Bart's hand, lifting her to her feet.

"Never kneel to me, Jorphy Bart," Varna said, "and you need never kneel to the Guardians, should you be lucky enough to meet one. We would meet your people, for I feel we have much to discuss."

Jorphy Bart nodded, eyes still wide.

"But who are you, Varna? Your aura is such as I have never seen before."

Varna shared a glance with Clay, who nodded with a smile, causing Varna to respond with a wry quirk of her lips.

"Clay and I are not from Ennaris," Varna said, to more gasps from the villagers. "The Children of Ennaris have returned, and I am one. Clay is Champion of the Light."

"The Prophecy! The Champion is one of the Nine!"

"The Prophecy will come to pass," Varna replied. "And we will be ready to do what is required, but we cannot do so alone. Your village, assuming you are not the only gifted ones, may need to play its part also. Your knowledge of the Prophecy seems to be better than most. I would hear more of your village and its past."

"If you know the Prophecy well," Clay said and smiled as Varna turned a withering look on him, "then you will know of Dharmoney, who aids in Ennaris' darkest hour."

Jorphy Bart turned to look at Clay, shock registering once again. Clay nodded to Varna and the older woman spun around again. Someone groaned and the spear that was still held clattered to the ground.

"Gee, thanks, Clay," Varna said with a voice that would turn water to ice. Clay laughed with genuine delight. "That will make everything much more relaxed."

The villagers had made their bolthole in a set of connected caverns that were almost at water level. They appeared to have been carved out of the solid rock by the actions of wind and wave long in the past, although Varna thought there were traces of machine-wrought excavation also, a fact that was confirmed later. The caverns, in fact, had been hollowed out long in Ennaris' past, well before the rebellion, and had been used for various purposes from camping sites to sightseeing. During the devastation of the rebellion's end, the former coast had collapsed and the ground had subsided while the water level had also changed dramatically. The caverns were, for a time, flooded before the water settled back to a slightly lower level. The ocean occasionally made its presence felt at high tide by slopping into the lower levels of the caverns.

The villagers - the cavern village was named Entar's Hide - established themselves in the caverns initially to protect against the rebels and then more permanently when there was a form of pogrom on all those with gifts. As the devastation became the new normal for the Ennarisi, and as the backlash against all those with gifts took hold in various parts of the land, more of the gifted people escaped or were rescued and were directed or brought to these caverns. The changes to the land had caused the coast to move further inland along a large swathe of the continent. These caverns had originally been inland but were now part of the new coastal cliffs. Subsequently, a large swathe of the cliffs further north had collapsed into the sea to form a rocky promontory and, in the same blow, removed one of the remaining primary access roads to the area, further isolating the refugees.

The small but growing group of gifted, therefore, formed their own village and became farmers of a range of crops, although only a part of them lived in the village itself. Crops were grown largely amongst the scrubby vegetation from the top of the cliff extending inland to the more heavily wooded slopes. By staying very quiet, over time their neighbours forgot that the people of the village had come from gifted forebears. And so it had continued for generations, the villagers at times seeking out partners from further away, but always seeking out those with gifts.

The old skills had dwindled somewhat across Ennaris, but they had never faded away and the small community ebbed and flowed in numbers. Always they were wary of strangers. At first that was because of the frenzy to punish anyone with gifts for the destruction of Ennaris. Then it was because the reason for hunting down the gifted had devolved into a superstitious belief that they were inherently evil and were the source of all ills that befell communities anywhere. Finally, the strong-men rose and carved out their own holdings and fiefdoms via the sword, and the people of the caverns adopted an even lower profile. Their gifts were hidden away but a tradition had grown, fostered by their early leaders, of ensuring that everyone with a gift had the chance to develop it properly. Watches were maintained to keep strangers away and to allow those with gifts to practice without being detected.

Jorphy Bart had been head-woman of the village for a long time now. She explained the history of the village to Varna and Clay while sitting around a fire that night, with the villagers arrayed around the caverns either listening quietly or occupying themselves with their own activities and the few children. She told Varna and Clay that she was a little more than nine hundred cycles old and, she assured them, remained in the prime of health and vitality. She had guided generations of gifted people, some with strong gifts and many with minor gifts, through their lives. Some lived for extended periods, others not so, but she ensured that all had the chance to practice their skills and work to the betterment of the community.

"For better or for worse," Jorphy Bart said, "most of our children are born with gifts aligned to either war, including the offensive skills or defensive capabilities, or healing and nurture. I guess that's only to be expected. The original group who created the village came from the school at a city called Resgalar, which was for those with gifts in battle, healing and agrarian pursuits. Healers are born occasionally, and there are several with other skills, but mostly we have battle gifts."

"Which is why Maygry warned that they did not need their spears," Clay nodded.

"Yes," Jorphy Bart replied. "And the last two generations are stronger than almost any before them. We have had occasions where practice has resulted in obvious damage as they felt out their strength, and we had a close call when a group of some vicious creatures tried to attack the village. We moved everyone to the caverns then."

"Were they half man and half beast?" Varna asked.

"Yes," Jorphy Bart said, surprised. "You know of these creatures?"

"They are ghazrak," Clay said.

"Ghazrak! The old tales tell of battles against ghazrak during the time of the rebellion. They've returned?"

"They have returned," Varna confirmed. "But from what we know they have been improved, if that's the right word. And there are flying ghazrak now, also, which there were not before."

"So, Goroth does indeed return," Jorphy Bart said sadly. "It starts again."

"No," Varna said. "It already started some time ago. It's out in the open now."

"The Prophecy told that when the Children returned it would be to help in the final battle for Ennaris."

"Yes," Varna said.

"The Prophecy also said that the Nine would arise and lead the Ennarisi, as of old. None have been able to determine what that means."

“It means exactly what it said, oddly enough for a Prophecy,” Varna replied. “The Nine are individuals who have specific skills and will lead the fight for this planet and its people.”

“And who leads?”

“Corm Ramesa,” Clay said. “He is the Faero, succeeding his father Intika, who was killed in battle with the ghazrak. Corm has the help of the Archmage and the remaining Mages.”

“An Archmage lives?” Jorphy Bart asked, interest sparking.

“As do a small number of the Mages,” Clay nodded. “They have held themselves apart for much of the time since the rebellion for the same reasons that you have done so. Their numbers have dwindled but their determination has not dimmed.”

“I heard a sweet chime a time past,” Jorphy Bart said, wondering, “as did most of the caverns.” She looked around and most of the watchers nodded confirmation.

“That was the Archmage receiving his Enchara from the Guardian Fernis,” Varna said.

“Fernis?” a younger voice chimed in. “The Guardian of life?”

“Indeed yes,” Varna said, turning to search out the owner of the voice, and finding a youth of possibly sixteen years.

“Kaphis is one of our number who maintains the gardens amongst the trees and bushes,” Jorphy Bart said, smiling to the young man. “He is proving to be very talented.”

“When this is over I’ll take you to Fernis’ Tree,” Varna promised.

“You’ve met Fernis?” Kaphis asked in an awed voice.

“I have, and I have lived in his Tree for a time while I was healed,” Varna said. “As did Clay. He was helped by Ogun, as was I also.”

A murmur went around the gathered villagers, most of whom identified more with Ogun than Fernis.

“The Guardians are real then,” Jorphy Bart said, almost to herself, and a single tear ran down her face. “For so long we have believed and called on them to help and wondered, and now you tell us they do exist and are real.”

"Many of the Guardians had to go from Ennaris to other places after the rebellion," Varna said. "Three of their number died in seeking to halt the destruction." A murmur rolled around the villagers. "Yes, the Guardians can die. The three expended their life force entirely to save Ennaris from total destruction. The Prophecy told that, were the Guardians to stay and attempt to take a further part, then Ennaris would die, so most departed until the time was right. And now they have returned. Some few stayed to do what they could," she said, thinking of Balgor, Fernis and Odruf.

Jorphy Bart thought for a while. "What is it you ask of Entar's Hide, Dharmoney?" she asked in a formal tone, her question silencing the few people muttering between themselves.

Varna and Clay shared a glance, and Clay smiled encouragement. Mentally, she drew herself up and replied with similar formality.

"I ask that all with gifts join with the Faero of Ennaris in opposition to Goroth and his ilk," Varna - Dharmoney-to-come - replied. "I ask that you assist Corm and the Archmage in the battle to come."

Jorphy Bart looked around the gathered group, searching out individuals to gauge reaction. Satisfied, she turned back.

"Entar's Hide will join with the Faero," she said formally.

Varna nodded, relieved. "How many may we count on?"

Jorphy Bart smiled. "We have twenty strong and fifteen of moderate battle skills, and twelve healers of differing strengths. Entar's Hide also has a number of other disciplines and lesser strengths who will assist. We number sixty-five gifted altogether."

"Well, that's a start," Varna said, slightly discouraged at the small numbers.

"Ah, but we have guests this night who wish to speak also," Jorphy Bart said with a smile.

At the back of the group a tall man stood. "Nortel's Hide will join with the Faero," he said, nodding decisively.

A second man stood. "Petar's Hide will join with the Faero."

And a woman. "Isant's Hide will join with the Faero."

"Marflin's Hide will join with the Faero," a third man said.

Varna looked from one to the other in shock as each spoke and, after a moment, Clay laughed, nodding his approval of the tactic employed. Jorphy Bart looked pleased at the effect.

"Now you didn't think we would be all alone out here, did you?"

8. Flin and the Demon

Bamjur was a small village, located off the main roads in what had once been orchard country. Some orchards remained, Flin was surprised to discover as he and Andira walked towards the village, or the descendants of the old orchards, rather. He remembered visiting this area long ago. The trees were somewhat scrawny where his memory was of row after row of fruit trees with fruit hanging off them in abundance. Then, they were assisted by Guides who would often joke about singing to the trees to relax them, so they produced better fruit. Flin smiled with the memory. But, of course, that was long ago, and the orchards now were a shadow of those of his memory.

Andira had been quiet as they walked, and Flin had been absorbed in his own thoughts. What happened at Resgalar had shaken him, for he was not given to raw emotional outbursts - not any more anyway. The force and energy that had flowed from him in his rage and anger and despair had seemed to be matched by a complementary force flowing into him, but he sensed that it was only a part of a greater outpouring from many. He could feel the twins join in along with Trabor and, in what he thought was a cruelty, he felt echoes of Marjory and even Halfgar before the surge of what could only have been the Guardians almost lifted him from his feet. Never had he felt anything like that before. It had left every nerve jangling, every hair in his arms and legs standing straight out. But now he had to prepare for what they might find at Bamjur.

Now he turned to Andira. "Andira, we're almost at Bamjur, and we must prepare. Are you able to sense anything like a demon in the vicinity?"

"No, Archmage," Andira replied, subdued. "There is nothing at the moment."

"Are you alright?" Flin asked, drawing Andira to one side of the road into the sparse shelter offered by a scrubby fruit tree. After a brief examination of the tree via his gift he plucked two crisp kuppies, just the right shades of red and green, and passed one to Andira. He took a bite and savoured the sweet-tart juices running down his throat as he munched.

Andira took a bite and then, summoning her courage, asked, "Archmage, what happened back there?"

"In Resgalar?" Flin grimaced. "I apologise for that. I think I just lost control for a moment. Resgalar was the place of my happiest memories. It was where I met my one and only love and had many, many friends. It was also among the first cities destroyed during the rebellion, killing most of those friends in a single stroke. And our son."

"How awful!" Andira's eyes were like saucers as she tried and failed to imagine what Flin must have felt at that time. "Was that aimed at you?"

Flin smiled wanly. "No, I was merely a young Mage at that time. Resgalar was where the Battle Mages were trained , as well as those dedicated to Fernis, as I am, and where many lived. By attacking Resgalar, the rebels destroyed part of the group that posed the most danger to them. They did not get them all, of course, and to their cost they missed my Marjory, who was the strongest Battle Mage. That ended up costing them. My memories of Resgalar were too strong, and my feelings of anger and despair welled up to the point where I could not control them. You saw the result of that loss of control."

The young woman was quiet for a moment. "Archmage, what I saw was more than just you, wasn't it? I could see the different colours breaking through, all the colours blending together. It was, well, beautiful. A little scary but beautiful."

Flin nodded. "I think inadvertently I drew the others in also, and I suspect the Guardians joined with us. Perhaps it was the catharsis we needed to prepare for what is to come. I'm not sure. But I'll strive not to lose control like that again."

Andira nodded, then gestured around her using the core of her kuppy almost as a pointer. "I've never had fruit like these. We have many others where I'm from but not these."

"Did you like it?" Flin asked. "It's a kuppy. This used to be an orchard area and it's good to see some remain, but they're a pale reflection of what had been here. Who knows, perhaps we'll be able to get these places back to something like what they were in time. Right now, we need to get rid of this demon and the idiot who's trying to summon it."

Andira nodded, tossing the kuppy core under the tree and wiping her sticky hands on her tunic. Both stepped back out into the road and started walking again. They had not gone far when the first small buildings came into view. A cottage with a separate shed was backed into the fruit trees. The cottage had a well-maintained but abandoned look about it, and Flin walked up the neat rock-lined path to the cottage door and rapped on its door. No answer. The shutters were closed, and he could not get a good look through the slats, but he had the impression of a neat and tidy interior. Shrugging, Flin walked back to the road where Andira waited. They walked towards the next small cottage on the other side of the road. This one was slightly less well maintained but was just as empty. Further along the road a cluster of cottages could be seen, indicating the start of the village proper, so they headed towards it.

Andira staggered slightly and she lifted one hand. Flin immediately clasped her hand and provided support. Andira's eyes were closed and a bead of sweat ran down from her forehead to her chin. She was trembling slightly.

"Andira?" Flin asked quietly.

"It's happening," she whispered. "Someone is summoning." She pointed towards the cluster of cottages. "Somewhere along there, probably past those cottages, it's hard to tell. But close, very close."

"Okay. Do you want to stay here?" Flin asked.

She shook her head. "No, I'll come with you. I may be able to do something." She laughed lightly. "I don't know what but maybe something." She had stopped trembling and her eyes were open, her expression at once scared and determined.

"Very well," Flin replied, dropping her hand and gripping his staff tightly. "Let's see what we can see."

The village was larger than it had appeared to be at first glance. The cluster of cottages marked the start of the village, as Flin expected, but the road passed through the cluster and swung to the left, dropping down into a small valley where the village centre was located. A small stream passed through the village, with a stone bridge that allowed the road to cross it just before the centre was reached. In the village centre Flin could see the usual tavern and smithy as well as what seemed to be some shops, all closed up. There were no people visible. Flin stood with Andira and examined the village with all of his senses.

"Over there," Andira said, pointing to a spot outside the village and partway up the valley's left wall.

Turning his attention to where Andira pointed, Flin was able to recognise the swirls of power. The looked relatively minor and somewhat confused to his Mage sight, but dangerous nonetheless. A thin spiral of smoke marked the spot. Flin could make out the presence of someone, but he could tell little else. He wished Varna was with him, with her enhanced aura-reading senses, but he had Andira and she had been able to pinpoint the location they sought. Together Flin and Andira headed down the road into the village, taking what turned out to be a surprisingly substantial trail, less than a road but more than the usual track that occurred away from the main paths.

The site from which the power emanated was a little off that trail, reached by what could have been mistaken as a game trail. A small hollow was revealed after only a short walk along the trail. Long grass clothed the floor and scrubby grasses clung to the sides. A small fire that was the source of the smoke was tucked in one corner. Standing in the centre of the hollow was a short man, shirtless in the chill air and wearing tattered breeches with equally tattered soft foot-coverings. He had a fleshy face, and shoulder-length dark hair. Andira flinched as they reached the hollow, and with a gesture and light pressure on her arm Flin directed her to stop and move back slightly. She did so, but moved forward again so she could see what was happening.

Flin strode toward the man, who was swaying and chanting in a low voice, moving his arms back and forth rhythmically. As he walked Flin used his staff as a balancing tool and Andira noted that the stone at the stop had stopped its usual swirling and was emanating a soft green glow.

"Stop this madness," Flin proclaimed in a loud voice as he reached the floor of the hollow.

The man started, opening his eyes to stare at the Archmage. His gaze moved from Flin to the green light coming from the stone to the trail where it entered the hollow and back to Flin. He seemed frantic, and Andira noted that the sense of demonic presence had not diminished. She started to call to Flin when the man started to speak.

"Who are you? Why do you stop me? The summons cannot be halted now." He looked to the fire where the smoke was thicker now and back to Flin. "You endanger us by interfering."

"You cannot do this," Flin said. "I forbid it."

"You forbid ..." The man stared anew. "Who are you to forbid me this rite?"

"I am the Archmage of the Council of Mages and I have every right to forbid this, this, abomination," Flin stated. "Stop it now."

The man laughed shrilly, staring at the fire, where the smoke was thicker again. Andira moaned quietly as he continued, "It's too late,

Archmage of the Council of Mages, whoever they are. My summons has been answered and my slave comes."

Flin glared at the man before turning to the fire. The smoke was thickening as he watched, and two red eyes peered from the smoke.

"You have summoned me once again, little man," a deep and mellifluous voice said from the smoke. "This time I come. What is your bidding?"

"See, it's too late," the man said to Flin, laughing once again. "I command you to make the orchards bear their sweet fruit once again, as was done in the days past," he said to the smoke, which was now a solid column.

Flin started. "You fool," he snarled, "the orchards were assisted by Guides of Ennaris, not demons or whatever this monstrosity is."

The eyes shifted their focus to Flin, and he felt himself to be subject to unaccustomed forces, very strong. Flin shifted his stance so he faced the fire. The thick column of smoke swirled as though from a breeze that originated within the fire itself. He settled himself, staff grounded by his side. The stone glowed stronger now and Andira could see it pulsing slightly.

And then from the smoke stepped a creature from Andira's nightmares. It was tall with jet black skin that was seamed and cracking. Something glowed red through the cracks as though its body was composed of flowing lava. Rivulets of smoke drifted from the torso. The creature's head resembled that of a horned gressa. It had a long snout with beady eyes separated by a bony vertical horn. A broad forehead and bony scalp were surmounted by more wicked-looking horns, curling outward and sharp at the points. The muscular torso was man-like, with thickly muscled arms and thighs, but the hands were more like claws with three fingers and a thumb and the feet were cloven hoofs. Naked, the creature had no visible sexual organs. The creature stared at Flin and the mouth below the snout separated in a predatory snarl.

Flin stared back, his distress at seeing what he faced only added to by recognising this creature as one on which Grensor's ghazrak were modelled. It was a Kindred!

The little man capered and laughed.

"See," he laughed shrilly, "I am as powerful as the old ones! I am able to summon and control a slave as of old. I will be the greatest on Ennaris. My orchards will be the best ever."

A Kindred! Flin knew the name from stories told of the time when Goroth and Grensor experimented with the dark arts. This was what Marjory had fought during the rebellion. It glanced at the cavorting man and with a sudden gesture snapped out one arm, grasped him with a claw-like hand and broke his neck. Andira gasped and ducked back when the Kindred turned to seek the source of the noise. She cowered against a large rock that marked the point where the trail dipped into the hollow. Not seeing anyone, the Kindred turned back to face Flin.

"You may summon me, little man," the Kindred said in its deep voice, "as you have tried many times, and have now succeeded. But you cannot control me." It laughed, the rumble coming from deep in its belly. "And you, Archmage of the Council of Mages, cannot control me either. Your puny powers are as nothing to me. I am Ghaz-tu and I claim this world for the Kindred!"

Flin shook his head as though to deny what Ghaz-tu had said, gripping his staff firmly. *Great, just great,* he thought bitterly. *Now I have Goroth and a demon to deal with.*

With a sigh Flin stepped forward with his staff held firmly before him. Its pointed foot rested on the ground. The stone continued to glow a brilliant green. It was somewhat fitful but maintained a constant glow. Flin concentrated, knowing that this was likely to be the fight of his life, and him not any sort of Battle Mage. From the stone came a beam of green light, brilliant and sharpening to a point where it met the Kindred. Rather than the unfocused beam Flin had flung at the Ghazrak at Escar, this time he tried to use the light almost as a sword. The Kindred's skin sizzled where the light touched and punctured it.

Red light leaked from the rent caused. Ghaz-tu recoiled but did not fall. With a snarl, it pointed one claw-hand at Flin and a shaft of red light speared at the Archmage, being deflected by a personal shield he raised just in time. Still, it caused him to be flung across the hollow, where he landed in a crumpled heap. With effort he maintained his shield even as he sought to stand. Never had he been hit with such force, and he thanked the foresight of his instructors who taught all Mages the shielding techniques, and of Marjory, who had insisted that Flin worked to strengthen his own shield.

Andira, peeking around the rock, saw Flin flung across the hollow and watched as the red shaft played across the thin barrier he maintained. Ghaz-tu was seeking a weakness that would allow him to destroy the Archmage. She moaned quietly, clearly seeing the demon building a second store of energy which, she was sure, would be used to finish off Flin. The Archmage appeared to be struggling. The demon raised its other hand, and the second shaft flew to strike Flin's shield in concert with the first. Flin was pinned back against the wall of the hollow, almost all of his power being used to hold the deadly shafts at bay.

Andira's thoughts spun wildly. Her terror of the demon warred with the fear of what would happen if it was to remain free. She thought back to her dreams, to the nightmares that she had experienced for much of her life, where she faced just such a creature. Could it have been a forewarning? In her dreams, she would hear, in the back of her mind, a kindly voice telling her to stand against the evil and believe and she would triumph. But how? She had no shields such as Drewflin. The Mage's barrier was being reduced as she watched. Ghaz-tu was laughing, a deep booming laugh of triumph, of disdain.

"This is the best you can do, Archmage of the Council of Mages?" it shouted at Flin. "My Kindred will strip this world easily if you are the best it has. And then we will take over this universe." A dreadful laugh reverberated across the hollow.

Aghast, Andira saw the demon drawing even more power into itself. The fire in the corner of the hollow flared. In a flash of inspiration, she realised that the fire was the source of the demon's power. She would have to do something, she knew, or it would defeat Flin, and that would be the end of everyone on Ennaris. Harnessing her fear, using it as a source of volition, and trusting to Flin to hold out for long enough, Andira crept back and carefully made her way around the edge of the hollow towards where the fire burnt unnaturally high and hot.

Flin, in the midst of the red flame, could feel it burning him even though his shield kept it at bay. But that was diminishing, he could feel it. The Kindred's energy battered against him and he was unable to do anything about it. His despair was making it hard to concentrate, to think of alternatives. Nothing he had could fight against the sheer power. Flin fought to hold the beam away, but he knew that it was only a matter of time. *At least*, he thought, *I will rejoin Marjory soon*.

Archmage Drewflin. The calm voice sounded in his consciousness. *Heal my planet, Archmage. Use your gifts to heal this place.*

With a start, Flin recognised the voice of Fernis. Heal my planet? Heal this place? How could he do such a thing? When he was helpless as a babe? The irony of his position washed over Flin like a wave of icy water. In raw terms, he was one of the most powerful Mages Ennaris had known, despite being mostly unable to use the pure destructive gifts, and yet he was trapped and helpless in the hands of this being from another dimension, or perhaps another universe. If he managed to get through this he would ask Fernis about that. The Kindred had said he would take over 'this universe'. Not that it mattered right now. He was unable to stand, let alone bring his healing gifts to bear. What he wished now was that he could be cocooned with Marjory in their own... Cocoon! Of course, perhaps he could do that! Of course, he still had to get away from this incredibly powerful creature before he could do anything.

Suddenly the hammering force ebbed as Ghaz-tu's attention wavered.

Andira, having made a wide loop around the hollow, reached the edge where the fire was burning. Trembling all over, she still was unsure about what to do. The fire seemed to be the gateway to where this thing was drawing its energy, so logically she had to extinguish the fire. How to do that? Water? She had nothing large enough to carry enough water, and the stream was too far away? Perhaps she could smother the flames? With what? Frantically, she looked around the surrounds but there was nothing she could use. But wait, maybe she just needed to disrupt the flow enough for the Archmage to break free. Maybe she did not need to put the fire out as much as just cause it to reduce in size. She gathered her courage, feeling it shredding even as she thought about what she needed to do. Then Andira had a brain-wave. She unfastened her long skirt and doubled it to make it thicker then, before she could think too much, she crept the last few spans towards the edge of the hollow. With a last look to see if the demon was watching, she scrambled down the bank towards the fire and flung the skirt over the flames.

Ghaz-tu felt the flow of power from the Kindred Realm waver and diminish. The red beam thinned and the strength of the beam waned. It could feel the Mage pushing back and sought to maintain the flow, even as it spun to look at the fire. There was another puny one standing by the fire and some form of cloth smothering the fire. With a shout of rage, Ghaz-tu separated its power streams, risking the Mage breaking free, and flung a second bolt at the second one. With some satisfaction it saw the beam strike and envelope this one, but satisfaction turned to shock and dismay as it merely splashed against this one and did no discernible damage. How could this be? Such a one as this could not stand against Ghaz-tu. This one had no power that Ghaz-tu could sense that would account for this!

In the moment that Ghaz-tu stared a second figure appeared alongside the woman. The newcomer turned to look at the fire, where the heavy material from Andira's skirt was smouldering and with a gesture reinforced the fabric so that it resisted the flames. Ghaz-tu could feel its power slipping away. A cry of rage erupted as it struggled to maintain both beams, finally allowing the second to fall away. The demon lunged at Andira, only to encounter an invisible barrier.

"You may not have her," the third one said. "She is under my protection. I am Dall."

Flin found that he could move again and with great effort he forced himself to his feet, all the while maintaining his shield. He did not look at Andira, although he was aware that she was safe. Slowly, imperceptibly, Flin pushed his barrier outward, away from his own body and towards Ghaz-tu. The demon tried to reinforce its power but was unable to do so as the fire dwindled. The danger had not passed, however, for the fire still burned, and Flin knew that he was approaching the limits of his own endurance. Sweat beaded his forehead and his arms felt heavy, but he maintained his defence.

Finally, after what felt like an eternity, Flin was able to deflect Ghaz-tu's beam and leapt to the side. The beam drilled a hole in the hollow's bank. Instantly, before Ghaz-tu could adjust Flin flung both hands up. From the left he flung a solid beam of green light, and Ghaz-tu instinctively dropped his red beam to defend himself, only to find that the green light was just that - light. But from his right hand Flin flung a protective energy, a growth energy, one of the many tools he had been taught long ago to protect large plants and animals from further damage by inclement environments or enemies. A cocoon of healing energy! The bands of energy wrapped themselves around the demon in solid sheets. At first it could rip through the sheets but gradually its efforts lessened and the wrappings became tighter and tighter, finally wrapping Ghaz-tu entirely, cutting the demon off from the still burning fire. With a grimace, Flin whipped Andira's skirt from the fire. He examined the gash in the fabric of the universe, with energies flowing between the two. Dimly he could sense other demons - Kindred - trying to use the same portal between the universes. Flin made a cutting motion. He used his gifts of healing to close the gaping wound that had been ripped open and through which Ghaz-tu had pushed, like he would do when healing a slash in a tree trunk.

There was a loud *pop!* and the wrappings collapsed. Flin stared at them for a moment to make sure the demon did not re-appear and then slowly he turned to Andira and Dall. Weariness was etched on his features. He bowed to the Guardian.

"My Lady Dall," he said evenly, striving to keep the extreme tiredness from his voice, "I thank you for your timely intervention. Oh," he continued, holding the skirt out to Andira, "and I think this is yours. It seems to have survived, somehow."

Andira gasped, suddenly realising she was almost naked from the waist down, and grasped the skirt. Flin smiled slightly and turned so he faced Dall entirely, leaving Andira some privacy.

"Did I hear you right, Lady? Did you claim Andira for your own?" Flin straightened slowly, realising that he had been hunched slightly, and pushed one knuckle into the small of his back.

"Indeed I did, Archmage. Andira has certain gifts I would develop further. But she must be with you at the battle with Goroth, for Grensor has opened commerce with the Kindred and may do so again."

Flin nodded. "Yes, I think he probably will. I'm sure you noticed the resemblance between Ghaz-tu and the ghazrak? Even the name? That commerce was opened long ago."

"Indeed it was." Dall stood tall, looking Flin in the eye, and smiled. "For a non-warrior, Archmage, you have some surprises still."

"It was Fernis, not all me," Flin objected. "He told me to heal Ennaris, and I realised that if I treated it as a wound I had things I could do." He shrugged. "It worked."

"So it did. It's worth remembering. I must go, Archmage, for we both have much to do." She turned to Andira, reaching out to rest one hand on her shoulder. "We will speak again, Andira, soon. I will instruct you in certain lore that you will be able to use to effect. For now, farewell."

Dall smiled once again, leaned out and gave Flin a kiss on his weathered cheek, and disappeared.

Andira stood perfectly still, stunned. Flin brushed his cheek where the Guardian had kissed him. He recalled that in legend Dall had a reputation of enjoying male company - a lot. Flin smiled slightly. He looked around him and then glanced to Andira.

"Come, child," he said kindly to her. "You've had a great shock. We should leave this place."

She nodded, looking from the fire to the wrappings that were now a shapeless bundle. "But, what did you do to him - it?"

"I wrapped it in a healing wrap, once I was able to get free. You interrupted its flow of power from its own domain when you threw your skirt on the fire and gave me the opportunity. You showed great courage in doing that, and I am very grateful. When I wrapped the demon it almost completely removed its reach for the power source, and then I could deal with the fire, which was the wound in Ennaris. Ghaz-tu lost power entirely and the link to the source of its power. Without that power, it was unable to sustain any existence as an elemental being of energy."

"So it's gone?"

"Yes. Had the fire stayed even partly alive it could have made its way back, but without that it just - expired."

"What do we do now?"

"We return to the Citadel. I've been away too long. But first," Flin grimaced and stretched again, "we find some food and have a sleep."

"What happens to the village now? Do we destroy it?"

"No, no, of course not," Flin said as he started to walk. "That fool was trying to invoke the demon to help him grow kuppies, as we did once here. But he had the stories all wrong, of course. I expect the villagers left when he started to experiment and, hopefully, they'll return. For now, food and rest, and then I take you to meet Corm. As Faeros go, he has promise."

The next morning, after a night where both slept well in a commandeered cottage, they started back. The walk from Resgalar to Bamjur had taken most of two days. The slower return took them into a third day. Flin was careful not to push too hard. He was honest enough to admit, when Andira asked, that he was more tired than he had thought, and the slow pace and frequent stops were as much for him as for her. On the fifth day after they had exited the portal gateway at Resgalar they returned, some short time after the sun had passed its zenith. But it was a different Resgalar to the one they had left. Andira stared, agog, at the changes and Flin looked around with an air of bewilderment.

The broad boulevard along which they walked, the Way of the Guardians, the same one they had used to leave the destroyed city, had been cleared of the rubble accumulated over the thousands of cycles since the city's destruction. The channel that ran down the centre of the Way bubbled once again with water, clear and clean. It bounced over the evidence of damage that could not be hidden. Flin stopped to stare at the water for a long moment, reading it with his senses, and then bent to scoop up a handful and let it play through his fingers. He took another handful, but this time raised his hand to his lips and drank, followed by a second. Immediately, he felt relief from the pains and bruises that had been caused by the fight with the demon, and with wonder he gestured to Andira to drink also. She knelt carefully, her own aches and pains making themselves felt, and drank, and then again, and the aches faded away.

After a moment the two stood, taking stock. Where only moments before they were hurting, now they felt no pain. Flin looked along the Way and could see the Ogunavid, the sight of which had been blocked by the remains of the buildings that had collapsed. He looked to the side streets, but they remained strewn with debris. He glanced to Andira, to see his own wonder reflected. As one they started once again to walk along the Way. At the Ogunavid, Flin halted once more. The square had been cleared of debris too, although signs of extreme damage were everywhere. Where the fountain had stood, in the exact spot where Flin had driven his staff and unleashed his rage, was a pool, with a clear spring bubbling from its centre and forming the source of the water running down the centre of the Way. Around the pool were five andary trees, with silver trunks already standing three times Flin's height. Glossy green leaves shot through with silver threads sprouted from thin branches that, in turn, sprouted from the trunks.

Standing in front of the pool were the twins, grinning at Flin's expression. When Flin turned his gaze on them both bowed formally, but the grins did not waver.

"Greetings, Archmage," Raglin said.

"Is this your work?" Flin asked, relieved his voice did not betray the shock and astonishment he felt.

"We have commenced the work to recover Resgalar, Archmage," Ragnor replied. "But I think the rest was your work."

"Along with pretty much everyone with any gifts across Ennaris," Raglin added, wryly. "I think you awakened every gift on the planet."

Flin was abashed and shook his head ruefully. "I lost control," he admitted. "It was like being here for the first time since the rebellion. Memories came flooding back, and with all that has happened it broke down the barriers."

"It was about time, old friend," Ragnor said. "We have awaited the Archmage in reality, not just in name. We have one, now."

Flin regarded the two Mages, two of his true friends, waiting expectantly, and nodded.

"Then let us return to the Citadel, for I feel our time of waiting has come to an end, or near to. Oh, this is Andira. Trabor brought her from the south. She has the ability to sense demons, among other things." He waited while the twins greeted the young woman. "That's where Grensor received the pattern for the ghazrak. He drew on the Kindred."

Raglin frowned. "The Kindred? Yes, we all thought that was the case."

"And we can expect him to have that contact still," Flin continued. "We must prepare for that also. The Kindred we battled was stronger than I, and it was only with the intervention of Dall that we subdued it."

"You defeated a Kindred, single-handed?" Ragnor stared. "That will be storied."

"Not single-handed by any means. I'll tell the story as we go. But the strength of that single Kindred was enormous. If Grensor brings others through we'll have great problems."

The four moved to the portal. As they walked Flin described the recent events dispassionately, and the twins listened, rapt. The small group entered the portal.

At Resgalar, the fountains continued to bubble through the ruins, and the healing waters flowed through the city and into the surrounding land.

9. Goroth Marches

Deep in the wastelands Goroth growled his dissatisfaction, but held his tongue. Grensor and Likud had been like a pair of hounds arguing over the same bone for the last two tendays when they should have been making sure of the arrangements for the army. Luckily, Goroth was able to enlist the aid of several of the northers. Their general, Morsen, appeared to be competent in logistics, even if his tactics were not of the same standard. Morsen and his command structure scouted out sources of food. The scouts had already located any water that could be found on the proposed route of march. Finally, Morsen had issued the summons to the northers that they should congregate in the wasted lands, and gave them the exact locations, bypassing the figurehead rulers whose forebears Grensor had established as kings and then largely ignored.

The numbers were as Goroth expected. However, that was the only element that was. The rebel Mage looked on askance as the northers arrived carrying a motley collection of weapons ranging from stakes and farm implements - Goroth could find absolutely no trace of a farm anywhere near the wasted lands, but he was assured they existed in a particular valley far from Grensor's compound - to swords, axes and knives. One norther family whose members did not follow the standard wiry norther body shape arrived with a cart carrying an array of ancient battle axes, apparently dating from some time two or three thousand cycles previously when the adjacent land had been ruled by a warlord. The family members were the only northers who were strong enough to wield the axes.

There were slightly more than thirty thousand northers, he thought, and Goroth was pretty sure that would not be enough.

"We'll have more than thirty thousand northers," Grensor said when Goroth voiced his concern. "And we'll have more from the east join us. We have promises of about twenty thousand from the Grokog."

"The Grokog?" Likud said disparagingly. "What sort of name is that?"

"Groks was the name of the Kindred we used last time. The easterners took him as some sort of god. The eastern region, what was once the region of Unscernis, is now a much smaller area on the other side of the eastern ranges, what we used to call the central divide. But they continue with the worship and the priesthood is in charge there." Grensor shrugged. "In any event, the northers and the easterners may make some difference, but it will be the ghazrak that carry the battles."

"Even so, only forty to fifty thousand in the army? We had ten times that number before in multiple armies!" scoffed Likud. "Is this the best you can do after all this time?"

"Yes, it is!" Grensor snapped. "You could have brought more of those useless disembodied Andorethi of yours had you thought about them, but you didn't. And back then the population of Ennaris was a hundred, no a thousand times more than it is today. We don't have large armies on Ennaris now. There just are not the people."

"What about the Kindred?" Goroth asked into the quiet that followed Grensor's statement. "And is Groks still around?"

"No, Groks was killed by Marjory before you were caught. Just don't tell the Grokog." Grensor sighed. "I've not been in contact with the Kindred as much lately. My strength is not as great as it was. I'm near two hundred thousand cycles in age, and I'm feeling it. I'm not sure that I could control a strong Kindred now."

"Well gather your strength," Goroth said bluntly. "I want you to make contact and arrange some further support."

"I told you I don't think that's a good idea," Grensor replied.

"Afraid, old man?" Likud sneered.

"Likud, grow a brain cell or two, just this once, and then use them," Grensor said wearily. "We used one of the Kindred to bolster us last time and we almost destroyed this planet. It was only Marjory who defeated us. She's not with them this time and I've been concentrating recently on making sure we don't have any new gifted children to worry about. The ghazrak, for my sins, have been killing the families as fast as we've been able to locate them. The Old Blood is thinning once again. It doesn't sit well with me, for we will need these skills once we start to rebuild Ennaris, but I couldn't allow them to be used by the Faero or Drewflin."

"Your point, old man?" Likud said dismissively. "So you've spent the last five thousand cycles killing children? And you're proud of that?"

"No, not five thousand cycles killing children, and no, not proud of it at all. I also made sure the northland remained loyal to us. I needed the raw materials for the ghazrak, and I knew we would need an army. That took effort that you would not recognise, given the level of subtlety required." Grensor grimaced and rubbed his sore right knee. "And I made a start on the winged ghazrak as well as the marine ghazrak. They took many false starts before I could get anywhere near usable specimens, given almost all of my equipment was either destroyed or useless."

"Wings and flippers? Why not just find one of the remaining bases and take over the old stingers and launchers?"

"Because there was an interdict against technology that Halfgar somehow made work. And, of course, I don't know where those bases are and had no way of knowing."

"Halfgar," Likud snorted. "That old fool. Why would he block the use of technology? That's ridiculous!"

"The better question to ask would be how?" Goroth intervened. "I know I would never be able to do that. I'm pretty sure neither Marjory nor Drewflin would be able to either, or any of the others from the old Council. And the reason is obvious - to stop anyone using the weapons still available, to take Ennaris back to a state that was more manageable. Would you have stopped using those weapons if you had the chance?"

"Me? No, I would have used everything I had," Likud replied boastfully. "No stopping, no holding back. Everything on the table. That's my style and it's worked for me for all this time."

"And yet you haven't won the galaxy, have you? We worked to help them but you subverted the people of Andoreth and turned them into some sort of wispy warrior race. But you didn't achieve the goal." Grensor tilted his head to watch Likud's reaction from the corner of his eye. "Why is that?"

"Bah!" Likud snorted dismissively, face tightening in anger. "I didn't count on the Union having a few good commanders and weapons designers over the last few hundred cycles. And my Andorethi are good at following orders but are not too imaginative."

"Because over the cycles you purged the trait from them," Grensor replied. "So, when they come across a situation for which you didn't prepare orders, they're unprepared and at a loss. How did you take over new systems, for example?"

"Went in there blasting away until defences were obliterated, then dropped the Andorethi to the planet and took over the minds."

"Subtle," Grensor commented. "No thought of espionage or creating a supporter base before taking over?"

"Of course," Likud replied. "I have many in the Union fleet working for me and quite a few of the politicians. They give me any amount of information in return for being allowed to take over the planets of their choice." He gave a short laugh. "And then I took the planet once they died anyway. These short-lived ones never realised they were dealing with me all the time. They thought it was a hereditary title. The Likud! I like that!"

"To bring us back," Goroth said, "I remain convinced that the army will be too light in numbers. From what you tell me, we have the north and the east with us, and they will provide armies. How many ghazrak do you have available now? It's been a further two tendays."

Grensor stared. Did the man not understand? The ghazrak were not made on an assembly line. There was no assembly line. There had been no advanced technology, but primitive power sources and tools.

"I told you that you would have fifteen hundred ghazrak shock troops, twenty more flying and ten marine. That is what you will have. I have several more growing and some may be ready if we wait a further two or three tendays, but that will be it. If you want to make an attack now then this is what you will have."

"Are there any further allies?"

"No. I've been unable to get into the southern lands much and the old stories seem to stick down there better than up here, for some reason. The ill feeling towards the Council that I was able to maintain for much of this time is not as strong there. Oh, there are a couple of places where my stories took hold, but there's nothing we could count on. If anything, my spies tell of the desert people building themselves up for war against us. They've been awaiting a new battle leader." Grensor paused and thought. "To get here they will have to take ship across the Broken Sea."

"Broken Sea?" Likud raised an eyebrow. "Nice name!"

"It was formed when the plates shifted and the western shoreline came down. The valleys were inundated. I can get my marine ghazrak to take care of the boats they will have to use. That should put paid to the desert people."

"Any others we need to worry about?" Goroth knew there was something missing but he could not quite find his way to it.

"Not of any real note," Grensor said testily. "We've been over this. We'll have the northern and eastern armies to feed into the front lines. That will create some damage to the armies of the Faero, with some of the ghazrak taking up the slack, doing more of the shock work where needed. The winged ghazrak will deal with the Rocs if they show up again. There can't be many of them or I would have heard stories. Drewflin will only have the knights and the Faero's army, with a few odds and ends from the northern continent. That will amount to maybe five thousand troops. The armoured knights look good and make a lot of noise but they run out of stamina and require their mounts, as we saw during the trial run at Escar."

"The plains people?"

"I've been working on them. My people there tell me that the clans are divided and at least some of them don't want to support Drewflin or the Faero. There's some ancient gripe, it seems. Even if they do, the plains people muster no more than a thousand fighters or so."

"Hmmm," Goroth mused. "And no gifted?"

"Other than Drewflin and the twins, and I think Trabor is around still, there are no Mages. There should be very few gifted children and none of the generations until now have been trained. Between the three of us, and a few of the northers who have some battle gifts, we should be able to deal with them. The ghazrak take care of the armies." Grensor paused to consider. "Of course, we don't know what the Children bring with them. And there is the Nine, which the prophecy says takes some sort of role."

"The Children are myths more than anything. If you want to fit most prophesies to circumstances you can do so," Goroth replied calmly, assured. "I'm more concerned about that fleet in orbit. If they take part, we may have problems."

"My fleet of Andorethi will take care of them," Likud said flatly. "*Qorv* is the most powerful warship on either side. The only one more powerful was destroyed more than fifty cycles ago. And when we need to, I can call the ships into the atmosphere to take part in the fight. We win this time!"

Goroth gazed at Likud's fixed expression, considering. Things were always black and white for Likud, and they were always overly difficult for Grensor. If he had a choice neither would be among those who he had with him, but it was what it was. So be it!

He had planned to have one or two cycles to rebuild support among the people of Ennaris and then start his campaign. The state of the planet and its people had made him rethink that plan. He would not wait.

"Very well. I want to start moving south in half a tenday. Grensor, get your preparations made. Likud, we'll start putting the finishing touches to the battle plan."

Goroth stood with a single lithe motion and strolled from the room.

Grensor stood at the pens in the northern sea port, at a point where a narrow passage remained free from ice in all seasons. It was part of a large inlet towards which the wasted lands reached a finger of desolation. To the north and east were the tundra and the icy regions. The pens were where his marine ghazrak awaited his orders. The huge self-armoured creatures had been melded from the leviathans of the deep with the techniques learned long ago from the Kindred and practiced using the northers and other creatures.

The old rebel Mage walked along the dockside, stopping occasionally to gaze at his creations. In many ways these were the purest of his creations, these ten specimens of his art. The leviathan was one of the least understood of the Ennarisi populaces. They kept their own counsel and were brilliantly insightful, but Grensor knew that there was ancient resentment in being penned to the planet rather than taking part in the explorations of the galaxy. He had used that resentment to good effect.

He had made contact with several of the leviathans over a thousand cycles ago, befriending several young and impressionable ones. From what he could gather, there were no gifted leviathans being born and the last of the Mages among them perished seeking to repair ongoing damage caused during the rebellion. *More blood on our hands*, Grensor thought sourly. After two or three generations, he had developed enough influence among a single small pod that they moved to be near his base, and it was then that he was able to start his experiments. It took quite a few failures, but finally he cracked the method and these were the results.

Grensor stopped his meandering walk along the dockside and looked over the side into the nearest pen, staring pensively. Floating partly submerged was one of the marine ghazrak, the largest he had developed. It was longer than twenty men stood one on top of the other were tall. It had giant flukes and a huge tail. From a point a third down the length of the body the creature was leviathan, or near enough. Some armouring enhancements had been made, but in reality, the original leviathan was there. The front third, however, was Grensor's creation. A sharp-nosed self-armoured carapace replaced the smooth and blunt leviathan nose and mouth. Huge bony ridges carved a path from that nose to the point where the armour ended, and great teeth were on show each time the creature opened its mouth.

The marine ghazrak had been designed as ship killers. The technology level of the last several thousand cycles was primitive. Wood and sail had taken the role previously held by advanced polymers, alloys and antigrav, and the boats were navigated by primitive methods. For the marine ghazrak, they would be no match. Oh, the creatures were clumsy at times, because of the many compromises he had been forced to make, and they had a tendency to lose some control under stress but, overall, he was pleased with his design.

With a thought, Grensor released the latches of the pens. Another thought implanted his instructions in the ghazraks' small brains - the much larger leviathan brain had been found not to be suitable, as it resisted Grensor's efforts to establish control. A third thought sent them on their way.

With barely a ripple the group of marine ghazrak oriented towards the strait that would take them through the heads of the large bay and into the northern sea, from whence they would make a quick path down the western side of the northern continent and into the sea that divided the north and south continents, where they would await their prey.

Back in Grensor's workshops, the last of the mature ghazrak were carefully taken from their tanks and prepared by Grensor's small cadre of helpers. There remained almost a hundred others, most in extremely immature states, but they would not complete gestating in time. Grensor returned from the pens in time to see the new ghazrak marching out after memories were imprinted from the usual template. The last batch probably was the best but, unless things went badly awry, they probably would be the last.

So, slightly more than fifteen hundred Ghazrak, which was an enormous number, more than three times what he had been able to prepare long ago when the rebellion was sprung on him earlier than expected. Grensor was sure that they would win the field. If Drewflin and the Faero had Battle Mages he would have been troubled, but they did not. In contrast, Goroth and Likud were battle trained, although they were not at the level of Marjory. They would be the difference.

As Grensor had said, there were a few northers who showed battle gifts, although nothing like the Battle Mages of old. Still, they could all wield shields, which may help, and most could at least throw things. A number of them could conjure and throw energy balls a good distance, but none could create Mage fire of any real strength. It was unfortunate that the north never really saw the level of gifts that were seen in other parts of Ennaris. Still, that could not be helped and he had made the most of those he had found. He had wasted a few of them trying to create gifted ghazrak but they all failed, usually quite dismally.

As he walked through the tunnels dug beneath the blasted land, with his few remaining Mage lights providing illumination, his reflections grew gloomy once again. The unceasing cycle of death and destruction played over and over and over in his mind. Well, once again, these laboratories would not be required after this, and he was comfortable with that.

He made his slow, halting way to his quarters. If he was to play his part in what was to come then he would need to rest.

It was four days later that Goroth gave the order to march. The motley northern army started its move towards the south, taking a slightly circuitous path through the sun-blasted land so that water could be obtained. General Morsen led the way with the Red Brigade and all three thousand regular cavalry and soldiers in good formation. Then followed four columns of more than seven thousand men and women each in roughly parallel lines, far enough apart that the dust raised did not cause too much trouble. There was little order in the groups but they held to basic formations. On each flank were the ghazrak, divided almost equally. Each of the groups of ghazrak were accompanied by Andorethi, including the three Andorethi Children. The huge ghazrak nominated as the Champion stumped along at the rear of one group. The Prophesy called for a contest between the Champions, and Grensor had put significant effort into creating this one.

From somewhere Goroth had found a hrss, and he rode between the four ranks of northers, while Likud walked by his side. Grensor had his light carriage - more like a sedan chair on wheels - which was pulled by four ghazrak. Far behind the columns of northers and ghazrak were the supply wagons, carrying weapons and foodstuffs plundered from wherever they could find it. The stocks of food for the remaining northers had been decimated, promising hard times for those left behind. There were few fighting age men or women left among them, however, and thus none to do the heavy work, so the older and very young would have to fend the best that they could.

The heat of the day was in full bloom as the combined army started out. The outcome of this campaign would reshape Ennaris for ever and Goroth was confident in the result. He had out-waited the others, even if that was not all his doing, and now he would have his revenge.

10. Citadel Preparations

The Citadel was a riot of activity when Flin, the twins and Andira stepped from the portal and walked to the main square. Flin stood atop the entry stairway of the administration building and watched as men and women in clothes of every style and colour imaginable milled around in the square. They seemed to alternate between getting in the way of carts carrying a huge range of materials and then finding themselves blocked by those same carts as they, in turn, reached another blockage. The noise was incredible. People shouted. Hrss-cart drivers cursed loudly as they tried to force their way through the mayhem. Animals were calling continuously. Trying to cross the square would be a mistake.

So, they went around it. Keeping close to the wall of the building they had just left, the small party made their way to the corner and safely wended their way through the confusion. They finally crossed the street to the tavern. Here, too, there was movement. Flin noted that extra tables had been brought in and the open front of the tavern had been extended further into the square than before. This caused further confusion as people had to move around or in some cases go between the tables and benches. Most of the tables were occupied but Flin led the way to an empty table near the side wall of the tavern and slightly away from the square itself. The noise level remained high but here it was a little more manageable, and they were able to talk with little chance of being overheard.

A slightly dishevelled server hurried to them after a short wait and took their order for ale. Flin and Andira dropped their packs against the wall and threw back travel cloaks. Flin watched the server move away, her back bowed slightly, and then regarded the milling crowd with interest as he turned to the twins.

"This is the most people I think I have ever seen in the Citadel," he remarked.

"You should see the grounds," Ragnor replied. "This is nothing! The Citadel has become the centre of the army preparations and there have been people streaming in. The Tellers have been passing on the stories as requested. There are as many adventurers here as there are people who believe in fighting for Ennaris."

Flin waited while drinks were served, thanked the woman who served them effusively for her service and gave her a silver coin, waving away change. Andira stared - the silver coin would have paid for the drinks more than three times over. Flin saw her expression and smiled.

"Servers in establishments such as this don't earn much. This tavern is better run than most, but still they will not pay well. That young woman is one of those Varna helped. She has three young children and will not accept charity. A tip, though, for excellent service is not charity."

Andira nodded slowly, while Ragnor grinned through the heady froth of the ale. Flin took a long, slow pull and sat back with a sigh.

"Now, I need to be brought up to date. Who responded to the call for troops and how many does Corm have? Have the Rocs visited? Do we have any information about Goroth's forces and where the battle will take place? What of Jalor, Blaine and Varna? And Dalresar, of course?"

The twins laughed as Flin's list of questions grew longer, but they set about answering them in some sort of order, speaking in turn as usual.

"Well, of the army recruits there have been many. We have people from the southern farmlands and the northern forests," Raglin said.

"The Faeronar, of course, have responded in force, and I expect the plateau has few fighting capable men or women left. But there are people from all over Ennaris here," Ragnor continued.

"Flin, the Tang arrived some days ago." Raglin reported, and stopped speaking to see what reaction came.

"The Tang?" Flin stared at the twins, both of whom nodded.

"Led by a warrior type named Murk," Ragnor said.

"They're all warrior types," Flin said, "from the time they're born. Sometimes I think they're born with sword in hand. Has there been trouble?"

"None at all. They're in the field, away from anyone else as far as they can be. Blaine and Helt have been to see them, though, and so has Almin Bor." Raglin smiled as Flin raised an eye-brow. "Again, no problems."

"Apparently Tanga came to them and instructed them to prepare for war. This Murk then brought his folk together and they have been training ever since," Ragnor explained.

"You mean they weren't trained before?" Flin said. "Thank the Guardians for small mercies then, because I'm not sure anyone could stand against them."

Raglin grinned. "Blaine did."

"Oh yes, that he did," Ragnor continued. "He took them on two at a time. Almin Bor said he knew Blaine was good but he never realised how good until then. Apparently, the Tang adopted Blaine and Helt then and there. Then they invited them to have a drink with them."

"Oh?" Flin was intrigued.

The Tang were notorious for their hard living, and anyone who had been to their slice of desolation would understand why. They had hired themselves out in ones and twos for centuries to those who wanted to carve out a larger piece of Ennaris. They were ruthless, tough and cynical, but they were peerless with one or twin swords. They would be valuable additions to Corm's army.

"That was six days ago," Raglin said, dryly.

"Ah," Flin rejoined. "And have we seen Blaine or Helt since then?"

"No," Ragnor said with a grin. "But Almin Bor visited for a while and then had to have a rest."

"Well, as long as they're ready when needed," Flin said, with a wry smile. "How's Corm doing?"

"He's going well," Raglin said. "It's early days but I think he'll be a good one. Already he's dealt with more of the domestic stuff than Intika did. He's visited each and every group of newcomers. So far none have left, so that's a good thing."

"And the Rocs?"

"They've continued to visit," Ragnor said in turn. "Corm had a platform built against the wall near the gate, pretty close to where we had the original one built when the Citadel was first constructed. The Rocs are happy with it, especially as they can visit with Balgor." He nodded at Flin's raised eyebrow. "Apparently, they knew Balgor lives in the wall, or protects the wall, or whatever that should be, and requested his company. So, when the Rocs are there, you may well find Balgor lounging with them. The Faeronar have become accustomed to seeing him and have adopted him." Ragnor sighed and shook his head. "When the people of the Citadel found that Balgor has been protecting them since before the time of the great destruction - well, let's just say he's the number one hero in these parts. To his embarrassment, of course."

"Interesting," Flin said. "After spending all that time not allowing anyone to know he remained behind, it would seem those times are done. I think that's a good thing, although I could wish we had been brought into the secret," he finished wistfully.

"But then, Archmage, you may have done something silly," a new voice broke in.

Flin twisted in his seat, recognising the tall figure standing behind him. The twins stood as one and bowed low, recognising what she was but not who. "Guardian," they said in unison.

"This is Dall," Flin said, gesturing. "Dall, Ragnor and Raglin. And, of course, you know Andira."

"Ragnor, Raglin. The twin Mages, of course," Dall nodded greeting. "May I join you?"

"Of course," Raglin replied, catching the eye of the server, who nodded. "Please, be seated."

Dall took a vacant seat and looked around. "I've not had the chance since my return to visit many parts of Ennaris," she said. "Is this Citadel typical of the planet in these days?"

"Yes and no," Ragnor replied.

"It's better than most and worse than some," Raglin added.

"Of course, Ennaris has devolved into regional differences, as you would expect," Ragnor said.

"It has been thousands of cycles, after all," Raglin finished.

Dall had been shifting attention from one to the other as they spoke and Flin laughed at her expression, which bordered on bewilderment.

"You'll get used to it," he said. "Just think of them as one person with two bodies and it makes it easier."

"Indeed," Dall said, and then smiled as a foaming mug of ale was placed in front of her. "Now this is something I have not had for a very long time." She took a taste and nodded. "Good!" Then, with a single long draught, Dall drained the mug.

Andira stared at the Guardian and Ragnor grinned broadly, gesturing for another round.

"To what do we owe the honour of your visit, Dall?" Flin asked. "Not that any of us object to one of the Guardians dropping in, but you tend to have reasons for doing things."

"We do," Dall replied, nodding to the server as she placed another mug of ale in front of her. "Hopefully we will be able to take a greater part in the life of Ennaris in the future, but we do have things to deal with. I have come for Andira, Archmage, as I said I would."

Ragnor and Raglin exchanged glances.

"It was Dall who intervened to protect us from the Kindred," Flin told the twins. "She laid claim to Andira at that time."

"And I have little time to impart to her what she must know," Dall said, drinking half her ale with appreciation. "This really is very good!

Anyway, I will only take her for a day or two at most, but I believe she will be needed."

"Andira is able to sense the Kindred," Flin said. "Actually, that's not quite right. I think Andira can sense the use of the dark arts, not just the Kindred." His eyes opened wide, and he stared at Dall. "The Eye of the Dark!"

"We believe so, and thus one of the Nine," Dall replied. "And I need to prepare her for what is to come. Andira, I will provide you with the knowledge you will need, but only if you agree."

With the weight of all eyes on her, Andira felt completely cowed and unsure. The encounter with the Kindred had left her shaken more than she had admitted. The businesslike way these people spoke of what to her were wonders and events of deep history left her feeling as though she were being forced into something highly dangerous, whether she wanted to do it or not. Flin recognised that.

"Andira," the Archmage said kindly, "this is not something asked lightly, nor is it something that can be forced. Confrontations with the powers of darkness and evil are always going to strain us, and current events leave us all feeling as though we are trapped rather than acting of our own will. At times, that cannot be avoided. I'm afraid this may be one of those times. As Ennaris needs its Faero and Corm happens to be in that role, and as Ennaris needs the Children and those three find themselves thrown into something they didn't expect, so Ennaris needs the Eye and it would appear that you have been chosen for that role."

"But, but, I'm just someone from a farm that Trabor found who could sense things," Andira objected in a small voice. "I'm not a hero to fight against evil like, like ..."

"Like us?" Flin asked with a wry smile. "Believe me, we're not heroes either. If any of us had a choice we would be somewhere else, doing something else. But we're not. We're here, and here is where we will have to stay. And given there's no-one else, and there hasn't been anyone else for a long time, it falls to us. I would greatly appreciate it if you joined us in our stand, but will understand if you choose not to do so."

Andira sighed, eyes closed as she fought her internal demons. She took a deep breath and opened her eyes again, looking to Dall. "Very well, Guardian, Archmage. When do we start?"

Dall nodded shortly and glanced to Flin, who gave a tight smile. She reached over to grip Andira's hand and said, "Right now."

The two women popped out of sight, leaving the Mages sitting at the table thinking their own thoughts.

It was the evening of the day when Flin returned to the Citadel with Andira, and not long after Dall had spirited the young woman away, when Corm Ramesa, Faero of Ennaris, leaned wearily on his practice sword and called an end to the sparring session.

An afternoon of sparring, combined with several short meetings with Almin Bor and leaders of various warrior troops, left him tired, sweating, and with a headache that he knew would get worse before getting better. And he was hungry! Surprised, he realised that he had not eaten since breaking his fast in the morning, early. So, with a wave to his sparring partners - Corm had progressed rapidly in skills and was facing two at a time now - he racked his practice sword and shield, strapped his own sword around his lean waist and strode towards the Citadel entrance. Briefly, he thought about his promise to Almin Bor and Jalor that he would be accompanied by his guard, but he dismissed the thought in favour of getting back to his quarters and eating. Thus, for the first time in a very long time, he walked alone through the gathering gloom.

Through the long passage leading through the main entrance gateway of the Citadel he walked, turning over in his head the various arrangements that he had discussed with the troop leaders during the day, and thinking about what that may mean for the morrow. He had to make sure that his army, made up of many elements drawn from all over Ennaris, would be ready to fight as a unit. Jalor, Almin Bor and Blaine had been working to meld them into a coordinated fighting force, but even minor misalignments could make all the difference.

Given that they would have to blend the army with the Knights from Escar, and the Rocs with their unique way of making warfare that had been demonstrated to Corm on two occasions already, coordination was key. He had confidence in Jalor but he also knew, from the studies he had been subjected to, that battles had a way of developing a life of their own, even though his own experience was limited to the recent defence of Escar.

He had passed through the gateway and was making his way towards the main square via a short cut without paying too much attention to his surrounding when he realised that his way was blocked by three men, all with drawn swords. Behind him he could hear others closing in. He quickly shook off the lethargy that he had embraced in preparation for a welcome day's end, turning his head to note the positions of the two men behind him. Five in all! He was a much-improved sword fighter but five to one was a little too much for him. Corm cast about for someone to assist but at the time there were few people about, and Corm had taken a short cut that was little used. His lack of thought would cost him dearly.

Corm put his back to the wall of the building and drew his sword, holding it low and inexpertly. He hoped to fool them into thinking he had few skills and thus they may be overly confident. That hope was dashed by the first speaker, one of the three who had boxed him in.

"So, finally we get you alone," the speaker said.

Corm recognised the voice, belonging to a relative newcomer to the armed forces, one who brought a small troop from a part of the southern continent. Or so he said. Almin Bor had been suspicious, but without saying why, and Corm had decided to accept the troop and take them at their word. It looked like he was wrong.

"Bunez! So, I take it you don't hail from Trebas, after all?" Corm asked, and almost winced to hear the fear in his voice.

"Not even close to it, Faero," Bunez replied scornfully. "We've not really had a home for a long time, though. So anywhere is good enough."

"Bandits and brigands, eh?" Corm said dismissively, trying to keep his voice even.

He had not realised how much he relied on the presence of others - Almin Bor, Jalor, Blaine and Helt, for the most part - to provide him with security and confidence. Without any of them he could feel uncertainty rise up like an unwonted companion, dragging him down. He tried to force it back into its hole.

"Not this time," Bunez said as he strolled towards Corm. "This time we're legitimate businessmen, all paid up and everything."

"You could forget about it and take double whatever you're being paid to walk away," Corm said, without really believing it would happen, even if Bunez agreed.

"Nope. We've been paid." Bunez smiled with an evil smile curling his lips. "And don't look for help from anyone. The rest of the troop is making sure we have this alley all to ourselves. The boy who would be king," he continued contemptuously. "I've been watching you being taught how to fight. It's time you learned how to die!"

"A Faero is not king," Corm replied, trying to keep Bunez talking. As he spoke a clash of swords from behind him could be heard.

"They're still trying to make you better than the rest of us," Bunez said with a snarl, listening to the sounds coming from around the corner. "Sounds like some of your friends have decided to join in. Too late!"

He leapt at Corm, sword swinging in an attempt to decapitate the Faero, only to meet Corm's broadsword as he swept it at an angle, diverting Bunez's stroke and bringing Corm around to face the first of the two men coming up from behind. With little thought Corm brushed aside the ineffectual sword-stroke and cut a deep slice from the next attacker's side. He ducked another stroke and leapt back from Bunez's follow-up, narrowly avoiding taking a severe strike, but wearing a shallow cut down his left arm instead. Shouts came from the other end of the alley now, and Bunez frowned. Corm could make out Almin Bor's voice and his attention wavered momentarily, coming back just in time to stop Bunez from driving his shorter sword right through him. As it was, he took another injury, a slice to the fleshy part of his right thigh. Pain erupted such as he had never known and lack of support from his leg caused Corm to topple to his right side, colliding with the wall he had been using to protect his back. His sword dropped and clattered away from him.

Bunez's sword stroke missed Corm's head by the smallest margin. Behind his attacker, Corm saw Almin Bor sprint around the corner, only to find the second and third of Bunez's team rushing towards him. Corm did not see what happened next for Bunez gave a snort of triumph and raised his sword, swiftly striking down at Corm's unprotected head. The sword rang as though it had hit an anvil, and its motion stopped a hand's breadth above Corm's head. Through the shadows that were closing around Corm's sight he thought he saw a bright figure walk from the wall alongside him, and then knew no more.

Blaine and Helt sprinted across the main square of the Citadel. Their boots rang on the pavement and merged with the assorted noises that swords and knives made even as they were being held in place by the wearers. The square was far from deserted even at this time, what with the large number of army recruits and associated companions and hangers-on, and they had to dodge and weave around various obstacles. They attracted quite a lot of interest as they made their dash. Up the broad steps they ran and through the entrance to the administration building and along the corridors until they reached Corm's rooms. There they encountered four stern-faced guards, holding spears and swords in a business-like manner.

"What happened?" Helt demanded as she and Blaine came to a halt in front of the guards.

"The Faero was attacked on his way from the practice grounds, Captain," one of the guards said. "He was alone at the time. The Commander fought his way through the attackers and managed to get to the

Faero before the final stroke could be delivered. The Archmage is with him now."

"Flin is here?" Helt gave a deep breath of relief. "Then all will be as well as possible."

"How many?" Blaine demanded.

"The Commander said there were nine all together. It was Bunez and his crew. The Commander" - the guard's eyes widened as he spoke - "he fought off five of them. By himself!"

"That's why he's the Commander," Blaine said. "Who else is in there?"

"Someone called Balgor," the guard replied. "He carried the Faero here. He seems to have helped the Commander."

Helt stared at the guard. "You're new here?"

"No, Captain. I've been here for half a cycle." The guard eyed Helt uncertainly.

"Then how can you not know who Balgor is?" Helt demanded. "He's a Guardian, you dolt."

"Guardian?" the guard all but squeaked. "I - I - didn't know they were real."

"Well now you do." Helt thought for a moment, staring at Blaine without seeing him. "Blaine, I think you can leave Corm to Flin and Balgor. There'll be hell to pay shortly though, if I'm any judge at all."

"Oh?" Blaine said in reply.

"The Rocs!"

Blaine's eyes went wide as realisation struck. "Oh, sh-!" He turned to the nearest guard. "You, come with me! The captain will hold your place." And he turned and ran back the way he came, followed after a moment by the uncertain guard.

Back out the door they ran, through the gathering crowd who now were aware that something was wrong, and towards the front gates. Through the night, high above the Citadel, there rang out the battle cry of an enraged Roc, a cry repeated by many other voices. Around the

Citadel, people stopped and stared into the night sky, unable to see the source of the cries but starting to panic nevertheless.

Blaine put on a burst of speed but knew he would not be in time to meet the Rocs and calm them. With a curse, he did the only thing he could think of. He drew forth the Golden Sword. Immediately he was encased in the soft golden glow and the armour grew along his limbs as he ran. Blaine shot ahead, a golden blur leaving the following guardsman far behind. Through the main gate the Warrior sped. He made it to the Roc platform just as Ky-rel landed in a flurry of wings and backwash, great red eyes spinning, wings held out and rigid. Above, with his greatly enhanced eyesight, Blaine could make out at least twenty of the great birds circling.

Ky-rel gave a short, harsh squawk, staring at the Golden Warrior. The call was answered by the circling Rocs, harsh and loud. Blaine sheathed his sword in a fluid motion, the golden glow dropping immediately, and held his arms out wide, hands open.

"He's alright, Ky-rel," Blaine shouted. "The Archmage is with him. So is Balgor. He'll be fine," Blaine continued, hoping he was right. "You need to remain calm now, so you don't give him anything else to worry about."

The agitated Roc was hopping from one leg to another as the guardsman finally made it to the platform. He stopped out of reach of the huge beak and watched uncertainly. Ky-rel's eyes continued to spin, but he stopped hopping and stared at Blaine.

"No, I haven't seen him," Blaine said, holding his hands out still. "But I'm sure that, with both Flin and Balgor assisting, he will be fine."

With a rush most of the rest of the Rocs landed on the huge platform, each taking a place where they could stand and yet be ready for instant launch. There remained a flight of four aloft, flying what Blaine could only think of as a combat patrol, gimlet eyes alert for anything that may cause a threat. A more intimidating sight Blaine had not seen for a long while.

A small group of Faeronar approached, carrying baskets of food and tubs of water and placed them around the landing in near proximity to two or three Rocs each. Gravely, each bowed to the nearest of the birds before retreating to the edge of the landing and waiting. The birds eyed the food offered and Blaine was sure they returned the bows before pulling haunches of meat from the baskets and carefully, almost daintily, eating what had been offered. After a while four of the birds launched and were replaced by the four who had remained aloft. Combat patrol, indeed!

It was about an Earth hour later by Blaine's reckoning that Corm, accompanied by Flin, Almin Bor and Helt, made a slow and careful way through the gates to the platform. Ky-rel hopped to the edge and awaited the Faero, who remained upright by willpower alone. Carefully, he shuffled to the great bird and leaned wearily against him with one arm slung across the great neck as support. Helt moved to stand with Blaine. Blaine looked to Flin who just nodded. Corm would be alright. For the first time that night, Blaine allowed himself to relax.

"Did any of them survive?" Blaine asked quietly.

"No. It seems Balgor takes his protection responsibilities seriously. It was he who saved Corm in the end and kept him alive so Flin could get there in time." Helt watched both Faero and Roc for a moment. "We found red gold on each of them, all nine. Lots of it." She smiled grimly, approvingly. "But Corm had already dealt with one of them and held off four before Almin Bor arrived."

Blaine just nodded. So, the enemy knew Corm was a threat and made his first attempt. There likely would be others. Watching Corm with Ky-rel and then Helt's set expression, Blaine knew the Faero would not be moving about without an escort, and a good one, again. Blaine wondered what Jalor would say about this. Blaine knew that had the general been at the Citadel then Corm would never have been allowed to walk unprotected. In a way, though, it was a positive outcome - it proved to the Faeronar and the army and allies that Corm was important enough to assassinate, but also demonstrated the standing that he had with the Rocs.

This would add some delay to their plans, but whether Goroth would take advantage of that delay was another matter. And where was Jalor?

The General of the Faero's army was wondering much the same thing. After returning from the steppes, a little after the twins, Jalor had spent a short time conferring with Corm and Almin Bor and then, with a small guard, had returned to the portal. This time the small band was rugged up, swathed in furs and thick woven cloth such that they were sweating as they awaited the portal's activation. But they were glad of it when they emerged from the gateway building into a fierce snow storm. Thick woollen bands with eye slits were pulled down over their eyes. Heads were encased by fur hoods that were attached to thick fur jackets. The team struggled to see anything at all, let alone those who should be awaiting them.

It took Jalor exactly ten seconds to decide to head back into the gateway building It was an incongruous structure in this land of ice and snow, constructed as it was of a seemingly indestructible stone-like material and impervious to the storm raging outside its walls. No sooner had they retreated into the large single chamber than they were followed by two others, who wore their protective furs much more easily than Jalor and his troop.

There was a momentary fumble as the guards sought to get swords and knives out, at which point Jalor waved them to stand down. The two strangers each held wicked looking spears that looked more like harpoons. Had they been hostile then Jalor and the guards would have stood little chance. The two stood quite still, looking around at the walls of the chamber, their eyes growing wide as they saw the images on the walls. Jalor had to admit that they looked impressive. One wall held a view of the ice from an elevated position, one that obviously did not exist in this time. A second wall showed a vista comprising a set of structures, very tall and thin, shaped like shards of ice. It was obviously a city. The structures formed an odd counterpoint to the next images of an ice-scape seen from ground level, with a close-up of a large white-furred creature that Jalor thought could have been a polar bear, except for the six legs and long whippy tail. The fourth wall, of course, was occupied by the portal gate and its screen.

"I am Jalor," he said, pulling thick gloves off his hands and pushing back his hood. "I bring welcome to the people of the ice from Corm, the Faero of Ennaris. And I thank you for taking the time to meet with us."

One of the two strangers shrugged. "Tine informed me that you would need to meet and discuss your war. She told me that you would have need of our help, but I'm not sure how that can be." He paused for a moment. "I am Xymin."

As he spoke, Xymin pushed back his hood and stripped his mittens off, deftly joining them and slipping them around his neck, allowing them to fall onto his chest. His companion followed suit. Xymin was no longer the innocent that he had been less than a cycle before. His people, the Junda, had taken some convincing about what he had seen, but the appearance of Tine at several meetings had put paid to that. Xymin had become a *de facto* leader of the ice dwellers, but they considered the whole idea of war with distaste. That had changed when they tasted the effects of the ghazrak for the first time. A whole community had been destroyed. This disaster was followed by a second one, also with no survivors. When a third community was attacked with the ghazrak retreating after killing every child in the small settlement, the Junda realised that they faced a foe that preyed on their most vulnerable members.

The Junda were gentle to a fault at times. They were persistent and patient on the hunt. They were skilled with the use of many weapons required for survival in this land that did not reward care but that punished carelessness or lack of skill. However, the Junda also were enemies to be feared. They were resolute and unforgiving. The ghazrak continued their depredations, but the Junda now gathered their people into larger communities and created a protective militia. Xymin led the militia, named the Junda-lar, with the Tinetings at its core, and they quickly relearned old skills, drawing heavily. on the lessons of Ogun.

They now practised old ways that had been downplayed but never really forgotten, just as the stories and traditions passed down through the long cycles had told them not to forget. Where those skills had devolved into games and contests of strength, agility and skill, now they returned to their roots of offensive and defensive skills. They had lost no more communities to the predations of the ghazrak but for the first time the Junda lost people to the defence of their own peoples.

Jalor learned their story and was impressed, and in turn imparted much of the story of the Faero, Ennaris itself and parts of the Prophecy of which Xymin seemed unaware. He reflected as he did so that he may not have been best suited to telling the tale, having come from the outside. Or maybe that made him better suited. Who could tell?

"Tine said one who came would be of the Children," Xymin said carefully.

Jalor merely nodded.

"You are of the Children of Ennaris?"

"I am," Jalor said, no longer sceptical of that claim as had been. "I'm from a world far from Ennaris, but a world drawn to civilisation by the Ennarisi long before the rebellion and seeded with Ennaris' blood. I and my companions will fight with the Ennarisi. In fact, we have already fought with the Ennarisi."

Xymin considered. This man was one who Tine had told him would be the leader of the forces and yet he did not come from Ennaris. "Why should you take up this battle?"

"It has been my battle for a long time, fought on many worlds. Goroth and his kind have infected other civilisations and my people seek to hold them back, to push them back, and to make all worlds safe from their influence. We protect our own children and those of others who are unable to do so. My companions and I are what we call Warriors of the Light. Ennaris' battle is our battle."

"And are there others who fight with you?"

"Yes, many. In fact, far above us, in the space around Ennaris, my fellow Warriors do battle right now with the forces of Goroth's ally, Likud. They seek to hold off those forces while we assist the Ennarisi to undertake their own battle here."

Xymin considered again, sharing a long and meaningful look with his companion, as yet not introduced. He came to a decision and locked eyes with Jalor.

"This is Zudor. He is my war second. The Junda-lar will support the Faero's fight. We will field one thousand fighters. Let us decide how best we do this."

11. Hunter

Well, she thought, *that's unexpected!*

Andira stood before a broad field of short, green grass that extended to fuzzy edges far away on each side. Was it real or invented by Dall? She was not sure. Facing her were ten Kindred, having little in common except skin that seemed to be splitting. Several had horns with wicked-looking points that seemed to gleam in the strange light in this place. Some had hooves instead of feet. Still others had large muzzles instead of noses and mouths while at least three had a third eye, right in the centre of their foreheads. Patches of fur, patches of bare skin, leathery reptile-type skin, even scales could be seen as she considered what she faced. One of the creatures appeared to have a bit of everything, including a tail.

Andira had been with Dall for two tendays now, or so it seemed to her. At first, she had been sceptical about what Dall told her. But after the first two days she realised that, not only had Dall been truthful, but that she, Andira, did have a gift that may be of use. Several more days of intensive learning sharpened her use of the gift and she was able to sense the use of the dark arts occurring quite a long way away. What was more, she even was able to pinpoint what sort of use was taking place. She was amazed at the variety of uses to which those dark arts could be put, and also the seemingly enormous power that could be unleashed. But she also knew that it was illusory. Yes, the power was there, but it most certainly was not limitless and it came with significant costs. Some of those costs could be put off for quite a long time, but the price would be paid. Usually, that involved being subjugated to one or more of the Kindred, these demons from another universe.

The latter concept had taken Andira a long time to get straight. The idea of parallel universes she still found difficult to grasp, so she tended to think of the Kindred's home place as a hidden world, one that was magically separated from the world in which she lived. Certain people were able to make tears in the thin wall that separated them. That was what Flin had repaired, with Dall's help, when they had faced the Kindred, Ghaz-tu, recently. It was like people's skin that needed to be patched and then held in place to make it firm once more.

So, the first tenday had been taken up in understanding what the Kindred were, and how to recognise either them or those who were trying to make contact with them. Andira was stunned to learn that many people had done so over an incredibly long time. The vast majority of them had failed, or they had suffered in some way as a result of a minor success. That may have taken the form of failed eyesight, or being rendered incapable of speech or their normal mental processes. In some cases, the summoner died, as had the one who summoned Ghaz-tu. For that was what they did - they summoned the Kindred and demanded their help. However, without adequate understanding or training, they were unable to control the Kindred and so suffered the consequences. In the days before the rebellion, when there were far more gifted Ennarisi, a clandestine team of Mages and Guides had maintained a watch for those who were misguided enough to make the attempt to communicate through the veil of fire and smoke. That team dealt with the summoner harshly, if there was anything left to deal with.

And they dealt with the Kindred that may have made it through the fire.

The second tenday taught Andira how to do that. She was amazed that she could do anything like that, recalling with absolute clarity the stomach-clenching fear that she experienced as Flin did battle. She recalled the resolve displayed by the Archmage even as he was being overcome by the Kindred, and then his ability to recover and take the initiative as soon as a small opening was provided. That she may be able to do anything similar she did not believe, and had told Dall exactly that. That she had scoffed at what a Guardian had told her was another sign of growth, one that Dall welcomed, although Andira did not realise it. And yet, after a single tenday, she had been given the knowledge of how to do that, and had been able to defeat a single Kindred, and then two at a time.

Dall had thrown her into different situations, with different types of demons, each of whom had their own ways of fighting. Inevitably, though, they began with intense mental pressures to weaken resolve and to induce fear, and then the demons sought to leverage that fear and the resultant mental chinks. The Kindred would then try to take control, either to destroy the summoner or to over-power them. The worst situation, as Dall explained to her, would be when a Kindred left its realm and took over a host. Inevitably that meant that she would have to battle both the Kindred's demon spirit and the host body. The saving grace was that the Kindred tended to be impatient and, usually, did not try to understand what its new host could do, but that could not be counted on.

Andira was intrigued that the Kindred had a single, neuter, gender. Flin had said that they were the model for the ghazrak, but Andira understood that the ghazrak were all male, so obviously the model had not been followed to the letter.

Now she faced what Dall told her would be her final test. She had been placed in the field facing ten of the Kindred. She recognised elements of each. Three of them were were-beasts. They would seek to rend and tear her mind, and then would do the same to her body if they could come to physical grips with her. Four were night-walkers, which was a misnomer for they could withstand daylight, even though they disliked it. They were weaker than were-beasts but if they could get close enough to drain an enemy of blood they would grow in power. Two others were reavers, which were similar to were-beasts but much more likely to seek physical confrontation. One was a sepok, a higher-order demon who could command the others and who would display far more intelligence.

Even while she thought about the foes that she faced, they attacked, launching a concerted assault on her senses and seeking to break through the barriers that she now had available to her. She resisted the onslaught, holding back the combined impact with a gasp. This was much more than she had experienced in the past and she knew that the sepok had not joined in the initial attack. Holding the mental attack at bay, she separated one part of her will - this had been the hardest thing to learn - and formed a sort of mental knife, almost a short sword, which she swung into position behind the demons and systematically cut the invisible cords that bound them to their plane of existence.

Six of the cords had been cut, and so six of the demons had died, before the sepok took a hand. Andira had been concentrating on the six that she destroyed when, with a wave of the Sepoc's hand, the sword was wrenched away from Andira's mind and destroyed. The aftershock transferred itself with shocking force through her senses. Prepared to some extent, but by no means entirely, for a possible backlash she recoiled physically, taking several steps backward before recovering any sort of poise. And that was too long!

The sepok blasted her with its own mental darts, sending them one after the other, rather than the crude shunt that the lesser Kindred had sent at her. She had to divert much of her attention to seeing and diverting or blocking those darts, which allowed the remaining night-walker to almost reach her. In desperation, Andira leapt aside, momentarily causing the sepok's darts to miss her, and turned her attention to the night-walker. The creature was close enough for her to feel its breath - why did they need to breath? she thought for no particular reason - before she could fashion a scythe that both swept its thin legs out from under it and then cut the cord. Using the same scythe, she swept back to sever the first of the reavers from its source of power.

But the sepok had taken the time to recover its poise and Andira now was barraged with dart after dart of power. They hit their mark time and time again. She could feel all of her control fading and she crouched as she tried to raise a thin defence. Andira gathered her will and tried to harden her control. She struggled as the sepok continued to fling mental darts, all the while advancing on Andira. Andira held her nerve, waiting until the sepok was close before reaching deep into her reserves and fashioning a razor sharp spike. As the sepok reached for her, Andira flung the spike into its chest before creating a thin knife from her own energy, rolling to one side and slicing through the sepok's link cord.

She had almost exhausted her own energy store. She tried to hold her shield to battle the last Kindred. But, it was too little, too late. With a moan, her last defence collapsed and the sole remaining reaver leapt at her, sharp teeth bared and dripping with venom. She fell to the ground and cowered as the reaver reached her ...

... And disappeared! Instead, Dall stood beside Andira and held out one hand. Shakily, with her hand trembling and her muscles refusing to work properly, Andira took the Guardian's hand and levered herself to her feet. She stood, dispirited and defeated, before the Guardian. Tears leaked from her eyes as she faced the fact that she was not strong enough to defeat the Kindred.

Finally, Andira looked up. Instead of the stern task-master that she had been dealing with for the last two tendays, who had pushed her to ever greater effort and made her work harder than she remembered working before, Dall was smiling broadly. Andira was bewildered.

"My lady Dall, why do you smile? I was defeated! How am I going to be of use to the Faero if I am unable to defeat the demons?" With a start Andira realised that she was almost wailing. Tears were now running freely down her face, even as she sought to hold back her emotions.

"Andira," Dall replied, still holding her hand, "I'm smiling because of what you were able to accomplish. You were never meant to win that battle. Rather, it was to teach you that even in defeat you must continue to fight, and to test how you would face that situation. I almost had to add fresh foes. I didn't expect you to deal with ten of them quite so effectively."

"Then that was not a failure?" Andira asked, brushing tears away only to have them replaced by a fresh supply.

"Not at all," Dall said. "You will rarely face more than half that number, if ever, from what I've been able to discover. The Kindred, even with a sepok to command them, don't co-operate well. But you must remember this. You have faced a sepok in your training and were able to defeat it, but don't believe they're all the same, for of all the Kindred they are the most intelligent, and thus the most feared."

The two women stood together for a short time while Andira recovered. Dall smiled once again.

"You're as ready now as you're likely to be. It's time for you to rejoin the Archmage. I fear he'll have need of your services." She placed her hand on Andira's forehead for a moment, then removed it again as Andira felt a slight pressure that immediately faded away. "You are the first of the Hunters of the new Ennaris, Andira. Come, I have someone you need to meet."

Still dashing away her tears, this time not to be replaced, Andira followed Dall across the field. When she looked back the remains of the Kindred had vanished - illusion or not, she wondered - and then she turned back in time to stop before bumping into the Guardian's back. And she stared. In front of Dall stood a Roc. But not any Roc. This one was almost pure white, with a crown of brilliant blue feathers. Andira had never seen a Roc and she was entranced.

"This is Ty-fel," Dall said, and Andira found herself staring into eyes like the deepest well she had ever seen.

I greet the Hunter, Andira felt rather than heard. *It is an honour to serve.*

12. Dharmoney Unveiled

Varna and Clay walked through the front gates of the Citadel. They had already been challenged three times as they crossed the broad sward in front of the fortress, and again as they entered the gates. Each time they had merely said that they were returning after a time away, and each time they were handed off to a guard for the next stage. Inside, they were met by the bustle of a busy city. Wagons were being unloaded and loaded. People shouted to each other as they fought through the masses. Hrss called to no-one in particular. The young guard who led their way watched them almost as much as he watched where he put his feet, for the street leading to the square showed the signs of much hrss traffic.

Crossing the square towards the tavern, the small party was halted by a loud call, raised above the general hubbub. Helt, resplendent in her silver armour and holding her helm under one arm, strode across through the crowd, forcing others to jump out of her way or be trampled.

"Ho, Varna, Dalresar," the warrior woman called. "Welcome back."

The guard stood uncertainly, his duty to escort the two to the guard sergeant suddenly looking to be less simple. Helt saw the uncertainty in the guard's face and grinned.

"It's okay Vellot, I can take care of these two miscreants," she said.

"Miscreants?" Varna replied, eyebrow raised.

"Ha!" Helt laughed as she enclosed Varna in a great hug, crushing the slighter woman against the armour. She reached out to clasp Clay's arm in a gesture of greeting. Vellot took that as a sign that the three knew each other and faded back into the crowd.

"Busy place," Clay commented.

"There's been a bit happening," Helt replied, a touch of tension leaking through. "Come on, you need to see the Archmage."

"What have we missed?" Varna asked, picking up on Helt's tension.

"Corm was attacked last night," Helt replied. "That's why everyone's a bit on edge. Oh, he'll be okay," she continued, "but only because Almin Bor and Balgor got there in time. The Archmage healed him and he's sleeping now."

"Someone tried to kill him?" Clay asked.

"He managed to get loose from his guard," Helt growled. "That won't happen again! And yes, someone tried to kill him. Red gold in their purses."

"So, Goroth's looking to remove him from the equation," Clay mused as they walked towards the main steps. "That makes sense. Corm is the one supposed to lead the battle, after all. If he was killed then the Faeronar would have to choose someone new, and that would take quite a while. I'm not sure who the nearest suitable relative would be, but there are not many of them."

"Well, we won't have that worry, at least," Helt said, nodding to the guard at the foot of the stairs and leading the way into the building. "We almost have everything ready to go. From what we can gather from the Tang scouts, Goroth is getting ready to move. We aim to meet him on the steppes where things can be in the open, so we'll be heading out as soon as Corm is well enough."

Clay nodded. "So, a couple of days, then."

"Probably," Helt concurred.

Clay stopped, forcing the other two to do likewise. "In that case, I have something I need to do." He looked at Varna who just nodded. "Major, please inform the others as you need."

"Aye, Champion," Varna replied with a touch of formality.

Clay turned on his heel and strode back through the doors. Varna turned to find Helt looking at her quizzically.

"Champion?" Helt asked.

"You don't need to mention that just yet," Varna said. "To anyone," she added. "Now, where's the Archmage? We need to have a chat."

Flin was in Corm's room, sitting in an easy chair under one window. In his hands was an old and battered book, its hrss leather cover bound by brass bands. He was looking out the window. Corm was sitting up in his bed looking like he wanted to chew on something.

"I'm fine, I tell you," he said as Varna entered the room. "Varna! You're back!"

Flin looked up, nodding to Varna and Helt. "You may not be fine, no matter how much you tell me you are. Nor how loudly. You very nearly died and we don't really know what Balgor's assistance will mean to you. There's something different to your aura and I need more time to work out what it means."

"Balgor's assistance?" Varna asked. "Helt told me he had helped, but why should that cause any concern? Where is he, by the way?"

"He had to provide some initial healing, which he said is not his strength. In fact, he quite openly said that he was not sure if he gave too much to Corm or not? He tried to give just enough strength to keep him alive until I could be there, but he was unable to judge clearly. As to where he is, you know better than that. He could be anywhere."

Varna looked at Corm, turning her enhanced sight on him. The Faero's usual aura, which was not much out of the ordinary in most regards, was a brown shot through with occasional spots of various colours. The latter usually indicated that there was something different about him, but not enough to cause significant gifts to be in evidence. Now, however, his aura included an overlay of pale grey, as though Corm's spirit was bolstered by the shadow of the Guardian. Varna stepped to Corm's side and held out one hand. To Flin's shock, the hand glowed as she moved it from Corm's head to his feet. The latter was held immobile by his own shock.

"He really is fine, Flin," Varna said. "But Balgor has, indeed, made some changes, although just what they are is hard to say. There's a shadow, a good shadow," she hastened to add, "over Corm's aura, which is what you can see. You, Faero, are very lucky. I think you would be dead had Balgor not done whatever he did."

"Oh, I just gave him a little essence," Balgor's voice said from the wall.

Varna sighed theatrically. "Would you stop listening in and just be here, please? And what is a little essence?" she asked just ahead of Flin.

Balgor appeared grinning, not at all abashed.

"Actually, I'd just arrived. Likki sends thanks, by the way," he said to Varna, who just nodded.

"Likki?" Flin asked, looking from Balgor to Varna.

"We met the last of those priests again," Varna said. "He tried to kill me as a sacrifice to whatever sickness he had." She frowned as the memory took her again. "He failed."

"That he did," Balgor said, smiling. "Most emphatically. One should always be careful when dealing with one of the Children. They can catch you out in peculiar ways."

"That's all very well," Flin said, deciding not to pursue that avenue just yet, "but what did you do to Corm? Varna tells me that he has some sort of shadow to his aura."

"Ah, yes," Balgor said with a wry grin. "You recall I did say I was not very good at that, yes? Well, I may have given him a little too much. Corm may have quite a long life, if Goroth doesn't kill him first, of course."

"Of course," Corm muttered from his bed.

"Why are you still in bed?" Balgor asked. "You're fine. Don't you have an army to run or whatever Faeros do?"

"See? I told you I'm fine," Corm said to Flin, throwing his bed clothes back.

"Very well," Flin said, rising. "Then I need to know what Varna has been up to."

"Not just yet, Archmage," Balgor said with a small smile. "But I'm sure she will tell you soon."

"What?" Flin asked, staring as Balgor grasped Varna's hand and both disappeared. "One day I'm going to figure out how he does that. Right, then!"

He turned back to find an empty bed and Corm nowhere to be seen. Helt stood at the door and jerked one thumb towards the corridor outside.

"He went that way," she said, laughing at Flin's expression. "How about I buy you an ale, Archmage? You look like you need one."

The following days continued to see the arrival of fresh forces to bolster the Faero's army. They came singly and in groups of five and ten, hailing from cities, towns and villages across Ennaris. Most arrivals had been from the northern continent until now, but more people from the southern continent and the eastern reaches, hard against the dividing range, started to arrive. Men and women, and occasionally whole families, made their weary way to the Citadel. Some arrived in hrss-drawn carriages that resembled small cottages on wheels but the majority were walking or riding. As they arrived they were assigned to areas of the great field in front of the citadel, which had now filled up.

A minor sensation occurred when a small group arrived from Kushnel. Led by a man of serious mien named Resta, when challenged he merely stated that Eresh had bid him to assist the Archmage. He was accompanied, he told the gate sergeant, by seven healers in training. The sergeant, recalling the effect of Drewflin and the Roc healers at Escar, immediately formed an escort of guards and instructed his under-sergeant to take the newcomers to the Archmage. The small procession of the escort and eight men and women wended its path through the growing mayhem until they reached the Administration building. Word had been passed ahead and Resta was greeted by Clofta, who Corm had retained as chief healer, before Flin was located.

The Archmage's relief was visible and profound to the curious bystanders. Healers! Jalor had told him that Eresh had agreed to assist the devastated Telsith, and the twins had passed on the news of the temple in Kushnel being converted to a place of healing, but he had not known that Eresh had found healers. Even though they were relatively untrained, they would be an enormous asset to Corm's forces. They were drawn into the administration building and Drewflin spent the rest of the day with them.

Enormous quantities of supplies had been laid in. Finally, the first of several trains of wagons was formed up, with its escort of mounted guards. Helt had elected to lead this first supply train, which meant that she would be the first of the army's leaders to arrive at the edge of the steppes between seven and ten days hence. The escort for this first wagon train was heavier than would be used for those following, as they would also form the advance guard for the army proper.

There were the inevitable problems. Several fights broke out about minor things like the order of march, resolved easily by Helt who strode along the wagons and, with an icy glare, informed the wagon drivers of their designated positions in the train. Her silver armour gleamed in the early morning light. One wagon broke an axle on an uneven part of the small outer square where they had been marshalled, and had to be replaced at the last minute, which added a small delay as essential items were moved to its replacement. A hrss was found to be lame and also had to be replaced. Finally, however, the train was ready to go. Under the watchful eyes of Corm and Jalor, with Almin Bor striding alongside Helt giving her last-minute advice from his own experiences in the past, they exited the Citadel at no more than a walk. In fact, several of the more experienced guards opted to walk with their mounts at this early stage, saving them for when they may be needed.

The route that they would take was well mapped out and passed through several small villages before coming down from the plateau in a series of switchbacks and then snaking its way through the forests and across several small rivers, before making a final run through an area of short scrubby bushes to the beginning of the steppes. Helt would select a good location for the camp and get it established, with one or two trains to follow each day. The volume of supplies seemed huge, but

Jalor did not want to rely on living off the land. He had seen only a few parts of Ennaris but its wildlife did not seem to be abundant and capable of sustaining a large body of people, a point with which Almin Bor agreed.

Now that the time for departure had come, time itself seemed to slip away. Corm was showing no ill-effects from his ordeal and the news had run through the army like wildfire that he had been healed by a Guardian. That seemed to lift the confidence of the army for, if the Faero was favoured by the Guardians, then perhaps things would get better. The news also ran through the newer member of the army that their general was one of the Children of Ennaris, which added to the positive morale. Still, Jalor was concerned that, while there was enthusiasm, there was little real experience. In fact, apart from Almin Bor, the surviving guard members who fought at Escar, the Tang and a small number who had fought in the last of the wars that had settled several of the current warlords' holdings, most had no more experience than occasional fighting against the scattered bandits.

Most of the supplies had been dispatched over the previous four days when the first of the troops moved out. Led by a mounted Almin Bor, the long line of a mixed force drawn from the many and varied recruits marched from the Citadel, aiming for the first of nine stopping points that had been scouted and marked out. The people of the Citadel turned out to wave and shout encouragement. Some were in tears, although striving not to show their fears. Paradoxically, however, despite the cheers it felt like a muted event.

Jalor, watching from the Citadel walls, thinking of other times where armies marched to war in a carnival atmosphere. In some of them there was parti-coloured bunting and celebrations, reflecting how little the populace understood what was to happen. That was not the case among the Faeronar. These people knew and understood. And, what Jalor had already realised but recognised anew, they accepted the need. They were the Faero's people, and they truly believed that they were the best hope for Ennaris, and they acted accordingly.

The atmosphere in the Citadel changed following the departure of Almin Bor's troop. The watch had intensified - the near loss of the Faero to assassination had been a shock and a wake-up call - and now the normal activities were overshadowed by preparations for the second and subsequent troop trains to leave. The second troop train would be led by Corm, over-riding objections by the physicians that he could not possibly be fit to make the journey, with a guard of the Old Blood and a mixed troop strategically selected from most of the regions of Ennaris. The third troop would be led by Murk, although the Tang would leave as soon as they arrived, to scout across the grasslands ahead of the expected battle. The fourth would be led by Blaine and the fifth and last by Jalor. Stragglers would be sent on as they arrived.

Sitting in the tavern as the last of the troops prepared to leave, Varna took stock. The Citadel had an almost abandoned feel about it. Where days before there had been hustle and bustle, now there was quiet but little calm. An undercurrent of anxiety permeated the place, and Varna could feel the effort being put into presenting a normal face by many of those left behind, women and men alike. Drawing back her senses, not having been aware that she had been using them, she realised that she was not alone. Across the table Balgor sat watching her.

"How long have you been there?" she asked.

"Oh, for a while," he replied with the slow smile that she so enjoyed. "You were a long way away, so I thought I would wait."

"I was just thinking of the Ennarisi, but the Faeronar more so and the Blood most of all. They are so stoic, so prepared to make the sacrifices that are needed. The fear that is being felt here is far more contained than I would have expected, and it *is* being contained."

"They've been raised knowing that they would be to the fore in the final battle against Goroth, so this is what they feel they're here to do." Balgor looked around the almost deserted square. "It's why I've spent the time to hold the Citadel safe."

"How will you spend the time when the battle is happening?" Varna asked.

"Oh, I'll be there, as will my brothers and sisters. We cannot take part directly, but we will protect Ennaris, as we have sought to do before."

"You'll leave the Citadel?"

"My time here is done. My role was to get the Faero and the Old Blood to this point, and here we are. And you?"

Varna grimaced. "I'm not sure I know what my role is going to be. Jalor leads, that's a given. Blaine is some sort of fighting whirlwind. Flin is going to need help, though, and I guess I can do some of that. But I just don't know."

"Your role will become clear," Balgor replied, his eyes glittering.

"Is that said as a Guardian or my - um -." She faltered, colouring slightly.

"Oh both," Balgor said with a wicked grin. "As both Guardian and 'um'."

"Care to give me a hint?" Varna asked with a slight edge to her voice.

"No, I don't think I can," Balgor smiled. "But know that the Children are instrumental to this battle, and you most of all."

Varna just nodded, looking to Balgor to make a comment about lack of clarity, only to find him looking past her. Turning, she saw an old woman making her somewhat unsteady way across the square, heading unerringly towards where Varna and Balgor sat. As the woman neared Balgor stood, facing the woman, and bowed to her. In turn, the woman gave him a wry smile.

"Still bothering the pretty ones, Balgor?" she asked in a surprisingly firm voice.

He laughed. "Not any longer."

"Ah, so you have found the one? I'm pleased for you, Balgor. Will you stay as witness, please?"

The Guardian bowed once again. "It would be my honour."

The old woman turned to Varna, who had watched the byplay uncertainly. What was going on here? The old woman obviously knew who Balgor was, and Balgor obviously knew the old woman and by his reactions accorded her enormous respect. And bear witness to what?

"Varna Barr, Child of Ennaris, I am most pleased to meet with you," she said, rummaging in a bag that Varna had not noticed hanging from her shoulder.

"Um, thank you," Varna said. "I don't believe we have met?"

"No, although we share much. You have come from afar to save Ennaris from its ancient peril. Do you accept the charge to protect Ennaris and the Ennarisi?" she asked. Her voice was clear and carried a formal note.

Varna looked from the woman to Balgor, who gave no sign of what she should do one way or the other. He just waited with a studiously neutral expression.

"Um, I guess so, yes," Varna stammered, feeling very uncertain.

The woman nodded and stared at Varna, once again. "Varna Barr, do you accept the charge to protect Ennaris and the Ennarisi, to the best of your endeavours, to the best of your capabilities?" Her voice had taken on greater overtones of formality.

Unconsciously, Varna straightened in her seat and then stood, facing the old woman.

"Yes, I accept," she said, nodding.

The old woman smiled, a gentle smile full of affection for one who she had never met before. She withdrew her hand from her bag, holding whatever it was in a small closed fist.

"Varna Barr," the old woman repeated a third time in a quieter voice, "do you accept the charge to protect Ennaris and the Ennarisi from all enemies for now and all time?"

Varna failed to notice Balgor start and stare at the old woman. *All time?*

"I so accept the charge," she almost whispered.

"So be it," the old woman said. She turned to Balgor, holding out her hand and passing what she was holding to the Guardian when he did likewise. "Would you do the honours, Balgor?"

Balgor gave her a long look and then merely nodded, turning to Varna. "Varna Barr," he said, in an odd tone that blended formality with the love that had blossomed between the two, "you have accepted the charge. Now accept this token of that charge."

He opened his hand to display a white gold chain, with a pure white stone as a pendant. Gently, Balgor lifted the chain and draped it around Varna's head, with the pendant coming to rest in the centre of her forehead. The stone flared with a pure white light that emanated from the centre of Varna's forehead and time seemed to slow for Varna. The people around the square moved slower than a snail's pace. She felt a warmth permeate her, and a sense of peace flowed through her whole being like nothing that she had ever felt before. Her senses, trained now and attuned to understand Ennaris, spread through the planet and into the surrounding space. Now she could *see* the fleets in space, could *see* the energies of the planet. She could sense the millions of Ennarisi, could see the armies of Goroth on the march. Finally, she turned her sight on Balgor. The brilliance of his aura now was bearable to her and was a vision of such beauty that she had never experienced before. Finally, Varna turned to the old woman to see a pure white aura, pulsing slowly, with a similar stone on her forehead.

The old woman smiled broadly with, Varna thought, relief.

"Varna Barr, I name you Dharmoney!" she said simply. Then, sitting abruptly, she turned to Balgor. "Guardian, my final task on this world has been accomplished."

"It has," Balgor said gently. "You have done well, Dharmoney."

"Dharmoney no longer," the old woman said, as her stone faded. "I am Meilani Gro Tillek once again. I have one final task, but my time on Ennaris is done and I ask a last favour."

"Anything that I may do for you will be my pleasure," Balgor said, smiling still, "Meilani Gro Tillek."

"I would be as I was for just a last moment."

"That is not something I believe is for me to provide, Meilani," Balgor said, with a small smile.

"But it *is* something I can provide," a deep voice said from the air, and Varna turned to see Odruf and Fernis appear.

As she watched the old woman blurred and, in her place, was a young and beautiful woman, with dark, lustrous hair that fell to her waist and framed an oval face with pale skin and liquid amber eyes, dressed in a tunic covered by an exotic blend of colourful fabrics that draped from shoulder to floor length. Meilani lifted one hand, no longer a wrinkled and aching appendage but now one that was firm and alive with energy, and felt her face. A single tear fell from one eye.

"You have fulfilled your charge, Meilani. You have the thanks of the Guardians and, were they to know what you have done on their behalf, all people of Ennaris. Your reward awaits you."

"Thank you, Guardian," she said, and faded from view, followed by Odruf and Fernis.

"No," Balgor said to the empty chair, "thank you."

Varna stood with tears sliding down her cheeks at the raw emotions that she had witnessed.

"Who was that?" she asked.

"Meilani was Dharmoney," Balgor said. "For so long she maintained her watch, through the long, long time since she was called. She watched her home collapse, her people fade and die. She lived through the rebellion and the aftermath and did not waver. All this long time, Meilani Gro Tillek protected the means for Ennaris to be reborn. She has gone to her reward now, her very well-earned reward." He smiled to Varna. "And I feel it's time the new Dharmoney took up the mantle. It's time for you to depart."

Looking around Varna found that time had resumed its normal pace. On the bench where Meilani had rested was a single veil of silky, translucent material. Varna stooped to pick it up, holding it for a moment. She knotted it around her neck and then nodded to Balgor. Together, Guardian and Dharmoney left the tavern.

It was time.

13. Field of Battle

Flin stood with the small group of leaders, watching the chosen field of battle closely. Varna, who had arrived with Jalor's column, gently touched his shoulder in support, and he nodded distractedly. He held the fully extended Battle Mage staff in his right hand with its metal-shod foot resting on the ground. The milky jewel embedded in its top roiled as though the contents were agitated. His attention was elsewhere. He stretched his awareness out as far as possible so that he could determine what sort of challenges would have to be countered. He was feeling increasingly unsure as the opposition mounted, for the forces arrayed by Goroth were significant.

Jalor regarded the staff's jewel and said, "Why has the staff changed? That jewel looks like it's come alive."

Flin started and looked at it. "I'm not sure. I'm not at one with the staff. It's not my calling and the staff knows that. Perhaps it's because the final battle is at hand."

Blaine had been watching the field too. Now he called their attention to the far end. "Something is happening over there. Looks like new forces."

"Well, that's not great news," said Jalor grimly. "We barely held our own at Escar but that was only a test, possibly even a mistake by Grensor or whoever led them. I was wondering what the main force would be. Looks like we find out."

"Yes, that's Goroth," said Flin. "I can feel his presence. I think this will be difficult. He's battle trained, as is Likud. This last battle may well be decided between him and me."

"From what you told me, he probably believes we have nothing and no-one who can stand against him. He may be over-confident and we may be able to use that against him." Jalor shrugged after making his statement. "Who knows?"

"It comes down to the realities of the situation, even if he *is* over-confident. The reality is that Goroth and Likud are the only battle-trained Mages left. The gifts have started to reappear but the young children are not strong enough or trained in any way. I'm not even sure *how* to train a Battle Mage, even if we had the time and enough suitably gifted people." Flin had not taken his eyes off the field, even though he was seeing via his extended perceptions. "And Goroth is bringing up serious firepower. There are a large number of ghazrak as well as a number of winged creatures. The northers are being kept back in the small hills and valleys on the edge of the steppes, but he must have all of them here. I didn't realise their numbers were so large!"

"Does Goroth have gifted people other than himself and Likud?" Blaine asked.

"Well, there is Grensor, of course. We keep talking about him as the creator of the ghazrak but he was also a Mage of serious power. Not a Battle Mage but many of the techniques of smelting and engineering can be turned to warfare, and that was one of his specialities before turning to genetics and health. I'm unable to sense at this distance if there are others. There may be some gifts among the northers." Flin grimaced. "If there are we face more strife."

"I count a further forty-seven gifted people among the northers," Varna said softly. "Most of them show the same signs as Goroth and Likud, although none have near the same power."

"You can sense that?" Flin asked, surprised. "Your strength has increased."

"Yes, since my doubts fell away, I've been able to use them more. Balgor tells me the barriers have fallen completely. So, I can sense the three older Mages, although one is in turmoil. And the others are trying to stay hidden away."

"The one in turmoil may be Grensor. I can't imagine either Goroth or Likud having second thoughts," Flin said sourly.

"And they are keeping the gifted ones in the back to keep them away from detection, I expect," Jalor said. "They will bring them to bear during the battle. That's what I would do. Keep them in a sort of reserve."

"Makes sense to me," Varna said evenly, thinking of the Hides making their way towards the field. "Surprise works in many ways."

Jalor looked at her. There was something that she was keeping to herself, he knew. He also knew that Varna was one with Ennaris now. Whether she remained a Warrior of the Light was for another time. If they survived all of this. Not for the first time, he wondered how the fleets were going. There were no portals near enough for him to get updates. It may be the final factor.

Blaine looked over to where Helt waited with the Faero's army. It was no longer a militia. The numbers had been boosted by recruits from all over Ennaris and now numbered well over five thousand men and women, mostly men. Almin Bor had done wonders in training and arming them. A veritable army of blacksmiths had been found and the well-armed troops stood proud with the Faero's banner waving lazily from standards raised above them. Helt stood out in her silver armour which still caused the occasional turned head at its figure-following contours. Beyond Corm's troops were the knights of Escar, all burnished armour and a riot of multi-coloured banners, standing close to where their mounts were picketed.

In a small hollow behind the main tents was the infirmary tent, with Clofta and Resta making their preparations. The men and women from Kushnel now wore utilitarian tunics edged with healer green.

Jalor pondered briefly how his team had been drawn into this, leading to complete disregard of the strictures on Warriors getting too involved, honoured in the breach though it often was, and then gave a mental shrug. Things seemed to have been stacked against them from the start and they were here now. Each of them was fundamentally changed in some way. In truth, he did not expect to survive the next couple of days, assuming it lasted that long. Flin was not a Battle Mage, nor were the twins or Trabor. Against them were two Battle Mages, one of them of great strength, and what seemed to be a number of trained lower order Mages, even if Flin did not like them being referred to as such. There were massed ghazrak which alone could overwhelm Corm's forces, a small regular norther army and large numbers of other northers, rabble though they may be when it came to fighting. But, assuming Goroth did what had been done at Escar they would be used as fodder to tire the defenders and cause as much damage as possible.

Well, he knew that they would have the Rocs on their side, which was a force to be reckoned with. Both the Rocs and their new partners were untried in battle but they were added factors and Jalor had planned their places with the wing-leaders. He grinned as he considered how appropriate that term was for flights of the great birds.

Occasionally, Jalor glanced around the grassy plains on which they were located. He had not heard from or seen the Clans since leaving their Gather, and was counting on their assistance. Every fighter would be important but the Clans were born fighters, and they were mobile, which the Faero's forces lacked, by and large.

Once again, he surveyed the arrayed forces, knowing that they were not enough. But, for better or worse it was what they had and they were as ready as they were likely to be.

Goroth also expanded his senses, seeking to understand what he was up against. His spies had reported the massing of opposition troops but he was more interested in the Mages and what they could bring against him. He did not discount Drewflin in any way, but he also knew that the Archmage was limited in what he could do in terms of warfare. The twins, also, were less able in the arts of war, but from what he had been told they had been inventive during the stupid fight for Escar, using the old masonry from Aberwin as weapons which, Goroth admitted grudgingly, he would not have considered. That only left Trabor, and he was not a first order Mage in Goroth's eyes. More importantly, nor was he a Battle Mage. So, from the Mages he expected little real opposition.

According to the Prophecy, though, he could expect opposition from the Children of Ennaris. He was well aware that none of the ghazrak who were thought to have met them over the past cycle had survived to tell the tale, so he assumed they had some sort of power or skills that he would have to counter. The few spies Grensor had in the cities could tell him little, and the ones that had been in the Citadel had been winkled out. Still, from what he had discovered they seemed not to have significant Mage powers. Their leader, Jalor, whose name Likud had recognised as a strategist of some repute, seemed to have no gifts at all, and the second was some sort of weapons expert. There were some reports from Escar that it was he who had turned into a fighting demon during the battle, but Goroth knew better than to take at face value anything men or women said in the heat of battle. The third of the Children, Varna, was a woman who seemed to have been ill in some way since arriving on Ennaris. She may bear watching, though, for often those coming late to their gifts had reactions similar to what was described for her, and she had not been seen for some time.

Goroth could identify the Mages in his expanded perception. Drewflin was obvious, even though he was dampening his aura. Not for the first time, Goroth was grateful that the Archmage was not a Battle Mage, for the sheer power he held was breath-taking. He could make out the twins, although he could not tell them apart, and Trabor's slightly weaker signature was included away from the others. There were glimmers of power in several parts of the army, but nothing Goroth was worried about. There were a few blank patches, which could be nothing more than aberrations, but he would have to be prepared for surprises. He withdrew his extended perceptions and turned back to his own army.

The ghazrak were a deep black presence, massed as they were behind one of the shallow hills, and behind another hill were the gifted northers that Grensor had been gathering, breeding, preparing for their roles.

Goroth hoped that they would be decisive and unexpected, as they had not been used before. Many of them were medium-low powers and a number were mid-range powers. There were no high-range powers so he would have to use several of them together. At least they had been trained in linking.

The northers were an unknown quantity to Goroth and he was unhappy with them. Unruly, undisciplined men and women, they would form the shock force, or so they had been told. In truth, as Grensor had done at Escar, Goroth had decided they were expendable and they would be used to wear down the Faero's troops. They had been kept to a deliberately low level of knowledge since Grensor had gathered them under his wing many generations in the past, and had been fed a steady diet of stories and assurances. They resembled members of a cult more than any sort of nation. They were fanatics in support of Goroth, who they saw as something akin to a deity, which Goroth disliked but Likud applauded. Despite outnumbering the Faero's troops by a factor of more than four or five to one, Goroth expected none to survive but he expected them to take many of the defenders with them. The norther army had its own role to play, though, and Goroth hoped that it would prove to be a vital difference.

Likud remained a loose cannon. He remained in some form of communication with his fleet and Goroth knew that he had some sort of plan in mind, but just what it was he could not discover. That was disquieting, for Likud had shown in the past that he would sacrifice everything rather than face defeat. All Goroth could get from him was that the Guardians would suffer for their arrogance and he had the perfect weapon ready to be used if it was needed. Goroth sighed. That Likud was unstable was undoubted. He just hoped his lieutenant would hold it together long enough, but Goroth was prepared to deal with him if it came down to it.

Grensor was more of a worry. The bio-engineer had never been a strong supporter of the rebellion. He had been drawn in more because he had few alternatives and would be ostracised, if not worse, for what he had done in his experiments to create a superior fighting soldier. Since his return, Goroth had noticed the changes in Grensor. Gone was the slightly distracted concentration on his experiments. It was replaced by a cynical perspective at what he had produced. Goroth knew that Grensor resented that he, Goroth, felt that his work was a failure overall, and that the ghazrak were seen as evidence of failure rather than any form of triumph. Goroth was not sure, but Grensor seemed to be less interested in continuing the aims of the rebellion. His relative reluctance to continue development of the ghazrak meant that there were fewer of the creatures than Goroth wanted. The original reason for gathering the northers was to act as raw material for the ghazrak, but Grensor had not used them as such to anywhere near the extent that Goroth had expected. True, as he said, breeding stock needed to be maintained, but there were plenty of northers available for that. If he didn't know better, and he was no longer sure that he did, Goroth thought Grensor was wavering in support. It was another thing to watch out for.

Goroth turned back to the field with a grimace. He was not satisfied with his forces, but would have to make the best of the situation. It was almost time for the action to start.

Grensor stood in front of the fire. His array of gifts included the artful use of fire and flame. In his younger days, he would delight in making patterns of the smoke released, and would experiment with burning different types of wood to produce different smoke and weave them together in patterns. He remembered those far more innocent days with regret, almost yearning, even though he knew that he could not go back to them. And yet, why not? He planned to use the flames to view the progress of his marine ghazrak in attacking the vessels that Goroth had been told would be crossing the sea between north and south, but he felt that he could indulge himself for a moment.

He turned his will on the flame. He tossed a few extra timbers onto the fire and gathered the smoke into a ball. With a small smile he stretched the smoke ball into a long streamer and twisted it into a series of shapes, starting with a circle and then moving onto a sequence of other geometrical shapes, twisting and turning it. Holding the smoke back in a ball again, he pushed and prodded it with his thoughts until he had the likeness of a hrss and with a whimsical thought made it gallop through the flames. The smoke hrss was followed by a flitter, the small insect with huge wings for its size that would buzz around swamps and marshes, and the flitter was chased by a fisher bird with its long beak and tail and stubby wings.

As the smoke dissipated at last Grensor pushed it into a final shape, that of a tall statuesque male, with a strong sculptured torso held up by thickly muscled legs. Similarly muscled arms emerged from the upper torso. The whole was topped by a well-formed head. It had natural armour instead of hair and an intelligent face, not quite formed in features but clearly displaying high intellect. Grensor snorted. His perfect warrior! This is what he had in mind all this time and still he was nowhere near what he wanted to do. While others had experimented with robots and mechanical devices, he had stayed with bio-engineering. And instead of his ultimate warrior he had the ghazrak!

With a grimace he dismissed the smoky image and concentrated once more on the fire. Without really concentrating on what he was doing, he caused a sheet of flame to form a curtain and images started to flicker to life as Grensor turned his talents to the task. He could see the inland sea and tightened his focus to the tiny dots that were ships making their slow way across the water. He sent out the call to his creatures who would be shadowing the ships and released them of his constraints. Had he done so earlier they would have attacked anything they could find, but now they would target these ships. After that? Well, assuming they survived he would be unable to take control back without great effort, and he would not have the time for that, so they would be loose until he could locate them and destroy them. After this phase of the rebellion, Grensor expected the marine ghazrak to be of no further use, no matter that Likud wanted to retain and further develop them. As Grensor watched, the sinuous lengths of the marine ghazrak approached their prey.

The attack that followed started as Grensor expected. Two ghazrak attacked and seemed to flinch, which made Grensor frown, but the first ship was destroyed before the occupants could do anything to save themselves, and Grensor almost dismissed the fire then. However, he forced himself to watch the rest of the fleet's decimation.

14. Battle At Sea

Marjory fretted. She stood at the prow of the fat, wallowing ship. She had never been a good sailor, and she was wondering for the umpteenth time if this was a good idea, although she had no real choice. The waters between the two continents should have been relatively calm, she thought. After all, the distance between them was quite short, although the ship's captain told her to expect two nights at sea. Well, they were not at all calm and that worried her. She wished that she had been within reach of a portal that worked so she could have avoided this sea trip. She wished she had *Fendaristil* so she could have made the journey in an eye-blink. Mostly, she wished Flin were here.

Looking to her left and right, Marjory could see the rest of her makeshift fleet. They had embarked in the small coastal city of Samkar, just to the north of the desert edge. She had ignored the advice of the captain that a storm was coming and pushed ahead. She was regretting it now, even though time was of the essence. On the ships, and sharing her misery, were the cream of the desert fighters. Those men and women who knew no fear in the desert were in a very different frame of mind now, and she could not blame them. The waves that occasionally broke over the sides of the vessels crashed against the ships repeatedly with a mindless but relentless malevolence. The gaps between waves seemed to be shrinking. There was no relaxation for those on board. The sailors went about their business with tense expressions.

Marjory stilled. There was something out there, and it was coming closer. She could feel it, she could sense it. There was some familiarity to whatever it was and yet it was different enough that she could not place it. There was something inimical about it, however.

Suddenly, whatever was out there was on them and Marjory yelled a warning. Then, rearing from the waters only five boat lengths ahead was a monster from nightmare. It was long with a huge head fringed by some form of spiky membrane that stood out from its neck like a stiff collar. It had a pointed face dominated by a mouth that was wide open and showed huge pointed teeth. Above the gaping maw were three tiny eyes, beady and black. The face was a mottled green-black and it sat atop a leviathan-like body that stretched and stretched as it thrust itself out of the water in the path of the ships. Marjory gaped before catching herself and gripped the boat's rail hard. The creature fell forward and submerged. Marjory watched as the long body rippled through the water like a huge snake. The enormous, sinuous body rose from the waves once again and then swept back down once more. It had some patches of armoured skin and had spikes along its length. The tail was like the flukes of an Ennarisi leviathan, large and flat, and drove the creature back under the waves with powerful strokes.

Marjory stared for a moment at the spot where the creature went under the waves, reaching out with her senses and finding it diving deep towards the back of the ship. With a muttered oath she ran from the prow, slipping and sliding. She was forced to catch hold of whatever she could among the ropes and rigging, the ship's rails and the deck's fittings, as she made her way to the stern. She made it just as the creature emerged again, looming high over the ship. As the desert fighters stared and shouted in fear, Marjory stood perfectly still, willing herself to move with the actions of the ship and freed her hands from the folds of her cloak that she had wrapped herself in.

The creature rose from the water until it was twice the height of the ship, and started to move towards the vessel as though to crash on top of it when Marjory lifted both hands and sent a crackling energy bolt into the long body, playing it along the length to the head, which was looming high over her. The creature gave a high-pitched cry and crashed backward into the waves before diving deep again. Marjory tried to follow it but her senses became confused as lengths of armoured skin roiled beneath the waves. It was with a shock that she realised that she was sensing multiple creatures, three she thought - no, five and then even more - and they were moving from the depths to attack her small fleet. Two of them breached at the same time, one behind Marjory's vessel and the second behind the farthest ship to her right. With despair, Marjory knew she could fight one of them but not both. Regretfully, she sent another charge into the nearest creature, which also flinched and retreated in pain, then turned to attend to the other, but she was too late.

With a high-pitched roar of challenge, the third creature crashed its length across the ship. The wooden ship was no match for the terrible bulk of the creature and was shattered. The creature broke the ship in half. Men and women were flung into the boiling water, while the waves still battered away at the remaining ships. Marjory watched, aghast, as the creature rolled back through the wrecked ship and rose again with three of the desert folk in its maw before diving once again. All around her, the desert fighters were shouting their rage and their despair, as much at being unable to fight back as at suffering the loss of friends and comrades. Marjory stood still, her senses outstretched and following the passage of the creatures.

The two that she had hurt had regrouped and were turning back to attack once again. This time, they were coming from both sides, targeting her ship, obviously having recognised the threat she posed. From left and right they rose above the waves. This time she did not wait but sent the energy discharge at the head of the left-side creature, only to see the charge shrugged off. Resigned to being able to deal with only one creature at a time, she gathered herself and as the creature rose higher the Battle Mage held out a single hand with the palm facing the creature. She let loose a solid bolt that struck the creature as it prepared to fall onto the ship. There was a load crack and the creature was flung back, as its long body convulsed and split open.

Aware of the cries arising from those around her, Marjory turned back to try to defend from the second creature. The Mage fire had drained her temporarily and she could only manage a bolt sufficient to stun the creature. Deep in the ocean, the third creature had finished its grisly feast and was returning, and two others were rushing towards the ships. Marjory sensed additional movement in the waters all around the fleet, four, five, more huge creatures rushing to the scene of the battle. She growled and the stone on her forehead flashed into view, glowing silver as she drew deeply on her power, knowing that she would have little in reserve.

The second creature attacked, driving its head against the side of her ship, and Marjory heard timbers cracking and felt the ship lurch sideways at the force of the impact. The creature slid beneath the ship only to drive its length high on the opposite side and, once again, Marjory flung her Mage fire at the creature, driving through the open mouth to explode through the back of the great head. The creature shattered. Bits of armoured skin and gore were flung in all directions as it flopped back into the sea, narrowly missing the next ship.

But Marjory was near exhausted. Such use of Mage fire took a huge toll, even for one such as she, and there was a third such creature from the original number, plus at least two others about to arrive but she knew there were more. Turning to face where she knew the third creature would emerge, Marjory gathered what remained of her power, seeking to shape it into the smallest volume that could carry the greatest force. She watched as the creature rose from the water like an enormous malevolent eel. From each side Marjory could feel other creatures drive themselves from the water, but she could not move her attention from this one. She prepared to expend her energy reserves but as the creature reached the top of its arc of attack it was assailed from all sides by sea creatures, leaping to tear strips of flesh, armoured and spiked as it was, while from the air came the ringing challenge of two Rocs as they dived onto the head, raking across its eyes with their sharp talons.

Finally, from the water between the creature and Marjory's ship came a leviathan, its massive flukes driving the creature above the water, where it appeared to hover for a moment, spreading wide its flippers as it did so. Marjory stared. From its immense forehead came the glow of a great blue stone and from its flippers came a blast of something like Marjory's Mage fire. The third creature exploded. The long body flopped onto the surface of the water and gradually, ever so slowly, sank beneath the waves.

All around the fleet the creatures of the sea battled against the horrendous creatures - Grensor's creations, Marjory thought through her rage. That rage gave the Battle Mage additional impetus. Another creature shrugged off its marine attackers and reared and Marjory flung another bolt of Mage Fire, joined by the leviathan as it once again launched from the depths. The two bolts tore the unnatural creature apart.

Marjory cast her senses wide, her hair streaming behind her as the energy she gathered sought to escape. Deep below the ships she could sense sea creatures fighting and dying, but Grensor's beasts died also. She drew deeper on the available energy around her, reaching even deeper into herself, almost as deep as when she had battled Goroth. She found and recognised a source of energy offered to her without reservation and drew on it, passing gratitude back down the link. Bolt after bolt of energy she sent into the depths, or into the beasts when they reached the surface. They still were intent on reaching the ships. With a concentrated spear, Marjory sent a bolt of energy through the depths. The water dissipated some of its strength, but enough remained to incapacitate the last of the creatures. The sharp teeth of the attacking sea creatures finished it off.

Marjory, exhausted, released the link with a further burst of gratitude. She forced herself to keep her feet as the agitated water slapped the ships hard, driving them sideways and rocking them violently back and forth. She could feel her innate energy slowly returning but she knew that if there were more of those creatures - ghazrak, she thought they must have been - then she would struggle to mount a defence.

The water settled and Marjory found that the light storm had dissipated, possibly because of the volume of energy released during the battle. The two Rocs surveyed the scene and darted to where a small number of survivors of the destroyed craft were struggling to remain afloat. Time after time the great birds dropped to the still unsettled surface, gripped survivors with their great talons and lifted them from the water to drop them on the deck of one of the remaining ships. In this they were assisted by the great fish, swimming under the desert people and pushing them to where the Rocs could reach them. Finally, when there were no more survivors, the Rocs alighted on the broad deck of Marjory's vessel. Plainly exhausted but also clearly elated at being able to lend assistance, the Rocs bowed low as Marjory approached them and in turn laid one hand on their great beaks in greeting. As they met, the huge snout of the leviathan emerged from the water alongside the boat, one great eye watching proceedings. Marjory remained in communion with the Rocs for some time and then turned to one of the desert dwellers.

"Grasdur, would you get someone to bring drinking water and some food for our friends, please? This is Hu-lor" - pointing to one, and then to the other - "and Ba-vel. They are Rocs, ancient allies of the Ennarisi against all enemies."

With a low bow to both Mage and Rocs, Grasdur hurried away to do her bidding. The Rocs, eyes swirling, turned to watch with interest as Marjory greeted the leviathan. What stories they would be able to tell this night, as a result of their patrol!

Marjory eyed the great creature which was now floating alongside the ship. Its long length outmatched the man-made vessel easily. A great flipper gently flapped the water and a spout of water emerged from the breathing hole atop its head. Marjory stared for a moment and then smiled broadly. To the astonishment of all watching, for the ships had all come to an unsteady halt and the passengers and crews had stopped what they were doing to watch the Rocs and the sea creatures, Marjory clambered lithely over the railing and down the side of the ship. She stepped onto the fin and from there clambered onto the back of the giant of the sea.

"Ooshmin? Is that really you?" she asked quietly, resting a hand on the leviathan.

A long warbling whistle emerged from the Sea Mage, unmistakably joyous and excited. The great flipper slapped the water again, drenching Marjory even more than the battle with the strange creatures had done.

"It *is* you! Ooshmin! I thought you were all dead." A pause while Ooshmin conversed with her mind to mind, although Marjory chose to speak aloud for the benefit of the listeners. "Yes, your timing was exquisite as always, old friend. How did you know to come?" Another pause, longer than before. "She did? Please pass my gratitude. We are seeking to reach the field of battle, although I fear we may be too late. Our Roc friends tell me that Goroth is in the field already." A third pause. "Very well, we can catch up when this is done. Can you assist us to reach the northern shore, my friend? I feel time is limited." A further pause ensued, and then Marjory rubbed the great head affectionately and nodded decisively. "You have Guides? That's wonderful. It was them who provided assistance?"

As they spoke the sea creatures rose from the depths and ringed the ships, several leviathans wearing blue stones or green stones. Among them were the smaller but more aggressive and razor toothed variety of leviathan, and swimming through the water were the almost as aggressive and much feared finbacks, their large fins slicing through the water as they swam.

"As you say," Marjory said, still in communion with Ooshmin. "Let us be on our way."

Marjory made her way back to the great flipper and stepped on it, after which Ooshmin lifted her so she could walk onto the deck of the ship. She turned to the stunned onlookers.

"This is Ooshmin, Sea Mage of Ennaris. He and his pod, the new Guides of the Sea, will help us to get to the far shore quickly. Make ready, for when we land we have a short march and then we may face battle. Pass this onto the others, please." She turned to where the Rocs waited, having drunk and eaten of the provisions provided them. "Hu-lor, Ba-vel, once again I thank you for your assistance. Please inform your battle leader that the desert dwellers will join the Faero as soon as possible." Again, there was a pause as Hu-lor spoke to her mind to mind. "Is that so? Norther gifted? Well, I think we can do something about that. We will feast after the fight, I trust."

Stepping back, Marjory spread her arms wide and bowed low to the great birds, who responded with bows of their own. Then with a cry to Ooshmin, answered by a great spout of water that wet everyone nearby, the Rocs leapt into the air and with great beats of their wings gained height rapidly and turned towards the northern land.

Marjory watched them depart for a long time, feeling comforted that the old allies remained, and then turned to Ooshmin. Many of the watching desert people had taken on trust that this was one of the most powerful Mages of Ennaris' history. They now believed without reservation. They saw her nod her head decisively, but were unable to hear her discussion with Ooshmin. But they all felt the wind pick up from behind the ships and saw the sails bellied out. Within moments the unwieldy ships were speeding over the waters between the two continents faster than they had ever gone before. The bow waves were accompanied for the initial part of the trip by water leapers, jumping and diving through the white water created by the ships' passage.

15. Junda-lar

Far to the north, where the ice and snow petered out and the harsh broken wilderness of the narrow tundra began, a small band of Ennarisi made ready for their roles. This group of Junda-lar, the warband of the people of the ice and snow, removed their heavy outer layers of clothing, carefully folding them and placing them in a well-hidden cave that had been known to the Junda but rarely used for centuries. Under those heavy garments, the Junda-lar wore nondescript, rust-coloured clothes - tunics and breeches - which came close to matching the colours of the broken lands into which they would move. Packs were carried made of the same nondescript materials, although the objects that they carried were far from nondescript.

A quick meal followed and then the warband of the Junda-lar were ready. Xymin moved to the front, squinting out over the broken and dusty terrain of the wilderness. He waved his spear arm once. The warband separated into four, each group staying close enough to the next group to provide support but far enough away to make attacks less concentrated. The warband searched out defiles and gullies, practising the skills that had been drilled into them for some time now. Despite Jalor's unspoken scepticism, the Junda-lar melted easily into the landscape.

For the first four nights of the trek, the warband allowed themselves a small fire per group. They remained in their squads after the fourth night, although the squad leaders gathered to plan each day. Sentries remained at their posts, rotating on a schedule that allowed each fighter to get some sleep, excited though they all were. Each day, they moved out before daybreak, after a cold meal, and were moving through the broken landscape as the light of day arrived. The fifth day brought heat and a wind that blew dust into their eyes. Several of the warband wrapped pieces of cloth over their noses and mouths to make breathing easier. Water, carried in precious clay bottles that were hard to obtain in the icy wastes, was sipped slowly. The band had been warned that springs were few and far between. They were heading for one such spring, located about half-way to their destination.

Despite being out of their natural icy element, the warband had adjusted and were alert. They constantly shifted their eyes from close to distant and parts in between, looking for movement while trying to show little themselves. Almost no dust was kicked up and the members of the war band almost flowed across the ground. The basic skills that had been learned long ago by their forebears and then passed down through the many cycles had been honed and made razor sharp. The Junda-lar had little sense of history these days, despite being descendants of the keepers of the records of Ennarisi exploration around what had once been the main spaceport in the north of the planet. Now, these men and women were lean and hard and carried their traditional hunting weapons into a different land. However, their intent was not to find food but to locate and deal death to their enemies, those who had trespassed into their icy land and had killed innocents without mercy. More than that, as they now knew, these creatures were doing the same across the planet, and the Junda-lar had committed to help bring that to an end.

In the lead, far ahead of the four smaller bands, Byrol stopped abruptly, going from liquid motion to perfectly still in a moment. Behind him, the foremost of each band noted the change and immediately followed suit. The entire war band became immobile in an instant, and then slowly folded into a crouch, searching out additional cover as they had been taught. Moving across their front at an angle, the band could see a group of people. These people moved without any discipline and wore ragged clothing, obviously heading for the same waterhole as themselves. This, obviously, was a band of northers, who Xymin knew were hard and vicious. Perhaps they were heading for the grasslands, or were deserters. Whatever they were, this band was making for the same waterhole as the Junda-lar.

Xymin, at the front of the second column, considered the situation. While proving themselves to be competent in this first true exercise of the skills they had been taught, the Junda-lar were not hardy enough to go without water in this harsh, dry land for any real length of time. He allowed enough time for the strangers to move into the distance. Then, Xymin signalled for the advance to start again, but their progress slowed now. They were wary about being detected and set upon, for Xymin's small warband, which was the part of the Junda-lar that was tasked with this target, were only a hundred strong and they expected that they were likely to be far out-numbered in any heated conflict. The rest of the Junda-lar were making their way towards an intermediate site where they would be joined by Xymin's band and then the Junda-lar would trek to the expected site of battle with Goroth.

Night fell rapidly in this wilderness. Forced to spend the nights in the open, the band made the best camp they could, even though they were running short of water and their food supplies were limited. Xymin tasked the best two of the band's scouts to get close to the waterhole and find out what was happening. Then he called the band leaders to a discussion. Once again, calm and order reigned, although there was some disquiet and uncertainty felt among the band. Most of the warband had never left the ice, so this was their first foray into what was an alien environment. However, they had been taught discipline from their earliest days, and so they were prepared to wait.

The first scout returned in the middle of the night, reporting that the group of northers had camped around the banks of the waterhole. Campfires were burning brightly but it seemed they had no guards out. By morning, the second scout had not returned and Xymin made the decision to move the warband closer to the waterhole. A small rise bounded the depression in which the waterhole lay. Xymin accompanied Hylog, the first scout, as he worked his way up the bank to the crest. Lifting eyes just above the level of the rise, slightly to one side so they were not at the precise crest, Xymin's mouth tightened as he surveyed the scene. A single figure, naked, could be seen laying on the dusty ground near the makeshift camp, which appeared to be abandoned. Arms and legs were pegged so they were stretched wide apart. Urzis, the second scout, was struggling weakly. With a muttered oath, Xymin started to rise, only to be dragged back down by Hylog who, with a gesture for silence, pointed towards one side of the depression.

Xymin subsided, his eyes searching out the area indicated. After a moment, he could make out a shadowed area that seemed to be out of place. A moment longer and he could see what looked like a spear tip. Working his way down from there, he could make out vague shapes crouching under what could only be netting. He nodded to the scout to show that he had seen it. So, a trap had been set and the bait was Urzis.

Silently, trying to still his rapidly-beating heart, Xymin studied the land around the waterhole. The depression in which it lay was not large, but was too big for a quick dash across the intervening space to Urzis. Motioning to Hylog to stay in place, Xymin carefully made his way down from the crest and crept back to the warband. Quietly he outlined his plan, drawing a map in the red dirt with a stick. A few suggested improvements were voiced by the band leaders, and then the four bands were in motion. One moved towards the location where Hylog still watched the depression, where they would act as a reserve and guard, but Xymin had another role in mind for them, also. The rest moved out in a wide arc to left and right. They would move around and come in from behind to attack the ambushers and rescue Urzis.

The stealthy approach was going well, Xymin thought. The three groups had made it to their designated points. One was behind and to the right of the ambush site. The second was behind and to the left. The third was slightly further back and between the other two, ready to act as rear-guard. The first two crept slowly through the low brush that bordered the depression, looking for the landmarks that Xymin had described. Settling into place, the members of the two groups closest to the depression looked for the hidden ambushers.

Nervous men and women found themselves rubbing clammy hands against their dirty tunics, which achieved little except to transfer dirt from one place to another. Several practised the breathing techniques that they had been taught during the long tendays just past in an effort to remain calm, but most had their doubts. The adventure had suddenly become real and quite possibly deadly for these tough but normally peaceful Ennarisi. This felt quite different to defending their communities from the ghazrak.

Xymin recognised the signs of nerves that were stretched tight. Still, he held them back while making sure of the situation. He led two others who he judged to be the steadiest in a scouting exercise. Their stealthy movements raised no dust and they made no noise at all. The three were close, very close, to the hide-away now but were unable to determine if the ambushers remained in place. It was just as Xymin was about to start back that he heard a faint scrabble as one of the waiting ambushers shifted his place, and one of Xymin's companions saw the faint movement as a spear touched and disturbed the netting. A touch on Xymin's shoulder and a pointed finger showed the location. Xymin nodded and signed to return, which the three did, once again taking their time. Dawn was now rising, and the attack would have to happen soon.

As the light of first sun touched the small hills Hylog stood to look over the depression. As planned, he allowed himself to be seen for a few moments before ducking down again. Below, Xymin could see the movement as the waiting northers prepared. Then, slowly, very slowly, the group that had been left with Hylog crept over the small rise and started to make a less than stealthy approach. They spread out across the width of the rise, making some small ceremony of their approach. Daylight was with them as they reached the bottom of the hill and approached the pool of water.

They regrouped to move around the edge of the pool furthest from the ambushers. Nerves were stretched tight as they made their slow way around the pool. The netting twitched as the waiting ambushers became impatient. The approaching Junda-lar halted and appeared to be arguing about what to do. One of them kept a watchful eye on the captured Urzis, who had subsided now. The small group started to move again, only to stop once more. The agitation among the ambush party was now such that Xymin could see that several were being held back. Finally, the pressure of waiting while being able to see their targets overwhelmed the always brittle norther discipline and the ambushers launched themselves from their hide, screaming defiance at the Junda-lar.

As one, the members of the small band wheeled to meet the threat, forming a tight defensive grouping with swords out. The few harpoon-like spears they carried were used as small pikes to push through a few gaps in the formation. Xymin gestured to his band, and they rose as a group and ran down the slope from behind the ambush. Several darted to where Urzis was bound. A moment later, the third of the small bands rose from the other flank and ran towards the battle. The Junda-lar, while having trained and trained for the moment, and despite successfully fighting off the few ghazrak they had encountered in the settlements, found that they were ill prepared for the reality of open warfare, as this initial clash proved. The Junda-lar met the northers from three sides but were uncoordinated, forgetting many of the lessons learnt. The northers, on the other hand, had been taught to hate anyone not of their own people, and to strike hard and viciously, which they now proceeded to do. Four of Xymin's warband were down, either dead or injured, within a few moments. Despite having superior numbers, the Junda-lar were on the back foot almost immediately.

The small battle became a test of defence for the Junda-lar as the northers threw themselves at those who they had planned to ambush but now met in the open. Rude and rough swords, pikes and weapons made from old ploughs or any length of metal were wielded with sometimes devastating effect. Xymin watched as one after another of his band were struck down, bloody, unconscious, some dying. But it was when the northers starting to attack those who were down that Xymin's rage took over and, without further thought he launched himself into the midst of the largest norther bunch, his better-quality sword taking on a life of its own. The other Junda-lar responded, recovering enough spirit to protect Xymin as he waded into the northers.

The response was too late to make enough difference, however. Too many of the Junda-lar were injured now, and confusion gripped most. The northers managed to regroup and had started to charge back into the Junda-lar when from behind a small hill on the east side of the depression, closest to the battle, yet another group appeared. Wiry, lean, of middle height to a man and woman, and brandishing twin swords that gleamed in the still young light of day, the new group fell on the northers like a thunderclap, shouting an incoherent war cry. Where the Junda-lar were unsure of themselves when they joined battle, these newcomers were in no doubt. First, they drove a wedge into the northers and then they extended the wedge into two small fronts, each driving half of the remaining northers back and away from the other half. With no quarter asked or given, and with the Junda-lar recovering to join the counter-attack, the battle was over quickly. No northers survived.

Xymin was shattered. For all of their training, for all of their sense of self-confidence, had it not been for the strangers' intervention they may well have lost the fight, even though they outnumbered the northers. There were seven dead Junda-lar and twice that number who were injured badly enough that they could not proceed further. Among the dead were several that Xymin counted as friends and who he had known from the time of sharing the communal cribs.

The one hundred Junda-lar warriors were reduced to about eighty and their confidence was severely shaken.

"Don't take it too hard," the strangers' leader said quietly to Xymin as the two stood together watching as the Junda-lar dead were laid out in a row. "The Junda are not known as warriors, and you did well for your first fight. Very well, in fact."

"And yet we required your assistance to prevail," Xymin said bitterly. "We were trained and trained for this, and to fail like this is soul-destroying. To lose friends and fellow Junda-lar is terrible, and a disaster for our people. And I am the one who led them into this fight." He shook his head sadly. "What have I done?"

"You've done what you must in this time when we all must cleave together," the stranger said firmly. "You're no longer inexperienced, but have been blooded in this fight for the survival of Ennaris. In this you have great honour, and your fallen will be remembered when the battle is done."

"I lost one out of five of my men," Xymin said. "I'm not sure of completing the mission given me by the Faero's general."

"And yet you'll continue," the stranger said wryly. "For you are Junda, and you don't quit because circumstances are hard or the fates play against you. Am I not right?"

Xymin considered. Tine had encouraged him to play this role, had assured him that it was right. She had never promised that all would survive, nor had she said that they would be successful. But she had encouraged the people of the ice to take part, even with the small numbers that they could put into the field. He thought on the history of the Junda, the hardships that were accepted as a matter of course, the endurance against the ice and snow, against the constant freezing temperatures, the recurring fight to eat, to be clothed, to have shelter, to live! Yes, the Junda did not give up.

"Aye," Xymin replied, standing straighter. "We shall continue." He turned to the stranger. "What of you? Would you join us?"

"It's a thought, but we have another purpose. For so long we have fought for others, now we fight for ourselves and our fellows. Like you, we are few. Like you, we have endured harsh lives, with many losses individually and as a people." He nodded to himself, his thoughts caught up in families that had been shattered as they tried to survive, including his own. "We have joined the Faero, as we were tasked with doing long ages past. We have led a part of his army to these grasslands in preparation for the fight to come. Our purpose now is to scout around the site of the battle to warn against surprises, which we have also done. We now go to re-join our fellows who have stayed with the Faero."

Xymin nodded pensively then held out one hand.

"How should I know you," Xymin asked of the stranger, "so that I may do honour to you and your friends?"

The stranger reached out and clasped Xymin at the forearm, smiling as he did so.

"We would appreciate your kind thoughts," he said. "I'm Murk, and we are the Tang."

"Murk of the Tang," Xymin said, nodding. "Go safely, Murk. I would share a flask with you when this is done."

"Aye, Xymin of the Junda-lar," Murk said. "I'm unsure how many of us will get through this, but for each of us there'll be many enemies missing also. And I'll take you up on the drink when we're done. If Tang lets me, anyway."

With a laugh, Murk turned away and gestured curtly. His scouts left their varied conversations and formed up loosely, hard men and women from a hard land. The troop of thirty walked briskly from the camp site. After a short distance, Murk held up a single hand, clenched it once and let it drop. The troop moved easily into a ground-eating trot, heading towards the grasslands.

16. Goroth and the Kindred

Grensor moaned as he watched the progressive defeat and deaths of his sea creatures. There was no mistaking the defence by at least one and perhaps two Mages. He thought that it was only one Mage, in fact. Then there was the surge of power as a leviathan led the maritime creatures into the fray. Grensor was shocked to his core at the power that was emitted from the leviathan, and the final destruction of his small ghazrak force. A sea-borne Mage! He had never considered that such existed after the rebellion! And then he narrowed the focus further to concentrate on the Mage on the ship and his shock was complete. Marjory! It could be no other. This was dire news, for she obviously was moving towards the chosen place of battle. Goroth had to be informed!

However, the repeated shocks had caused Grensor to loosen his control over the fire. His haste to view the effects of the marine ghazrak on the small southern fleet had caused him to pay less attention to what he was doing. As a result and without thinking, he had used the same cantrip to establish the flame screen as he used to link to the universe of the Kindred, and Ghaz-ti took the opportunity to make its move. This particular Kindred had been forced to provide this puny man with information and assistance for a long, long time, all to create these abominations. This one then dared to consider them to be in the image of the Kindred! The fire was the conduit to the universe of the Kindred and Ghaz-ti had been waiting for the time when it could use that channel. It had prepared, gathering to itself as much knowledge of this Mage as it could. Its vicious expression turned to a sneer at the thought that one such as this had been able to force its will on Ghaz-ti, a sepok of the Kindred. Now, with shock after shock, the puny one's attention was drawn elsewhere. Ghaz-ti struck!

Through the flames the Kindred quickly pushed itself. Grensor realised his danger and tried to counter, but Ghaz-ti had prepared well. Its first attack drove a sharp spike at Grensor's mind, punching through the weak shield and rendering him as good as senseless. Ghaz-ti pushed its own essence through the link that was thereby established, leaving its old physical shell to burn where it left it. It occupied that of the puny one, dismissing the remainder of the previous spirit without compunction. With a further thought, Ghaz-ti extinguished the flame, revelling in the sensations of this new body, and it looked around the world with interest. The grass and hills were so different to the desolation of its former home and it was sure that it could rule this soft land easily. Then it looked down at its new body and was dismayed. This one was aged and in a poor state. There were injuries that it had not realised existed during the past struggles for power. In fact, Ghaz-ti could not understand how this one could have stood up against it for so long. So, somewhere there had to be power, and Ghaz-ti would find it and use it. Grensor's face smiled evilly as Ghaz-ti started to rummage through the memories left behind.

Andira staggered slightly before being caught and steadied by another member of Corm's support team. She straightened and turned to stare across the enormous grassy plain to the hills in the far distance. Chills and heat alternately ran through her. She now knew that feeling! She knew what it meant! A demon had been released into this world! And this one was far stronger than the one that she had sensed before. How she knew that she did not know, but she knew that this one was far stronger. She had to tell the Archmage!

It was almost time, Goroth thought. Three nights had passed with the forces facing each other. He decided to test the water and see what happened. He ordered the first of the norther forces to attack the Faero's forces, around five thousand of them. A small force of fifty ghazrak were sent to accompany them, along with two of the precious winged ghazrak. The regular army was held back. Goroth stood on a small rise to watch progress, using both his eyes and senses to track the course of the battle. He had no illusions that this would cause victory, but it may well cause enough damage to his enemies that the next battle could be decisive.

As expected, the northers showed next to no discipline at all. Screaming invectives as loud as they could, they made their unruly way towards the lines of defenders. Many wielded rough and ready swords that were similar to those used by the ghazrak, and many more brandished scythes or crude spears. Goroth watched proceedings. With a frown, he noted that the ghazrak seemed to be uncertain. They were holding back rather than trying to lead the way into battle. Grensor was not paying attention - the ghazrak needed to be guided at the early stages and then they could be let loose.

Ghaz-ti, as Grensor, was led to Goroth, who immediately knew he was dealing with someone - something - else. That was a problem. Whatever was occupying Grensor was strong, although Goroth knew - hoped - that he was stronger.

"What are you?" Goroth demanded, projecting his power, feeling the resistance immediately.

"I am Ghaz-ti, puny one!" the Kindred replied as Grensor's face sneered its disdain.

"You have taken over Grensor's body?" Goroth asked.

"This form is mine now," Ghaz-ti said. "It has interesting memories that I am tasting. With these memories, I will take over this world and make it mine."

"No," Goroth rejoined. "This world is not for you to take. But," he continued, thinking quickly, "I will allow you to have part of it if we are victorious. But for that you must follow my orders."

"I follow no orders," Ghaz-ti boasted. "I follow my own way."

"No," Goroth said flatly, noting that Ghaz-ti was building its own energy in Grensor's body and understanding what it presaged. "If you don't do as I say, I'll cut you off from your source, and you'll die."

"I have removed the need to maintain such contact, puny man," Ghaz-ti said. "You have no control over me."

Ghaz-ti suddenly send a bolt of pure energy at Goroth, who was ready for it and had his own shield ready. The force rocked him but his shield, made of the pure power of a strong battle-trained Mage, held firm. In response, Goroth sent a tendril of power at Ghaz-ti while looking for some trace of a tie to a power source. And he found it. It was not through a fire, as would be the norm for these creatures, but was via Grensor's unusual ability to tap into the planet's magnetic field and manipulate it. This ability was what had allowed Grensor to understand the mechanics of the world so much better than most others. It was his development of engineering techniques drawing on the magnetic properties of Ennaris that had brought him to some prominence when young. Ironically, it was that elevated prominence that led to his other activities in bio-engineering being noticed later, and that had led to his own disciplinary actions by the Council of Mages.

Now, Goroth had a lever to use, and he did so ruthlessly. He crafted a barrier that he knew would block Grensor's access to the magnetic field. Goroth threw the barrier into place between Ghaz-ti in Grensor's body and the planet faster than Ghaz-ti could react. Of a sudden, the Kindred found itself without a power source and immediately started to wane. Eyes wide, it made a sharp thrust with what strength remained, which Goroth batted away, and then slumped.

"Now," Goroth said, holding the barrier in place with some effort, for Ghaz-ti continued to probe despite giving an impression of defeat, "I will allow you to have access to your power again if you agree to follow my commands."

Ghaz-ti looked at Goroth through Grensor's eyes. Hatred was mingled with grudging respect at being bested, and it nodded once.

"Very well," Goroth said, knowing that was the best he would get. He made the barrier looser, allowing Ghaz-ti to get to some of the power, but kept the barrier's form in place, ready to be made solid once again. "I need you to direct the ghazrak to attack the enemy forces."

"They are weak imitations only, not worthy of being called Ghazrak!" He pronounced the word with a subtly different inflexion.

"Perhaps, but they are what I have to work with, and they must be directed. That was Grensor's role and now it is yours."

With a growl, Ghaz-ti looked to where the ghazrak were making their slow way behind the norther forces. As Goroth watched, the ghazrak stopped, stood straighter and then increased their pace, pushing after the northers. Ghaz-ti sent a glance to the two winged ghazrak, which also showed sharper movements and greater intent.

Goroth nodded and turned back to watch the progress of the encounter to come. Internally he grimaced. This was not good! He would have to deal with Ghaz-ti and he had no doubt that the Kindred demon would be trying to work around or through the barrier. But he needed the creature for now. Blast Grensor for falling now of all times. And where was Likud?

17. First Skirmish

Battle was joined by the ragged wave of norther men and women rushing the defensive lines of the Faero's army. Jalor watched as the motley force crossed the intervening distance, shouting curses and insults, and clashed with Almin Bor's more disciplined army. The immediate losses to the northers were large, and they continued to mount.

The northers had no tactics except to rush into the defensive lines waving whatever weapons they wielded. They risked damage to their fellow northers as much as to the defenders. As a result, the attackers were relatively easy pickings for the more disciplined defenders. However, the sheer weight of numbers of the northers was the concern. Attacking losses mounted rapidly and Jalor noted that they were concentrating their efforts on the left edge of the line. With a shock, he realised that the bodies of the attackers were being used to form a ramp of sorts. The large number of dead and dying northers were making it harder for the defenders to maintain their stations.

Inexorably, the defenders on the left flank were forced backwards by the weight of numbers, curving the line. They suffered relatively few losses at this stage as the line still held, but Jalor could see how it wavered. Almin Bor was alert to the problem. As Jalor was about to send an order, Almin Bor ordered a break to be opened in the defensive line, and he called the mounted fighters through. As the last of the hrss-mounted soldiers passed the line, it closed again. A small number of northers who had managed to squeeze through were dealt with by a roving troop before they could cause any damage behind the lines.

The mounted troops charged through the attackers, slashing and cutting to left and right. They succeeded in driving a wedge through the force, offering some relief to the defensive line. When they started to take their own losses, the hrss-soldiers swept in a well-practised arc through the attacking ranks to their rear. Then they turned and charged back through the attackers, turning to parallel the defenders until they reached the edge of the fighting, where they took their exhausted mounts through the small gaps that were opened to receive them.

It had taken a remarkably short time, but Jalor could see that the effects of battling large numbers was setting in. The men and women of the Faero's army were tired, the effects of sudden intense fighting wearing them down rapidly. A shout and pointed finger turned Jalor's attention to the ghazrak force about to enter the fray. Wondering why they were so far behind the norther force, Jalor turned and barked an order. On the pole behind the command position a set of flags was raised. In response, on the right flank the banner of Escar was raised and the line opened to allow a force of knights to thunder through. Their mounts were much larger and heavier than those of the hrss-soldiers. Sweeping around the lines of norther attackers, the knights concentrated on reaching the ghazrak before they reached the battle.

While the carnage continued between the northers and the defenders in the line, the knights and ghazrak came together with a resounding crash. Rather than trying to stay mounted as they had at Escar, the knights dismounted after the initial clash and waded into the midst of the ghazrak force. They were outnumbered by the berserker half-men, but attacked nevertheless. A first foot charge of metal-clad knights against bone-armoured creatures resulted in several ghazrak being killed or injured badly enough for them to be out of the immediate fight. The knights received no significant injuries from the charge, after which they adopted formations that allowed them to alternately defend and attack. The knights all bore sections of armour made for them by Hunder, using the same material as he had used for Helt's armour, and this time the knights were able to absorb blows that would have caused serious damage previously.

Jalor watched the melee develop. The defenders of the line were holding, although under pressure from the enormous numbers of attackers, and the ghazrak had been diverted and were being held in check. Above, the two winged ghazrak - Jalor found the small number of the creatures to be significant - were circling, obviously waiting for something to happen. Turning to one side, Jalor searched out Blaine. The Warrior was standing near Helt and was splitting his time watching the battle play out and Jalor. The latter held up one hand, and Blaine nodded. He turned to Helt to say something and then strode away towards a smaller mounted troop held in reserve. Jalor had decided to bring this battle to a decisive end.

Behind him, Corm and Flin waited, as did the twins and Trabor, the engineer Mage who had been spending as much time with Hunder as possible, using his own gifts of fire and metal to reinforce the smith's work, adding additional strength to the composite and metal pieces used by various members of the combined force. Andira was with Trabor. She had an indefinable poise that had not been evident when Jalor first met her. Flin had noted that she seemed to be both more confident and slightly detached, which he put down to her time with Dall. And she had arrived on the back of a Roc, which gave her celebrity status immediately.

The left flank of the defenders rolled open as Blaine led his mounted force into the fray. These were the most experienced of the mounted fighters, those who Almin Bor had selected as the steadiest and best of the army. Several of them had been soldiers for hire in the infrequent but bloody wars that had shaped Ennaris in recent times, and all had been blooded in battle. Formed as a blunt wedge, with Blaine at the point, the idea was to have a mobile hammer that could be swung into action and thereby relieve pressure, which they proceeded to do. Into the remaining ranks of the decimated attackers Blaine led his lightly armoured troops. This reserve scythed through the melee, cutting down the northers still trying to reach the defenders. There was little the northers could do against this new threat, and instinctively the attackers moved further to the right, thus relieving the pressure on the left part of the exhausted defensive line and pushing numbers closer to the line of gullies that bounded the field.

To Jalor's dismay, a horn sounded from those gullies and a swarm of creatures erupted from the depths, straining to reach the banks. Once there, they launched themselves into the action. It took a moment for Jalor to realise that the newcomers were attacking the northers, so stunned was he at what he saw. The creatures were enormous reptiles - he could only think of them as relatives of Earth's alligators - and standing on the broad back of each was a small figure, clad in little more than loincloth and red tunic and wielding blow pipes and knives.

The Waslit - Jalor was told their name by Trabor as he watched - controlled their terrifying mounts using some sort of rein, and the enormous crawlers dashed into the side of the remaining norther force, twisting, snapping, rending flesh, tearing limbs from torsos. The norther fighters who had been single-minded about reaching the defenders were confronted by this terrifying new threat and wavered, then wilted. The remaining attackers, in ones and twos, and then in handfuls and finally all that were still able to do so, turned and fled, dropping weapons as they were harried by the crawlers. Blaine held back his troop, but the Waslit allowed their mounts to pursue the fleeing northers. Few of the northers survived.

"General," a voice called from behind Jalor.

He turned to find a woman, dressed in normal Ennarisi attire but with a red tabard adorned with the Faero's sigil and holding a standard also bearing the Faero's sigil. Behind her were more than a thousand armed women and men. She bowed.

"Likki sends her greetings. The Waslit have come to support the Faero's defence."

"And you are?" Jalor asked.

"I am Credar, Guide of Likki."

"Welcome Credar. Your followers have made quite an impression."

"The Waslit do not follow me, general. They allow me to lead." Credar gave a small smile. "There is a difference."

Jalor nodded and turned back to watch the battle. The northers had succumbed to the greater skill of the defenders and, in the end, to the terror of the giant water crawlers.

The ghazrak troop, on the other hand, were superior in numbers to the knights of Escar and had started to inflict significant damage. Ghaz-ti was proving to be better at tactics that Grensor had been. The ghazrak had been given different instructions and were more effective than at Escar. Several knights were down and not moving as the battle became a fight of attrition. Helt, watching from her mount, saw one knight have his legs taken out from under him by one ghazrak only to have two others attack him with their hooked swords, literally trying to chop him to pieces. The sight was too much for Helt, who could see her father and those she grew up with being assailed. With the defensive lines holding from the northers, and the Waslit still chasing the attacking army off the field, Helt looked to Jalor and raised one silver-clad arm, pointing to the melee. Jalor merely nodded and waved agreement. Helt handed the reins of her mount to an attendant, unhooking the short shield that had been made to her specific needs by Hunder, and started to walk towards the melee.

At the half-way point she broke into a trot, a distance-eating gait that took her rapidly to the fray. Closing her visor, the warrior princess unlimbered her new Hunder-wrought broadsword and charged, the one-woman assault shouting insults as she did so. The two closest ghazrak turned to face her, only to be cut down as she raced past them, one single great swipe as she pirouetted between them serving to decapitate one and severely damage the other. Into the midst of the battle she waded, shield and sword moving in unison, slashing, parrying, blocking. She placed herself between two ghazrak and a knight who had been forced to his knees by the force of the beasts' blows. She deflected the stroke of one while she thrust her sword through the gap between armoured chest and bony head of the other. She then removed the sword arm of the first, leaving it to the knight to finish it. She took another ghazrak from behind as it raised its blunt sword to brain a second knight, only to feel a shattering buffet on her back, the force of which was partly absorbed by Hunder's armour. Still, she was staggered and her reflex to turn with her shield in front of her was all that allowed her to turn the next blow. She responded with a sharp blow of her own that cut through the bony armour of her attacker, but she then had to defend as it roared defiance and rained a flurry of blows at her, ignoring the injury. Finally, with her arm throbbing from holding the shield in place during the barrage, she saw the ghazrak waver and Helt pushed the final blow aside and swept her sword in a swipe that severed one arm, the reverse stroke removing the beast's head.

Helt looked for her next opponent but found none. The ghazrak troop had been destroyed entirely, and the creatures littered the ground around the site of the fight. Many knights were injured and as many killed. Helt located the king and started towards him as above the battle ground the two winged ghazrak swept in to launch their own attack. Held back until the defenders were exhausted, and designed to knock the remaining confidence from those defenders, the winged ghazrak made a low sweep over the heads of the defensive lines, before making an arcing turn, gaining altitude and swinging in towards the group of knights. A cry alerted Helt of the danger and she rushed towards the king's position as the first of the ghazrak snapped open its wings to their greatest extent, with the razor sharp leading edges angling towards the knights' position. The second positioned to follow it in.

The knights turned to face the new threat, knowing there was little they could do to combat this foe. But this was the Rocs' element and from a great height four thunderbolts dropped as one. The first ghazrak was close to the group of knights and Helt was charging towards the king, when the battle cry of the Rocs rang out across the field. The first ghazrak was slammed from above by two of the great birds, one on each wing, snapping the thick bones easily and causing the creature to tumble into the field, carrying one of the Rocs with it. The second ghazrak swung away from its prey to face the threat. Its great wings were beating to thrust itself into a turning climb through the air above the knights, several of whom were running to the fallen ghazrak and Roc so they could kill the beast and try to rescue their ally. The remaining three Rocs swept around the ghazrak, staying away from the sharp-edged wings while seeking to locate vulnerabilities.

Jalor decided that this was a good enough time to try the latest of Hunder's weapons. A signal flag was raised and from behind the lines two Rocs launched into the air. Each wore a harness modelled on those remembered by Kunas from long ago, and strapped into each harness was a member of Corm's Guard, wielding a cross-bow. Designed by Blaine and built by Hunder and his now numerous workshop assistants, these cross-bows were made from a combination of hardened wood and a simple alloy drawn from Ennaris' past that was strong enough to handle the strains required. The bolts were solid steel, but tipped with arrowheads made from the same composite material as Helt's armour. Rising rapidly the two birds strained to reach their fellows who continued to harass the ghazrak. As they approached, the three separated, clearing the field of fire, and the two newcomers swung in so that their riders could target the creature. The first missed, the bolt flying into the distance before arrowing into the ground. The second struck the ghazrak along its armoured side, punching through the armour to bury itself deep in flesh. Both riders recharged their cross-bow quickly, and both fired a second bolt as the ghazrak staggered from the first hit. Both bolts found their mark. One lodged in the joint between the wing and torso, and the creature tumbled from the sky. Once again, several knights rushed towards it, dispatching it before it could bring its remaining working wing to bear as a weapon.

With that, the battle was over but Jalor had no illusions about the result. While beating off a significant force of northers and ghazrak was a win, Goroth had committed but a small part of his force. Had the Waslit, riding those huge reptiles, not arrived as they did, the result may have been less complete. The defenders had many casualties, and the knights had taken a beating. Overall, the defensive tactics had worked and could be refined, but the overwhelming numbers of Goroth's forces were yet to be felt. The Mages on both sides had taken no part in the battle as yet, so that remained a factor to be considered also. It was the reason that Jalor had held back the Council Mages from taking any part, knowing that they were unevenly matched, no matter the apparent strength of Flin.

It was only later that Jalor discovered that Almin Bor was among the injured and that two of the troop commanders had been killed. According to Almin Bor they had been singled out for attack. The tactic may have worked had the troops not been as well-drilled and disciplined as they were. The two commanders had been experienced, as much as the relative peace of Ennaris' last hundred cycles allowed, and their losses would hurt. Now they had to rebuild their lines, re-establish the command structure and prepare for the next onslaught. Jalor was far from satisfied with his position.

Goroth *was* satisfied, however. He had forced the enemy general to show his hand and a second sortie would probably destroy the resistance. Goroth then would be able to win the battle with what he expected to be the third and final attack. *That one is good*, he thought as he reviewed the brief battle. *Certainly better than Likud. Maybe as good as me. But he doesn't have enough of a force, and I doubt he ever faced a battle-trained Mage, let alone two of us.*

18. The Compound

It was well after the middle of the day when Xymin spied the landmarks he sought in the distance. The maps provided by Jalor were very detailed, and the small set of hills were clearly marked. Atop one of the low hills was a small shed, while at the base of a second hill there was what appeared to be a wide entrance, perhaps for a mine shaft. Now, five days after the disastrous battle, they approached their goal.

The Junda-lar had buried their dead by the side of the small lake, marking the spot with a cairn. They left the injured with enough food and water to last until they returned. They had found that the small redoubt where the northers had laid in wait was dug deep into the small hillside and had enough shelter to keep the injured from the sun, especially with the camouflage netting offering a varied shade pattern. While it was heart-breaking to have to leave them behind, the men themselves were adamant that their fellow Junda-lar had to finish the job. Seventy-eight Junda-lar continued their journey.

Now they were upon their target, which were the workshops for the ghazrak of the outlaw Mage, Grensor. Jalor had warned that there were likely to be guards and even ghazrak, which caused Xymin no end of concern. However, over the last day it seemed that the anger of being almost bested by those undisciplined northers, and the humiliation at having to be rescued by the passing troop of Tang scouts had settled into grim determination that this job would be done, and done well.

Swords were gripped tightly in hands that had grown sweaty. The Junda-lar separated into their designated groups. Three separate teams would investigate several features that could have been entrances to the underground lair and deal with anything they found. The first team moved to the left as they approached, to come in from behind the nearer hills. The second moved to the right to do the same from that side. Xymin took his third team directly into the small settlement.

Eyes darted left and right as the warband searched out signs of life and found none. Alert for any movement, especially for signs of ghazrak, Xymin and his twenty Junda-lar moved into the space in front of the two small cabins and halted. As prearranged, five of the number moved to the first cabin, and a further five to the second. Xymin nodded shortly and the two cabins were assaulted, men fanning out as they went through the doors. In short order, both teams returned, reporting no occupants. However, the team leader from the right-most cabin signed for Xymin to come in with him, and led the way back inside.

It took a moment for Xymin's eyes to become accustomed to the gloom. He saw that they were in a two-room cabin. The room they were in obviously was being used as a utility room. The other room, he surmised, may have been for sleeping. The walls of the utility room were covered in maps. Many of them were hand-drawn on parchment and the whole number were tacked into place. The maps showed the northern continent. To the western edge there was the sea, and towards the top of the map was a large bay with some strange markings, like pens. In fact, as he spent more time looking at the maps, Xymin realised they were, indeed, pens. Given that the old Mage had been experimenting with people and turning them into these creatures, it was logical to assume that there were marine examples as well. Xymin thought for a moment but, with no way to get messages to anyone, he filed it away for future use and continued to search the maps.

The smaller maps seemed to show their current location, although they were not as precise as the one Xymin carried. What these cruder maps did show, however, were the locations of the workshops. Xymin examined the maps for a short time and then walked to the door and quietly called the team leaders and their seconds into the room. All three groups had rejoined in the open space before the cabins.

"This map shows where the workshops are," Xymin said once the men were all gathered, standing in a half-circle in front of the map. "Look, we are here, and there are at least fifteen locations marked on the map." He pointed to the locations one after the other. "We need to make sure that we get them all, so I suggest we split up as planned and target them three at a time."

He looked around the faces, seeing agreement, as well as fear. Well, so be it. This was why they were here.

"Did either of you find anything as you came in?" Xymin asked the leaders of the two columns that went to east and west.

"What may be a large mine entrance in that hill, although it seems to be flat so it can't go far in," Fertil, the leader of the western team, said. "We didn't go in, and it's not on the map."

"We can check it after we deal with the workshops that are marked," Xymin decided. "Senbir?"

"Some of these entrances marked on this map are over that way. They look like cellars covered by some sort of door." Senbir looked at the map. "I think we will take these five," he said, placing his hand on the map such that the eastern hills were covered. "We get in, find what we need to find for each one and then light them up."

"Agreed," Xymin nodded. "Fertil's team can take this lot," he continued waving his hand over the markings, "and we will take the rest. As Senbir said, get in, check them out, fire the workshops and get out. And be careful. If this is the workshops area where those creatures are made, then we may find some of them. Remember where General Jalor said that they are vulnerable."

The teams separated again. Xymin led his group towards the first of the locations marked. He had taken the precaution of copying the locations onto Jalor's map. Within a few minims of leaving the cabin and briefing his team members, Xymin and his twenty arrived at the first one. A flat door, no more than a large metal panel - unusual enough for Ennaris where current metalworking capabilities could not create such large, thin panels - lay flat against the ground and it took two men on each side to lift it. It had no hinges, so it was less of a door and more of a covering. The men awkwardly carried it to the back of the opening. Xymin looked into the depths that were revealed. He saw a ladder heading down, with very faint illumination staining the deep darkness below.

Xymin looked around the waiting men and then, with a deep breath, reached for the ladder, only to find his way blocked.

"No, Xymin," Zushi, one of the men said, "we'll go first. You're the leader of this squad but also of the Junda-lar. The risk will be ours."

Xymin stared at Zushi for a moment, recalling Tine's words about allowing others to share the responsibility, and then nodded. Zushi stepped to the top of the ladder and with no fuss started to climb down. He was followed by three others before Xymin could get onto the ladder. The first four and Xymin made it to the bottom, deeper than Xymin expected, and turned to look around. The first four moved out into a scouting formation and Xymin moved away from the ladder, making room for the others to climb off it.

They were in a large space, easily twenty paces from the left to the right wall as Xymin stood, and possibly thirty paces front to back. The ladder emerged roughly in the centre, travelling the last stretch without the chute to support it. It was, Xymin noted, secured to the strange floor, which was made from a flat, grey material that he could not recognise. The ladder itself was made of a type of light-weight metal that Xymin also could not identify. The chamber was dimly lit by a means that, again, Xymin could not fathom, until he remembered that the owner of the workshops was a Mage from Ennaris' distant past - the lights may have been a manifestation of his power. In any event, the light was even across the room, apparently emanating from panels in the ceiling.

Ranged around the walls were twelve large containers - vats, Xymin thought - roughly twice as long as a Junda male and half that length in width. *That*, Xymin thought, *probably holds a single ghazrak*. Tentatively, holding the others back with repeated gestures, Xymin stole towards the nearest vat. It contained a liquid which Xymin decided probably was not water. The surface was still but reflective. There was a silvery sheen atop the liquid, or the liquid itself was some sort of silvery concoction. Xymin could not see below the surface. In any event, he was unable to see if there was anything in there or not. Looking around, Xymin saw a pole with a paddle attachment, likely used to stir the contents. Well, stir the contents was what he would do.

Gingerly, Xymin slid the paddle into the tank until he judged that it was half way to what should be the bottom. He moved it gently back and forth. He was tense and holding his breath, and he forced himself to release his muscles. Glancing to the members of his team, and then swiftly around the chamber, Xymin took a deep breath and then moved the paddle in a long sweep, angling it so that the paddle's face pointed into the centre of the tank. The liquid resisted the movement, as though it was composed of a heavy mixture. Xymin had no idea what that could be or what it meant, but the paddle encountered no obstructions.

Xymin removed the paddle from the tank and nodded to Zushi as he took a deep breath.

"Okay, this one seems to be empty. Let's mark it and prepare to burn it." He looked around the large underground area. "I'm not too sure a lot of this will burn. If not then we may have to just destroy the tanks. We'll do the same for the rest of the tanks and then see if we can start it burning."

Zushi nodded shortly and reached into his pack. From it he removed a small cylinder made by the blacksmith Hunder to Blaine's specifications and passed on to Xymin by Jalor while planning was under way. The cylinder had a single button on top. It was to be placed as close to the object to be destroyed as possible. Each of the Junda-lar carried a small quantity of the devices, while two from each team carried about twenty of them in a reinforced pack. This cylinder was placed against the side of the tank.

Xymin led the way to the second tank, gesturing to others to find things to use on the other tanks. This one likewise produced nothing, nor did the next. Two others had found lengths of materials. One was wood. The other was something else that was smooth-skinned and shaped like a narrow pipe, although the material was thinner and stronger than anything Xymin could imagine being made on Ennaris. Each had tested two tanks when Bugol, he with the strange pipe, encountered resistance. Bugol called out urgently as the liquid roiled inside the tank and then cried out as a misshapen head with horns that were mere nubs emerging from the skull appeared from below the surface. The ghazrak, still embryonic and poorly formed, nevertheless obeyed its base instincts and sought to clamber from the tank and attack.

Standing, the ghazrak shed the silvery liquid, revealing half-formed armour and little in the way of the usual muscle development. A distinct join was evident low down the torso. Like two creatures joined together, Xymin thought. A moment passed as the Junda-lar stared at the creature, but the moment passed as it started to clamber from the tank. Swords were produced and five of the Junda-lar moved in to stab and cut at it, coming close to causing almost as much damage to their fellows as to the ghazrak. With a strangled snarl, and leaking copious amounts of blackish blood, the ghazrak staggered back and collapsed, sliding below the level of the liquid. Small globes of black blood floated sluggishly to the surface.

Shaken, the Junda-lar looked to Xymin. He nodded in acknowledgement of the efforts of the men, then signalled to check the rest. The work proceeded slower than previously but nevertheless all tanks were checked within a short time. Given that they had four chambers left to check, Xymin chaffed at the time that had been taken. Still, the five cylindrical devices allocated to this chamber had all been placed quickly once the last tank was checked and cleared, and Xymin gestured most of the men up the ladder. He took a single look around and then he and Bugol moved from device to device, pushing the top down as they had been shown. Rapidly they moved towards the ladder. Xymin waited for Bugol to clamber up before following.

As Xymin reached the roof of the chamber, the first of the devices exploded, sending a gout of flame across the room. It rolled across the ceiling and caused Xymin to gasp and climb faster. The flames did not reach up the ladder after the fleeing men, but Xymin heard the remaining four explode one after the other and the resultant heat chased Xymin and Bugol up and out of the ladder pit. A bright red-yellow glow from the depths of the pit told of the extreme heat that was generated by the explosives. Xymin doubted that much would have survived. After a careful look down into the chamber showed nothing but flame, Xymin led the men to the second pit.

The work proceeded smoothly from there. Each of the teams reported encountering multiple ghazrak in similar malformed states and each was dispatched quickly with no injury to the Junda-lar. All of the cylinders had been deployed with the exception of two carried by Xymin and each of the chambers was alight when the three teams met once again, outside the bounds of the small workshop settlement.

Fertil nodded as Xymin offered praise to the teams.

“Yes, it’s been a success, Xymin,” Fertil said, “but we still have the chamber dug into the hill to investigate.”

“That’s right,” Xymin said in response, nodding his thanks. “I almost forgot that one. Lead the way, Fertil. I have two of the devices left that Jalor gave us. And it’s getting late, so I’d like to be away from here sooner rather than later.”

Fertil led the Junda-lar around the hill to a spot where there was an opening. A set of crude wooden doors leaned against the opening but did not completely cover it. One was easily dragged aside. The dark was not unexpected, and Xymin was almost disappointed when the magic light did not come on as they had in each of the ghazrak chambers. One of the men pulled a fire-stick, covered in some sort of strange paste, another gift from Jalor, from his pack and Fertil struck his flint to create a spark. The paste ignited and burned strongly, startling Fertil. The men chuckled uncertainly at his surprise, and Fertil laughed shortly. A second and then a third fire-stick were produced and lit from the first.

A guard of twenty-five men was left outside the cave while Xymin led the rest inside.

Xymin realised that the cave was more like a cavern. It extended well back into the hill. In fact, he thought, it must have occupied the hill almost completely. The walls were square and regular and were of some strange sort of manufactured material. They were smooth to the touch and appeared to be slightly translucent. There was a scattering of furniture like stools and a couple of small cupboards, crudely made of old wood, and scraps of different materials stood in small piles.

But it was what stood at the back of the cavern, placed about the same distance from the left and right walls, that brought them up short. None of them had ever seen anything like it. It was a craft of some sort. It was squat and somewhat ugly, resting on long skids similar to skis with which all of them were familiar. The craft was much longer than the sleds that the Junda used and was like a large box, with a pointed nose. It was made of silver and black materials that the Junda-lar had never seen, and it crouched like a beast waiting to strike. Dark windows could be seen in the front. There was what could have been a door in the side. At least, it was some sort of different panel. The Junda-lar moved around the craft carefully, keeping their distance in case of they knew not what.

Xymin, though, decided that they needed to know more about it and approached the panel of different material. A small black panel was alongside the large one. Tentatively, curiously, Xymin reached out and touched the panel with one finger. It came to life. The Junda-lar sprung back from the craft. A strange voice spoke strange words and the small panel pulsed for a short time before settling into a dull creamy glow. Gathering his wits together once again, Xymin moved back and stood in front of the small panel. The strange voice spoke again.

"I am unable to understand what you say," Xymin replied.

More strange words were emitted and the panel pulsed again. Maybe it wanted him to touch it again, Xymin thought. So, cringing inside, he reached for the small panel again and placed a hand upon it. The panel illuminated briefly and turned red. At the same time, a tone sounded that the Junda-lar found ominous.

"Move, get outside, now!" Xymin shouted.

The Junda-lar turned and ran from the cavern like their lives depended on it which, Xymin thought, they well might.

Swiftly, Xymin took the two remaining cylinders from his pack and placed them both under the pointed nose of the craft, pushed down both of the charging buttons and sprinted for the opening. Behind him a piece of the craft's nose dropped away and a short, stubby tube pushed forward. Waving his men away from the opening, Xymin made it to the doorway as a series of blasts sounded behind him. He felt his shirt being plucked to one side as he skidded around the doorway. The Junda-lar sprinted along the path leading from the settlement, up the small incline, and stopped at the crest of a small hill on the south rim of the hollow. Xymin was the last and he turned, gasping and wheezing at the exertion, to look back. As he did, the two cylinders exploded in twin pops that were now familiar to the Junda-lar. What was not so familiar was the massive explosion that occurred only moments later. The cavern disintegrated and the roof was blasted off. A fire-ball leapt into the air.

At almost the same moment, the ground around the settlement shuddered and gave way under the extreme heat generated within each of the chambers. The entire area heaved, and the chambers collapsed in sequence. Fire spurted high into the air as the flames fed on the strange liquid that had been spilt from the tanks onto the caverns' floors and was encouraged by the fresh air it now had available to it. The Junda-lar watched, stunned, at the destruction that they had wrought. Never had any of them seen or felt anything like the force of these explosions and fires.

They stood for a time, watching the flames spurt from the collapsed pits higher than the level of what had been the ground. Then Xymin thought of the second of his directives, this one from Tine rather than Jalor. He gathered his men in close so they could hear above the continuous roar from the demolition of the ghazrak breeding tanks.

"Vinca Jalor, the general of the Faero, charged us with the destruction of the place of breeding of the ghazrak," he said to his men. "We have done so." He paused, nodding, as several of the men cheered. "We have injured men to be assisted back to our homes. But Tine gave me another charge, to assist General Jalor and the Faero to overcome the evil of Goroth. That I intend to do. I ask for those who wish to accompany me."

He was gratified when every one of the Junda-lar declared himself ready to follow Xymin.

"I am unable to take all," he said. "Some must assist our injured and carry the message of our dead and this great victory to our people." He looked around the faces of men who he had known all his life. "Tondir, Volxin, Yinsel, Gorfil and Xintel, you must stay behind. This is no disgrace," he said as the five named men started to remonstrate. "This is necessary, for the Junda-lar and the people of Junda. Tondir, I name you leader of this, our fourth team, and in the event we do not return you are the leader of the Junda-lar. Tine will be proud of you all. We," and he gestured to the men standing around him, "will be proud of you all. Take care of our comrades, our friends."

There were a few further remonstrations and complaints, but Xymin was not swayed. Among those being left behind were the younger siblings of some going. Several were the least experienced, although with this journey they had all been blooded together.

Finally, after the arguments had been made and lost, the five dejected Junda-lar moved away towards the lake where they had left their fellows. Xymin waited to make sure that they would not try to double back before turning to his troops.

"We have little food left so it must be rationed. We have the map from General Jalor that shows water holes, and we can refill our water skins from them as we go. The rest of the Junda-lar await us. I estimate that we will make it to where General Jalor expected the battle to take place in seven days." He looked around the group once again, and seventy-four Junda-lar looked back. Several carried light injuries. "Let's go. Form into teams. We go this way."

Xymin checked his map once more, oriented towards the grassland of the south, and led the way. The three troops followed, separating slightly, and adopted the long, easy stride of the ice people.

Behind them the flames continued to burn, flickering above ground level from time to time. The smoke rose in a thick column.

19. Final Orders

The first battle was lost, and yet Goroth was content. Yes, a large number of the northers were lost and a number of the ghazrak along with them. But that was their job. Grensor had been taken over by a Kindred - that was a larger problem. From what Goroth could tell, the losses were quite high among those armoured fools, and the intelligence provided by Grensor's spies had ensured that the army leaders were targeted. Hopefully, that had worked and there were fewer leaders than there had been.

Goroth held back from another attack for the rest of the day, to let the fear grow. He decided to do the same for the next day, for the same reason. His remaining force outnumbered Drewflin's pitiful army by a large margin, and all would have seen that. Perhaps he would allow Likud to order in a strike from orbit. But no, that would only make matters worse. From what he had seen there was no need for such an action. Drewflin had his allies, but not many.

What should be done, though, was to take care of the fleets around Ennaris. He could not afford to have this Union, whoever they were, play a part once the battle was decided. Thought became action, and Goroth sent a runner for Likud, who wasted little time responding to the summons.

"You wanted to see me?" Likud asked as he approached Goroth.

"It strikes me that we have the upper hand here," Goroth stated. "But I'm not so sure about what's happening up there." He jerked a thumb upwards. "Do you have any idea?"

"The Union fleet seems to be holding station. My fleet can handle them, though," Likud said confidently. "My commanders know what to do. They have plans for each of the enemy ships."

Goroth stared at Likud and shook his head in disbelief.

"You have a plan for each ship?"

"Of course. The ship commanders need to know what to do and that's the best way." Likud smiled thinly. "They all know what will happen to them if they don't follow my orders, and I have my own loyalty officers on each ship to make sure that happens."

"And if things change?"

"They won't. I've thought of everything." Likud shrugged. "But if something does happen, I can communicate with the fleet commanders and give them instructions from here, now that this so-called technology bar seems to be non-existent."

"Well," Goroth said after a moment spent thinking about the folly of having rigid plans for warfare, and then he realised that it was all he had available for now. "Why don't you get that space battle started. I don't want to have to worry about that other fleet."

"Agreed," Likud said. "It's about time. I'd like to be there to see that fleet admiral's face when his fleet is decimated. He's caused me trouble for too long now. I've ordered some more of my Andorethi down here also. We may need them to hold things in line, only these will be properly armed."

"Fine, but make sure that you keep them in reserve. We'll use the northers and the ghazrak as the primary troops. And if Grensor's easterners arrive they can be used the same way. We'll have to get rid of the ghazrak anyway once the fighting is done."

"Maybe we can keep them, or some of them? Put them into a stasis field and keep them just in case?"

"No," Goroth said. "They're too hard to control and we just won't need them. Get started on the space battle and then we can finish this."

20. Grokog

Xymin stood atop a tiny rise in the land, trying to make sense of what he saw. He had his map held loosely in one hand. He knew which way to go, but all he saw in every forward direction was grass. He had heard of the grasslands, of course, but the reality of them staggered him. All of the Junda-lar were similarly affected. After a lifetime of living among the ice, the recent days of moving from the ice through the tundra, then into the blasted and wasted lands to Grensor's ghazrak factory and then further through that ultra-dry, dusty landscape to this sea of grass had opened their eyes. It caused distress for some. The dislocation that they all felt was exacerbated by the knowledge that more of them would likely die here, so far from home.

Still, what they came to do was to help the Children of Ennaris and the Faero, and in order to do that they needed to cross this grass. Xymin gave a mental shrug and turned to give the order to proceed when he saw Byrol hurrying towards him. The scout had been on the eastern side of their line of march.

"Xymin," he called when still a short distance away, "there's an army coming towards us from the east. I've never seen people like this. They're on foot and don't look to be very expert but there are maybe four thousand of them."

"How far away?" Xymin asked, turning to look in the direction indicated.

"Less than half a day's march at the pace they're going."

"Can you tell if they are for the Faero or against him?"

"Well, they're carrying banners that show what can only be a demon. Bright red, horns, ugly as sin. They look like the ghazraks we fought in the ice and what we saw at Grensor's workshops, but worse. On that basis alone, I would say they are against."

"But you can't be sure. Anyway, we are only seventy-five. Against four thousand we stand no chance." He quirked his lips wryly. "And we aren't exactly the best fighters anyway."

"No," Byrol agreed. "If we press forward faster, we should be able to stay clear of them. We can move quicker than they are. And they don't seem to have any forward scouts out more than a short distance."

Both were distracted by a drumming sound coming from the west. A small dust cloud was moving towards them. Xymin glanced to Byrol, who shook his head in a mute gesture that he did not know what was coming. Xymin gestured and the Junda-lar quickly formed a defensive circle, each of the three troops taking a segment. Xymin moved from the small rise to stand in front of his men with Byrol at his side and awaited what was coming.

From the small dust cloud came three men, riding the first hrss that any of the Junda-lar had seen. The Junda-lar eyed the newcomers with interest but warily, for the war-like exploits of the hrss-riding Clans were legend. The three wore dull coloured clothes, loose fitting but functional. Broad-brimmed hats were held on their heads by straps that were similarly coloured and all wore dull brown boots made, Xymin realised after a moment, from hrss leather. The hrss themselves were of as much interest as their riders. Each of them was of the same dull brown colour and were almost as tall as a man from sharp hoofs to top of blunt-nosed heads. Long manes waved as they trotted towards the Junda-lar, with alert eyes and pointed ears forward. These creatures were as much on guard as their riders, who regarded Xymin and his men grimly.

With no ceremony the riders drew rein before the defensive circle. One pushed forward, almost to the point where Xymin stood.

"Who are you and why are you in the grasslands of the Clans?" the rider asked bluntly.

"I am Xymin, leader of this warband of the Junda-lar," Xymin said evenly, letting his hand rest easily on his sheathed sword. "We have come from the ice to assist the Children of Ennaris and the Faero in his war against Goroth."

"Well, Xymin of the Junda-lar, you are far from home, and not taking a very direct route," the mounted speaker replied. "You came from the waste land. Why?"

"Who are you to challenge the Junda-lar? Who are you to challenge the first acolyte of Tine?" Byrol glared at the three riders.

"I am Horint," the rider said quietly. "I am an acolyte of Lak, Guardian of the plains people. This," and he motioned forward one of the other riders, "is Ferelas, elected war leader of the Clans at this time, and this," and the other rider moved forward, "is Marelas, war second of the Clans. And these grass plains are our place. So, we have *every* right to challenge anyone who comes to this land, especially those who come from the waste."

Xymin glanced to Byrol, who returned the glance, abashed. Xymin nodded and made a signal, at which the Junda-lar moved from their defensive formation into their three teams.

"Well met, Horint," Xymin said. "Allow me to apologise for the harsh words spoken just now. The Junda-lar are not natural warriors and we have lost men, friends, on this mission. This has made us wary. We come from the waste lands because we were tasked by Vinca Jalor, the general of the Faero, with destroying the ghazrak factory of Grensor. This we have done."

"You have destroyed the place where the ghazrak are hatched?" Horint looked at the men with new eyes, as did his companions. "Natural warriors or not, that is a feat to celebrate."

"Perhaps. In doing so we killed a number of ghazrak who were growing still, but more importantly we destroyed the tanks and equipment used to make them. As to whether we celebrate or not, Byrol, our chief scout, informed me as you arrived that there is an army of four thousand approaching from the east. They appear to march under the banner of a demon. We were debating what to do."

"We had word this army approached," Horint said. "We believe they'll join with Goroth, and we intend to stop them from doing so before we then join the Faero's army. Do you wish to fight with us?"

Xymin considered, turning to his team leaders. All three nodded. Xymin turned back to Horint.

"We'll fight with you. We're not riders, and have no hrss. We have swords and spears but are not warriors as the Clans are reputed to be. Can you fit us into your battle plan?"

"We'll set our plans accordingly," Ferelas said, grinning with an odd light in his eyes. "It's not usual for us to match mounted fighters with infantry, but we've done so before. In this case I believe you'll be the bank against which these intruders will break. Let's make our plans now, quickly, and get this done. I itch to move onto the main battle."

The Grokog marched in four irregular lines. They were well into the grasslands and were stretched out across a significant distance, but the lines travelled quite close together. Hardog was comfortable with the progress they were making. By the scale of the map, he expected to be near enough to where the great Mage Grensor wanted him to be in three or four more days, at which time he would send out scouts to find them and make his final approach based on what was found. He intended to play an important role. His nearly four thousand men were sure to prove a decisive force. They had been marching across this grass for what seemed like forever, but that should be over soon. At least there had been no further disasters since leaving the foothills of the dividing range.

For a moment, Hardog thought about his future. Getting here had been a trial, but with Groks' help he had done it. His men had been outfitted with their fighting equipment and had met no opposition since the storm, which was not a surprise given that he had four thousand still available to him. That was a force to be reckoned with. With these men he would carve out his own domain, build his own temple and be the Prophet of the west. So far, the western side of the mountains was not proving to be very fertile, but he was sure that would change. This interminable grass, after the difficult terrain near the mountains, could not go on forever, and the soft westerners would feel the iron of the Grokog and surrender. He would build his temple on a hill where he could survey his lands and watch the people toil for the greater glory of Groks and the priesthood. His mind drifted to the pleasures he would enjoy. He would have to find a new source of the drugs used to subdue the people, but that should not be a problem. And the Temple Assistants would have to be replenished and made to serve his wishes, which again would not be a problem. It would be a grand outcome.

Those pleasant daydreams were interrupted by his lead Temple Assistant.

"My lord, can you hear that noise?" he asked, sitting on one of the very few hrss left to them.

Hardog shook off his thoughts and brought himself back to the present. They were, after all, in enemy land. He could hear a faint drumming, somewhat like the drums of a Temple ceremony. For a moment, he felt irritated at the thought that another had beaten him out here, Bernis perhaps, but then he realised that it was not drums. He shared an uncertain look with the Temple Assistant, who shrugged to show that he had no idea. By now Hardog could *feel* the drumming, even though he was mounted. The hrss were trembling and trying to shy and both men had to exert additional control.

"Is it a ground shake?" Hardog asked.

"I don't think so," the Temple Assistant replied, looking around at the flat, grass covered plain. "What's that?" he said, pointing towards the back of the column.

Hardog turned and stared. A pall of smoke - no, it was dust - was approaching the column from the rear. A sick feeling came over Hardog. Not again!

"Get the men closer together. We're being attacked. Move!" Hardog shouted as he started to move among the trudging men. "Move into formation, you men. Get into the defensive positions you've been training. Hurry!"

The Temple Assistant joined into the shouting and cajoling, joined by the volunteers who had been made officers. However, the men were tired and lethargic after days of walking through this hard land. Most did not want to be here, anyway, and very few were capable soldiers.

"Move or die!" shouted Hardog as he moved back and forth.

It was too late and the columns were too long, too stretched. The drumming was louder now. The shouting of Hardog, the Temple Assistants and the officers were joined by cries of terror from the back of the columns. Hardog stood in his stirrups to see what was happening. The heat and bright light of midday on the grasslands caused his still untrained eyes to have problems, and black specks danced in his vision. He concentrated harder, blinking to sharpen his gaze and stared. Far to the back the dust cloud had spat out dozens, no, hundreds, of hrss-men who were charging through the marching men, dealing out death. Men were being hacked by swords, or impaled by hand-carried spears. The charging hrss cut swathes through the extended lines of men. The few hrss of the Grokog at the rear of the columns were riderless already. As he watched, the Grokog further back started to run. One or two officers tried to force them to stop and form into their defensive formations, but to no avail, so they joined the rout.

It had been only moments since the attack started, and the men near the front of the column had started to move faster. There was no thought of obeying the commands to stand and fight. These were not soldiers, Hardog thought bitterly, and none of them were really ready for this. The fleeing men from the middle of the column caught up to those few at the front who had been forced into defensive squares. The terror etched on the faces of their fellow Grokog was enough to make those few formations that had been formed waver. Then, from behind and *above*, came that chilling cry that was remembered so well from the tunnel. The black specks resolved into the giant birds, each with a rider, spearing from the sky. The lead rider was the one with the bright light shining from his staff. The Grokog broke.

What was a steady march only a short day-dream ago was now a ragged, chaotic and terror-riven mass of fleeing men. The imagined triumph was a rout. All along the length of the Grokog army men fell. Hrss charged through the mess with riders striking to left and right, or holding those strange spears level and steady and impaling men on them. From above, fire balls and metal bolts were reaching out and dealing death from the giant birds. Hardog's hrss panicked. It turned so sharply that he lost his hold on the reins and was pitched from the saddle. The hrss vanished into the grassland. Hardog landed heavily and for a moment lay winded, before picking himself up and joining the fleeing men, many of whom had thrown away their weapons and were merely running in blind panic.

Hardog was unsure about how many of his army remained alive. He had no idea about which officers remained alive. He could not think of any tactic or strategy, and he was not a military strategist in any event. He *was* sure that his dreams were dead, but at the moment the fight or flee instinct told him to flee, which he did. Men streamed past him as he staggered on. He had a brief thought that the hrss riders and huge attacking birds were driving the army onward, dealing out death on all sides and forcing the fleeing Grokog into an arrow straight line. Then, from the haze in front of them emerged a series of banners, standing straight and fluttering slightly. Hardog had enough presence of mind remaining to recognise the red banner with the Faero's sigil, but the others he did not know.

A cry rang out, a command, and from the grassland in front of the fleeing Grokog another force emerged, rising from the crouch that they had held since the attack had started. The hrss-men continued to harry the remaining men, and the Rocs - Hardog would never know what they were called - swooped while the men on their backs released bolt after bolt from their cross-bows or sent those strange balls of cold fire into their midst. The first men reached the line formed by the new force and screams of terror and pain floated back to those following. Lines of spears had been thrust into the ground, forming a death-dealing barrier onto which the fleeing army impaled itself. Those who evaded the first line found themselves running into a second and then a third. Those who evaded the third were faced by grim-visaged men who took full toll.

The charge faltered as the Grokog sought to avoid this new threat, but the hrss riders gave no quarter, offered no mercy. Hardog looked back and, for as far as he could see along a swathe of crushed grass, there were the bodies of his army. His four thousand men had been reduced in short time to the few trying to avoid the blockading force, and as he watched the mounted force swept to the side and charged into the remaining men. From behind him came that chilling battle cry. Hardog turned to see a giant bird, whose intelligent eyes were focused on him, glaring at him. The last thing Hardog saw was the figure on the bird's back release the bolt. The impact to his chest threw Hardog backwards and flung his body to the ground, lifeless.

A few cries were all that were left as Horint dismounted nearby and walked to where Xymin stood. Both surveyed the battleground, although to Xymin it represented a slaughter more than a battle. The Clans had received very few injuries, and the Junda-lar none beyond scratches. Ferelas was instructing the hrss leaders in what to do. Most of the riders were dealing out death to the remaining Grokog in the vicinity, mostly as mercy, for the wounds were grievous. None remained upright. Xymin and his men who had manned the spear barrier stared at the carnage as they moved out into what was left of the field of battle, and from above came the cries of victory from the two battle wings of the Rocs that had come at the request of Horint. The Junda-lar had never seen the like and watched, caught between being sick at the death they had helped to deliver and awe at being in the presence of the legendary Rocs.

One of the giant birds landed nearby and the rider dismounted, strolling across to where Xymin and Horint waited.

"Ho, Horint," the rider called. "The wings will sweep back to the mountain and then head back to home base to restock. Any of the bolts you can recover would be appreciated, as we have relatively limited stock although Hunder's workshop is churning them out now. Who's this?"

"Wensil, well met," Horint replied. "This is Xymin, leader of the Junda-lar."

"Junda-lar? I know of the Junda, the ice people. Not of the Junda-lar, though." Wensil turned his attention to Xymin.

"We are the warband of the Junda," Xymin said, taking in the utilitarian garb of Wensil and wondering what it must be like to fly on one of those great birds.

"Good job setting and manning that barrier. That took nerve," Wensil said, then turned slightly as though receiving a message. "Ah, For-na tells me you that are the chosen of Tine, as Horint is the chosen of Lak. It is my honour to make your acquaintance," Wensil continued, bowing slightly.

"We will move towards the further end of the grass plains, Wensor, where we expect to find the rest of the Junda-lar," Xymin said. "We need to help gather the javelins first. We'll gather your bolts and leave them behind the battle lines. Go well, my friend."

"Aye, go well indeed. Good hunting, Horint of the Clans and Xymin of the Junda-lar. I look forward to sharing a good ale with you both when we are done."

Wensil turned back and clambered lithely aboard For-na who shook his wings once and launched into the air. Xymin, along with many of the Junda-lar and the Clans, watched as the Roc arrowed higher and higher, merging into one of the two formations of Rocs. With a loud cry that reverberated across the plains, the battle wings wheeled as one and accelerated towards the mountain heights.

"They do like to show off," Horint said with a smile. "But they make an impressive sight."

"That they do," Xymin said as watched the birds become tiny dots in the distance and then disappear from sight. "That they do."

"Well, I know what you told Wensor, but will you march with the Clans, Xymin? As you said, we will gather the javelins, including those you used for the barrier, and any cross-bow bolts we can find. It's a bit gruesome, but we need them. And then we can find the rest of your Junda-lar."

"Aye, I think we will," Xymin replied on reflection. "There are only seventy-five of us at the moment, so your numbers will keep us safer."

"And we know the way," Horint grinned.

"That, too!" Xymin replied with a smile.

21. Fleets Engage

"Admiral, *Qorv* is powering weapons, including that big central one, whatever it is," Ensign Porlis said in a steady voice from the sensor. "The rest of the enemy fleet is also powering weapons now. Starting to manoeuvre."

"Very well. Looks like they got tired of waiting. Those two damaged ships that joined the Empire fleet may have had something to do with it. Signal the *Freekam* and *Grestil* to execute the wide hit and run plan, get all wings aloft, *Starfire* and *Moonbeam* to the fore. Weapons free for all ships, but stay in formation as long as possible."

High Admiral Bard moved to the command chair and sat calmly. He watched the screen that showed dozens of ships moving in coordinated dance steps that were designed to obtain advantage over the enemy that was attempting to do the same. The Empire's smaller ships started to run towards the Union fleet. It was a feint, Bard thought, designed to make them react. That was a standard Empire tactic, and if there was one thing about the Empire commanders that Union commanders relied on, it was that their tactics rarely changed. Usually, they relied on overwhelming numbers and firepower, but here they were almost evenly matched after the skirmishes that had occurred.

Freekam was a smaller, nimble gunship, based on a tug. It was less than half the size and weight of the small frigates that made up most of the Union fleets, but had almost the same engine configuration, a heavy concentration of offensive weapons but only relatively light armour. *Grestil*, *Freekam*'s sister ship, had a similar configuration but with a heavy defensive weapon fit-out and extremely strong shields. The two ships were designed to work in tandem, acting much like a single larger ship. Keeping close company as they had trained many times, flying almost belly to belly, the two ships darted from the Union fleet formation, rapidly moving perpendicular to the two facing fleets, preparatory to launching their attack. At the same time, several of the screening ships for *Qorv* shifted their places to move out along a long arc. Almost as one, the Empire ships began a bombardment, with the enemy capital ships targeting the smaller Union ships.

"Admiral, both *Griffin* and *Hydra* are being targeted, same as *Nova* and *Quasar* were. Targeting the launch bays mostly. Both ships are manoeuvring to avoid but are being bracketed." Porlis' eyes darted left, right, up and down constantly, trying to make sense of the huge number of inputs hitting his screens.

"Stay calm, Ensign," Kiri said from her station. "You can't do everything, so stay with what you can do. Leave the rest to others. You're doing fine."

Bard glanced to Kiri and smiled to show approval of her words. "Colonel, *Moonbeam* and her fleet are to take the offensive. I want the Empire frigates hit hard."

"Aye, sir," Kiri said as she bent to communicate the instructions. "*Moonbeam* responding. Fleet Two ships are firing. Multiple hits on two frigates, severely damaged and likely out of action. Three others damaged but fighting still. *Fendaristil* is entering the field. Oh my," Kiri breathed. "*Fendaristil* has fired some sort of plasma weapon and it just destroyed one of the smaller frigates."

"*Griffin* and *Hydra* have both been hit," Ensign Porlis called. "Launch bays are damaged and both ships have taken significant damage. Heavy casualties on both ships. Enemy ships are now targeting *Moonbeam* and her screen ships."

"Colonel, move *Starfire* to screen *Griffin* and *Hydra*. If they need to abandon then get those people over here if possible. What's *Qorv* doing?" Bard tensed as his orders were carried out, while he watched his ships take damage and his people being killed or injured.

"Nothing, Admiral. *Qorv* is just sitting and watching." Ensign Porlis switched his attention to another part of his screen. "*Freekam* and *Grestil* are starting their run."

From above and far to the open space side of the battle, the two ships hurtled towards the Empire fleet. This tactic was something that had been developed almost two hundred years earlier but was rarely used, so it was likely that the Empire commander had not seen it before. Inventive tactics was a standard means of dealing with them. They learned and managed to work out counters to Union tactics over time but when the Union created new tactics the Empire fleets were unable to react easily. That seemed to confirm the lack of imagination and independent thought that Union intelligence continued to report as characteristic of the Empire commanders. The two gunships flung themselves at the Empire fleet, the pilots of each ship performing synchronised manoeuvres so that the ships appeared to be anchored together. It took great nerve and unswerving faith in the other pilot.

Grestil had her massive defensive shield, which was powered by her over-sized engines and covered both ships, cycling rapidly to allow *Freekam*'s energy weapons to fire through minute gaps created in those shields. *Freekam* targeted two cruisers as she swept through the outer reaches of the Empire fleet in tandem with *Grestil*, in a breathtaking display of pilot skill. The sustained fire from *Freekam* created havoc on the two cruisers, destroying hard points on both ships and reducing their fire power dramatically, although both ships remained operational. In passing, *Freekam* laid fire on the two smaller vessels that had shown damage when they arrived with *Qorv*, and both of which now were destroyed. The two Union gunships swept through the Empire fleet and out the other side, apparently unscathed.

"Admiral, *Qorv* is firing its main cannon," Ensign Porlis called out urgently.

Energy beams speared from ships of both fleets, impacting on defensive screens with varying results. Ships moved in patterns designed to make them less liable to be hit repeatedly. But those energy beams paled as *Qorv* rolled and fired its main weapon from the ship's belly. The amount of energy released was such that the Empire dreadnought was pushed backward in reaction. The enormous blast of energy engulfed both *Freekam* and *Grestil* as they exited the bounds of the Empire fleet and overwhelmed the sensors of the Union fleet momentarily. When the sensors recovered, neither ship was to be found.

"Admiral, *Freekam* and *Grestil* have disappeared from sensors," Kiri reported in a shocked voice. "Both are just gone."

Bard nodded, appalled at the event but unable to spend much time on it right now.

"Understood, Colonel," he said crisply. "That was a planet-buster they fired, and that's not something they would usually do. It seems they have someone on that ship who has a clue."

"*Qorv* has started to recharge, but it looks like it'll take a while," Ensign Porlis reported. "That was a massive energy release. That would cut through any screen on our side, sir."

"Then we need to get this happening sooner rather than later. All ships are free to manoeuvre at will. Keep an eye on *Qorv* and that weapon's status. *Starfire* will target *Qorv* and the two cruisers *Freekam* attacked. *Moonbeam* is to take the other cruisers." Bard watched the screen. The scintillas of energy beams reflected on it as ships were impacted. "Let's hope Admiral Jord finds something useful."

"Admiral, incoming ships," Ensign Porlis called urgently. "I make it fourteen signatures."

"Whose ships?"

"Uncertain at this stage, Admiral." Porlis maintained a watch on the energy signatures approaching the battle zone, even while trying to hold a view of the engagement.

"Kiri, stay alert on those incoming ships. I hope they're friends."

"Aye, Admiral. We're being pushed around a little here, Admiral. The Empire fleet now outnumbers us by a margin and the rate of fire is pretty high for them. Most of our ships are being hit from two or more directions. We're outgunned."

"Something new for them," Bard nodded. "Someone over there definitely has a clue. Keep the fleet in motion. It's our best bet for the time being."

"Admiral, incoming ships identified. It's ..."

"*Starfire*, this is *Sirius*. Permission to join the party?"

On the bridge of *Sirius*, Admiral Mika Sancer didn't wait for permission to be granted. Targets had been laid in as the ships from the Fourth Fleet approached.

"Tactical, all weapons released. Launch stingers. All ships, open fire!"

22. Tued Arrive

Marjory almost laughed at the expressions of relief on the faces of the desert fighters as they disembarked from the ships. The small docks of what was now a small fishing village, but whose site was once an inland city, were crowded as almost a thousand men and women milled around seeking their clans. The situation was made even more confused as the sand-hrss were brought from the holds. The situation looked to be chaotic but Marjory, with a practiced eye, knew differently. Within a short time, the clans had formed, each of them missing members from the ship that had been destroyed. Marjory had promised them time to mourn, after the evil of Goroth was defeated.

The people of the village stood and stared as Marjory, once again wearing the robe of a Mage of the Council, walked to the front of the mob and raised her hands. Within moments the docks fell into silence. The only sounds were the creaking of the boats that remained tied to the bollards and the odd cry of a gull.

"Well, we made it across," she said clearly, enhancing her voice so all could hear. "We faced challenges and we have come through. It's now time for us to take the last step. I'll be leading you to the great grasslands of the north, where we will do battle with Goroth and his army of renegade Ennarisi and his creatures of nightmare. Your swords will drink deep before this is done."

A roar greeted her words, accompanied by waved swords. Like children, she thought as she looked around the village. She recalled that there was a portal here but could not see anything remotely resembling one. Calling over a boy who was watching raptly, with open mouth and wide eyes, Marjory smiled and opened her mouth to ask him some questions.

"Are you a Mage?" the boy asked before she could say anything.

"Yes, I am," Marjory said. "Do you know ..."

"Are you going to kill everyone?" he asked, wide-eyed.

"No," she shot back. "Why would I want to kill everyone?"

"I thought that was what Mages did," he replied, as several of the desert fighters chuckled behind Marjory, although when she swung around their faces were suspiciously smooth.

"Well, we don't," Marjory said shortly, turning back to face the boy. "Uh, no more questions," she continued with one hand raised as he opened his mouth to ask more questions. "What's the oldest building in this village? Probably made from some sort of stone that can't be broken."

The boy considered and then pointed to a lookout tower at the back of the small square fronting the docks. "The tower was rebuilt last year. It was the oldest building then. It's made from strange stone that no-one could chip or break down, so the new one is built on top of the old one."

Looking closer, Marjory could see that the viewing platform seemed to extend from a lower structure, what she thought had been a lower floor or foundation. Nodding in satisfaction, the Mage walked up to the base of the structure and examined it closely. Someone had done a thorough job of building a framework and wooden cladding over the old stone-like work, for whatever reason. Through a few cracks Marjory could make out the older facade, built not of stone but of a material devised long, long before. The twins would know what it is, she mused, but dismissed the thought. The door into the portal would be facing the square, she thought. The square was old, of a much older city than the surrounding village buildings, and public portals always were built facing onto a square.

Marjory turned and gestured to a few of the desert fighters.

"Can you tear down this side of the facade?" she asked. "We need to get through to the portal inside."

With a brief nod the fighters attacked the wall, bringing wails of protest from a short, rotund individual who had just arrived on the scene.

"What do you think you're doing?" he yelled as he approached at a slow waddle. "You can't do that. I just had that ugly old thing covered up."

Marjory turned to face the newcomer while the cladding started to come down in earnest.

"I need to get to that ugly old thing," she said firmly.

"Who do you think you are to just destroy the property of this village?" he demanded, standing straight and almost reaching Marjory's shoulder.

"I am Marjory nar Drewflin, and we need to reach the field of battle on the steppes," she replied evenly, her eyes flashing in a sign that many of the past would have heeded. Not so this man.

"Well, the steppes are a long way away," he said. "That way." He pointed into the distance to the right. "Stop doing that!" he demanded of the men stripping the planks away.

"Wrong!" Marjory stated. "The steppes are a short distance away. That way!" She pointed at the wall of the building that was coming into view as the thin covering was removed.

"You're destroying it! You'll have to pay for that to be replaced." The little man was apoplectic, red in the face and hopping from foot to foot.

"Again wrong," Marjory said. "The portals are under the care of the Council of Mages, not you."

"Council of Mages? Who cares about them. They don't exist and if they did why would they want to come here? I am the mandar of Grellar, and I order you to stop." He was now shouting at full volume, and a small crowd had gathered.

"The Council of Mages exists," Marjory said, nodding in thanks to the men who, in short order, had pulled down one wall of the pride and joy of at least one person in the village. "And I have need of this portal."

She stepped towards the seemingly solid wall, examined it closely and reached out to touch what seemed to be a single stone. It flared into light and cracks appeared in the wall, widening as great doors grumbled open for the first time in millenia. The crowd stared, transfixed, and the mandar stepped back, aghast.

"Who, who are you?" he sputtered with all resistance gone and truculence replaced by fear.

"I am Marjory nar Drewflin," she repeated in a ringing tone. "Battle Mage of Ennaris!"

She turned and made her way into the gateway chamber that was revealed as the doors opened to their fullest. Lights came on as she entered and she looked at the murals on the walls, telling of the city that had stood here for ages before the rebellion, with tall buildings that overlooked a long, green valley. Shaking her head at what was lost, Marjory walked to the panel on the further wall, where a single point of light was the only sign of power. She touched the panel, which changed from black to grey.

"Recognise Marjory nar Drewflin of the Council of Mages." The formal tones of the portal AI were replaced by the warmer tones of the Council Assistant. "Battle Mage! You were reported lost! It's pleasing that you are alive. You should know that the Archmage has gathered with the Faero at the Field of Mist in the steppes."

"Thank you," Marjory replied. "What's the closest portal to the Field of Mist?"

"The portal of Ishtel is the closest." A map appeared on the screen, with the portal indicated as a flashing green diamond. "The distance to the Field of Mist is fifty-seven sendils."

"Very well. Establish connection to the portal of Ishtel, and hold it open." Marjory turned to face the clan leaders who had followed her into the room and were looking at the walls, entranced. "Yes, this place was not always a sea-port. Once this was a city on the wall of a deep valley running through the middle of Ennaris. Now, we'll pass through this gateway to the steppes. From there, we'll make our way to the battle ground. I'll go first to make sure the area is safe. You'll have to lead your sand-hrss. There's nothing to fear with the gateway."

The desert leaders gave firm nods, acknowledging the trust implicit in their battle leader. Marjory turned back to the wall. A large silver-grey patch stood where previously it had looked to be solid stone. The stone above her brow flared silver as she gathered her power, and she strode firmly through the portal.

23. Arrival Of the Hides

Jalor looked over the field of battle, considering the events that were almost two days past now. The first skirmish had shown pretty much what he expected to see. The northers had swarmed forward as shock troops, but not in anywhere near the numbers he had expected, or that they had available. Still, they had caused damage. The follow-up by the ghazrak had added to the damage. Significant losses had occurred among the Faero's lesser-trained soldiers and Flin and the healers, those gifted and those with traditional skills, had been very busy. But it was the enemy gifted that were his concern. At least Goroth had not taken the field as yet, and the larger body of winged ghazrak were being held back for some reason, although one of the creatures flew a tight circle above Goroth's camp. In fact, he could not understand what they were waiting for. He would have followed up his advantage and launched a second attack quite soon after the first.

The knights had proven their worth, beating back most of the ghazrak attack, but had taken losses and injuries. Only half of their number had been committed, however, so they remained a viable force. Blaine and Helt had stood firm against the rest with the Faero's army. The Rocs had dealt with the two winged creatures, while losing one of their number, the first Roc casualty of this war. Corm had been visible. The Faero's banner, as expected, had come under heavy attack and had been defended by a mixed bag of the Faero's guard and the alliance's forces. The sight of the long, scaled water crawlers, as they were called - he could only think of them as alligators, although he knew they were not - with their riders standing on the broad armoured backs, would stay with him for ever.

The twins and Trabor had stood with Flin to deflect the magic attacks that had not eventuated. They did not expect to succeed when the time came. They knew that they would not be able to retaliate with any sort of effectiveness. And that meant major trouble. A troop of Warriors of the Light would not go astray here.

Jorphy Bart stood atop the small rise that overlooked the part of the steppes where the initial skirmishes had occurred. She could see the torn and trampled grass. Above the whole, she could see one great winged beast circling which, from what Varna had told them, would be the winged ghazrak, abominations returned to Ennaris at the behest of the evil ones.

To the north were the forces of Goroth, drawn back as preparations continued for the next fight. To the south were the forces of the Faero, with various flags rising and fluttering above the tents. In the centre, atop a tent no larger than any other, was the red and gold standard of the Faero of Ennaris.

Jorphy Bart turned to look at the group standing just behind her and nodded.

"So, this is where we return to the world, it seems," she said, smiling slightly. "Shall we see what sort of welcome we get?"

Her words were greeted by nods and grimaces. The Hides had deliberately stayed away from the world of Ennaris for all of the time since the rebellion, and they had hidden themselves very effectively for the most part. What had started as a form of protection had become part of their way of life, separate and apart. This was not because of false pride but because they did not feel the need to take part in the petty quarrels and fights of the people with whom they came into occasional contact. Because the people of the Hides tended to live longer as their gifts manifested, and because most had some form of gift and thus enjoyed that longer life, those petty concerns tended to be seen as short-term trifles.

With a sense of theatre, the Hides formed into the societies they had maintained over the cycles of their existence, drawing on the Guide guilds of ages past. Dressed in the guild colours and tunics that carried designs handed down from those long-gone days, the Hides moved onto the steppes and turned towards the Faero's camp. Jorphy Bart walked at the front of the train, trailed by a standard bearer with the standard furled still. They were a short distance into their march when a warning came from behind. Jorphy Bart looked over her shoulder towards the enemy camp to see the winged beast rising higher into the air and beating towards them.

So, they faced one of Grensor's misbegotten creations as their introduction. From the Faero's camp came a figure in silver armour on a hrss, racing across the beaten down grass towards the group. With a calm that most experienced warriors would envy, Jorphy Bart halted and gestured. The Hides moved without hesitation into a defensive formation and awaited what would come.

Helt could see the winged ghazrak reach its usual attack height and turn towards the newcomers. Who they were she had no idea, but she knew that they would be caught in the open and slaughtered by the ghazrak. She tried to boot the hrss into greater speed but it was at its limit and she knew that she would be too late. In frustration, she cried aloud in an effort to distract the ghazrak, drawing her longsword from its back scabbard as she did, but with no effect. There was little she could do but stare, aghast, as the ghazrak started its dive.

As one the people of the Hides crouched low, while around the edges of the defensive formation five stood, facing the oncoming beast. They stood firm and apparently calm and watched the ghazrak commence its dive. Jorphy Bart stood at the centre of the formation.

The ghazrak was gripped by excitement. It had watched its nest mates as they tried to deliver death to their enemies two days past before being killed. It looked forward to adding to the tally of ghazrak victories with these puny creatures. The ghazrak revelled in the fear it created as its targets crouched down low, obviously seeking to avoid the sweep of its great razor-edged wings. It revelled in the knowledge that such a tactic would be of no use. The silver one would not reach the scene in time to cause any inconvenience. It was strange that not all of the targets were cowering, but that just meant that they would be the first to die. It spread its wings wide and opened its mouth to cry out its victory.

As one the five lifted one hand, and as one five bolts of energy erupted from the hands, targeting the ghazrak. The five bolts punched through the creature which stopped in mid air as though hitting a wall. Uncomprehending, the ghazrak struggled to move and watched as the one standing near the centre pointed. A single sizzling and crackling blast smote the ghazrak and it disappeared in a great blast. The carcass was consumed by a blistering hot fire that erupted from within. Nothing was left to fall to the ground. Helt pulled her mount to a halt and stared as the formation broke apart once more. But now the one in the lead nodded to the standard bearer who tugged a string, and the standard broke open and floated in the still air as though being blown in a stiff breeze. The group started to march to the Faero's encampment once again.

In the camp Flin had been watching, knowing that there was little he could do, even as Helt had jumped onto her hrss and started across the long distance to the party. He, too, had watched as the ghazrak started its attack run, and he, too, had been astonished at the events that unfolded. Standing alongside Flin, Ragnor started as the standard was unfurled and fluttered. From the distance he could see the broad green banner, with the insignia fluttering proudly.

"Flin," Ragnor said in a stunned whisper.

"I see it," Flin replied, as stunned as Ragnor. "I don't understand it, but I see it."

Corm came up behind the two, accompanied by Raglin and Trabor, both of whom joined their fellow Mages and watched the approaching party with wide open eyes.

"What banner is that?" Corm asked of no-one in particular.

It was Trabor who answered. "That, Faero, is the banner of the Mage Academy of Resgalar."

"The Mage Academy? Resgalar? But didn't you say ..." Corm trailed off.

"Yes," Flin said. "Resgalar was destroyed by Goroth in the early days of the rebellion, as was the Academy."

"Archmage," Ragnor said. "I believe it is for you and the Faero to greet the newcomers. It would appear we have some allies."

Flin nodded thoughtfully before turning to where his pack lay outside Corm's tent. Reaching in, he drew forth the stub of his staff, extending it to its full length with a thought. The stone at the peak of the staff burst into life. The green glow of the staff stone matched that of the Enchara that now flared on his brow. Glancing at Corm, who nodded unspoken agreement, Flin led the way to where the party would approach the camp. On the way Jalor joined them, as did Blaine, while the other Mages trailed behind. Walking past the outer row of guards, Flin halted and surveyed the newcomers.

The woman leading the column had been the one to deliver the final blast. She was wearing the tabard of Ogun, her tunic adorned with the thunderbolt grasped in one hand. She had the indefinable air of one of power. Behind her Flin could see others wearing the same tabard, and still others with the Tree of Fernis, the flame of Menra, the eye of Dall, and the two hands of Appanu, one of the guardians who had lost their lives. A number wore no tabard.

The woman walked up to Flin. She stood tall as she looked from the staff to the glowing stone to the Enchara and finally to Flin's face, which he held impassive with some effort. She smiled and stood quite still. Behind her the column separated into five sections, representing members of the five Hides. Each section included those wearing tabards of different guilds.

"Archmage?" the woman asked in a low, even voice, one eye cocked.

"I am Archmage Drewflin nar Marjory," Flin answered, his eyes drifting to the banner floating still behind Jorphy Bart. He gestured to Corm, standing just behind him. "This is Corm Ramesa, Faero of Ennaris."

The woman nodded to Corm after an appraising glance, and turned her attention back to Flin. "My name is Jorphy Bart. I speak for our leader, Maf, who will join us when he is able. We would assist the Faero, as was promised to Dharmoney. The Hides of Resgalar return, Archmage."

The woman bent to kneel on one leg, her clenched left hand striking her chest, followed by the members of the Hides, who all gave the ancient salute. Flin looked across the group, recognising the gifts and the strength present in several. This was a boon he had not expected, and it could make all the difference.

Goroth, however, was furious. He had stood and watched as the winged ghazrak had been destroyed by a strength that he had been assured did not, could not, exist. Grensor's error, again. Flin now had a store of Mages, obviously battle trained. He recognised the banner of Resgalar, viewing it across the huge field with an exercise of one of the basic skills all Mages were taught early in their training. Resgalar! Likud had assured him that he had destroyed the Academy and all of the trainees. Another failure!

He may need to bring to bear some of the norther gifted ones immediately, although they were not trained as he would wish. If necessary, he would use Likud as his attack hound and allow him to drain them of their power. However, he preferred to hope that they would be able to fight and so split the attention of Flin and the others. Still, there was no Marjory and it was unlikely that there would be any of the newcomers fit to fill the gap left by her loss.

And, of course, he had Ghaz-ti. Like most Kindred, the demon was vicious and existed only to destroy. Goroth would give it the chance to do so, but it would have to be given a good target. Goroth had several in mind but he could only choose one. He doubted Ghaz-ti could reach Flin and the Faero would be better targeted via the battle field. But there were many candidates for Ghaz-ti. Goroth turned away from the field deep in thought.

24. Battle Mage Returns

It was the early evening of the same day. The leaders of the Faero's army were standing at a slightly higher point where the field of battle could be seen.

"I think that demonstration may well force Goroth's hand," Jalor said pensively. "We can expect the next attack to come soon. I have no idea why Goroth waited this long."

"Probably trying to build the levels of fear in the army," Blaine replied. "The Hides would have been as big a surprise for Goroth as they were for us. It may force him to commit the gifted northers, and possibly himself and Likud."

"Well then, if that's the case, let's see if this thing wants to cooperate," Flin said to no-one in particular. He was referring to the Battle Mage staff, and ignored the sudden rustle and murmuring of the people who gathered behind him.

Jalor smiled gently. "You've not been able to wield it with effect so far, and nor has Jorphy Bart, even though she could sense its power. She appears to have much more complete war skills than you. It's as though the staff is resisting, as you said. Why would you try again? Perhaps it's time for plan B."

"Well," Flin said with a shrug. "She certainly is better suited and I thought for a moment that she was the one foretold to me who would take up the staff. But not so. It needs a true Battle Mage, I'm afraid."

"Then perhaps you should allow one to wield it, Archmage," said a voice from behind, one Flin never thought to hear again.

Slowly, Flin turned to stare at the speaker. Marjory stood straight and tall, looking Flin in the eye, smiling enigmatically as she surveyed the Mage. Trembling, Flin walked toward her, standing immediately in front of her and, ignoring all around, threw his arms around her and hugged her closely with tears streaming down his face.

Marjory cried and returned his embrace fiercely in return, the two holding tightly to the other for a space of time that felt like an eternity but that was all too brief. As they parted, Marjory visibly brought herself under control and, dashing away her tears, spoke gently to Flin.

"We will discuss why I did what I had to do," she said, as Flin also brushed away tears. "Meanwhile, it looks like we have a problem to deal with. And that's my job!"

Flin nodded to both statements and, with great ceremony held out the staff with both hands to Marjory. Jalor was interested to note that the milky stone was roiling faster than it had been, as though excited.

Then, as Marjory grasped the staff and Flin let go his hold, the stone flared into silvery brilliance, accompanied by a clear, sweet tone that all of the gifted could hear clearly and that reverberated across the field of battle. Goroth paused his planning of the second assault in confusion, unsure of what the tone presaged. At the same time the stone in the centre of Marjory's forehead also flared, a brilliant silver that cleared rapidly to settle into a gentle glow. The stone on the staff now glowed silver, with coruscations of white running through it occasionally.

Quite clearly Varna heard Fernis, Hollow Branch, declare, "Marjory has returned! The Battle Mage of Ennaris has returned!" Then, more gently, "The time has arrived Varna, for Dharmoney also."

Standing to attention, Varna said, "Admiral, Specialist Major Varna Barr reporting." She saluted.

Marjory smiled, formally returned the salute and said, "As you were. I'm an Admiral no longer, Varna. As you see, I've returned to a prior role. You have done well, I'm told, but now this is my task."

"Not alone, Admiral - Marjory, Battle Mage." Varna replied with certainty.

With a thought the white stone flared on Varna's forehead

Marjory glanced at the stone and, startled, looked up again to Varna. "Oh, my child! I knew you would be important but never dreamed ... The white stone? Is that...?"

"I am Dharmoney," Varna said simply as Marjory stared.

Marjory stared for a moment at Varna and then glanced at Flin. "Dharmoney! Any more surprises for me? I thought I'd been brought up to date but it seems not completely."

"Oh, one or two," said Flin, back to his old self. "I believe you would recall Jalor and Blaine? Blaine is the Defender. Jalor commands the Faero forces."

The two moved forward, stiffening to attention as one and saluted, holding it until Marjory had returned it. They both stood easy as she examined them and waited for her to speak. She gasped when she spied the swords slung to their waists, but more so the golden sword strapped to Blaine's back.

"Both of you, too? How is that possible?" Then she started laughing. "Halfgar! And I thought I was being so clever manipulating the bloodlines to get a team with the purest Ennaris blood as I could."

Flin started again. "Halfgar? What about him?"

"Ah, yes. Halfgar was - is - a Guardian. All that time we thought he was the oldest of the Guides he was a Guardian, guiding *us*, helping *us*, guarding *us*. Halfgar is Odruf."

On cue, a ball of light formed in front of the group. The bright light flared and cleared to show Halfgar ambling towards the group.

"So, reunion going well?" he asked, smiling. "Flin, you're looking old. The years have not been kind, it would appear!"

"Halfgar!" Flin trembled slightly as he regarded his old friend and companion. "All that time, you were with us and we never thought you were any more than the oldest of us. But why?"

"In truth, I *was* the oldest," he said reasonably. "As to why. Well, why do you think we call ourselves Guardians? And I'm afraid I need to break this up. It's time for this to end. The fleets have engaged and

Goroth and his minions are planning to wreak havoc on everyone and everything if they can. He's another who didn't believe," he said, with a sly smile at Flin. "He will now!

"We're not permitted to take part in this battle. We *are* allowed to make sure that this world is not destroyed, as we were permitted once before. We have been allowed greater leeway than we had in the past. The Nine are almost all present, as it was foretold."

"Nine?" Marjory looked around. "I count five with Flin and myself, Varna, Jalor and Blaine."

"Nay, for the sixth is and has always been the Faero of Ennaris, whose responsibility has ever been to protect as well as to oversee."

Halfgar gestured the young Faero forward, whose uncertainty was plain to see.

"Fear not, Faero of Ennaris," Odruf said in formal tones. "Know that you are the one to resolve the question when the time comes." Corm straightened as he was addressed, nodded to show he understood, or at least that he accepted the responsibility. "You will understand when the time is right," Odruf said, smiling in sympathy.

"So, that's six. And the seventh, eighth and ninth?" Jalor was beginning to suspect.

"The Eye is here," Halfgar said, gesturing to Andira and then addressing her. "Recall your lessons and you will prevail." He turned to Marjory.

"Two more, then." Jalor said.

"You have need of a champion, as was also foretold. One who surpasses all in feats of arms and skill while yet being bound to Ennaris."

Helt stood forward, leaning on her sword and still exhausted from her race across the field only a short time before.

"Nay, warrior princess, 'tis not your place at this time. Know that you have the honour and regard of the Guardians but this is not your battle." Odruf walked to the crowd of people watching intently and stood before Clay, hooded and wrapped in his heavy cloak. "Come forth, Champion."

Clay nodded and threw back the hood, then shrugged out of the cloak and handed it to one of the watchers. He was wearing the black tunic and heavy trousers of a Warrior of the Light, with the *Sunburst* insignia patches on each shoulder. Strapped around his waist was his belt with the tied down needler and blaster, one at each side. He stepped forward to join the group. Instinctively, both Jalor and Blaine came to attention once again, only to be waved to relax by Clay.

"No need for that Jalor, Blaine. Admiral, it's been a while. Reporting for duty, at last!"

"Clay," Marjory nodded as though it was a run of the mill meeting. "It's good to see you again."

"Well, I guess I lose my apprentice then," said Flin. "It probably is time, anyway." He sighed theatrically and turned to Odruf. "And now what happens? We are missing the ninth."

"The Protector has been named and will join when the time is right. For now, I think it's time the true Archmage joined us, don't you?"

Flin nodded and a green blur enveloped him. Varna saw a brilliant flare in Flin's aura and in a moment the old man was replaced by a slightly taller, much younger-looking version, clad in the brown tunic and breeches with a short cape trimmed in deep green. The Enchara, the great stone of green with the imprint of the Tree, was centred on his forehead, suspended from a silvery chain. The stone pulsed for a few seconds and settled to a steady muted glow.

"It is done!" Odruf declared.

25. Second Battle

The second battle largely went as Goroth planned, at least at the start.

He committed almost half of the remaining norther army, another ten thousand of them, and almost half of the remaining ghazrak. He was resigned to not having the easterners that Grensor had promised him. It was yet another failure of the aged Mage, but it would not matter. This was meant to strip most of the defenders away and leave the rest vulnerable.

There were a few changes to his original plan as a result of those five gifted ones appearing and then that strange tone. Something had happened, and he was taking no chances. Goroth ordered the norther gifted to be brought to the front and deployed behind the army, well clear of his oversight position in case they were attacked. He positioned Likud with them.

Goroth decided to deploy Ghaz-ti also, with a special target.

Watching from the Faero's pavilion with Marjory, Flin saw the norther forces start to move, with the body of three hundred ghazrak moving into formation behind them. Accompanying the ghazrak were a small number of Shadows, the first time any of them had taken the field. Jalor, watching with Flin, could not make out the detail as the Mage could. As Flin described what he was seeing, Jalor realised that this still was not the whole of Goroth's force. So, this would be a second attack intended to decimate defences with the third to finish the thing.

"This still is not the final battle," Jalor said to Flin. "From what the Rocs told us, there are many more ghazrak over there. And a large number of northers still. And we don't know where the regular army is. The Tang scouts reported that there were several thousand of them, and they won't be the rabble that we just faced."

"And according to Andira there is some sort of powerful demon also," Flin replied.

"And there are gifted moving into place behind the army," Marjory added from her place with Flin. "There aren't many of them, and none of them are first order Mages, but they may cause problems."

"Raglin and Ragnor, and Trabor, can you stand ready to provide shields?" Jalor asked, eyes half closed as he worked through the strategy for the coming battle. "I think we hold Marjory back for now. Clay, I think you become sort of a roving reserve if you can. Take command of the Guard, please."

The twins and Trabor nodded, and Clay smiled as he nodded also. Not long ago, Jalor had stood to attention when Clay made his identity know, but now he was the general, and in his element. He was, Clay thought, a good choice. Was this why Jalor was there? He was one of the Children but had also been named one of the Nine, but the Nine did not include a general. Shrugging mentally, Clay moved off the find the Guards and form them into a roving reserve.

Along the Faero's line the various forces made ready. The knights of Escar were fewer than before, even with multiple healers working their gifts. They tightened cinches on their hrss and mounted using steps designed for the purpose. The jungle Waslit with their nut-brown bodies glistened in the oil that each had applied to make gripping more difficult. They controlled their huge reptilian mounts easily, although the troops around them were not so sure. The urban Waslit and militia stood with Joplin and Maxnil at their front, slightly behind the front lines from where they could launch their javelins and then join the front line. The Faero's army stood behind various barriers and were ready to break out when needed. Archers with long bows waited further back. Many of them now carried Hunder-made arrow tips specially designed to target the ghazrak, with their bows reinforced by a new sort of flexible material that gave them more force.

The desert dwellers stood as a large group, uncertain as to their purpose in this company. Topil looked around before stalking to the Faero's pavilion and standing in front of Marjory. While there was a certain deference, the Battle Mage saw grim determination on his face.

"Topil?" she asked, smiling slightly as she recalled his challenge.

"You were presented to us by Morrig as the battle leader of the Tued," Topil said with anger resonating through his voice. "And yet with battle coming you are not with us. Do you forsake your role? Do I lead the Tued home again?"

Marjory stared with her eyes wide as Topil spoke. She had promised Morrig that she would be the battle leader. But she also had a responsibility to Flin and Ennaris as a whole. The desert people were not as numerous as the Faero's army but she knew that they would make a significant contribution. They also valued honour and commitment, as did she. She nodded to herself.

"Topil, I agreed to lead the Tued in the battle." Marjory turned to Jalor. "General, my place is with the Tued for this battle. You wish to hide my identity for a little longer, but I must fulfil my duty to them."

Jalor nodded. "Aye, Admiral," he said, and watched as Marjory gave Mavin Serra's slow smile. "Take your place."

Arrayed behind the main lines were three small groups of those from the Hides with battle skills. Jorphy Bart stood in the middle group. Instructions had been given. Their awe at having been instructed by Marjory, the Battle Mage of legend, had faded as they prepared for their tasks. The Hides' healers had been sent to the healing tents set up to deal with the injured, and the relatively few engineers were being given last-minute instructions from Trabor and the twins. Several others had joined Hunder's workshop to assist the blacksmith.

Corm had joined his own army, standing under the banner of the Faero and thereby making himself a target. Corm knew that would be the case. It was a measure of the man he had become, Jalor thought, that he accepted the responsibility and the reality of this role.

Aloft and circling over the Faero's forces were the four regular Roc battle wings. Two of the wings carried their riders in the new harnesses and one of the other wings had strange bulbous attachments slung beneath them. These latter were Blaine's devices, worked out with Hunder and Senasarra, the almost sentient sensor array that he and Jalor had encountered what seemed like a long time ago. The Rocs had their own instructions. Far above them, far enough that only other Rocs could see them, Ky-rel circled with her flight, watching.

In the middle distance the northers started their advance, if such it could be called. They were an undisciplined mass, relying more on numbers than skill to overwhelm their enemies. The ragtag army bellowed incoherently or shouted insults that were lost as they ran. Behind them loped the three hundred ghazrak as a ragged group.

From the small number of norther gifted came bolts of fire, arcing over the attacking force to land in front of the Faero's army. The twins and Trabor set their shields. Their energy levels were bolstered by the engineer Mages from the Hides. A second set of energy bolts were better targeted and much stronger as Likud took a hand. They were aimed at Corm and his Guard. The shields flared as the bolts fell on them, and the attacking energy was dissipated.

The northers were no more than fifty spans away when Almin Bor, who was injured but had been healed enough to partake in the battle, lifted and then dropped one arm. Almost two hundred bows released their shafts in an arc that ended amid the running norther army, followed by a second wave and then a third wave. Gaps appeared in the attacking force as enough shafts found their marks. The urban Waslit used the third wave as a signal to launch their first javelins, followed quickly by their second. More gaps appeared.

The charging army closed on the front line of the defenders, becoming even more ragged after running such a significant distance. The archers continued to pick off individuals. At a further signal from Almin Bor the archers broke off their barrage. They each drew from a second set of arrows, notched them and waited.

Corm nodded to a bugler standing by his side, who sounded a single tone on his horn. The defensive line split at four points and through each of the gaps thundered forty mounted soldiers, lances levelled. They met the line of advancing northers, charging through the front lines after impaling their chosen targets, after which they drew their swords and lashed out to left and right, maintaining their momentum as they did. A wave of energy bolts fell in the midst of the norther army. Although they were aimed at the light cavalry, the impacts killed and injured Faeronar cavalry, hrss and northers indiscriminately, tearing through bodies and throwing others tumbling through the air.

Corm nodded again and a second horn blast sent the cavalry, now almost through the charging army, speeding to the sides, away from the now approaching ghazrak. Further bolts of energy followed them and, while most missed their targets, the cavalry took more losses. Only two-thirds managed to make their way to the edges of the battleground.

The front of the norther force reached the defensive lines, charging into the line of lances and spears that were dug into the grassland at the last moment. Dozens, then hundreds more northers died, but still they charged forward, waving their rudely-made iron swords and farm implements inexpertly. Further spears were thrust through the line, accounting for even more of the attackers, but weight of numbers was forcing the defenders back, as had happened during the first battle.

From above came the awesome battle cry of the Rocs as the two mounted wings swept across the battle-field. The riders dealt out death as fast as they could operate their crossbows. Directly into the massed northers they fired, before soaring for the heights once again. Bolts of energy followed them. However, the norther gifted ones were unable to establish a suitable aim. The bolts landed in the attacking lines again as the Rocs made a second pass. More northers died.

Behind the mounted wings came the wing carrying those strange bulbous attachments. They split into two sections. The first section of Rocs swept across the attacking line, releasing their attachments as they did. The attachments were special bombs devised by Blaine, carrying explosives in a light-weight metal case and with simple and very basic impact fuses. The second section swung to pass over the ghazrak and released their bombs on them. Each bomb exploded and the case became a cloud of shrapnel. The bombs caused massive carnage among the northers, although they had been dropped towards the rear to protect the defenders from the shrapnel. The ghazrak withstood the shrapnel better, losing only thirty dead and with around the same number carrying various wounds.

With the bomb run done the Faero's army counter-attacked desperately, needing to deal with the northers before the ghazrak made it to their lines. Corm led the charge from the centre, so that the twins and Trabor struggled to maintain their shield above that part of the line. All three were wearying, even with the help of the Hides engineers, but then the bolts from Likud and the northers were much lower in intensity and strength as they were also becoming exhausted.

On the left flank, the desert fighters surged forward as Marjory led them in a direct charge into the right flank of the northers. The flashing scimitars of the desert people cut a swathe through the attackers, whose cruder weapons were far more unwieldy. Marjory, holding her twin Mage swords, flowed through the forms she had been taught such a long time ago, a slender sword in each hand. The black uniform of the Battle Mage glowed in the battle and she led the Tued, as she had promised to do, and they followed their battle leader. Deep into the flank of the northers the desert fighters tore a deep wound, before Marjory turned outward and the Tued mopped up the stragglers, those who were slower or more wearied from the sustained charge and so were at the back of the attacking force. From there she could see the ghazrak, who had most of their numbers intact and were now loping towards her. With a thought she reinforced the swords' blades and moved to meet them.

On the right flank the Waslit released their crawlers. In a flash the huge reptiles were on the northers, tearing and rending flesh in a frenzy. Standing on their scaled backs the Waslit fitted darts to their blowguns and with deadly accuracy sent poisoned death into the northers, time and again. Many of the Waslit died as they were unable to defend from the iron swords, but that only released their crawlers who turned berserker and charged into the remaining northers.

There were very few of the northers now and they died rapidly, but they were serving their purpose. Suddenly, from the centre of a knot of of the remaining norther attackers burst a strange figure, an old man wearing the remnants of a dirty grey tunic and sandals. His ragged pants were hacked off below the knees. His remaining iron-grey hair was wild, standing out like badly worn reed brushes. He charged through the defenders, throwing them aside with feats of strength that were completely unexpected for one looking like he did. Directly through the defenders he rushed, ignoring Corm, who was the logical target, and charged towards the small rise where Jalor stood with his small guard, surveying the field.

From the corner of his eye Jalor saw the commotion and turned in time to see the old man charge through the back of the defensive line. Trabor sent a bolt of energy at him but, to Jalor's astonishment, it hit and bounced off. Jalor's guard arranged themselves between the sole attacker and Jalor, while from one side Jalor saw Andira come running. The old man shouted a guttural challenge in a strange language. Above, a Roc shouted a challenge in reply and Jalor was shocked when the old man lifted a hand and a blast of red fire shot out and engulfed the Roc, incinerating it in an instant. Jalor now understood. This was the demon, and Andira would not arrive in time. The old man turned his attention on Jalor's guard and with a wave of his hand blew them aside, all four of them tumbling to form untidy heaps to left and right.

Jalor stood waiting, realising that sword play would not avail. He turned to bluff, hoping to gain time for Andira or one of the Mages to intervene. That proved to be of no use as the demon pointed one finger at Jalor and spoke a word, just as Andira skidded to a stop between them. Jalor felt a surge of some sort through his whole frame, then pain that coursed and twisted through him from head to toe. He could feel someone, probably Andira, engage the demon enough to reduce the force that had been delivered, but by then it was too late. Jalor wilted where he stood, collapsing. Even as he did so, he saw the ghazrak reach the defenders and launch into the exhausted lines of men and women. Despair overwhelmed him as the numbers of ghazrak began to take a grisly toll. It was the last sight that Jalor saw, as blackness closed in around him, and the world dwindled to nothing.

Andira stood over Jalor's body and faced the demon, recognising it as the sepoc she had sensed being released. This was a higher order Kindred of significant power, even though it had possessed an old man's body. That old man, of course, was a powerful Mage. Sepocs could only be summoned by someone with real power, so Dall had told her, and some sort of connection would be maintained. In the moment she faced the demon, Andira sought for the demon's link to its own universe but could find nothing. That meant that it had physically left its world, and its source of power. For it to maintain its strength it must have an alternate source.

"So, little girl-child, you wish to match strength with Ghaz-ti," the demon growled in a voice no Ennarisi could ever have. "Already you are too late for your so-called general, your Child of Ennaris." Ghaz-ti sneered as it flexed Grensor's arm and leg muscles. Flabby and weak as they were, they were growing smoother, larger and more firmly muscled as the Kindred fed its own power to them. "You will die. Better yet, I will take your body and when I am finished with it, I will give it to one of my followers from the Kindred. This body has interesting memories that I will digest and use when I am done with you."

A wheezy laugh was followed by a solid blast of yellow power directed at Andira's face. Without hesitation, Andira raised a shield as Dall had taught her, angling it so the energy hit it and dissipated into the air. Ghaz-ti growled again and sent a second and third blast after the first. Both were handled by Andira, although the second shoved her back slightly. Her heel came up against Jalor's leg, and Andira glanced down to see if Jalor breathed. It appeared not. A fourth slug of energy hit the shield, although it was not as powerful as before, and Andira straightened.

Andira, she heard Trabor's voice inside her head, *the demon has possessed Grensor. You must not allow it to use Grensor's gifts.*

She acknowledged the message and felt Trabor leave, returning to the defence. Trabor had merely confirmed that Grensor, the rebel Mage who created the ghazrak, had been possessed. She had been told that the ghazrak were modelled on the demons, but she now saw that they had not been replicated very well.

Another bolt reached her, slightly weaker still and easily deflected. She smiled, deliberately, looking to goad the demon into reacting rather than thinking. Dall had called them almost elemental, in that they reacted to the immediate more than they planned and considered.

"You weaken, demon," Andira said, taunting. "You have taken the body of an old man and must give it your own energy to maintain it. You have left your world and that makes you weaker still. You are unable to defeat me."

The last boast was given as a throw-away insult, diminishing Ghaz-ti's worth for all to hear. The demon was outraged that such as this would challenge it and renewed its attack.

"Bah, I have more power than you know," Ghaz-ti bellowed. "I do not need to link to the Kindred's universe as this body has its own tap into this world's energy and I can use that. Like this!"

Blast after blast was directed at Andira and she could feel her shield slipping. Her own control was shaking. One of the blasts was reflected into a small group of troops standing by to do whatever they could to help, and Andira moaned as they were literally blown apart. Her fault, she thought, because she could not hold this thing in check. The last of those blasts carried something else with it, something not of Ghaz-ti. Grensor, Andira realised. It was starting to use Grensor's own powers, possibly without realising it. Andira needed to end this or the demon would prevail.

"You start to fail, woman-child," Ghaz-ti said, gathering power from somewhere. "It is my time soon. I will take over this world and then this universe. Ah ha ha ha!"

Without realising it, Andira had moved into a crouch, the better to maintain her shield, to protect Jalor's body and to limit her own energy needs. She trembled as her shield absorbed blast after blast but, she realised in wonder, that tremble was not caused by fear. Rather, it was from anger at the thought of someone being stupid enough, venal enough, to allow a sepoc into this universe. Dall had prepared her well. Her momentary doubt was pushed aside. Now she stood and deliberately moved to the right, away from the front of the command tent, away from Jalor and the downed troops. Further away she moved, ignoring Ghaz-ti's taunts, as long as the creature followed her.

"Scared, little woman-child," Ghaz-ti taunted as it stamped after Andira. Both of them moved further away from the downed Jalor. "You have reason! I will draw your life force from you slowly, and savour every morsel as you die. I will suck your brain dry. I will give you agony such that you have never felt, and it will last forever."

Andira ignored the inconsistency of Ghaz-ti's taunts, as she now ignored the Kindred's energy bolts. She felt that she was far enough away from the command area, so she stopped moving away and stood perfectly still. She stared at Ghaz-ti, looking to find the link. It used Grensor's link to the world, Ghaz-ti had told her, so not the same sort of link through a medium into its own universe. In a flash, Andira realised it literally was a link to this world, one that Grensor had forged and so had some sort of dependence on Ennaris itself. With that insight, she narrowed her focus and saw it, the tendril of power that Ghaz-ti drew from Ennaris itself. Undoubtedly Grensor would have had other ways to maintain and build his power, but Ghaz-ti had not located them. Yet!

Ghaz-ti stopped advancing, slightly perplexed by the fact that Andira had stopped. Its innate arrogance led it to believe that Andira's fear had caused her to panic and freeze in place. Grensor's face shifted to a wolfish grin. Its eyes blazed a deep red. Andira dropped her shield.

Ghaz-ti roared in victory and rushed to cross the intervening space, shooting energy spikes at Andira. Andira reached out her right hand and, with a thought, created a sword of pure energy, as Dall had taught her, glowing softly. Her left hand now held a new shield, also of pure energy, square at the top and bottom and slightly curved to form a concave surface. The spikes flared as they impacted the shield, but this time Andira withstood them. Once again Andira sensed the use of more than the sepoc's own power. She had to end this.

Ghaz-ti was unable to check its charge. Grensor's body was proving to be less than capable physically, despite the reinforcement provided by the demon. Andira drew on her lessons, then drew on the energy forces that were all around her. She rolled to one side, the shield folding to cushion her. As Ghaz-ti charged past her, Andira swung her sword horizontally, slicing through both of Grensor's legs just below the knees. The glowing sword severed bone and tissue easily. Andira felt Grensor's connection to Ennaris snap. But that was not enough yet.

With a burst of power Andira surged from her roll and rose into the air, dragging Grensor's damaged body with her. Ghaz-ti roared and tried to reach Andira, but she held the Kindred away from her easily. Grensor's body contorted and twisted, its skin rolling and limbs contorting. In a paroxysm of rage, Ghaz-ti burst through the fragile Ennarisi skin, shredding and then shrugging it off. The demon was revealed, a sepoc in all its grisly glory, twisting and fighting to be released from the tight bands that Andira held firmly.

Its deep red head shook and rolled. The sharp-pointed horns in its head glowed and shot out tiny bursts of energy. Ghaz-ti roared again and tried to leap for Andira, but without effect. Andira floated well above the ground, holding the demon tightly at the same height, maintaining her hold over Ghaz-ti for all to see. The Kindred thrashed its limbs. The horned hoofs tried and failed to find a purchase so that it could launch at its tormentor.

The Kindred's rage changed to concern, and then fear. Ghaz-ti had destroyed Grensor's body, Andira had severed its source from Ennaris, and the Kindred had removed its own link to its universe. It could feel its power dwindling. With a loud bellow it unleashed a powerful blast of fiery energy, enveloping Andira. Ghaz-ti roared its victory before realising that the restraint had not lessened. The fire dwindled away to show Andira floating, unharmed.

Long enough, she decided. She allowed her shield to dissipate, and lifted her left hand. Ghaz-ti floated towards her. Its own energy levels were dropping disastrously. The thrashing limbs were slowing. It stared at Andira, looking for any sign of weakness that it could use to its advantage. It found none.

"Begone, demon!" Andira said quietly, pointing her glowing sword at the floating Kindred.

The sword extended, spearing through Ghaz-ti's chest and emerging from its back. The muted white glow of the sword flared into brilliance, engulfing Ghaz-ti, who bellowed a final challenge. A massive explosion came from the intense light, accompanied by a concussion that threw all near, except Andira, to the ground. The glow faded to reveal Andira once again holding the sword. The sword faded in turn, leaving Andira floating high above ground. She turned her focus on the battle where the Faero's army fought and died, and then to the group huddled over Jalor's body, and her heart constricted.

The ghazrak fell on the front line of the exhausted defenders, roaring and waving their heavy, misshapen swords. They slashed left and right. There was no thought of charging through the lines, although they may have succeeded in that had they mounted a determined effort. They wanted to kill, and these puny ones would be what they then fed on.

Above, five of the winged ghazrak squawked their own harsh challenge before swooping on the Faero's men. Corm seemed to be everywhere, encouraging his people, pushing into difficult spots to reinforce temporarily, intervening to save a life here or take one there. The standard of the Faero travelled with him and made him a travelling target, which Blaine recognised could be used to advantage, although he did not like it.

What he did like, though, was what Corm had become. He was a leader and, assuming he survived this, would be a good one, perhaps a great one. He inspired the troops to greater effort and helped to repel attack after attack. It helped that he was accompanied by Clay. The Champion of the Light, and Champion of Ennaris, carried a new sword made by Hunder of tempered steel melded with the lightweight alloy that had proved effective in Helt's armour, and the arrowheads used by the archers. Dressed in the Warrior blacks, he made it his job to keep Corm's back clear of the enemy, and was very effective.

Weight of numbers was against the defenders, though. Ghazrak were being killed but not fast enough. These constructed beings, whose only reason for existing was to destroy the Ennarisi, inspired fear and dismay in the defenders. That slowed reaction times and reduced the energy available to the troops. Not for nothing were they referred to as shock troops - the shock was in their animal ferocity as much as their appearance and the difficulty in killing them.

Blaine knew that Jalor had been targeted and injured by some sort of demon. He had been informed by a runner sent by Flin. He could only assume the right people were taking care of it. He and Jalor had worked out the strategy, and when Marjory had been revealed to be Grand Admiral Serra - that clicked a lot of things into place - she had made suggestions that improved the plan. It relied on timing, and that was to be managed by Jalor. Blaine and Marjory would have to deal with this.

The ghazrak were making inroads and the front line was about to wilt. Blaine made a signal to his mounted troops and dismounted. The small cavalry troop moved away on their designated mission, while Blaine strode forward. This was the point to apply a shock to the combatants, the first of two or three that Jalor had thought up. Blaine was all for psychological warfare, although he knew that he was not great at planning for it. Jalor excelled at it. Marjory made Jalor look like an amateur. *Although*, Blaine considered, *she's had much more time to practice it.*

Blaine reached the front line. Left and right the line was suffering. Men and women died or were severely injured. The knights were being battered as they became exhausted and their hrss did likewise. The Waslit and their creatures were darting in and out of the fighting, but there were far fewer of those than had started. Blaine saw two ghazrak coordinate their attack on one of the giant crawlers. One ghazrak acted as bait while the other killed the Waslit rider and then drove its huge sword into the crawler's head. That these ghazrak were able to plan and execute a coordinated attack like that gave Blaine cause for concern. If these were smarter ghazrak then they were even more trouble than their numbers suggested.

Marjory remained with the desert fighters. She stood out in the garb of a Battle Mage, and the all-white of the desert fighters made them easy to locate. They were taking losses also, being largely unarmoured and carrying mostly the scimitars as their primary weapon. They were more than capable fighters, Blaine knew, and some were exceptional, but against the ghazrak they would be far less effective.

He unlimbered the golden sword. Immediately he felt the surge of power. The warmth spread through him, making him preternaturally alert. Limbs and muscles were suffused with new strength. Temporary this may be, but it was why he had been granted this gift. With a giant leap, Blaine cleared the front line in a particularly vulnerable point. The golden armour enveloped him and gleamed in the clear early afternoon light. The great broadsword felt as light as a feather. It was an extension of Blaine himself. Blaine landed in a nest of ghazrak and became a blizzard of destruction. Broad swipes of the sword took off arms, legs and at least one head, but those swipes were done with an inhuman speed such that the ghazrak had no time to react. Seven were down and dead or ready to be finished by the defenders. Blaine moved!

The Golden Warrior became a blur. Blaine dashed into the mass of ghazrak who were trying to get at the front lines. Slashing, stabbing, swiping - he cut a swathe through the ghazrak in a diagonal path of destruction, taking pressure away from Corm and becoming the new focus of attention. That tactic worked and many - most - of the ghazrak turned from the front lines to chase after him. That relieved the front lines somewhat, although there remained enough ghazrak to deal with there that the relief was only brief.

Blaine took his fight further into the field away from the lines. It was time for part two of their plan.

26. Battle Mage of Ennaris

Goroth saw his plan unfolding as he expected it to. His Mage-enhanced sight allowing him to make out the detail at long range. The northers were cut down, of course, but enough of them managed to get to the lines to cause significant damage to the defenders. Even more, they exhausted the Faero's army. With Likud chafing amongst the norther gifted, and the relatively small number of gifted northers recovering from their exertions, he was relying on the ghazrak to do most of the damage.

He watched with satisfaction as Ghaz-ti broke free of the melee and rushed towards the hill on which Jalor - Goroth had learnt the enemy commander's name a short time ago - stood and watched. Goroth smiled and Likud cheered and laughed as the Child of Ennaris collapsed under the onslaught of the demon's energy shaft, but smile and cheer faltered as they recognised the power that challenged Ghaz-ti. A Hunter! Where did Flin find a Hunter? Grensor had assured Goroth that no gifts existed. Already the fool had been proven wrong by those six powers that had destroyed the Ghazrak after the first battle, although Goroth had been relieved that they had not taken the field this time. They must have been drained as his own gifted were. He had the beginnings of a plan to deal with them next time.

Switching his attention back and forth between Ghaz-ti and its assailant and the battle, Goroth was able to follow the Faero, Corm, and his small group as it moved around the battlefield, a seemingly unstoppable small force. He was impressed with what he saw, even though he had wanted the Faero removed from the battle as soon as possible. This was not the dissolute, primping simpleton that Grensor thought Corm to be, but a leader. But almost immediately the ghazrak hit the lines and the battle changed.

"Find the Rocs," Goroth called to Likud. "They made a few passes over the northers and then disappeared. Find out where they went."

Likud nodded, having forgotten the Rocs. He realised that it was unlike them to leave the battle like this. He cast his senses wide, but was unable to locate any sign of them. He frowned. That can't be right. He sharpened his focus further, examining the land around the grasslands battlefield. It took time but he seemed to sense something, as though there was some sort of cloak. He settled down to penetrate the cloak.

Meanwhile, Goroth noted that the front line looked like it would collapse soon. *A few hundred ghazrak will do that*, he thought. It would not be that easy, though, not if he knew Flin. He could see the Archmage's aura near the hill where Ghaz-ti fought the Hunter, and assumed Flin was trying to save Jalor. Knowing the Kindred as he did, Goroth thought that was unlikely to happen, even for one of Drewflin's immense strength and talent. The twins and Trabor were maintaining a shield of sorts over the defensive line, but that was all. It was a weak one, which demonstrated that they were tiring also.

Goroth's attention was drawn to the golden figure that appeared. What in all the hells was that? A thrill of apprehension went through Goroth as memories of the old battle legends came to him, along with lines from the Prophecy that Grensor had given him. *The defender clad in gold!* Goroth now understood the reference. The Defender was one of the oldest Ennarisi legends, going back an unimaginable distance to stories of a time when Ennaris was threatened by others who came from the stars to conquer. Like most Ennarisi, Goroth had not believed that it referred to a real person, but rather was more of an allegory for those who performed heroic deeds. Uneasily, Goroth thought of other legends, and again of the Prophecy. Was this Hunter the Eye?

The golden figure caused havoc in the ghazrak lines, although there remained more than two hundred of them. That should be enough. But then the golden one - the Defender - drew the bulk of the ghazrak away from the front lines. Goroth estimated only about a hundred remained behind, which the defenders should be able to deal with. Goroth was uneasy. There was a strategy in play that he could not quite understand, with revelations coming at intervals that were a concern.

This move, the Defender successfully making the ghazrak follow the shining golden threat, felt like one of them.

The timing was fortuitous. Andira held Ghaz-ti up for all to see, and the sight had mesmerised many, including many ghazrak. The Kindred was revealed in its menacing form at the last. Obviously, it was held in thrall by the woman who floated aloft with it. The brilliant light flashed as she ran Ghaz-ti through with her light sword, and the massive explosion told of the Kindred's destruction. With a cheer, the remaining defenders renewed their efforts, while the demoralised ghazrak remained stunned. More, they lost the disciplined control of the Kindred.

At the same time, Almin Bor released the archers once again, and flight after flight of arrows that had been strengthened by Hunder's forged alloys flew over the defensive lines and fell into the ghazrak that had been lured away by Blaine. These arrows were heavier to provide greater force, with heads fashioned from a similar alloy to that used for the armour and Clay's sword. Modelled on the arrows that Blaine had brought from *Starfire*, Hunder had created arrows and bolts that punched through the armour-like skin of the ghazrak torso when fired from the Faeronar long bow or the Roc-based cross-bows.

Having been released from the shield created by Trabor and the Hides gifted, the Rocs swept across the battle front and their riders released a withering wave of crossbow bolts. The battle wings then reached for the skies to avoid the winged ghazrak that moved in to attack. Not all were successful. The last batch of the winged ghazrak were the most advanced of them all, with innate abilities to anticipate attacks and determine when to wage their own offensives. The Roc battle wings suffered casualties to both Roc and rider.

The ghazrak were suffering losses, but they were creating chaos in the defensive lines. With Jalor down it fell to Blaine to direct the action for the defenders, but Blaine was involved in his own battles. Thus, it fell to Helt, as Blaine's designated second.

"Sound the second signal," she commanded.

The court trumpeter expected the command to come from Jalor or Corm, and hesitated. Helt glared at him.

"Are you deaf or stupid? I said sound the second signal."

"The signal is to be called by General Jalor or Captain Blaine," the trumpeter stuttered.

"Jalor is down and may be dead. Blaine is doing that golden thing," Helt shouted, unlimbering her great sword. "Sound the second signal or your successor will do it!"

The second signal sounded. It sounded a little strained to those with an ear for such things, but was close enough to be effective. Immediately the front line disengaged as much as they could, in some cases literally running backwards from the ghazrak that they had been attacking moments before. A noticeable gap opened in the lines, as the defenders had been left in no doubt that what came next would not differentiate between friend and foe.

Jorphy Bart had been growing increasingly frustrated. The battle-trained adepts of the Hides had been held from the field, behind the front lines, to allow for this moment, and she thought they were being held too long. At last, the signal sounded. Jorphy Bart glanced around her circle and then looked along the line to the other five battle adepts. Each had a circle. At her waved signal, the other five adepts stood. They linked to their circles, from whom they could draw power, and started to fling Mage fire bolts into the midst of the ghazrak that were attacking the dwindling front line. Bolt after bolt they flung, each of the bolts destroying ghazrak, whose numbers at the attacking line diminished swiftly.

Jorphy Bart switched her attention to the ghazrak attacking Blaine. Once the final ghazrak at the defensive line were accounted for, the five other battle adepts did likewise, although with reduced vigour as their circles were becoming exhausted.

The warnings about over-using the golden armour were coming home to Blaine. His movements were more than the ghazrak were able to handle still but, to him, they were becoming sluggish. He had to disengage or risk being caught. This was not yet the final battle, that much was obvious, and he would be needed given the losses the defenders had suffered. But he faced almost a hundred ghazrak still! So many had been killed already, but Blaine's energy levels were running down. The bolts coming from the Hides battle adepts were helping but he needed to get away.

Helt realised the situation and ordered the third signal. This time the trumpeter did not hesitate and sounded the call to action. Immediately, the defenders, the relatively few who remained able to fight, split and the knights charged through the lines. As they cleared the line of defenders the charging knights formed two lines, less than ten paces apart. Fifty paces from the milling ghazrak both lines lowered their lances, the tips of which were reinforced with the new steel and alloy. The sound of the clash of the lances against ghazrak reverberated across the field. The charging hrss from the second line trampled the first group of fallen ghazrak while more of the creatures were skewered. The charge was not without loss, and of the hundred knights deployed more than thirty had fallen by the time the charge was done. But almost a third of the remaining ghazrak were killed or wounded badly enough to be out of the fight.

The jungle Waslit, having recovered sufficiently from their earlier exertions but with markedly fewer remaining to take part in the battle, targeted the remaining ghazrak with their huge crawlers. However, there were too few of them to kill all, and as the battle proceeded cavalry, jungle and urban Waslit and Faeronar suffered extensive casualties. Blaine continued to battle through the ghazrak ranks. His strength was waning. His reactions were slowing. His energy levels waned alarmingly.

The Hides sought to re-engage but their efforts were reduced in strength as their teams literally ran out of available energy to share.

Helt, watching from the hill where Jalor had fallen, was about to order the remainder of the Faero's troops to help Blaine when the desert fighters swarmed from their own battle front and descended on the ghazrak. Shifting, spinning, dancing, the desert fighters showed the skills they had developed over many cycles but rarely used in battle, their scimitars found gaps in the armour bred into the ghazrak. Led by Marjory bearing her twin Mage swords, the desert people slashed and stabbed their way into the midst of the ghazrak.

Finally, Marjory reached Blaine, and stood with the exhausted Warrior as his golden armour retracted. The desert fighters continued to struggle against the ghazrak, striking and then flitting away. From the skies two of the Roc wings returned to the fray, their crossbows twanging as they sent bolt after bolt into the ghazrak, although their efforts were hampered by the need to avoid causing harm to the Faero's forces and his allies.

The final ghazrak was dispatched. Blaine dropped to the ground. All of his energy was exhausted. By his side now stood Clay and Varna with sword and extended battle staff in hand, having fought their way to the Warrior. Both were covered in multi-coloured gore from ghazrak and defenders. Both were nearly exhausted.

But a cry rang out from the command hill and Marjory turned to see what looked like a hundred more ghazrak storming across the battle field. Looking around, Marjory saw there was little to stop the new force, even though a small part of Goroth's remaining force. There was only one answer.

"Enough," Marjory said. "This ends now."

She reached down to remove the nub of the staff that had been attached to her belt while the battle raged in more conventional ways. She stalked from the defensive lines towards the onrushing ghazrak. A panicked call to return to the line was met with a look that caused the call to fade out.

Finally, she decided that she was far enough from the lines to ensure that the remaining defenders were not damaged. With a thought the staff was extended to its full length. The milky white stone at the top of the staff was quiescent, only roiling mildly. She waited until the first ghazrak were forty paces away, and then unleashed the power of the Battle Mage of Ennaris.

Five, ten, twenty, fifty bolts of Mage fire shot from the staff that now floated free, or from the silver stone on Marjory's forehead, or from Marjory's hands. The front ranks of the onrushing ghazrak were incinerated, and the rest slowed their charge. Half the remaining ghazrak were felled by the Rocs and their riders' crossbow bolts as they swept across the field once again. But Marjory was not prepared to wait for any other forces to attend. In a moment, she reduced the staff to the short nub and attached it to her belt. With another thought she shot into the space above the ghazrak and sent bolt after bolt into them. All were destroyed.

Still aloft, Marjory lifted herself higher, detaching the staff and extending it once again. Facing Goroth across the battle field, she lifted the battle staff high. The stone flared star-bright. A silver glow stretched across the entire field for the space of ten heartbeats before fading. And Marjory announced herself.

"I am Marjory nar Drewflin, Battle Mage of Ennaris. Surrender and you will not be mistreated. Continue this fight and you will be obliterated!"

27. Allies

General Morsen was having a bad day. The day before he had led the regular army of the twin kingdoms away from the main battle field, as the great lord Goroth had directed. He was about to turn back to add his troops to the shock wave that would be the ghazrak attacking the Faero's lines. The plan was that his smaller force of regulars would attack from behind the lines while the massive irregular force and ghazrak attacked from the front. That required him to go in a large loop. Somehow, however, his scouts had become disoriented in the endless grass and led them away from their target rather than around behind it. Now they were trying to make their way back. Morsen feared that he would not be there to play his role. Worse, he would not be able to emerge with glory to ensure that he had a favoured position when the great lord Goroth was victorious.

His four scouts had returned only a short time ago and immediately fell into an argument about just where they were and in which direction they should go. Morsen's temper was short already, and this argument added fuel to the fire. Aware that his whole army was watching, Morsen stalked to the knot of scouts, whose argument subsided as he approached.

"Where are we?" he growled. When there was no reply forthcoming, he pointed to one and continued in a voice suffused with anger. "Jursik, we're meant to be with the great lord Goroth now. It's likely that we're missing the decisive battle. It's likely that several of us will not survive the aftermath of missing the battle. So, one more time. Where are we?"

"Sir, I believe we're in the centre of the grasslands and now about a half day away from the battle field," Jursik replied, glaring at his fellow scouts. "We've been moving away from the battle field for the last half day instead of back towards it."

"How?" Morsen could feel his temper fraying, slipping the tight control he was exercising.

"We followed a meandering path to avoid deep gullies and dry watercourses," Jursik said. "In taking that route we became disoriented. When we came to the point to turn back towards the battle lines, I believe that we turned back on our previous path. Worse, the trodden area that we crossed some time back was our own path."

"So, you have taken us across our previous line of march and didn't notice?" Morsen's voice was raised now, his words clipped as his anger broke through.

"Yes, sir," Jursik replied in a low voice. "We thought it must have indicated a well-travelled area and thought no more of it."

The five men stood for a moment. The general glared at the scouts who all found something else to look at. Finally, Morsen ended the stalemate.

"Where do we go?" he demanded. "Remember that your life depends on this answer."

"In that direction, sir," Jursik replied, pointing back in the direction from which the army had just come.

Jursik glared again before turning back to his command group. In frustration he looked up to the sky to entreat the cosmos for an answer. That was when he saw the Roc.

Jel-nar soared through the warm air that lifted off the grasslands. His flight of two were a forward scout for the two wings of the Alnar-kun led by Hel-nor. They had been watching what looked like an army wandering around the grasslands for most of the morning. They appeared to be moving away from the site of battle, and yet Jel-nar had seen the standard of the norther kingdoms. He had no idea why they were there.

After discussing it for some time, the two Rocs could only assume that they were lost, especially after they crossed their own back trail. Jel-nar then sent Kro-mel to report to Hel-nor and the Protector while he maintained a watch.

On a whim he rose higher, so that he could see further. In the middle distance, riding along a large, shallow fold in the ground that hid them from view but also hid the norther army from their view, was a large number of hrssmen. Many carried double, it appeared. They were heading arrow-straight for the battle site and were moving quickly. Jel-nar considered options even as he watched a single rider crest a small rise and head towards the tight column. These would be the Clans that had destroyed the easterners. Perhaps they could be brought into action against these northers, also. Jel-nar dipped his right wing and turned away from the norther army.

Ferelas had been musing on the recent encounter and the impact of the Rocs on the outcome. It had been a battle to remember as the easterners were destroyed. Who knew? Perhaps he would meet another Roc after the battle toward which they rode. The Clans of the grasslands all wanted to play their part and were anxious that they did not miss it. A shout brought Ferelas back to the present. One of the scouts was returning at pace, which could only mean that there was a problem.

"Norther army!" the scout shouted as he drew rein. "That way. About twelve rods."

He started to point to the east when a huge shadow swept overhead, followed by a cloud of dust and grass, as Jel-nar landed close to the small knot of riders that had formed. The entire column sat straighter in their saddles as the Roc swept his gaze along the column before settling on Horint, who stood beside Ferelas. This was the one who spoke with Hel-nor. Horint walked to meet Jel-nar and held out a single hand as he had been taught. The Roc bobbed his head so Horint could rest his hand on the great curved beak.

"I am Horint, acolyte of Lak," Horint said aloud.

"*I am called Jel-nar,*" the Roc replied through the link with Horint. "*I have come to inform you of a norther army to your east side.*"

"Our scout has just returned with the news," Horint said. "But I thank you for the warning."

"*Not a warning, Horint acolyte of Lak,*" Jel-nar returned. "*My flight mate goes to bring Hel-nor's battle wings of the Alnar-kun. I thought of our recent joint battle with the easterners. I thought you may wish to join with us once again.*"

Horint thought he could detect anticipation from Jel-nar. He turned back to the watching group.

"Ferelas, Jel-nar invites us to join with the battle wing to attack the northers. What say you?"

Ferelas glanced around the small group and then beyond to the riders awaiting their orders. Many carried double, of course, as they had the full force of the ice men riding with them. The small group of Junda had acquitted themselves well, and perhaps this larger group could serve the same purpose. He turned to Xymin, who had joined the group and was staring at Jel-nar, entranced.

"Xymin, are your Junda-lar prepared to join with us and our Roc friends once again?"

Xymin tore his gaze away from the Roc and nodded. "That we are," he replied. "Only a small number of our full troop have been blooded, however."

"That will change," Ferelas said, before turning back to Horint with a hard grin. "We will join with our Roc allies."

Horint passed the message back to Jel-nar.

"*The wings come,*" Jel-nar said after a moment. "*I have informed the wing leader and he has agreed. He suggests a different tactic.*"

Morsen swung around at the shout. His gaze swept higher to follow the pointing finger and he saw the two flights of Rocs soaring high above. He lost count twice before giving it up and settled for an estimate of around forty of the huge birds. He had seen what only a few could do to the winged ghazrak. What could that many do to his troops?

"Mount up, form into defensive positions," Morsen shouted.

His men stared for a moment before his order was repeated through the ranks. The small cavalry troop swung into their saddles and settled themselves, while the regular troops hustled into their formations. Morsen's problem was that they faced a potential enemy from the air, so which way did the formations face?

Another shout and another pointed finger. In the distance there was a dust cloud that appeared to have come from nothing. A third shout and pointing in the opposite direction. Another dust cloud! What was happening? Morsen thought of the Clans. Being caught out of position when facing the Clans had always been his chief fear. Perhaps it was coming to pass. Oddly, the dust clouds appeared to be staying the same distance from Morsen and his army. Now a fourth shout, this time pointing back towards what Morsen thought should be their true path. He pulled his eye-glass from its sheath and held it to his eye. In the distance there now stood a line of men. No, Morsen corrected himself, there were two or three lines. So, a defensive formation, maybe three or four hundred men only. He worked through his options furiously.

The small force stood between his army and the main battle field, he was sure. The two dust clouds remained almost stationary, for what reason he could not fathom. Perhaps there was a threat there and perhaps not. The two flights of the great birds were a definite threat, no matter which direction he moved. Or, indeed, if he stayed in this camp. He also needed to get to the battle ground. Should Goroth be victorious, and every indication was that he would be, then Morsen needed to be by his side when victory was won. He made his decision.

A short conference with his sub-commanders was followed by a flurry of orders. The cavalry troop formed their twin lines and rode away to the south to swing around and flank the smaller opposing force. At the same time the infantry separated into their three columns and turned to face the standing enemy. With a nervous glance to the skies - were those damned birds lower? - Morsen gave the order to march.

Xymin had been watching the norther army for some time. All had gone as Hel-nor and Ferelas had predicted. The small cavalry force may have had some success had they ridden to attack the Junda-lar where they stood, but they probably would have been destroyed completely. Logically, then, they would be the flankers, either north or south. South it was. That meant the main army of more than three thousand trained men would be directed at them. Ferelas had been sure that the northers would not want to confront the Clans, which the norther commander would assume was what was causing the large dust clouds. It seemed he was proven right. Xymin looked left and then right. All of the markers were in their right positions. Not long now! Xymin turned to the one chosen to raise the standard and nodded.

Morsen's confidence was growing. His troops were making good time. Away to the south, his cavalry would be starting their turn. This was a manoeuvre that they had practiced many times. He took another look through his glass and stared. Flying above the heads of the enemy troops was a flag, probably held by one of them. It was red with a design on it. With a thrill he realised that it was the benighted Faero's standard. So, he would be engaging the true enemy after all. At just the right moment, a shouted command caused the three columns to increase their tempo of march and bunch slightly. The centre column would assault the centre of the defensive line while the other columns would turn the defenders' flanks and force them into a progressively smaller formation. The cavalry would complete their flanking move and attack from the rear.

Xymin ordered the pre-arranged signal to be given. The Faero's standard was waved back and forth repeatedly. At the same time the remaining Junda-lar, who had been crouched in a shallow depression, rose to take their places in the defensive line. The northers now faced nearly a thousand men and women.

Morsen saw the standard waving. His heart sank when the hidden Junda-lar stood, and he turned. The dust clouds were gone. Unknown to Morsen, the six Clansmen who had been tasked by Ferelas to create the dust clouds had dropped the bunched lariats that they had dragged behind themselves as soon as the main norther army had started to move. Now, half of the Clans riders approached the tail of the norther central column. To the south Morsen heard screams and clashes of swords. The cavalry! Morsen swivelled his head to the north where a new dust cloud had appeared, but this one was coming closer. Dreading what he would see, Morsen turned behind and looked up. As he did, he saw the two wings of Rocs swing into formation and start their descent.

“Attack!” Morsen shouted, waving his sword. “Attack!”

It was a choice of attack and die or defend and die, Morsen thought. So, attack it would be. The men started to pick up their pace and the norther army became strung out as the faster runners moved ahead.

The north-most Clansmen reached the norther lines first. Javelins were thrown into the norther ranks, creating instant chaos. Men were impaled or tripped over those who had been impaled, or sought to avoid incoming javelins and collided with their fellows. The attack run became a ragged stampede towards the Junda-lar. Now the Clansmen who had decimated the norther cavalry as it swung to the south added their own javelins to the confusion. Casualties mounted. The Clansmen swung through the norther column and then returned with their swords and knives, darting into the mass of fleeing men and then out again. Finally, there came the dreaded cry from above as the two battle wings of the Alnar-kun swept overhead. The men and women strapped to their riding harnesses chose their targets and fired their crossbows. Maf, riding Hel-nor, held his staff high and a brilliant white light flared forth, followed by bolts of Mage fire that reached out for their targets. Behind Maf came his fellow Hide Mages, all using their own gifts to cause mayhem and destruction, and the non-gifted using their crossbows to devastating effect. Individual Rocs extended their great clawed legs and wrenched unlucky northers from the ground, lifting them high as the flights soared up at the end of their attack run and dropping them onto their running comrades.

The Clansmen came around for another run into the body of the fleeing norther army as the first elements reached the Junda-lar line. They met a nest of spears. Those who had been in the first bloody battle against the easterners held the centre, while the unblooded were to left and right, and formed the bulk of the icemen. Gone was Morsen's grand strategy of the centre delivering a decisive blow while the flanks swung in a pincer.

Xymin, following Jalor's advice, stood back to better see the battle. The northers may have lost discipline but they remained trained soldiers with soldiers' weapons. The first ranks of the Junda-lar shuddered as the northers collided with them. Spears were dropped after doing as much damage as possible and the fight became one of swords and knives. Xymin watched with a dry mouth as his friends and fellows stood against the onslaught. Many fell. Some relief came as the Rocs swooped back into the fray, this time coming from behind the Junda-lar line. Crossbows fired and were recharged to be fired again. Several of the Alnar-kun had their own javelins and these were thrown into the melee also.

Xymin turned to the standard bearer and ordered the signal blown. A mournful call rose as the standard bearer blew into his short bone horn. The two flanks of the Junda-lar now moved into their own pincer formation and swung into the flanks of the northers. The Clansmen drove the survivors forward now, and norther numbers dwindled rapidly. Finally, the Clansmen met the Junda-lar line. The noise of sword clashes died away, to be replaced by moans and cries from both sides. Xymin moved from where he stood and joined Ferelas as he dismounted. The Clansmen battle leader, like all of the riders, was covered in blood and gore and dust and dirt. Almost all carried injuries of some kind, as did many of the Junda-lar. Many had fallen from the ranks of both, for these had not been a rabble as the easterners were, despite their panic.

The Rocs landed a short distance away and Maf leaped from Hel-nor. As the Alnar-kun riders all went about the grisly task of recovering as many of the spent crossbow bolts as they could, he strode to where Xymin and Ferelas stood. Horint reached the small group at the same time.

All four stood looking out over the field of battle. In the distance, a single hrss wandered aimlessly, for Morsen and his senior officers had been early targets - they stood out as the only three with hrss among the foot troops. Where the other two hrss were was uncertain. The Clansmen went about their equally grisly task and dispatched wounded northers efficiently. This time Xymin was able to look on the scene more dispassionately.

"Hel-nor informs me that healers and repeaters come," Maf said into the silence. "Gather your wounded and we will heal as many as we can."

"The final battle awaits still," Horint said. "We have many dead and injured among both the Clans and the Junda-lar, however."

"The battle has begun," Maf replied, tilting his head in a listening posture. "The Alnar-kun will join our fellows shortly. Hel-nor reports that the Defender is in the field, as is the Archmage." He smiled and continued with momentary pride. "The Hides have joined the battle and destroyed winged ghazrak. There are, however, many more ghazrak remaining. A demon has struck down the Faero's general."

"Jalor? Dead?" Xymin asked in horror. "He's one of the Children. How can he die?"

"I know not that he's dead," Maf replied, "only that he's been struck down. Ah! The Eye has dealt with the demon."

"The Eye?" Horint exclaimed. "The Nine have gathered. Your place is with them, Protector."

"Aye," Maf replied. "We will go soon. It seems the second battle has not gone as the Faero's forces had hoped, but the northers have lost many."

In the distance, too far away for ordinary men and women to see, came a series of many sharp blasts. Maf's head jerked up, for he recognised that sound. It was the blasts of a powerful Battle Mage unleashing full power. Then came the most unexpected of announcements, rolling across the grassy plans.

"I am Marjory nar Drewflin, Battle Mage of Ennaris. Surrender and you will not be mistreated. Continue this fight and you will be obliterated!"

"Marjory!" Horint exclaimed.

"Battle Mage!" Xymin said.

Both looked at Maf, however, for the Protector had gone pale. Helnor squawked in concern as shock gripped his rider. Maf finally worked through his shock to exclaim a single word.

"Mother!"

28. Sunburst

"Admiral, *Starfire* reports taking damage," Rork reported in a flat voice.

"How bad?"

"They're defending the planet from the main weapon on the enemy dreadnought. Colonel Kiri describes it as a planet buster. *Qorv* has already destroyed *Freekam*, *Grestil*, *Musar* and *Truben*. Apparently, the latter two placed themselves in the way of the beam to protect the planet." Rork looked up. "Both ships report many casualties, even though the captains largely evacuated the ships beforehand."

"How far away are we?"

"We will come from behind the moon in thirty seconds. Admiral, we're being cloaked somehow, probably by the moon's installations. I have no idea how."

"Can you drop the cloak, Mr Rork?" Jord asked evenly.

"I don't think we need to do that, sir. The cloaking device is interfaced to us - again, no idea how - and it's preparing to drop the cloak at the same time." He took a moment to look at Jord. "We really need to meet whoever built this," he said.

Jord just nodded in response. "Kurzil, we will emerge from some sort of cloak in a few seconds. On my command I want Hammer and Shield to target the Empire cruisers and frigates."

"Both squadrons, Admiral?"

"Both squadrons. *Starfire* and her ships are suffering, so let's give them cover."

"Aye, Admiral. Ready when you are."

"Five seconds, Admiral," Rork reported.

"Weapons status?"

"All weapons on-line, Admiral," came the reply. "Admiral, we have primary, secondary and, ah, tertiary power on line."

"Tertiary?" Jord said. "Never mind! Later! Target the dreadnought as soon as we get a sight of it. Weapons are clear."

"Cloak dropping, Admiral," Rork said. "They can see us."

Jord nodded once again. "Hammer and Shield, go!"

On the bridge of *Starfire,* Denton Bard was watching the Empire ship as it positioned itself once again to fire whatever that beam weapon was on the planet below. The two Union cruisers *Musar* and *Truben* drifted to port and starboard, dead in space and breaking up in slow motion. They had intercepted the beam before it could impact the planet but at huge cost. And now it was *Starfire's* turn. All weapons were firing at the Empire flagship but it seemed to absorb the damage, as could *Starfire* if it had room to move, Bard mused.

"Admiral, we have a ship emerging from some sort of cloak. It's coming from the dark side of the moon." Ensign Porlis on the sensor station was trying to emulate Rork and almost managed to sound detached, but the slight break in his voice told a different story.

Kiri was staring at her monitor. "Admiral?" she called. "Admiral, the signature of the ship..."

"*Starfire*, *Starfire*, stand clear of *Qorv*. I repeat, stand clear," came the voice of Jord. "*Starfire*, this is *Sunburst*, stand clear."

"...it's *Sunburst*!" Kiri finished.

"Helm, take us down. Hard to port. Weapons, select your targets away from *Qorv*," Bard said without a moment's hesitation. "We'll leave it to our big sister." He smiled grimly. "*Sunburst*, he's all yours. I hope that old scow can handle it."

"Affirmative, *Starfire*, handling it now," Jord replied drily.

The monitors displayed the enormous ship moving sharply into the battle zone, with a swarm of fighters accelerating to join battle with the Empire fighters and fleet.

"Oh my! *Sunburst's* weapons are, um, well ...," the ensign stuttered to a halt.

"Well, what are they?" Kiri asked irritably.

"They're impossible!" the ensign said. "Just impossible! Sir!"

"Impossible how?"

"Railguns. Multiple huge railguns. But they're only theory at that size," the ensign said. "Um, on screen now, maximum magnification."

On *Sunburst,* the newly upgraded weaponry was deployed fully. Large sections of the hull retracted and the muzzles of six enormous weapons, looking like cannons from ancient water-borne ships, poked their noses through the gun-ports, forming a ring around the blunt nose where a main energy weapon was located. All weapons oriented like no old-world cannons could ever do, as did the huge array of defensive railguns studded along the flanks and the upper and lower surfaces.

Starfire hustled to get out of the way, while still remaining between *Qorv* and the planet.

"*Qorv's* weapons are powered, Admiral. They're preparing to fire again," Kiri called urgently.

"*Sunburst* is firing," Porlis said, almost in a whisper.

A blizzard of metal and composites leapt from the muzzles of the huge railguns as well as the small ones, charged bullets that were relatively light individually but were accelerated massively. They developed enormous kinetic energy as they were spat from the guns and sped on their way. And, impossibly, the railguns kept firing, without pause as the tertiary power system bolstered the usual secondary power plant. Wave after wave of huge charged bullets crossed the distance between *Sunburst* and *Qorv.*

As the first bullets reached the mid-way point, *Fendaristil* decloaked above *Qorv* and fired burst after burst of the strange plasma weapon. The defensive shields of the Empire flagship sputtered out where the plasma bursts impacted. It was only moments later that the leading edge of the metal hail reached *Qorv's* remaining shields and half a moment later the shields collapsed under the combined plasma and railgun bombardment. *Qorv* was shredded in slow motion.

At the same time, *Sunburst* fired bank after bank of missiles. Most were targeted at *Qorv*, but a significant minority were sent towards other vessels. The missiles winked out as they micro-jumped, re-appearing much closer to their targets.

The railgun bullets discharged their accumulated energy in wave after wave of impacts against *Qorv's* massively reinforced hull, and the thick alloy plating was battered away. External weapons were destroyed as kinetic bullets ripped through their mountings. External pods were destroyed, causing the loss of sensors and targeting ports, so that *Qorv* was partly blinded. Stabilising nodules were perforated and *Qorv* started to roll. The missiles arrived and added their destructive force as they impacted along the length of the dreadnought. The force of the railgun bombardment did not abate.

Bard was stunned at the energy being expended, for *Sunburst's* railguns continued to fire. He was struggling to understand. While railguns had been invented long before, their limitation at ship size was the power requirement and the fact that any gun would have to pause and recharge. The recharge period became longer and longer as time passed. Even *Starfire's* advanced weapon suffered from that limitation. That problem appeared to have been solved on *Sunburst*.

"Admiral, *Qorv* is firing!" Kiri called.

And so it was, but it had lost stability controls and now faced away from Ennaris and the energy beam, a solid shaft, lanced from the ship's belly. But, rather than destroy the planet, the beam cut through three Empire ships that had been racing to *Qorv's* aid. The beam died quickly but the three ships had been sliced open and were rocked by explosions that were eerily silent in the vacuum of space.

Qorv lost its first massive armour plate as the weight of bullets from the railguns finally took its toll. A second plate soon followed as the missiles arrived. The plates torn from the hull looked more like sheets of paper that had been nibbled by rodents than the thick reinforced alloy panels that they had been. The bullets from *Sunburst's* railguns could now make their way into the ship. *Qorv* was being destroyed from the inside now. The pellets charged through the initial breaches and others that followed. They decimating anything and everything they encountered.

Across the back of *Qorv* sped *Fendaristil*, firing the strange plasma bursts that now chewed through the exposed skin of the dreadnought before burning through the vessel's interior.

Sunburst stopped firing. The last bullets were like the edge of a curtain being draped over *Qorv*, ending the job. *Qorv* drifted with the force of the strikes, showing no energy signature at all.

On *Sunburst*, the small bridge staff stared in shock at the destruction visited on their enemy. Jord was the first to recover.

"Rork, keep a track of the debris and let me know if it gets in the way. Where are the fighters?"

The fighters had been busy. Both squadrons had sprinted ahead of *Sunburst*, spreading out into the standard Union form of an attack formation. Their targets were the remaining cruiser class vessels, each of which had a screen of fighters that leapt towards the oncoming Union vessels. The Empire ships were no match for the Ennarisi fighters, either in speed or weaponry, but they were in the way and had to be dealt with.

"Hammer and Shield, weapons clear," Squadron Captain Kurzil said in a deliberately matter-of-fact voice. "Break into flights. We punch through the screen and go for the cruisers and then the frigates. Don't forget these aren't the boats your mommas flew. They probably bite harder when you screw up also."

Each of the squadrons divided into flights of five fighters. Each flight closed up and formed a diamond pattern with one ship in the centre, a standard Union attack pattern. They laid down a withering fire as they approached the Empire fighters. The first flight to open fire found that their weapons were far more powerful than expected and thus their range was longer. The pilots were not slow to realise that fact and all flights opened fire well before the Empire fighters could close to their own weapons range. The sharp energy bursts reached across the diminishing distances and fighter after fighter from the Empire fleet was destroyed. The Union fighters burst through the defensive screen with only two stingers lost to lucky shots. As the remaining Empire fighters scrambled to turn and chase, the Union fighters approached the two remaining cruisers. Each of those ships responded with a hail of rail-gun pellets, followed by point-defence energy blasts as the small railguns recharged.

The two squadrons split apart like a cloud of hornets as they tried to dodge the kinetic pellets and the blaster shots. Five didn't make it. Squadron Captain Horwen was one who flew past the cloud of railgun pellets only to be bracketed by blaster fire. Her fighter disintegrated. Smoothly, the four remaining members of her flight reconfigured into a tighter diamond and pressed the attack. Another flight lost two, while two flights in Hammer were reduced to four members. As they moved closer the defensive fire became more intense and the squadrons suffered greater losses.

In Andar-9, Grechsly snarled as he saw his left side wingman destroyed. Instinctively he gripped the control stick harder and tried to jink to avoid what he could not see or react to in time.

"*Grechsly, let go of the control stick,*" the ship AI said.

"What?" Grechsly yelled. "Not now! I'm busy!"

"*You will be dead if you do not,*" the ship replied. "*This is my job.*"

"You can deal with all of this?" Grechsly asked, quieter.

"*It is my function. You will have to initiate the attack, though.*"

"Damn!" Grechsly thought hard as he dodged and weaved without knowing if it achieved anything. He could see the squadron had been reduced by about one-fifth and they still were too far to open fire. What the hell! "Okay, the ship is yours."

The tactical display on the dash lit up showing the targets, the Union fighters and the defenders who had swung around and were pursuing, and through it all were the clouds of pellets ejected by the enemy railguns and the bursts of energy fire.

"*Energy fire pattern established,*" Andar-9 said. "*Would you like me to manage the vectors of the squadron?*"

"You can do that?" Grechsly asked as his ship slipped sideways and he saw a burst to the right, exactly where he would have been.

"*Yes, I can handle up to one hundred vessels.*"

"Okay then." Grechsly thought fast then pressed a stud. "Kurzil, we're getting smashed here. My AI thinks it can help us but it needs to take control of the ships."

"What?" Kurzil grunted as he swung his fighter in a tight loop without knowing if it was effective or not. He grimaced as two fighters exploded to left and right. Well, they were supposed to be advanced.

"Okay," he replied, "take it."

Andar-9 did not wait for Grechsly. Immediately the control systems of every remaining fighter were slaved to Andar-9. On *Sunburst*, as *Qorv* lost its fight to survive, Jord watched his fighters get pummelled and prepared to go after them to attack the larger ships remaining. Suddenly, the fighters reconfigured their approach to both ships. Each squadron swung wide apart so the railgun bursts passed harmlessly between them then swung back as the energy bursts filled the gaps and the railguns recharged. But now the attackers were dodging the bursts, flying around them. The fighters formed into two wide cones, with a single fighter at the point of each and as Jord watched the cones reached their targets.

"*All ships,*" Andar-9's AI transmitted. "*Weapons have been configured for offence. Targets selected. Execute!*"

The pilots saw that their almost familiar controls display a new icon. The weapons systems now showed a brilliant blue readiness icon where they would usually show green. Without any hesitation, the pilots pressed the studs on their control pads. The cones, with each ship offset from those around it such that they did not get in each other's way, all fired at once. Half of the ships had been set to target defensive weapons, and those targets were obliterated by firepower that the Union fighter pilots had only ever dreamed of having. The other half swept along the length of each cruiser, destroying sensors and communications pods and then concentrating fire on the engine nacelles. Each pilot mashed the missile icon that popped up in blue as they swept past the cruisers on their way to the smaller frigates. The small missiles sped forward and then swung around. Andar-9 maintained locks on each of them as they flew into the engines of the cruisers.

Grechsly could not see what happened as the squadrons sped past the stricken cruisers. On *Starfire* and *Sunburst,* the admirals did see, and they stared open-mouthed as the cruisers were blown apart. The remaining frigates followed suit. Andar-9 steered the attacking swarm, which now included *Fendaristil*, into what was left of the Empire formation, quickly analysing and then predicting the firing pattern for the defensive bombardment and allowing the fighters to punch holes in the defensive net and then to destroy the ships.

In little further time, the battle was done. Stricken ships floated through the vacuum of space while remnants of other ships did likewise, threatening to cause additional damage even while rescues were under way. *Starfire* had sustained heavy damage because of the need to hold station and defend rather than manoeuvre through the battle zone. It had lost both of its cruisers and every ship had sustained injuries of some sort. *Moonbeam* was venting from multiple injuries and had lost screening vessels. *Sirius*, oddly, had fared best of the Union flagships and held station while mopping up operations took place. On the Empire side, the destruction was overwhelming. *Qorv* was lost entirely, as were all cruisers and frigates. All fighters had been destroyed and almost every ship was dead in space.

Like a heavy-weight fighter dealing with school bullies, *Sunburst* positioned itself between the remnants of the two fleets, with its weapons targeting the few small Empire ships that yet showed any offensive capability. *Fendaristil* took station alongside *Sunburst*.

"Admiral, message from the Empire commander," Rork reported to Jord. "Vice-Commander Ertur-y-Troos requests terms for surrender and medical aid."

Jord nodded. "Acknowledge the message. Tell the Vice-Commander to stand down the remaining ships. Inform Admiral Bard of their surrender and request boarding parties. How many ships ..."

"Fresh message. Stand clear! Auto-destruct has been initiated on all ships and cannot be stopped." Rork stared at Jord. "The Vice-Commander did not initiate the auto-destruct, sir. Looks like some sort of programmed response."

"Time?"

"None left, sir," Rork said flatly and pointed to the screen.

From the five remaining Empire ships escape pods erupted but all were engulfed in a series of detonations that blew the ships apart. Two of the severely damaged Empire ships followed suit.

Jord swore bitterly. The Empire had been the enemy for his whole life, but still the commander had surrendered and Jord would take that at face value. He had been left with no chance to do so.

"Very well," he said in a tight voice. "Track all debris. All weapons systems to protect the remaining ships. See if there are any life signs from the enemy ships that didn't blow. How many escape pods do we have out there?"

"Only about two hundred and eighty," Rork replied. "Tracking them all, but some of them are heading for Ennaris entry. We may not be able to retrieve them all before they hit atmosphere. Ah, sorry, retract that. *Sunburst* is targeting them all."

"Targeting?"

"*Sunburst* is painting them, Admiral. Ah, some sort of tractor beam is emitting from the moon and capturing them. It's taking them in tow. There's a door opening on the moon's surface. Wow! That's huge! The pods are being drawn into a dock or something." Rork stopped, stunned. "That's amazing!"

"Well, Mr Rork, when we have this cleared up you have my permission to go over and take a good long look at it, but for now, let's get that clean-up happening."

"Aye, sir," Rork replied, shaking his head as though the clear it, too. "Message from *Starfire*, sir."

Jord touched a stud on the arm of his command chair and Bard appeared on the screen. A pall of smoke was visible in the background.

"Sir, do you need assistance?" Jord asked.

"No, we have pretty heavy damage but it's being attended to. There are some fairly stunned people over here, what with *Sunburst* and now those pods being rescued. Good job, by the way. And whoever directed the fighters gets my personal congratulations." Bard smiled. "But we have too much damage to welcome the fighters on board, including our own. Can you handle them?"

"Yes, sir."

"Good. Get them landed and ready to fight again. I don't think this is over yet, and I want to be ready. The fleet has taken a battering but we'll have to be ready to defend the planet. There's something going on down on the planet's surface, strange energy readings. And," Bard said with the almost predatory grin that Jord recalled all too well, "it's time we took a hand in whatever's happening down below."

29. Champion

"I am Marjory nar Drewflin, Battle Mage of Ennaris. Surrender and you will not be mistreated. Continue this fight and you will be obliterated!"

Likud was nonplussed but at the same time he was beside himself with anger. Goroth merely stared at the glowing figure hovering above the plain. Marjory! Alive! Goroth had based his strategy on the fact of her death, and yet here she was confronting him yet again. Grensor was mistaken in his assessment of so much of what was happening, and of so much that had happened. Those mistakes would cost Goroth dearly, of that he was sure. He snarled, all his composure lost. His anger boiled over. Likud had his fleet in orbit still. Could he use that? No, a more rational part of his mind told him, as that would cause even greater damage than the last time. Even in the depths of his rage, Goroth did not want his home world to be destroyed.

He had alternatives still but needed some time to work out a strategy. He had the rest of the northers still, but where was his army, and those norther battle gifted? And the remaining winged ghazrak?

Behind the remaining norther army, which was gathered in a depression in the land that hid them from sight, and hidden behind a screen laid by three of the norther gifted, the Andorethi waited. Thirty Andorethi remained of the number that Likud's forces had dropped and periodically reinforced over the last ten cycles. Starting as a planet that had been colonised by Ennaris untold millenia ago, for the last five thousand cycles they had known Likud as their ruler. This was not the mythical being that he had become on Ennaris, nor was he a benevolent legend like many people created as their civilisations reached their own awakening. Likud was real to the Andorethi. And true to character, Likud did not want to be worshipped as a god, but obeyed as an absolute emperor.

As Grensor had chided him repeatedly, over those millenia Likud deliberately bred opposition out of the Andorethi population, ironically building on genetic traits that Grensor had modified. Those who opposed Likud were destroyed, and their families were destroyed. Those who raised objections to Likud or his tactics were destroyed, and their families were destroyed. Those who failed at a given task were destroyed, although their families may be spared, or not, as Likud willed. Hundreds of generations of repression, and the forced removal of those who would or could think independently, resulted in a population that retained much of its native intelligence but little in the way of initiative. Usually, it was the brighter minds that objected to Likud's unimaginative solutions to a range of problems. It was the brilliant that were removed as a consequence. Nearly all those who remained followed Likud's direction blindly.

Their emperor had been found to be incorrect many, many times. He was impulsive and emotionally-driven, as well as strategically and tactically lacking in his planning capabilities. Likud made up for those deficiencies by applying numbers to the tasks. He found that most of his poorly planned initiatives had some form of success if he just used overwhelming force. His secret police was a much larger force than may have been needed by clearer thinkers. His manufacturing capability became much larger than may have been required by others and thus caused greater problems for those planets and locations selected for his huge factories. His fleets often were much larger than the Union opposition fleets and, where they were not, he quickly bolstered them via his bloated manufacturing industries so that they were. His casualties in battle were significantly larger than would be considered normal, especially in the last few hundred cycles, but he made up for that by a forced breeding program.

In all aspects of Andorethi life Likud took a hand. He made key decisions and expected that they were carried out to the letter. In everything from food supply to sanitation to the manufacture of any number of items and onto the conduct of war, Likud decided what to do and his decision was, quite literally, law. Deviation from Likud's law meant destruction to the offender and his or her families.

Now, the remaining Andorethi on Ennaris were gathered in a tight mass, awaiting Likud's summons. Undoubtedly, they were to control the remaining ghazrak in battle, using the mental capabilities that Likud's breeding program had enhanced from a normal communication device into a weapon, although at terrible cost. Where they originally had the ability to fade into a non-corporeal state to escape danger, which was the natural trait had been expanded by Grensor, these Andorethi were now trapped in that state. The Andorethi found ways to adapt, and not all of the population lost their corporeal form, but their population growth had slowed and then reversed. Without some form of intervention, they would die out in the near future.

All of this Clay had learned from Ogun, and it passed through Clay's mind as he watched the tight group of Shadows from the top of a rise a short distance away. Secure behind his personal shield that the Shadows could not detect, he could see them floating in place, their cloaks fluttering slightly in the tepid breeze. A small group of seven were separate from the rest, which puzzled Clay enough to make him wait a little longer while he considered his moves. He knew that the Shadows were not to blame for Likud's ambitions and drive to conquer, but he also knew that they were dangerous in their own right, and even more so as ghazrak controllers. So, they would be stopped.

A short time earlier, Clay had slipped away from the Faero's lines, muttering to Varna that he had something to deal with. He had observed that the later ghazrak charges were accompanied by a proportional number of Shadows, although the demon obviously had been controlling almost all of the second, larger charge. Given that what seemed to be around half of the ghazrak remained behind Goroth's lines, it stood to reason that a number of Shadows remained also. So, he had commandeered a hrss from the Faero's stock and travelled a wide loop to come in from the rear. Security was lax this far behind the front and he had reached his current location with little trouble.

His face was untroubled as he considered the task of attacking the Shadows from where he lay atop the rise that formed the northern end of the shallow basin. Getting into their midst would be the least of the problem. Killing them would be somewhat difficult. Getting away may prove to be the real problem. Clay had no quibbles with the idea of laying down his life for the right reason, but he had the feeling that his presence would be needed in the near term. So, suicide charges were out.

A small commotion caught his attention. One of the norther gifted - Clay assumed he was one because he wore a coarse version of the Mage robes worn by the twins - walked around the corner. A small guard of northers attempted to intercept him, only to be flung aside by an unseen force. Clay smiled thinly. Assumption verified! One of the battle-trained, then, and one who was confident enough to deal with his fellow northers with contempt. He walked to the group of seven and gestured abruptly, angrily, for them to follow, then turned his back again and stalked away without looking to see if his directive was followed. It was. The seven Shadows drifted after the summoner, moving past the small group of guards, who had just regained their feet, and then out of sight around the bend that formed the path into the bowl. The guards stared after him ruefully but did not attempt to intercept him or the following Shadows. So, twenty-three remained. And the three guards.

Clay checked the charge indicators on his twin weapons. Both were full. He prepared to rise from his concealment when another gifted appeared, walking below where Clay lay. Clay smiled a half-smile. Change of plan, one of those fleeting opportunities to improvise that made the difference between the Union forces and the Shadows. Allowing the man to walk past, Clay rose into a crouch and followed. He angled down the small hill. He was careful to make no noise and raise no dust. He had no idea why this one was out of the camp alone like this, but it was an opportunity too good to pass up. Clay closed on the gifted norther quickly.

Something betrayed Clay's presence. It might have been a slight noise, or even the light vibrations from Clay's stealthy but rapid steps, or his gift may have given the man a warning of some sort. For whatever reason, the norther stopped abruptly and turned, with Clay no more than five paces away. His mouth opened and he raised both hands - perhaps another battle trained one - but Clay was too close. He struck the norther with considerable force in the middle of his chest with the heel of his right palm, holding little back from the thudding impact. The norther stopped and his jaw dropped open. The strike over the heart was one of the most effective silent disablers among humans, and Clay expected it to be the same among Ennarisi, as the physiology was almost identical between the two peoples. Called the touch of death, if the strike occurred at the right moment in the heart's beating rhythm, and was delivered in just the right way and with full force, the heart's function could shut down immediately. If either timing or delivery method was slightly out, the effect may still be lethal, but the effect may be delayed. Clay was an expert. He caught the man's body as he collapsed, laying it out on the ground gently, quietly.

Swiftly, Clay stripped the man's robe from his body and slipped it on over his own clothes. It would be hot in the robe as well as his own clothes, and it appeared that this fellow had avoided bath water for some time, but it should serve the purpose. Clay did not really resemble a norther, but it would provide time enough to get him to a good position. There was nowhere to move the body, so Clay left it where it was. He moved back up the slope and checked that nothing had changed, then went back down the hillside and walked rapidly to the opening into the bowl.

Approaching the guards, Clay adopted the supercilious sneer that he had noticed on the faces of those wearing those robes. Without pause, he swept past the guards, not deigning to even glance at them and stalked towards the Shadows. The thoroughly cowed guards shuffled their feet nervously, then turned to face the opening, leaving Clay to his own devices. As he approached the gathered Shadows, Clay grasped the needler and blaster and deftly thumbed the settings up one notch. Shadows were notoriously hard to kill and he did not wish to waste time. With a brief hope that the hills would muffle the already muted sound of the weapons, the Champion of the Light went to work.

Muzzle blasts erupted from just inside each sleeve. Individual needles or bursts of pure energy were emitted in repeated blasts as he thumbed the firing button. The Shadows fell in waves as Clay's continuous fire marched through their ranks. This was what being Champion meant, being at the highest level of expertise with any number of weapons. He had been on Ennaris for more than half his life, and had not used these weapons much beyond recent practice, but he had maintained extreme levels of fitness that were now honed to a level even he had thought unattainable. For Clay, the weapons felt like extensions of himself. His aim followed his eyes and his thumbs mashed the firing buttons seemingly without volition. He did not count. He realised there were no more of the Shadows alive when there were no more black cloaks floating upright, so he stopped firing.

Swiftly, he turned to the guards who were staring mesmerised. Belatedly one of them realised he was supposed to guard the now dead Shadows. He raised his sword even as he opened his mouth to call for help. He was far too late, far too slow. In a movement, Clay returned the expended needler and blaster to their belt mounts and grasped another tool of death with his left hand. Faster than the eye could follow, he brought both hands together in front and, in a smoothly repetitive action, threw three star knives. The guard opening his mouth died first, the shout gurgling in his throat where the first star knife now was lodged. The second and third guards followed less than a heartbeat later.

Clay glanced around to make sure that all Shadows had been accounted for. Then he darted to the three guards and swiftly dragged their bodies into the basin fully, out of sight of passers-by. Finally, breathing easily, he walked from the basin and retraced his steps to where the norther battle-gifted's body still lay and then into the hills beyond. The commandeered robe was removed and Clay confidently started the return journey to Corm's camp. With luck, Goroth would have trouble controlling the remaining ghazrak, which may prove to be an advantage of some sort to the greatly diminished defence.

30. Dire Straits

"Flin, it looks like Goroth is sending the rest," Raglin said as he strode into the tent. "We'll need you out here." He paused, looking at Jalor laid out on the pallet. "Anything?"

"No," Flin said as he turned to face the entrance. "There's something I can sense but he's so far gone that I'm unable to bring him back. Varna tried things I don't even understand and could do nothing either. I don't think there's anything we can do for him."

"Well, we have a fight on our hands now, so we need you and Varna out here." Raglin shrugged. "We have very few able-bodied men and women left to us. The healers are doing what they can but we don't have the time."

"Marjory?"

"She's waiting for you, along with Trabor and Ragnor." Raglin straightened. "The Council awaits, Archmage."

Drewflin nodded to his friend and drew a deep breath. Did Jalor's death mean the end of things? The Prophecy said nothing about one of the Children dying, although then again, maybe now it did. Who knew? What he did know was that the last battle was at hand and Goroth had played his hand well enough.

"Varna, we must go," Archmage Drewflin said kindly. "The others will need us."

He led the way from the tent, trailed by Raglin.

A small group stood watching the far side of the field of battle. Flin could see a number of northers that exceeded the last lot. Goroth still had a significant number of ghazrak and winged ghazrak. Then, of course, there was Likud and the gifted northers. Flin still was surprised that they had been hidden for so long but then, he thought, the Hides had done the same. Looking towards the defensive line, he could see Helt chivying the remaining soldiers into battle order. The knights had only about a fifth of their original number and all were battered. Most carried some sort of injury. The jungle Waslit were effectively out of the fight. Most of the crawlers had been killed or maimed by the last ghazrak attack, and the Waslit handlers had been largely decimated. The urban Waslit were down to swords and knives and they were reduced in numbers also.

"What do you think?" Flin asked Marjory as he walked up to the group.

"He has about fourteen thousand or more northers, probably no better than the others. The ghazrak number around five or six hundred and there are the remaining flying creatures also. Not sure about the number of gifted, as they stay shielded effectively enough. But there's some sort of commotion happening that's stopped the attack, at least for now." Marjory shook her head. "I have no idea what that could be."

"Well," Clay said as he stepped up to the same group, "it may be that the group of Shadows who had been held back to control the ghazrak were all found dead."

Marjory turned to regard Clay with one eyebrow raised.

"And you know this how?"

Clay merely returned her gaze, oblivious to the stares directed his way by the others. Marjory's lips quirked and she nodded.

"So that's where you were. How many were there?"

"Twenty-three, but that was after seven had been led away somewhere. I'm not sure where or why."

"Twenty-three? And they're all dead? How did you get a team in there to do that?" Corm asked.

"No team," Marjory said to Corm. "Just Clay." She looked to the open-mouthed Faero and shrugged. "The Champion is a little more than most can handle."

"But we do have a problem, Admiral," Clay said. "The remaining northers are a little better armed, although not greatly. They do seem to have a little more discipline from what I could see when I scouted, but I'd still not rate them too far above those we have seen so far. There are thousands of them and we don't have enough defenders to meet them. But the biggest threat still is the gifted being held behind that low set of hills. I expect most of them to be battle trained to some extent. If the ones I saw up close are anything to go by they have little experience but I doubt many are much less than middle powers."

"They'll be the ones flinging the fire bolts, although Likud took part last time. And there are only a few of us to withstand those powers," Marjory said quietly into the silence that followed Clay's comments. "The Hides and I will have our hands full dealing with them. The Hides adepts are tired and their circles are close to exhausted. We have, what, about a thousand fighters able to take the field?"

"About that, yes," Helt said, joining the conversation for the first time. "We could bring back a few hundred of the injured but the rest are too badly hurt to make any impression. The knights are almost non-existent - only about thirty remain in fighting form. And Blaine is exhausted, too. He's recovering, and the Hides healers are trying something they call regenerative therapy to help him regain strength, but we may not get him back at full effectiveness."

"We do what we can do," Flin said calmly, glancing at Marjory and smiling fondly. "The defenders will be tasked to defend the Battle Mages, and the rest of us will feed them whatever power we have, as was done before. Corm, please ask the Rocs to ride continuous sweeps across the field and do what they can. And to keep those winged ghazrak off us."

"What about Goroth and Likud?" Trabor put in. "They won't just stand back and let us do this."

"They will be my job, I think," Marjory said. "Likud will be the easier to handle. I almost guarantee he'll do something stupid. Goroth doesn't think clearly when the stress gets too high, so partly we need to raise the stress levels. How to do that when he has overwhelming numbers, I'm not sure." She shrugged. "I'll think of something."

"Think fast, Marjory," Varna said from her place slightly away from the main huddle. "They're coming."

Strangely, the advancing force slowed to a stop shortly after they started to move. The northers milled around as though uncertain of what to do. From their midst floated the seven Shadows, who formed into a line and continued to advance. Further movement amongst the northers saw them peel apart in the centre. From their midst strode an enormous ghazrak, towering over the norther men and women. It stumped forward on tree trunk legs. This one wore nothing but a loin-cloth and its musculature was immense. Hugely muscled arms ended in massive clawed hands that each held a heavy ghazrak sword as though they were toys. Its barrel chest and broad back were sheathed in giant bone plates. The torso narrowed below the chest but its girth at the hips still was that of two men. The ghazrak gave a roar as it reached the Shadows, who parted to allow it to pass through their midst.

"What's happening?" Goroth demanded.

Likud had a single Andorethi with him still and he listened for a moment before replying.

"Apparently Grensor had told the northers and the ghazrak that they would be victorious when their champion defeated the Faero's champion. It seems the Prophesy called for the champions to do battle."

"Well, get them moving," Goroth demanded, growing enraged.

"I'm told the ghazrak will attack after the battle of the champions, but not before. The northers too."

Goroth and Likud merely stood and watched their entire force milling around the battle field. Goroth built his power in preparation to launch his own attack but, oddly, it was Likud who held him back.

"Let them do this," Likud said. "It won't take long, assuming the other one responds, and then we get on with it."

The ghazrak champion stopped.

"Chump - ee - on," the giant ghazrak shouted in rage.

The watchers on the far side of the field stared, fascinated.

"Oh, I hope there are no more of these," Ragnor said.

"Chump - ee - on," it shouted again before it started to march towards the Faero's line once again.

"I believe I'm being called out," Clay said calmly.

"Those seven Shadows..." Varna started to say.

"Are there to mess with our minds," Clay said. "Or with my mind, anyway. I believe this is my fight."

Clay glanced quickly around the group, nodded to Marjory and Flin who were standing together, and walked unhurriedly towards the huge ghazrak.

"So, what's the plan," Varna asked from his side.

Startled, Clay turned to see his fellow Warrior matching him stride for stride.

"What are you doing?" Clay demanded.

"How good are your mental defences?" she asked in reply.

"I should be able to withstand them," Clay replied.

"I can do better than that," Varna said confidently.

"I'm surprised that haven't started to attack us yet," Clay said.

"They have," Varna replied. "I'll keep the Shadows off you. You deal with Goliath."

The Warriors separated. Clay continued to walk towards the enraged ghazrak giant while Varna moved to take a position well to the side. She kept an eye on the norther force, too, but they seemed to be rooted in place. Odd.

A ripple passed through the Shadows. As one they turned to face Varna, as though recognising a greater threat. Smoothly, Varna separated her shield into seven threads and wrapped each Shadow in one of them. She held them immobile while Clay and the giant ghazrak approached their meeting point.

"Chump - ee - on," it shouted once more. "No! I chump-ee-on."

Clay appreciated that he faced a ghazrak that was not only larger than the others, but also one that was more developed than any that he had faced to date. That did not worry him but it did add a level of care. The two rough swords seemed to be toys in its hands. When seen up close, it was a fearsome creature although, oddly, Clay felt that this ghazrak seemed to be better proportioned that the others. It was as though it had grown into the armour plates and large bony skull.

When it was twenty large paces away, the ghazrak broke into a lumbering run. The ground shook at each step and dust rose from the grasslands. The enormous cloven hoofs left deep indentations in the ground.

The two swords made deep *swoosh* sounds as the ghazrak swung them from side to side, almost like a scythe. The norther army cheered and then cheered again when Clay skipped back a pace to allow the swords to flash past him. When the two swords were at their furthest extension and the ghazrak was about to start the reverse swings, Clay darted closer. His much finer sword flashed and flicked like a slither's tongue. Then he slid back once again to be just out of reach. The ghazrak sported deep wounds to both arms and black blood trickled down the huge arm muscles. The only acknowledgement of the injuries was a deep grunt.

Again, the ghazrak swung both swords, hard. Again, Clay waited until just the right moment and then darted closer. His sword flashed and flicked again before he stepped back. More wounds glistened with black blood, this time on the giant's thighs and torso below the chest armour plates. No sound came from the ghazrak this time, but it swung its head back and forth ponderously. It attacked a third time with the same result. Its endurance was suffering, Clay thought, for its movements seemed to be slower, but his attention never flagged, which was just as well.

The next attack started like the other before it, but this time instead of swinging both swords at once the ghazrak alternated them, making it difficult for Clay to get close. An experimental poke of his sword was met by one of the ghazrak's sword strokes in a ringing clash, and Clay felt the impact to his shoulder. He skipped back to check on his sword.

It had acquired a deep nick but remained serviceable, he thought. The ghazrak rumbled what, to Clay, sounded like a satisfied growl.

Varna, meanwhile had turned her full sight on the seven Shadows. Each of them showed a grey aura, edged with deep red. This, she thought, was what she had noted before. Now, however, she could also see a spot of even deeper red hovering behind the front of their black robes. With a thrill, Varna realised that this may be the controlling device that Flin had warned her not to touch. She tightened her vision. She could see that each device was sheathed in bonds of pure energy as she expected a glamour would do. The energy wrappings had hooks that delved into the Shadow's non-corporeal being and was held in place by them. It would be, she thought, painful physically but she expected that it was even more painful to the Shadows' spirits.

Gently, one by one, Varna disengaged the hooks from the closest Shadow. With that done she lifted the device from the Shadow's robe and floated it towards her. As she did so she saw the Shadow's aura lose the red edge and settle into a uniform grey. She thought the Shadow floated slightly more easily, even though it was wrapped in her shield still.

"*Balgor!*" she called through their mental link.

"*I'm here, Dharmoney,*" the Guardian replied immediately. "*I've seen what you did.*"

"*Would you tell Odruf please? It's possible that the Shadows on their home world have been forced like this also.*"

"*I have done so. What will you do now? Remember these beings have been raised as your enemies.*"

Varna gave no response, that knowing Balgor remained with her. Instead, she turned her attention to each Shadow, one after the other. The evil-bound control devices were unpicked from each and floated to Varna. Each time, the red tinge to the Shadow's aura faded almost immediately. Now, with the seven Shadows still bound, she reached out one hand to grasp the seven devices, which were shaped like disks and had demon images etched on them. They felt slippery to the touch and she felt the malevolence, the *evil*, with which the devices had been imbued. Had she taken hold of that device from the Shadow at Old Bastion before Flin intervened, Varna knew that she would have been badly damaged. Now, however, she drew the evil energy out of the disks and turned it into ... nothing!

Once again, Varna turned to the first Shadow. She could *see* the telepathic channel that linked the Shadow to its fellows.

"*How are you called?*" she asked the first Shadow.

"*Mistress, my name is Derusilasa,*" was the response via what Varna thought of as a sequence of images more than sounds.

"*Derusilasa,*" Varna repeated the sequence that made up the Shadow's name. "*How did you come to be wearing this device?*"

"*The Emperor gifted me to the one called Grensor. Grensor bound the controller to me to enforce his will on the ghazrak. Even though Grensor is no more, the controllers continue to operate. Goroth assumed that control.*"

"*So Grensor is dead?*" Varna asked. "*That was his body that the demon occupied?*"

"*The Kindred Ghaz-ti destroyed Grensor when it took over that body,*" Derusilasa confirmed.

Varna considered her next move.

"*I have removed the controller from you and your fellows,*" she continued. "*If I release you from the shield, will you consent to being held behind the battle lines and take no part nor cause any damage to our forces?*"

"*We have been forced into this duty by Likud, our Emperor,*" the Shadow replied. "*Our families are held to ransom. Should we not obey his commands they will be destroyed.*"

"*Likud will not be destroying any more families,*" Varna growled across the link. "*Of that I make you a promise. If you and your fellows provide assurance that you will not oppose us, I will release you to be held in safety. Then I will make sure that you return to your home safely.*"

Derusilasa was quiet for a few moments before replying.

"*May I commune with the others?*"

"*You may,*" Varna replied and loosened the shield on all of them, enough for them to communicate.

Immediately, she sensed that an animated conversation erupted. Seemingly, all seven were "speaking" at the same time. She did not try to intercept any of the thoughts but could see that the telepathic links were all active continuously. Amazing! She thought to herself. It was only moments and the stream dwindled away.

"*We have communed,*" Derusilasa sent to Varna, who sensed that all seven remained in the link. "*Vasinesula is the only one of us without family and he is a believer in the Emperor. He objects to our surrender.*"

"*And the rest of you?*"

"*We submit, Mistress,*" Derusilasa replied, followed by five other touches of affirmation.

"*I do not submit,*" the seventh sent.

"*Very well,*" Varna replied to all of the Shadows.

Her reading of them showed her, surprisingly, that she could trust the six who had submitted to keep their word, while the seventh was open in his objection and would not conform. There was no guile and little subtlety, which she thought was strange until she realised that, with such direct communication, they would be unable to hide much, if anything, from other Shadows. It was something to bear in mind. She dropped the shield from Derusilasa and the other five who had submitted. Vasinesula she left shielded but able to communicate. She pointed back to where the Mages waited.

"*Make your way to my friends over there and follow their direction,*" Varna ordered them. "*I charge you to keep Vasinesula from causing problems. He remains shielded. Can you carry him with you?*"

"*We shall do as you command, Mistress,*" Derusilasa replied. "*And we will be able to transport Vasinesula. We offer our thanks, Mistress.*"

Watching the display, Goroth was nonplussed to see the seven Andorethi quiescent beside the woman. He turned his Mage sight on her and drew a short breath as he saw the vivid colours of her aura swirling together. He saw her remove the controllers and frowned. He had been unable to fathom how Grensor had produced them, although he knew that the old Mage had blended Mage skills with Kindred-style binding energies, and he could no longer ask Grensor. How had she been able to release them? And what now? The answer came moments later as six of the Andorethi seemed to gather the seventh and float towards the Faero's defensive line. Likud, it seemed, had not even noticed, for he had concentrated on the conflict between the two champions. Goroth felt a chill as he looked back to the woman.

Varna turned back to Clay and the ghazrak. Her attention had been divided while she dealt with the Shadows, all of which had taken no more than thirty seconds or so. She was in time to see Clay slide his blade into a gap left by the tiring ghazrak giant and draw even more black blood. In the few seconds that she had been side-tracked, Clay had picked up nicks to both arms but they appeared to cause him no discomfort. The ghazrak stepped toward Clay again. Its motions were more sluggish than they had been but Varna was not fooled. These creatures had endurance beyond any she had seen. And then, disaster!

Clay made a thrust at the same time as the huge ghazrak restarted his attack. Clay's sword blade was caught by both of the crude but heavy ghazrak swords and shattered, despite being Hunder-wrought. Immediately, Clay skipped back out of reach, while the ghazrak roared in victory and the norther army responded with its own roar. With a shrug, Clay tossed the hilt of the shattered sword to one side, all the while maintaining his watch on the ghazrak. He took several steps back, flexing his right hand that had taken the shock when the sword broke.

The huge ghazrak started forward again, breaking into a shambling run. Varna frowned but saw that Clay, while concentrating hard on the giant, appeared to be unworried. Seemingly from nowhere, Clay produced two knives, one for each hand, took a single step and vaulted as though to pass over his opponent. The ghazrak could not stop its forward momentum and its efforts to redirect its massive sword swings caused it to stumble. Clay landed lightly on its shoulders, reached down to jam both knives into each side of the ghazrak's torso where the bony armour plates met, and then flipped off to land behind the ghazrak. The ghazrak roared anew, in pain and frustration and anger. It turned clumsily to confront Clay again and roared in challenge. It now had the two knives sticking out from each side of its torso, and was bleeding copious amounts of black blood from the wounds, while other blood was leaking from the lesser wounds to arms, legs and torso. It swayed as it regarded Clay with an unwavering glare. Clay backed up further. He glanced to Varna and shrugged, hands held wide to show no weapons.

Finally, the ghazrak started toward Clay again. The Champion ended the fight. Both hands smoothly swept down and came up holding the needler and blaster. He fired one shot from each weapon, taking the ghazrak in the forehead with the needler and through the neck with the blaster. The ghazrak continued its forward momentum as it fell, crashing to the ground with a loud thump. Clay glanced to Varna and then over his shoulder to the norther army, now standing in stunned silence. As one, they both turned back towards the Faero's defensive line. They reached the lines moments before the norther army raised another shout and started to charge across the field.

31. Jalor and Dharmoney

He was dead! Of that Jalor was sure, although why he would be *able* to be sure of that, to have any thoughts at all, he was not so sure. He could no longer feel the extreme pain that he had felt as the creature that inhabited Grensor's body blasted him with some sort of strange energy. He knew that Andira had twisted that weapon somehow, but not enough, it would seem. He opened his eyes - or senses that approximated eyes - and looked up at nothing, a vague grey-white space that seemed to extend into the distance on all sides. Nothing, there was nothing. Was this what death was like? If it was, there were a lot of people who Jalor had encountered during his life who would be disappointed, in one way or another.

Perhaps this was where one waited for judgement, assuming that tradition was correct. Or was this where souls went to await rebirth, as other traditions asserted? In fact, Jalor recalled Flin implying that people would be reborn, a sort of reincarnation. Maybe he was being prepared for that via this dreamscape of sorts. It was uniformly grey and fuzzy at the edges so that his eyes refused to adjust. Featureless. He lay where he was for a short time, staring into the grey. Then he snorted. He was staring at the roof of a tent.

Strangely, he could feel some odd sensations, and could sense something equally odd. He puzzled that out. If he was dead then he wouldn't feel anything like that, like anything, surely. Of course, to his knowledge he had never been dead before, so he didn't know. But this was somehow familiar, like a signature that he remembered seeing after a long time. Jalor decided that worrying about it was of no use, so he settled into something like patience. He knew the battle was being lost, and that his death would not help matters. He knew he truly was a gifted strategist, but he also knew that others would carry his plan on without him. He floated for an indeterminate time.

With a sigh he levered himself into a sitting position and then stood, looking around to get his bearings. Flin stood nearby, staring at something behind Jalor with an expression that could only be termed as bitter and helpless. It was as though he was faced with something that even he could not deal with. Jalor turned to see what Flin was staring at. Now it was his turn to stare, stunned. Lying on a pallet, his skin pale and almost translucent, was himself.

Crouched beside the pallet and leaning over him, holding out one hand that was glowing intensely as she moved it back and forth from his head to his navel, was Varna. Beside her, weeping her own bitter tears, was Andira. With a visible scream that Jalor could not hear, Varna sat back on her heels and turned to Flin, tears running down her face, saying something that Jalor could not make out. Flin replied, shaking his head sadly. One of the twins entered to speak with Flin, after which the two Mages and Varna left the tent, Varna with great reluctance. Again, Jalor was unable to hear what was said. In fact, he could hear nothing! There were no sounds of people talking, no camp noises, no noises of the animals that were held behind the healer tents. A war camp always had a cacophony of noises, but Jalor could hear none of it. Panic rose and he stamped it down ruthlessly.

Jalor checked himself for injuries. Nothing. Then again, there appeared to be no physical injuries on his body lying on the pallet. He forced his racing thoughts to calm. He recalled a few references by Flin and others that implied some sort of afterlife. Was that what this was then? Was he dead? Or a ghost?

That sensation again, as though someone tried to reach out to him and could not get through whatever barrier this grey-white stuff represented. Was that Varna? Or Flin? Jalor dismissed the speculation once again, for he had a sense that something was happening, something or someone was coming. The grey-white shifted, like air currents moving a gas around, or like the wake of his old single-seater as he powered through the outer reaches of a nebula, which was something he had always loved to do.

Whatever it is, it's almost here, Jalor thought. *At least I'll know. Am I dead? Awaiting some sort of judgement?*

The shifting, wispy stuff was pushed apart from behind him, like a bow wave being shoved out of the way by a bulky ship.

"Neither of those are yet for you, Vinca Jalor, Child of Ennaris," a melodious voice said from behind him.

Jalor turned his head to see the speaker. Another surprise.

Well, he thought, *that was not what I expected.*

A stunningly beautiful woman stood behind him, and he turned completely to face her. His first thought was that he could hear her, so why not the others. His second thought was that he had seen no-one like this woman during his time on Ennaris. She was dressed in flowing, colourful silk that seemed to fall from one shapely shoulder, leaving the other bare. The folds of the sheer material were clasped on one side by a jewelled broach of some sort and fell almost to floor level where sand-coloured sandals partly clad her feet. The woman's fingers were dressed in an array of rings. Each band was inlaid with a small stone that appeared to glow gently. Jalor recognised an emerald on one ring, an amethyst on another, then a ruby and a garnet, and others that he did not know. His gaze travelled back to her face, which was a perfect oval framed by dark hair that was held back by a gold band and then fell in tresses down to the middle of her back. Smouldering dark eyes set off by long dark lashes held green tints that, in turn, held Jalor's own gaze. For a long moment he just stared at this woman before bringing himself back to the present.

"Can you tell me what has happened? How is it that I can hear you but not my friends? What's happening?" Jalor tried to hold his fears at bay, but his questions betrayed the anxiety that he was feeling.

"You were attacked by a Kindred, a being from another universe that had no place here. The demon has been destroyed by the Eye of the Dark, who you know as Andira. But it was able to deliver a killing blow to you before she was able to intervene." The woman gazed at Jalor intently. "You are in a place between. To you falls a decision to be made, one only for you. You may continue to leave this world knowing that you enjoy the favour of the Guardians and The One and be reborn accordingly, should you wish to do so."

"So I'm dead but not fully dead yet," Jalor replied, to which the woman nodded with a slight incline of her head. "And I can choose to leave. What's the other choice?"

"You can choose to stay. You can choose to continue the fight against Goroth and other evils that beset Ennaris and other worlds."

"How do I do that?" Jalor asked. "Do I just go back to what was before? Continue to be Corm's general? From what I've seen on Ennaris, I doubt that it's that simple."

"It's not," the woman replied with a smile, and the warmth lit the green flecks in her eyes till they glowed. "Your path, should you choose to remain, will be difficult. You will be feared even while you are lauded. You will see many who you know and love fade and depart. You will see whole peoples, whole worlds grow and die. But you will be able to help many to resist the evils that are here now and that will be in the future. It's a difficult road to travel," the woman said with a sigh, "one that needs a person of inner strength and deep character. But it will continue your story until you are released from your duty, it will allow you to battle those who would damage or destroy or ruin the worlds of this universe."

"You speak as though you understand," Jalor said, intrigued by this woman.

"I am Meilani Gro Tillek, I am Dharmoney-who-was," the woman said proudly. "I have withstood where most fell. I have held the sacred artefacts of Ennaris safe against time and strife. I have watched my people die and others less worthy take our lands. I, who once travelled to the stars, whose passion was to protect those who were unable to protect themselves, was tasked with these things by The One and I have completed almost all of those tasks. I am the oldest being of this universe with the exception of the Mages and Guardians, and others of their people. There is one task to complete before I am released and can re-join my own before being reborn."

Jalor bowed to this woman, recalling Varna's story of meeting Meilani, and the regard in which she was held by the Guardians.

"I am honoured to meet you, Meilani Gro Tillek," Jalor said. "Tell me. Who is The One you talk of? Is it Odruf? Another of the Guardians?"

"The One is the maker of this universe," Meilani said. "The Guardians are to The One as the smallest insect is to the Guardians. They work to protect its creation, as have I done in my own small way."

Meilani and Jalor gazed at each other. There was a common feeling, a pull that Jalor felt towards this woman, a purpose that they shared. He, too, had devoted himself to battling the various forms of evil and ill-intent that the Union had encountered. In Ennaris and the Ennarisi Jalor felt that he had found that elusive home that he had never really had, that place where he could centre. Ennaris would change, of course, as a result of the events under way at this moment, but the planet and its people had created their own chains that held Jalor fast. But what Meilani suggested went far beyond just being a Warrior of the Light. It went far beyond being the general of Corm's army until Goroth was defeated. Did he want to watch all these people die while he did not? Did he want to see civilisations rise and fall? His sense of duty had brought him to this point, but could it sustain him in what was being asked? He was not even sure of what that ask entailed.

"Time grows short, Jalor. Would that we had more time to spend together, for I feel a oneness between us that in another time I would explore." She smiled wryly and shook her head, every movement redolent with the grace that Jalor thought would have been inherent in Meilani. "However, we have some time now and I would use it accordingly. We are in a place where time stands still. Afterwards, however, events will move on in the living world and you must make your choice."

There followed a time, caught between the frozen seconds, that Jalor would treasure for ever. While not a stranger to female company, he had not found anyone with whom he could see a long-term future. Now, on the edge of death on this planet that had wrought such changes to himself and his team, Jalor found that one. He knew the time would be fleeting, for Meilani would end her own time on Ennaris once this task was complete. They talked about themselves and their experiences, about their hopes and dreams and expectations. Time, frozen as it was in this place between, stretched and allowed these two people to meet and to join. Meilani Gro Tillek had been a warrior for Ennaris far in the past. She had been one of Ennaris' best pilots. In Jalor she found a fellow spirit. Their discussion was at times intense and at other times light-hearted. At their core, however, was a call of duty. Meilani had lived her duty for thousands of cycles, while Jalor had devoted himself to his duty for only a blink of time in comparison. And yet they recognised common cause. Finally, the sense of duty caused them to bring this joining to an end.

Meilani held out her hands. Laying across them was a sword in a black scabbard. Folded beneath the scabbard was a pile of black cloth. Jalor knew that she had held nothing a moment before but it did not matter.

"The time of choice is now, Jalor."

"Another sword?" Jalor asked with a quirk of his lips. "And I take it I need to dress up to make this happen correctly?"

Meilani laughed, a genuine laugh that was out of keeping with the solemnity of the moment, a final moment between the two.

"The sword is of a time when these roles were mapped out. It's more evocative than an energy weapon, don't you think? As for the garments, they are more for a sense of theatre in this case. Your friend's golden armour protects him as much as it defines him. You will not require the same. However," and a wicked twinkle appeared in her eyes, "I think you'll look good in black."

32. Dreadlord

Andira gasped as the pallet, suddenly, was covered in thick black mist. Jalor's body was enveloped and disappeared from view. She stood to run to tell someone, anyone, when the mist started to thin. As it faded, she stared at the sight. Where Jalor had been wearing standard Ennarisi military attire when he had been laid low - breeches and shirt with a hardened leather breastplate, sturdy brown boots and a utilitarian sword that now stood against the tent wall - what was revealed was a Jalor in black.

Everything was black. His breeches were now made of a well fitted black material that she could not identify. The shirt was looser than previously and made of a shimmering jet-black material that again she could not identify. His boots were a dull black but of such quality that the black almost shimmered. Again, they were of a material that she did not know. He had no breastplate or any armour at all, but around his waist was a jet-black sword belt, with the attached scabbard lying along the length of his leg. The scabbard held a sword that, to Andira's newly enhanced senses, radiated menace but not evil. All she could see was that the hilt was a deep black, and embedded in the pommel and the quillons that formed the guard were jet black stones. Andira did not doubt that the blade would be a similar hue.

The woman who had recently stood against and defeated the most powerful demon to have been summoned to Ennaris gave a short cry and ran from the tent, directly into the melee of preparations for the attack that was developing. Looking around frantically, she saw the small group of leaders who were preparing to move in their own directions. Andira ran down the small slope, waving frantically.

"Archmage," she called urgently. "Archmage!"

Drewflin and the others turned to face the running woman, who was pointing back up the slope.

"Andira? What -"

"It's Jalor," she stammered, breaking in on Flin's query. "Something happened. A sort of black smoke just covered him and now he, um, well..." She ground to a halt as she turned to look back to the tent.

"He what, Andira? Quickly please, we must go."

"That!" Andira said, pointing.

As one, the group turned towards where Andira pointed. Striding through the camp towards the battle field, Jalor was a dark vision. His all-black garb was offset by a band of black that held his suddenly longer hair back with, centred on his forehead, a jet-black stone that seemed to drink in the light. The group gasped as each of the stones they wore flashed, as in greeting. The people running back and forth preparing for the fight to come stopped and made way as their general walked - stalked - through the camp.

"Hold the army back until I say," he ordered in a strangely hollow voice as he walked past the stunned group of Mages and warriors.

"Jalor," Varna said as she passed him, returning with Clay.

He glanced at her without stopping and nodded solemnly.

"Dharmoney," he said in acknowledgement. "Meilani said to tell you it's time to take your place."

Stunned, Varna simply stared as Jalor continued to walk towards the battle line, past the group. She turned her other sight on him and gasped anew.

"Flin, his aura!"

The Mages all turned to follow Jalor's progress. Flin's eyes opened wide as he saw what Varna saw - a jet black aura that was shot through with even deeper blacks somehow, with silver and gold shooting and darting. He made the connection.

"Dreadlord!"

At the site of the battle with the norther army Hel-nor called urgently to Maf.

"Protector, the Dreadlord comes. We must join our fellows."

Maf nodded and turned away from his discussion with the leaders of the Junda-lar and the Clans. His shock had passed, mostly, and intent shone forth. It was time for this to end.

Overlooking the field of battle Marjory looked from Flin to Jalor and back to Flin, then to Varna, who had joined them. She nodded decisively.

"So be it! Helt, hold the army until Jalor gives his signal. I think we'll know it. The remaining knights should be ready to back up the infantry. Corm, I want the winged ghazrak taken care of as fast as possible, and then the Rocs are to fall back. Jorphy Bart, the Hides battle adepts... No, not adepts. Your Battle Mages" - Jorphy Bart stood straighter at this acknowledgement - "are to engage the enemy gifted ones. Raglin and Ragnor, Trabor and Andira, provide the Hides your support please. Andira, Trabor will show you how. Varna, stay with Drewflin and me, please. And someone find Blaine and get him over here. Clay, you're with Corm." She looked around at the group staring at her. Flin smiled as the Battle Mage took charge. The Grand Admiral made her appearance. "Move, people!" she barked.

"Aye, Admiral," Clay said wryly, sketching a salute as he joined Corm and the group scattered.

Jalor moved swiftly through the camp, through the lines of fighters awaiting orders, ignoring the pointed fingers and stunned comments. Almin Bor, swathed in bandages but nevertheless leading the Faero's Guard - the Old Blood - bowed as he passed, one hand over his heart in the Blood's salute. His salute was followed by all of the Blood. Jalor acknowledged the salute, nodding to Almin Bor as he walked through the ranks, which closed behind him.

In the distance, he could see the norther army advancing towards him, towards his own lines. Large balls of blazing energy were cast across the battlefield by Goroth and Likud, drawing on the linked gifts of the moderately powerful norther gifted, to be met by the shield raised by the Council Mages. In reply, the Battle Mages of the Hides flung their own bolts, targeting the norther gifted rather than either Goroth or Likud. The power available to the rebel Mages diminished as the northers tried to raise shields. Not all succeeded and the number of norther gifted dropped rapidly.

Onto the field of battle Jalor stalked, alone. And yet not alone. He recalled those last moments with Meilani, the soft kiss she placed on his lips that told of connection made at the worst time, the depth of her gaze and the deep green flecks in her eyes that drew him in.

"Take your place in destiny, Vinca Jalor, Child of Ennaris, Dreadlord," she whispered to him as she embraced him tightly. "I feel that we will meet again, perhaps when I am reborn. Look for me! Wait for me!"

And with that, Meilani Gro Tillek, Dharmoney-who-was, had faded to accept her own reward as promised by the Guardians and The One.

So, Jalor thought as he continued to walk towards the approaching horde, not alone. For he had the memory of Meilani with him. And, of course, he had the others! Blasts of Mage fire were targeted at him as he walked, to fall against the shield extended by Marjory over the Dreadlord. He was untouched.

Jalor stopped walking. He stood and waited as the northers and the remaining ghazrak charged towards him. Above, he knew, the Rocs would deal with the flying ghazrak. The Mages would deal with the diminishing quantity of energy bolts from Goroth and Likud. Still, his reduced army was unable to halt this number of attackers, even with the most powerful Battle Mage Ennaris had ever seen and the unexpected but very welcome battle trained ones of the Hides. But he - the Dreadlord - could! With a single, fluid action Jalor drew the jet-black sword and held it high. A brilliant lick of flame chased along the blade before it settled to a dark glow.

A ripple passed across the battlefield. Watching from behind the Faero's army, Varna cried out aloud as she saw what was happening before most of the others could, and they only indistinctly. But those of the Blood, those whose people had stood firmly behind Ennaris' Faeros for such a long time through dark and darker times, were also gifted with the sight and as they realised what they were seeing they also raised their swords and cried aloud before Almin Bor led the Blood onto the field.

Arrayed behind Jalor now stood an army, the likes of which had never been seen. In a line to left and right of the Dreadlord was a row of battle standards, each of them that of the Faero of Ennaris, and beneath each banner stood one of the Faeros who had distinguished himself or herself in defence of Ennaris, who had died in doing so either in battle or after long service. Not all of the past Faeros stood there by any means, for not all Faeros had so distinguished themselves, but many had. And behind the Faeros were the Blood of the past, those who had spilt their own blood with honour over countless generations to protect Ennaris, to support their Faeros, those who had lived and died doing so. Goroth and Likud ceased their waning onslaught, caught in shock at what they were seeing.

"So, Dreadlord," Intika Ramesa said from his position to Jalor's right. "The Children call on the Blood."

"Aye, Faero," Jalor said quietly, but all assembled on the field could hear, as could those watching from the lines. "The Blood will defend Ennaris."

"That we will, Dreadlord. That we will, as we have always done."

Intika Ramesa raised his sword, his action mirrored by the line of Faeros. The front line of the army was joined by Corm Ramesa, Faero of Ennaris, who raised his sword likewise. The living members of the Blood joined with their fellows of the past behind the Faeros. Tears streamed as Corm watched his father lead the defence of his beloved Ennaris. Jalor and the Faeros waited until Jalor spoke.

"Now!"

"The Blood of Ennaris!" Corm Ramesa roared.

"The Blood of Ennaris!" Intika Ramesa roared.

"The Blood of Ennaris!" the line of Faeros past roared in reply.

"The Blood of Ennaris!" the assembled Blood soldiers present and past replied in a single thundering voice.

High above, the survivors of the battle wings of the Rocs had swelled to many times their number, and the thunderous battle cry of the Blood was matched by the battle cry of the Rocs of Ennaris ringing out from the sky above. And into the mix came the last of the battle wings, led by Hel-nor and Maf, wielding the Protector's blazing staff.

The Dreadlord dropped his sword to point it at the closing horde. The Blood charged. They *flowed* across the field of battle. From the sky the Rocs dropped like thunderbolts. Throwing restraint and a good measure of common sense aside, Corm charged into the fray followed by all soldiers of the Blood, those fully healthy and those with many different injuries. Helt held the other soldiers in their line by the liberal use of her parade ground voice, learned from association with Blaine and Almin Bor, and watched, spellbound.

The stupendous clash as the Dreadlord's army met with the attacking northerners and ghazrak could be heard far and wide. The Faeros and their people had awaited this time for many, many lifetimes. Each of them had been taught, and each of them believed, that they would be the ones to defend Ennaris. They had died knowing that they had not been able to do so, knowing that they were leaving it to others, to their children and their children's children, to do what they all believed was their duty, their honour. The pent-up generations of anger, of frustration, was put into this moment. Goroth's army stood no chance in standing up to this army, for the dead were dead and could not be killed again, while the living of the Blood fought with their own and for their own.

Like a swarm of honey-stingers, the Faeros and their army swept through the northers. Like a scythe through grain stalks, nothing could stand in their way. Swords, spears and pikes slashed and stabbed and swiped though rude weapons and occasional shields. Northers died in their thousands, their lack of fighting skill and poor weaponry leaving them with no other outcome. Above, the Rocs dispatched the remaining aerial ghazrak in short order, each of the winged horrors finding itself the target of a wing of the great angry birds from the present and the past. To the fore was the Protector, whose staff shone bright all the while and spat fire at the enemy. The rest wreaked havoc on the ghazrak that charged as an unruly pack behind the northers. The great birds rent the ghazrak, whose inbuilt armour stood no chance against these creatures from the past, while the talon tips of the Rocs of the present had been sheathed in new razor-sharp steel. The staff of the Protector rained death on the ghazrak, while other Alnar-kun from the Hides threw their own bolts. The ghazrak made no impression on the Rocs drawn back from the grave, and little on those still among the living, and were decimated.

In a surprisingly short time, the battle was done. Neither northers nor ghazrak remained alive. Jalor reflected, dispassionately, that it was possible that the norther people as a sustainable population had been destroyed. He watched from the place where he had stood as the battle was waged, the place from which he had launched the Blood's offensive, for he had taken no part in the fighting itself. He held his jet-black sword by his side. Now he was approached by the Faeros with Corm standing by his father's side, and was surrounded by the army of the Blood.

"We are victorious, Dreadlord," Intika Ramesa said, to a rumble of agreement from the assembled Faeros. "Our task is done. I fear you have yet to undertake the final accounting with Goroth, but that was always to be the task of others. We thank you for giving us the chance to recover our honour."

"Your honour was intact, anyway, Faero," Jalor replied. "Faeros," he corrected himself to chuckles from the assembly. "The Blood has acquitted itself well, as no-one doubted they would do."

"We would rest now, Dreadlord. Our time is done. First, however." Intika Ramesa turned to Corm. "Know, my son, our son, that we are proud of how you have taken on the role, much earlier than I had planned. And by we, I mean all of us." Another murmur of agreement followed. "You will have the choice to make, and we have no doubt you will make the right one." More murmurs of agreement. "I wish I could stay to add my support, but that cannot be."

Corm just nodded, his expression stoic although Jalor knew he was close to tears. "It has been my honour to fight alongside my ancestors," he said in a tight voice. "I wish you well in your future lives. I swear to you that I will uphold the honour of the Blood in whatever is to come."

The Faeros nodded in acceptance of the speech and, as one, turned to Jalor.

"It is time, Dreadlord," Intika Ramesa said.

Jalor nodded. He looked around the assembled men and women of the Blood one last time, and sheathed his sword. The Faeros and people of the Blood bowed to him as one, and faded away. Above, the Rocs issued a mighty cry that reverberated across the field before most of their number faded away. Corm and the living soldiers of the Blood were left standing with haunted expressions. Corm came to his senses first.

"Come," the Faero of Ennaris said, "we have much yet to do."

He led the way from the field. The men and women of the Blood formed on Almin Bor in a column of two to depart the field of battle. Jalor remained for a moment longer, looking across the field to where Goroth stood on a small rise, wondering what came next. Then he looked up.

On high the battle wings of the Rocs entered into their formations and swung into overlapping patrols. All except Hel-nor, who broke away and spiralled towards the knot of people who had watched the events spell-bound. The great Roc landed in a flurry of dust and grass and his rider dismounted lithely. He paused to share a moment of silent communion with Hel-nor before turning and striding through the still flying dust towards the Mages.

Marjory and Drewflin, with Trabor, Raglin and Ragnor behind them, awaited him.

"This is Maf," Jorphy Bart informed them all, "leader of the Hides. Named Protector of Ennaris."

It was Marjory who realised first, and she gripped Drewflin's arm hard in shock. Maf walked up the small rise to stand before them. For a long moment the three stared at each other. Then, with a sharp cry of immense joy, Marjory released Drewflin and enveloped Maf in a hug, followed a moment later by Drewflin. Andira turned to Trabor, at whose side she was once again, only to see the Mage openly weeping as were the twins. After a short time, Trabor glanced to her.

"This is Marflin, the son of Marjory and Drewflin. It was thought that he was killed when Resgalar was destroyed," Trabor said as tears continued to flow.

"He's their son? Maf told us that he and a small number of others were sent to help a community that had been severely damaged by the rebellion," Jorphy Bart breathed. "They were away when Resgalar was destroyed. When they returned the city was in ruins. They fled, as they thought they would be pursued by the rebels and hid in a series of caves which were held prepared for disaster relief. While they were in the caves, the land around Resgalar broke and the cave openings collapsed. They were able to navigate through the cave system after many tendays and found openings that had been created during other upheavals. When they emerged, they decided to remain hidden for safety. Later they were told that all Mages had perished and any that were found were being killed, so they stayed hidden."

Jorphy Bart stared at the tableau, transfixed. She sighed.

"All this time, he thought he was alone. At least he has found someone again."

Trabor smiled to the Hide Mage. "You have all found someone," he said. "You are Mages of Ennaris. You are part of us. You will help to rebuild the Mages and Guides. The gifts have returned and they will need guidance. Together we will rebuild Ennaris."

33. Battle's End

Goroth stared at the tiny figure of Jalor, the Dreadlord, disheartened and incensed. He, too, was pondering what came next. He had spent his last years, discounting the time sent in stasis, trying to take Ennaris into a better direction. It would be less reliant on the old Mages of the past and more on the vision of the future that he had. He wanted to lead the Ennarisi to take their rightful place in the galaxy and to directly influence the emerging peoples. He did not believe, as Likud did, that these subject people should be conquered, but they most certainly would benefit by knowing the Ennarisi directly, intimately if that should occur.

These battles were not what he expected. He had endured shock after shock since his return. He found a planet that had been all but destroyed, a civilisation that had forgotten what it had been and that had no capability to reach that peak again for a very long time, if ever. His own name was reduced to dire myth and legend, children's tales. Ennaris had been surpassed by at least two of its client civilisations, one of which had provided the means of his defeat. To find that the Guardians did exist was a far greater blow, an existential shock that still reverberated through him. To further find that Halfgar, the old Mage whom Goroth had always treated with barely disguised contempt, was in fact Odruf was shattering.

Grensor had gifted him overwhelming numbers and a divided set of enemies. But Grensor was no soldier. His ideas did not result in a trained and well-armed force suited to the final battle that Goroth had envisaged. His ghazrak were never perfected, nor were there the numbers that Goroth required. Worse, Grensor was gone when he needed the old Mage's strength the most.

Legends, so old that they were deemed to be fictional, had returned to life. The golden warrior could only be the Defender. Goroth did not doubt that it was the Dreadlord who stared at him from across the battle field. Goroth felt neither hatred nor even anger from this one, merely a calmness that gave him even more cause for concern. The sole Kindred had been defeated easily by one who could only be the Eye, who could sense when rifts opened. Goroth was not sorry to see that particular problem dealt with. His own dealings with the Kindred, in the days of planning and fighting his rebellion, were such that did not wish to have them anywhere near Ennaris. Was the one with the Rocs the Protector? Perhaps so.

So, it came down to Goroth, Likud and the surviving hand-full of partially trained norther gifted against Marjory, Drewflin and a few others. Would those legends take part again? Possibly not. They appeared to be suited to the field of physical battle, which this would not be.

He had a thought. Where was Likud? The impulsive Mage needed to be controlled. Goroth turned to spy his comrade staring across the battlefield. All vestiges of calm were gone from Likud. Pure rage leaked from every pore. His stance was one of aggression and challenge as he stared. Goroth had a moment of terrible intuition as he saw Likud draw back his long sleeve to reveal a communication device and press a sequence of buttons. He then pulled the device from his forearm and throw it to the ground, grinding it under his boot heel before unleashing a bolt of Mage fire on it.

"What have you done?" Goroth shouted as he strode towards his lieutenant.

"What I should have done all along," Likud replied angrily. "What *we* should have done all those thousands of cycles ago. This planet doesn't deserve to live if they refuse to give in to us. Well, now they won't."

"What have you done?" Goroth repeated in icy tones, gripping Likud's arm in a vice-like grip.

"I've given *Qorv* the order to bring the main cannon to bear on Ennaris and obliterate this planet." Likud shook free of Goroth's grip. "Let them see what Likud can do! Let them see what happens when they defy me and all of my might." Likud's eyes were feverish, his voice rising in pitch and volume. "Let them all die!"

"Stop it," Goroth shouted. "Likud, stop the attack, now. You can't kill the planet. This is what we fight for, to guide the people, to lead them to new heights. Not to destroy it."

"It's too late! I've given the order that I prepared when I came here and then I destroyed the communicator. You can't stop it!" His bright eyes looked to the sky, and he capered from foot to foot in excitement. "Look, here it comes."

Goroth stared at Likud, then with a sick feeling followed the direction in which his finger was pointing. To the west the sky was roiling. Thick, black-edged clouds were created and then pulled apart as the atmosphere objected to the forces being applied. Goroth knew what this was. He had seen it before. A large space ship was entering the atmosphere.

"Now we see who is the strongest," Likud snarled, actually licking flecks of spittle from his lips. "Now they pay for not taking Likud seriously."

On the far side of the field the Faero and his troops also watched the strange turmoil in the sky. Flin looked to Marjory and moved to stand with his life mate, and Maf joined his parents. They were joined also by the twins and Trabor, with Andira in tow. The Council of Mages drew together. All knew what this presaged. Likewise, Jalor and Blaine, with Clay, watched, fascinated as much as dismayed. None of them had seen a capital vessel enter the planetary atmosphere, at least not from below. Varna also stared, as she tried to penetrate the roiling energy surrounding the ship. Her stone pulsed as she applied her own power to the task of viewing the approaching ship, before her visage smoothed in relief. Seeing Clay watching her she merely nodded, before giving a small smile. Silently, she moved away from the small crowd.

Corm and the Ennarisi had no idea what they were seeing. Nothing they knew could explain what was happening nor what they should do. Several of the hrss broke free of their restraints and charged away from the camp across the grassy plain. No-one tried to stop them. Jalor stepped across to Corm.

"This is a ship from space entering the atmosphere of Ennaris," Jalor told Corm.

"Who is it?" Corm asked, striving to remain calm when his own nerves were jumping alarmingly.

"I think it could only be the Empire," Jalor said sadly. "Union capital ships are not designed to enter the atmosphere. They can't maintain propulsion and lift enough to do so, although they can help to control an emergency landing."

Corm shook his head, having understood nothing that Jalor had just said. He looked around to see the Ennarisi watching him. He stood straight.

"Hold, Faeronar, Ennarisi," Corm called. "Hold where you are. Maintain your watch for tricks. The Archmage and the Guardians will protect us from whatever this is."

The troops, who had all seen things that they never thought to see this day, nodded and turned to watch the field, although all kept twisting to see what was happening.

"See," Likud shouted, amplifying his voice so all could hear. "See what comes! The might of Likud comes to destroy you all!" His voice trailed off in a manic laugh.

"He never did have all of his senses in a straight line," Trabor said to those around him, smiling gently and wrapping one arm around Andira, who had stepped close to him for comfort. "It sounds like they may have departed altogether."

Marjory turned to look across the short distance to where the Hides gathered. Jorphy Bart looked back at her and the two exchanged the briefest of nods. With a few words, Jorphy Bart chivied the Hides Mages into a peculiar formation suited to provide maximum power transfer. Marjory nodded approval.

"Archmage," she said formally. "I request the support of the Council."

Archmage Drewflin smiled ruefully and nodded. "Here we go again," he said softly.

The remaining Mages of the Council linked. Their stones pulsed rapidly, in sync as the meld formed. Marjory prepared to draw as much power as she could to either fight what was coming or try to handle the destructive force that Likud had threatened to unleash. It was strange that the Guardians had not appeared, but they would do as they needed.

The boiling sky came closer. Clouds formed, dissipated and shifted from moment to moment. A roar accompanied the visual display, a dull roar that grew in intensity. A strong wind picked up, blowing loose objects around in swirls. Eyes narrowed or closed as dust blew up and swept through both camps. The ship emerged from the cloud like a great leviathan cresting the ocean, casting a huge shadow over the ground. It took a moment for eyes to adjust to the sheer size of the vessel as it dropped below its self-generated cloud. It's energy shields sparked as the dust of the planet impacted them. And the huge ship logo was lit by powerful spotlights.

"Admiral Serra," Marjory's forgotten wrist communicator sparked to life. "*Sunburst* reporting for duty. Need a hand?"

She started, so caught up in preparations for a desperate defence was she that it took a moment to register that she was staring at her own former flagship, which had been forgotten in the moment. As she and the rest of the Ennarisi watched, *Sunburst* disgorged flight after flight of stingers.

The sight broke Likud completely. He stared, unable to comprehend that the ship that had come at his call was that of his enemy. An inchoate scream of rage ripped from his throat. Lightning sparked from his clawed fingers as he lifted his hands and screamed again. He looked across the field of battle to where Corm stood and before Goroth could intervene Likud, belying his lesser Mage power in his rage, lifted from the ground and moved across the field with his arms spread out before him.

"Uh, Marjory," Andira said, breaking the spell that had seemed to bind her.

"Yes?" Marjory turned, seeing the approaching Likud. "Ah, it seems Likud wants to have a chat. I'll take care of this and be back shortly."

"No Battle Mage," Balgor said from behind the group. "On this occasion this is the Guardians' role. It was Likud who sought to destroy Ennaris the first time, and again today. It will not be allowed a third time."

"Who?" Marjory asked.

"Why, our newest Guardian, of course," Balgor said, nodding towards the battle field.

All turned to see that Varna had already walked beyond the defensive lines. The glow from her Aldenthrush pendant, allied to the stone that was visible on her forehead, lent her a distinctive aura. She *glowed*! Her blonde hair shone as it streamed behind her. She had removed the cloak to reveal a simple green tunic above breeches that were the same colour brown as Flin's robe. Soft brown boots seemed not to crush the ground at all as she walked calmly to meet the raging Likud.

"Varna!" Drewflin breathed.

"Dharmoney," Balgor corrected him. "The last Dharmoney, in fact. We hope."

Likud charged. He saw Varna and sent blast after blast of his Mage energy, backed by thousands of cycles of rage and frustration and hatred at her. The energy bolts struck her repeatedly, but she walked through them. Her attire changed and she wore the white jump suit of a Warrior of the Light. Likud recognised the uniform. The change should have warned him but it only served to raise his ire even further. Varna - Dharmoney - spread her arms as though to embrace Likud and rose effortlessly to his own level. The rogue Mage continued to send blast after blast at her, none of which had any effect.

"I am Dharmoney," Varna said directly into Likud's fevered mind, but broadcast so all could hear it. "This action has caused far too much death and destruction. You have been much of the cause."

She brought her left hand to face Likud and a brilliant shaft of light speared into the oncoming Mage, stopping his onrush abruptly. The light spread, too bright for any but a Guardian to see, a brilliant flaring sphere that seemed to cover the entire field of battle. The shaft of light winked out and the sphere of brilliance faded. Likud was gone.

Varna looked across the field and vanished from sight.

Goroth looked around and found himself alone. No norther army remained, no ghazrak, no Grensor or Likud. The small cadre of surviving norther gifted stood in a knot a distance away and watched, terrified, but did nothing.

Goroth turned back to find Varna standing a few paces away. They stared at each other for a count of five before Varna spoke. Goroth realised two things immediately. This woman was utterly luminescent, in a way he had never seen before. And he was unable to feel his powers.

"I am Varna Barr, Warrior of the Light of the Union of Sentient Planets and Child of Ennaris, born of Earth which you know as Ordoreth. I also am Dharmoney, protector of Ennaris from those who would harm her. I have sealed you from your gifts."

Varna waited calmly, watching Goroth, before speaking directly to his mind.

You are the one who led the rebellion, who caused such destruction, who wanted to enforce your will on a planet and a people who objected to your and your followers' behaviour. You are the one who would have destroyed Ennaris and who caused Ennaris' civilisation to regress millions of cycles in a cynical and callous disregard for the welfare of the Ennarisi, who subsequently died in their billions. In doing so, you caused the deaths of three Guardians and yet the Guardians were restrained from doing you harm.

Goroth stood and stared. Whatever this woman did, however she did it, he could never describe. But Goroth *saw* the effects of the breaking of Ennaris. He *saw* the efforts of the Guides and Mages on land and in the sea to hold back the worst effects of the destruction that he and Likud had wrought. He *saw* the Guardians - the Guardians were real! - providing their own support to Marjory and Drewflin as they tried to simultaneously fight against the horrendous weapons the rebels brought to bear and to deflect their worst effects. He *saw* the three Guardians use themselves up in their efforts and just ... cease to exist. He *saw* the millions and then billions of Ennarisi die because of the upheavals of the land, the changing coastlines, the fracturing of the sea floors. He *saw* the almost overnight descent of the shining civilisation that had been Ennaris into barbarism , a fall that took scant generations. He *saw* the remaining Mages trying and failing to hold this, their planet, his planet, together. Enormous numbers died that should have lived. Even more were not born that would have been influences for good in the galaxy and, somehow, he recognised the losses of potential.

Goroth felt shame. He felt great humiliation. He had no answer. He had no excuse. Grensor had tried to tell him of his own shame and sorrow at being part of the rebellion, but he had dismissed them. He had seen the destruction, walked through the dry, dusty and broken land that such a short time before in his memory had been lush and full of life. But he remained Goroth, he reminded himself from the depths of his despair, he remained one of the most powerful Mages that Ennaris had ever produced. The Guardians existed but still they could not touch him. They had constraints that he had not realised existed, as he had not believed the Guardians existed. But those constraints bound them still.

I am not bound by those constraints.

With a thought Varna and Goroth vanished, only to re-appear in front of Drewflin and the small group who had gathered with him and Marjory. They all stared at Goroth. No-one attempted to attack him, although had the glares directed at him been knives he would have died on the spot.

"Drewflin, Marjory," Goroth said after a moment, bringing his extensive training to bear to force calm into his voice. "I was told you were dead," he said to Marjory.

"Not dead," Marjory replied evenly, her own calm restored. "I had to leave Ennaris to stop Likud."

"Likud?" Goroth felt that he had missed something.

"Yes. In a way I wish I could have informed him that he had been fighting me all those cycles. It was me who made sure the Children of Ordoreth, Earth as they call their planet, had the technology to halt Likud's expansion and fight back." She smiled. "He destroyed the Andorethi in seeking to exercise dominion over the galaxy. But I could ensure that he did not do the same to Earth."

Goroth nodded.

"He did talk about a number of people who seemed to thwart his plans. I take it you were one."

"Oh, it's likely that I was several of them," Marjory said. "But we'll never know who he meant now. Not that I regret that. And now it comes to you. Drewflin and I restrained our instincts and desires when we battled before. Now is the reckoning that we should have had then."

"It's not your decision to make, Battle Mage, Admiral," Varna said. "You do not speak for Ennaris, but for the Mages wronged by Goroth and his ilk."

"I speak as a parent whose child was destroyed, or thought to be destroyed, by this monster and his friends," Marjory replied in an icy calm voice. "I speak for all the parents who were unable to protect their children, who watched them die in agony before joining them. As Drewflin and I were unable to do."

"Nevertheless, it is not your role to speak for Ennaris and the people of Ennaris. That task falls to the Faero." Varna turned to Corm and gave a slight bow. "Faero, the decision is yours."

"Why is it my decision?" Corm asked in a low voice, directed to no-one and yet to everyone listening. "Marjory and Drewflin, the twins and Trabor, you and your lost Guides and Mages have fought against this evil and its effects for more lifetimes than most here can imagine. This should be your decision."

"Nay, Faero," a new voice cut in as Odruf appeared, flanked by Fernis and Balgor. "For this decision must be made by one who speaks as the leader of Ennaris in spirit, and that has ever been the role of the Faero. Your role has never been political or military, but nor has it been ceremonial, no matter that it became all of them at times. Rather, it has been and is to be the spirit of Ennaris, to apply the spirit of Ennaris to such decisions."

"The Prophecy said that the decision would be made by the first of the Blood," Balgor said. "Thus it has been my task to protect and as necessary guide the Faeros. Now is one of the times for which you and your forebears prepared, Corm. The decision is for you and you alone. The Guardians will ensure your decision is enforced."

"Do I get a say in this?" Goroth asked, through the shock of seeing Halfgar, who he had always treated with disdain as an aged Mage, in the form of a Guardian.

"No," Odruf said. "You lost any chance of that when you restarted your campaign of terror when you were returned to Ennaris."

"That is your decision, then?" Goroth said, sneering, more to buttress his own courage than to demean the Guardian.

"No, as a matter of fact," Odruf said easily. "This was the ruling made by The One."

"The One?" Goroth looked uneasily around the gathered group. "Who is The One?"

"Ah, Goroth," Odruf said. "You've never really understood, have you? The One is who we, the Guardians, answer to. The One created this universe. The One is who we called on when sealing the rifts that you and Grensor created between universes, thereby threatening this one. The One decided that the Faero makes the decision as to what to do with you."

Goroth looked ill. Not only were the Guardians real but they answered to the Creator. And the Creator, it seemed, had been inconvenienced by Goroth's activities. He, Goroth, was not the powerful one. He was, in fact, one with no power at all. This Varna Barr, Dharmoney - he flinched from that name - had seen to that. He was at the mercy of one who had no reason to be merciful.

Corm walked away from the small group. He understood that his decision was to determine Goroth's fate. But what to do? He could just kill Goroth, of course, which would remove him and, hopefully, his influence from Ennaris. Corm did not take life easily. If he was threatened, he would fight back but he did not go looking to cause or be part of strife. He could have Goroth resealed in some sort of container, but all that would do is push the problem down to a future generation. That would not do! There appeared to be few alternatives though. Corm walked slowly with his head down, deep in thought.

He was unsure how long he walked. From the small hill where the leaders of his army stood, he walked a meandering path, unaware that he was shadowed by Helt and a team of her most experienced and most trusted guards. Above flew Ky-rel and a flight of warrior Rocs, likewise unnoticed. Without thought, his path took him around the hill and away from the battle field. After a time, he found himself standing at the edge of a small gully, which obviously was a water course when the infrequent rains fell but which was bone dry now.

Corm stood quite still and watched as a small rodent pushed out from a burrow high up the gully's opposite bank with its long nose twitching as it scented the air. Seemingly missing Corm entirely, the rodent exited the burrow, followed in short order by three pups, all scampering up a shallow path carved in the earth of the bank. Reaching the top, the three pups scampered off but the mother turned to look at Corm, without any fear. Corm and the mother rodent locked eyes. Corm read trust that he would not come after her and her children. The mother rodent seemed to nod before breaking eye contact, turning and hurrying after her pups. Corm stood for a time longer, staring at where the mother rodent had stood. The trust that she had shown him stayed with Corm for all of the trip back to the tent.

His return path took him past a small gathering where Jalor, Blaine and Varna were surrounded by a number of men and women wearing unfamiliar uniforms. Corm realised that these were the comrades of the Children. In fact, all of them were Children of Ennaris, too, he thought, all descendants of the people who were raised by the Ennarisi. Varna called him over.

"Admiral, I would like to introduce you to Corm Ramesa, Faero and leader of Ennaris and the Ennarisi." Varna smiled to Corm. "Faero, it is my pleasure to introduce Admiral Denton Bard, commander of the Union First Fleet and its flagship *Starfire*."

"Admiral, it is my pleasure," Corm said, bowing slightly.

Bard came to attention and bowed formally. "Faero, the pleasure is mine," he said before relaxing. "Is there anything we can do to assist? I've already given orders for my medical teams to provide whatever assistance you need."

"My thanks, Admiral. Is that your vessel still hanging above us?" Corm looked up.

"No, Faero, that one is *Sunburst*. That was the flagship of the First Fleet under Grand Admiral Mavin Serra long ago. I feel we have lost that one," he continued with a rueful smile.

"Lost?" Corm said, confused. "But it's right there."

Bard gave a chuckle. "You know Mavin Serra as Marjory. It seems she designed *Sunburst* using advanced plans from your own planet. When *Sunburst* was evacuated Admiral Serra was the last off the ship. It seems as Marjory she claimed *Sunburst* as salvage for the Ennarisi fleet before leaving. I'm fairly sure one can't abandon one's own flagship and yet claim it as salvage, but I'll leave that for others to worry about. I'm also sure that your Battle Mage is the only one who really knows what she can do. Certainly, there was surprise after surprise for the crew who boarded her."

"Like the ability for a capital ship to enter the planet's atmosphere and hold in place?" Jalor asked. "I'm not sure I've seen that before."

"Yep, that's one of the things," Bard said, nodding. "Some of the weapons systems are so far ahead of our weapons as to make us look backward. And, apparently, they were installed or planned for when she was built and we never knew. Just needed to be activated and armed, mostly. Oh, and the ship has a mind of its own that we also were unaware of." He shook his head. "I'm planning on leaving all that to others to work out."

"It has been a pleasure to meet you, Children of Ennaris," Corm said, having understood little of the conversation other than that Marjory had been known to the Children under another name, "but I must leave you for now."

"Yes, I understand that you must make a difficult decision," Bard said.

"How do you make hard decisions, Admiral?" Corm asked as he started to turn away.

"Ah, I was taught to think about the pros and cons, work out the best and the worst, and then sit back and let it wash over me. Then go with your gut!" Bard smiled. "It works for me."

"Gut?" Corm was nonplussed.

"Instinct. Feelings," Bard said, placing one hand over his heart. "When you have the facts and they don't give you the answer then step back and let instinct take over. Usually, you know the answer and have been trying to work out why it is the answer or why you don't like it. But often, that is the right answer."

"Who taught you that? It sounds both wise and simple at the one time."

"Admiral Serra told me that when I was a young ensign," Bard said. "I have used that advice repeatedly and have not yet regretted it."

"Thank you, Admiral," Corm said. "I will think on it."

He turned away, consciously allowing his mind to drift. Through his thoughts came recent events, the tragic circumstances of his elevation to Faero, the destruction that he now knew had occurred, the people who had caused it and those who had come to help his planet. Rocs flew.

Ghazrak snarled. Demons attacked. Oddly, his thoughts kept returning to a small rodent, trusting him not to hurt her family, her children.

34. Decision

The leaders were gathered in Corm's tent. It was after dark and lamps had been lit. Guards surrounded the tent in case any remaining northers tried to rescue Goroth, but no-one thought that was really likely. Nor did Goroth, who stood quite still as the tent filled.

Corm stood silently in the centre of the tent. He was flanked by Jalor, Blaine and Varna, the Children of Ennaris. Balgor stood beside Varna wearing a carefully neutral expression. To one side stood the remaining Mages of Ennaris with Drewflin and Marjory slightly to the fore. Andira crowded close to Trabor and the twins. The leaders of the allied army stood as a group on the other side of the tent. Almin Bor and Helt occupied front positions. Goroth stood alone between Corm and the tent door. He looked at no-one and nothing, sunk in deep despair. Corm, likewise, was withdrawn, staring but not seeing.

With a pulse of light Odruf and Fernis appeared.

"I see everyone who needs to be here has convened," Odruf said without preamble. "It falls to Corm to decide Goroth's fate."

Corm stirred, turning slightly to face Odruf.

"Why is it my decision?" Corm asked quietly, repeating his earlier question. "Goroth caused great ill to Ennaris. Billions died. Every part of this planet was damaged and every segment of Ennarisi society suffered great damage. Why does it fall to one man to make this decision?"

"The decision is for the Faero, I'm afraid Corm," Odruf replied kindly, with a tilt of his head. "The most important decisions have been the Faero's for long eons. That was the role your forebears accepted as leaders of the oldest blood of Ennaris. I'm afraid it cannot be shirked, it cannot be passed to another. Every Faero has carried the chance of this being required. It falls to you, however, to make this particular decision, as others have made difficult decisions in the past."

"Others have made such decisions?" Corm asked. "Who and when?"

"The occasions have been few, thankfully," Odruf said gently. "In the third eon, the Faero Mellis made the decision not to annihilate the Grucellae, a ruthless space-faring people who sought to destroy Ennaris and caused great destruction. Many died as a result and Ennaris was directly threatened with its own destruction. The Defender led the defence of Ennaris and defeated the Grucellae, ultimately capturing their leader in single battle. Mellis decided on leniency after she had spent some time with the survivors."

"What happened to the Gru ... Gruss ... the enemy after that?"

"Most of them departed this galaxy, or the remnant of them did, but only after they had overthrown their military leadership. They settled far, far away and rejected warfare and violence. Their civilisation has thrived since then, as I was given to understand it, but their ambitions have remained small."

"That's one example," Corm said. "Are there others?"

"Yes, several. All were required to deal with the aftermath of dire threats to Ennaris." Odruf watched Corm. "None of the decisions were simple. While the Faeros have often been war leaders, so too have they exhibited compassion as a defining trait. Not all decisions resulted in forgiveness, however."

Corm nodded.

"Thank you, Odruf," he said, bowing to the Guardian. "I would very much like to know more about my forebears should you be able to spend some time with me after this."

"It would be my pleasure," Odruf said with a smile.

"And I have come to a decision," Corm said, looking around the tent before settling his gaze on Goroth. "Varna - Dharmoney - would you release Goroth's binding, please?"

Goroth's head came up sharply as he stared at Corm. His surprise was mirrored by most of those assembled although not by the twins.

"Are you not afraid of what I may do?" he snarled in a low voice.

"No," Corm replied. "Varna, please?"

Varna regarded Corm for a moment with a slight smile tugging at the corners of her mouth. She nodded to indicate that the bindings had been released.

Goroth took a deep breath as he felt his powers return. He stood still, however.

"How are you so sure?" he asked Corm, the growl replaced by puzzlement.

"You truly have no choice," Corm said. "You have no allies. You're surrounded by those who can take control in an instant, and if you did manage to escape you would be tracked down and caught easily."

"Very well," Goroth nodded. "What is your decision? Do you have one of these kill me?" He jerked his head to indicate the Mages.

"No," Corm said thoughtfully. "There's been enough death among the Ennarisi. And despite everything you have done, you remain an Ennarisi and thus one of my own."

"Surely that's a reason to kill him," Helt broke in. "He's one of the strongest Mages and used his power to kill so many and almost destroyed Ennaris. He deserves nothing less. His victims deserve nothing less."

Her words were met with nods from many onlookers.

"All of that is true, Princess," Corm replied. "But I don't wish to cause his death even so."

"So what do you wish to do, Faero?" Fernis asked.

"I would speak with The One," Corm said evenly.

This time everyone was shocked, including the Guardians.

"I don't believe The One has ever spoken with any in this universe but us Guardians," Odruf said quizzically.

And then his eyes opened wide in shock. At the same time Varna felt a presence that just appeared, an enormous pressure that threatened to overwhelm her but, instead, wrapped loving arms around her spirit. Balgor reached out to grip her arm, even while mirroring Odruf's shock.

"You wish to address me?" a voice seemed to say from everywhere and nowhere. "I would hear what you have to say, my child. I am listening."

Corm appeared stunned, as much with the fact that The One appeared as with the terrifying power he felt. The Mages reacted similarly, although those without gifts appeared to be less affected. Strangely, it was Corm who recovered first.

"Uh, yes," Corm said, diffidently.

Those watching the Faero saw as he shook his head as though dismissing a thought. He stood straight and tall, allowing time to pass while he considered his next words.

"You have left this decision to me, as the Faero of Ennaris, of this world," Corm said. "Why is that? Why leave this to a single man?"

"We have found that decisions of weight require one invested in the outcome," the disembodied voice said. "My first children have exerted their best efforts to protect Ennaris and this galaxy. But they are not born of this planet, or of this galaxy. We felt that one born of this world would be the best to make those decisions. We tried other methods in other situations but the results were not suitable."

"You keep saying 'we'," Corm said, puzzled. "Did you and the Guardians make this decision?"

"No," The One said. "My siblings and I made this decision."

"Siblings? But, you're The One!"

Corm's expression was mirrored by everyone except the Guardians. There was more than one of these beings!

"That is what my children call me, yes. My siblings have often discussed the different methods to manage our inventions. Where we allow free will we also must allow free decision, but the right people must make those decisions." The One paused. "Your forebears agreed to make those decisions, them and their descendants. Thus, it is for you to decide."

Corm nodded, staring at the tent's floor, lost in thought. Ne nodded again. He raised his head, decisively.

"Your siblings. Do they have their own worlds?" Corm asked.

"They have their own universes," The One replied.

"Then I ask that Goroth be exiled from Ennaris, from this universe, to another where he will have no special powers but will have to live like all others in that universe. Is that possible?"

Goroth stared at Corm, shocked. Death he was expecting, even when Corm announced that he would not have him killed. Exile from Ennaris he could understand and would be able to deal with. Exile from this universe?

"It is," The One replied. "One of my siblings has agreed to this. Are you sure that this is what you wish?"

"It's my decision," the Faero of Ennaris replied firmly. "Goroth will be stripped of any special powers and exiled to another universe of your choosing. For it's not only me who has a stake as Faero of Ennaris. It's you who have a stake also, as creator of this universe."

"So be it!" The One said, and Goroth disappeared.

"I thank you," Corm replied.

"You have done well, Corm of Ennaris. Varna, my newest child, we welcome you to our Guardians. We will converse further."

The presence abruptly vanished.

Epilogue

Corm surveyed the former field of battle. It had been a tenday since Goroth had been bested, to great loss among the Ennarisi. Many of Corm's army and almost all of the norther army had died or been incapacitated. The Ennarisi healers - Drewflin, Maf, the Rocs and several from the Hides, as well as the followers of Eresh and one highly gifted healer from the city of Frelor - worked long and hard to heal as many as they could. The medical teams from the Union fleet took one look at what the Ennarisi could do and started to shuttle their seriously wounded to the planet, joining forces with the Ennarisi.

Goroth was gone! The end had been almost anti-climactic. What was left was an enormous amount of work to repair the damage that had been done. It was too late to help all those who had died as a result of Goroth's rebellion. It was too late to bring the land back to what it had been. The Guardians had decided that they would not try to do so, but they would make such repairs as would help the Ennarisi to take their own civilisation into the future.

In this Corm would need help. The Union of Sentient Planets, which Corm now knew was a federation of planets that spanned a significant although not massive portion of the galaxy, had made overtures for this previously unknown planet with people of strange powers to join, but Corm and his new Council had yet to respond. Already Marjory had made Ennaris' claim to the entire system, as well as several nearby ones that had been used as a buffer in the long distant past. In this she had been supported by the four admirals, whose fleets were now configured to screen the entire system. All nearstations and farstations blazed like beacons in space, reinforcing just how powerful this world had been, and could still be. The Council of Guides had been re-established formally, and Drewflin occupied the leadership role as Archmage.

The army of the Faero had largely disbanded. The southern desert people had started on their return - not by sea - but by portal, for the Vale of Morrig had been found to also hold a portal. The Waslit, who had suffered grievous losses, had also departed, as had the Tang. Escar's leadership was a little confused as King Ensert had announced that he would step down in favour of his daughter, who was heard, clearly and loudly, berating her father in her own unique style about leaving his people to rebuild. Helt and Blaine had then disappeared, to recuperate Corm had been told. Blaine, it appeared, had decided that Ennaris was his home.

Likewise Clay, Champion of the Light and Champion of Ennaris, had decided to stay. He also had disappeared, but had made sure that Corm knew how to find him. The Faero now had a brand new communication device with which he could make contact if necessary, once he worked out how to use it properly.

Ennaris and the Ennarisi would have to change rapidly, Corm knew. He snorted to himself. They would change whether the Ennarisi wanted it or not. With the best of intentions, the Mages who had lived through the rebellion and the impossibly long aftermath wanted Ennaris to take its place in the galaxy again. The concepts of universes and galaxies were becoming easier to understand, and Corm had been taken by Flin to the Council Chambers, where he was introduced to so many new ideas that his head continued to spin when he tried to bring them together. Likewise, Ennaris' new friends from Ordoreth - Earth - were so familiar with what, to them, was modern and normal that Ennaris was only seen as a backward planet, despite the nascent military strength. Even the three Children were of that culture, no matter their acclimatisation to Ennaris. If their friends saw Ennaris in that manner, then those seeking to take advantage would do so even more.

Varna was with the Guardians now. She *was* a Guardian now. This young woman, who had struggled to survive on Ennaris, had become one of its most important figures. While she would do what she could and, in her own words, was less bound than the other Guardians in what she could or would do, still there would be limitations. She already had told Corm that she would assist and support, but the Ennarisi had to drive change in order to survive in this new order.

Several of the Guardians had left Ennaris again, with promises that they would return, and often. With the approval of The One, they were spread through the galaxy to repair the damage that Likud had caused. Two, at least, were on Andoreth. The Likudian Empire was no more but it had left the Andorethi badly damaged, and the Guardians were intent on repairing and, where possible, reversing that damage. The Union had been asked to provide assistance and had decided to do so, to the surprise of some. Some of that may have had to do with Odruf appearing during a heated exchange of the Union parliament and informing them that, if Ordoreth did not assist, then the Guardians would complete the job of lifting the Andorethi properly and the Union would have a worthy opponent. It seemed that the policy of non-interference by the Guardians had ended. Some of the change of attitude may also have been caused by the uncovering of a major cell of Empire supporters in the parliament itself. These were the ones who had consistently sought to undermine the Union Fleet.

Corm had passed his eighteenth name day with no-one noticing. It was not something that bothered him, where once it may have done so. He had too much to do to worry about trifles. He was Faero of Ennaris, but he now knew that his responsibility covered the galaxy, and he would need all the help he could get.

Admiral Vinca Jalor (Retired), newly promoted to the position just before handing in his retirement notice, stood on the shady knoll and overlooked the small valley. He had left Ennaris soon after the battle concluded, leaving the aftermath to those who were better suited to dealing with it. He had a lot to process and needed to be alone to do so, he thought.

Well, now he was alone, on a planet with few resources that were needed anywhere in the galaxy and with a single, very small, human settlement. Behind him, perched on the only level ground he had located in this part of the deep wilderness, was a needle-nosed Ennarisi craft, near enough to his old stinger to be comfortable but so far in advance of his old craft technologically that he smiled every time he thought of it. He had had an exhilaratingly fast trip from Ennaris to Korstel-8, which was far off the usual routes for interstellar travel and was much safer now that Likud's Empire had crumbled overnight.

He had sought solitude. The events on Ennaris had been profound and Jalor struggled to bring the pieces together. The personal changes for himself were matched by the effect of the events on the galaxy as a whole. For the first time that he could recall, the identities of the Warrior team had been made known. That Ennaris existed was a minor sensation, but that it was a cradle of the galaxy's civilisation had been met with incredulity and then, as realisation that it was true set in, a range of outcomes across the spectrum from despair to ecstasy. Then there were the Guardians that had been overseeing the safety of multiple planets, including Earth. Topping it all off was the existence of The One.

Established religions collapsed remarkably quickly, and new ones arose. Opportunistic law suits targeted those old religions as being frauds while the media, never subtle at the best of times, went into a feeding frenzy. Within days of the news breaking there was a veritable armada of media and pseudo-media vessels heading towards Ennaris. Intelligence leaks remained, it seemed. Corm had been worried, of course. He and the leaders of Ennaris had to both recover from the impacts of Goroth's last stand and then start to modernise the planet and its people, hopefully without destroying what Ennaris had become. Marjory had given assurances that Ennaris would be given that time. Oddly, as they approached the planet en mass, the swarm of media ships found themselves with navigational challenges that rendered them unable to locate Ennaris.

Jalor, of course, had been besieged. His personal communication channels had been hacked or sold by someone - investigations were continuing in that regard - such that he disabled them all. His promotion and subsequent retirement became fresh fodder for the over-excited media and it was obvious that his privacy would be non-existent. He felt the need to be apart from all that was happening. The twins, who always were adept at understanding the inner turmoils that people faced, suggested a means to achieve that end. Marjory made that end happen. A special ship, based on experimental materials and technologies from the time before Goroth's rebellion, remained intact in the depths of Escantil, Ennaris' moon base, and it was prepped and made ready for Jalor's use. It used materials such that no scan received a return signal, nor could it be tracked by its heat signature or any other electromagnetic emission. It was the ultimate in stealth ships and had been gifted to Jalor. That was the ship parked behind him on Korstel-8.

But Jalor now faced an unexpected problem of his own, and this was not one that the Mages or Guardians could help with. While he sought and now had seclusion, he realised that he looked forward to a long existence where he would likely be alone. He was realistic enough to understand that the media storm would fade relatively quickly, but it remained likely that he could never be completely unrecognised with the artificial intelligence capabilities available to anyone. It would be a simple matter for those media or other organisations to do a set-and-forget search that would identify him when he went anywhere. He smiled as he considered having some fun with that, turning up somewhere far from Korstel-8 and then disappearing again, and then watching what happened. But he turned sombre again as he pondered the reality ahead of him.

Oddly, he thought with a wistful smile, no story that he had ever read showed the hero at the end standing on a lovely knoll on a near deserted planet contemplating life alone. A sense of crushing loneliness was fended off with considerable effort. He had been told by Meilani Gro Tillek that his choice would leave him with a very long life, even if the isolation had not been included in that discussion. Recalling their conversation and her last smile, Jalor realised that Meilani had, indeed, understood what he faced, for she had done likewise. With a pang, he recalled again that sense of connection that he had never felt before and expected never to feel again.

Jalor heard a rapping sound and turned to find Balgor and Varna standing by the stinger. Balgor had just knocked on the craft's skin as though on a door.

"Hello, anyone home?" Balgor asked breezily as the two walked forward.

"Hello," Jalor said, smiling.

"Love what you've done with the place," Balgor said as he and Varna reached Jalor and looked out over the valley. "Used to be flat, wasn't it?"

Varna laughed and Jalor joined her. Balgor was Balgor, no matter where he was.

"We thought we'd drop in and see how the hero of the last battle is getting on," Balgor said with a side-ways glance at Jalor.

Jalor snorted. "Hero!" he replied. "Let's just say that it's not all it's cracked up to be."

"Well, let's see," Balgor continued, undeterred. "You have the undying gratitude of the entire planet, the Guardians and The One, the majority of the galaxy and, in fact, anywhere in this universe where the events have been made known. You have a life span that means that you will be able to experience this -" he waved his arms as though to encompass all around "- everything, however you want to."

"Yes, that's true," Jalor said. "And I get to do that with hordes of people chasing after me anywhere I go, without a moment's peace. I get to outlive everyone I care for, except for the very few Guardians and Mages on Ennaris."

"You can come to Ennaris any time and will be very welcome," Varna said quietly, laying a hand on Jalor's arm.

"Oh, I know that, and I'll do so," Jalor continued with a smile. "I know I'm being selfish here and I shouldn't be. Meilani told me what would happen. She told me of her own experiences and what it had meant to her. I did know what I was getting into, or thought I did. The reality of it is a little overwhelming, that's all."

"Hmm. Well, there may be the odd job for you to do here and there. But that's probably not enough. We will visit from time to time, of course, but what you need is someone to share it with," Balgor said. "Someone who understands." He paused, tapping his chin, as though musing. "I wonder who that could be?"

Jalor gave Balgor a pitying look. "Balgor, you're about as subtle as a brick going through a plate glass window. What's going on?"

Varna laughed. "I keep telling him he's not subtle."

"Like a great big red demon stalking through the Citadel," Jalor agreed.

"It was an excellent demon, if I do say so myself," Balgor said in mock outrage. "Very well. There was another who was promised a reward for the service she gave. It seems her reward was not to be reborn after all."

Balgor turned and Meilani Gro Tillek walked from behind the stinger. Jalor could only stare. Meilani looked anxious, as though unsure of the reception she would get.

"I was offered a new life, Vinca Jalor," she said in her mellifluous voice, "but I felt that you and I are meant to share this one. If you feel the same, of course."

Jalor found his voice at last. "I, er, um, I," he stuttered.

"He normally can speak with whole words," Varna said to Meilani, with a smile.

Jalor bestowed a withering look on his former fellow Warrior before turning back to Meilani.

"I would be honoured to share this life with you Meilani Gro Tillek," he said. "Never have I felt a connection such as the one we experienced."

"Things tend to get a little more intense in that between life," Balgor said. "You can't hide anything, so the real you is on display. Personal connections, if made there, are stronger than others."

"Is this a one-way decision for Meilani?" Jalor asked. "What if it doesn't work out for us?"

"I have every confidence, Vinca Jalor," Meilani said. "But yes, this will be my final decision if you agree." She glanced at the stinger then turned to Jalor with a quirk of her lips. "Besides, I see you have the experimental Grassfer model. I recall watching it being developed. I can show you how to really fly it, if you wish."

"Well," Jalor said with a slow smile, "it is a two-seat model."

About The Author

James K. McVey is an author living on the New South Wales Central Coast, in Australia. The four novels that comprise *Children of Ennaris* are his first published works.

Visit www.jameskmcvey.com.au for further information and updates on these and other works.

www.ingramcontent.com/pod-product-compliance
Lightning Source LLC
Chambersburg PA
CBHW070427170726
48291CB00002B/384

* 9 7 8 1 9 2 3 2 1 1 0 3 2 *